DARK
OF THE
WEST

DARK
OF THE
WEST

Joanna Hathaway

TOR TEEN

A Tom Doherty Associates Book

NEW YORK

This is a work of fiction. All of the characters, organizations,
and events portrayed in this novel are either products
of the author's imagination or are used fictitiously.

DARK OF THE WEST

Copyright © 2018 by Joanna Mumford

Edited by Elayne Becker

Map by Jennifer Hanover

A Tor Teen Book
Published by Tom Doherty Associates
175 Fifth Avenue
New York, NY 10010

www.tor-forge.com

Tor® is a registered trademark
of Macmillan Publishing Group, LLC.

The Library of Congress Cataloging-in-Publication Data
is available upon request.

ISBN 978-0-7653-9641-9 (hardcover)
ISBN 978-0-7653-9643-3 (ebook)

Our books may be purchased in bulk for promotional,
educational, or business use. Please contact your local bookseller
or the Macmillan Corporate and Premium Sales Department
at 1-800-221-7945, extension 5442, or by email at
MacmillanSpecialMarkets@macmillan.com.

First Edition: February 2019

Printed in the United States of America

0 9 8 7 6 5 4 3 2 1

For Nyema and Kirstin,
who first believed in this story—and in me

Acknowledgments

I've discovered it takes a small army to get a rookie writer off the ground and flying in the right direction, and I'm forever grateful to those who, at different stages, have challenged me, encouraged me, and breathed great life into this story: Radhika Sainath, Jack McBride, Katie Bucklein (my "Delta"), Hafsah Faizal, Kristen Ciccarelli, Dylan Matthews, Reza Hessabi, Rachel Medlock, Kirstin Lindstrom, Stephanie Vaillant, Rose Hathaway, Colleen Mumford, Isabel Ibañez Davis, Jennifer Todhunter, Sarah Dangar, Alli Smith, Jim Window, Lindsay Diamond, Peter Callahan, Alyson Bowen, Timothy Vienne, Diana Pho, Zohra Ashpari, Kamerhe Lane, Hema Penmetsa, London Shah, Mike Kern, Michael Mammay, Michella Domenici, Snowfall, Brenda Drake, Alex Cabal, Samuel Hathaway, Scott Struthers, Dorina Moldovan, Louba Podvoiskaia, Sarah Kim and my entire Pitch Wars class.

Endless thanks to my fantastic editor, Elayne Becker, and everyone else at wonderful Tor Teen, including Kathleen Doherty, Seth Lerner, Lucille Rettino, and Patty Garcia. Thank you also to Marisa Aragón Ware for creating this truly beautiful cover. As well, much gratitude to the brilliant team at Curtis Brown, Ltd: Tim Knowlton, Holly Frederick, Maddie Tavis, Jonathon Lyons, Sarah Perillo, and Sarah Gerton. A special thank-you to my incredible agent, Steven Salpeter, who makes this journey better than I ever imagined.

And finally, thank you to my family—I love you beyond measure.

SANTIS   SOELDAN

PETRI

THE EMPIRE:
LANDORE

ETANIA
●Hathene

CLASSIT

LALIA

Norvenne ●

THE HEIGHTS

Roier ●

Havenspur ●

Hady

RESYA   Beraya   *Thurn*

Izahar

Madelan

MYAR

ETANIA

LOYALTY BINDS US

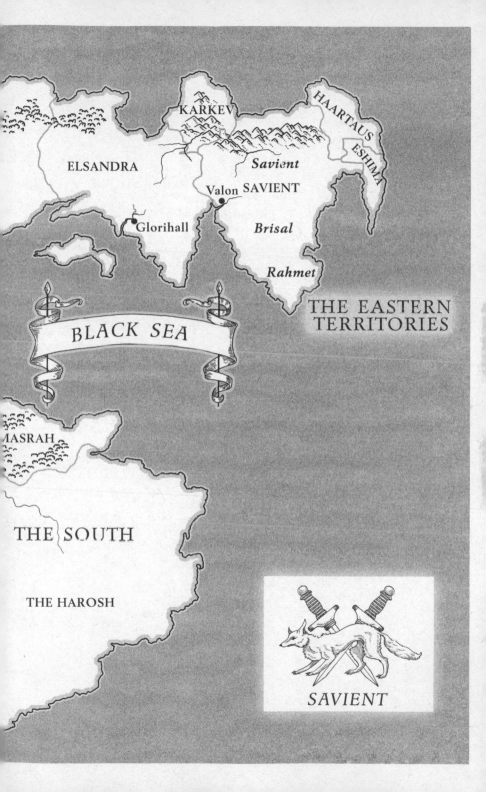

KARKEV

HAARTAUS

ESHIMA

ELSANDRA

Savient

Valon SAVIENT

Brisal

Glorihall

Rahmet

THE EASTERN
TERRITORIES

BLACK SEA

MASRAH

THE SOUTH

THE HAROSH

SAVIENT

DARK

OF THE

WEST

PROLOGUE

War is no good for the young, or for love.

The Commander learned this long ago, that it's the youngest and most in love—with life, with the world—who splinter quickest beneath its weight. Yet here he stands at the door of a crumbling sandstone building, its once elegant pillars destroyed by mortar fire, a feral dog panting on its steps, and he's wondering if he might still be in love.

Behind him, three dusty trucks idle, leaking petrol. White flags hang adrift in the sun. It's a ceasefire, the long-awaited truce, but it feels hollow and anticlimactic somehow. He knows, now, he could just as easily be fighting for the other side. Enemies to allies. Friends to foe. He's seen it all, and his soldiers keep their weapons drawn and ready, their eyes skittering across the rooftops of this battle-scarred town. The world—North and South—has been torn apart and left weeping. An entire generation of wasted courage.

He might still be in love.

The local children emerge from hiding, eyeing his uniform, the fox and crossed swords symbol on his cap. The Commander looks too young for his rank. He *is* too young for it, but this war has bled his family dry and here he stands. The little faces watch, waiting—blue eyes, brown eyes, a garden of curiosity. They can't see the long-ago mountains behind his gaze, the ache of her smile in his heart. The girl who once promised to love him for a thousand days.

The girl who brought them this ceasefire.

Alone and uncertain, he imagines what his brother would do, then strides through the shell-strafed entrance to meet his fate. A deserted foyer greets his leather boots. Its ruined walls sag in defeat, a fractured chandelier wobbling above and winking near a hole of blue sky. There are ghosts of another life everywhere. Mangled photographs. Abandoned trunks. Ceramic vases like floral tombs. Everything is withered in the heat, forgotten and left behind beneath the whistling panic of mortar shells.

He walks, following the ghosts, his steps as those of one to a grave.

Seath of the Nahir waits for him in the parlour. The aging revolutionary sits at a table covered in silt and debris, a rifle resting across his lap, his lean body lounging in one of the only usable chairs remaining. He has a greying black beard, a steady hand on his open map. Weary triumph on his sun-worn face. The girl seated beside him is much, much younger. She has her own gun, her own expression, but the Commander only allows himself to see her as a phantasm to the right of his vision—in his mind she is exactly as she once was: raven hair long, breaths gentle, posture straight and formal, a princess.

He doesn't dare behold her fully now.

Aeroplane propellers growl in the sky above, rattling the damaged roof. They belong to the young Commander, a memory of strength and a reminder of the power he once held in a time long past. The thrill of the engines that once gloried in his veins. And yet here, today, the sky can't save him from the earth.

Not from this negotiation that belongs to Seath.

With no proper chair, the Commander is left standing before the table, sweat along his pale neck, weighed down by illustrious badges that shouldn't be his, listening as Seath discusses the Nahir's terms and speaks about lines on the map he wants for his people, the helpful things he will do in exchange. The ways he will help the Commander defeat their new, shared enemy.

The Commander eyes the map, wondering what exactly he's to keep and what he can surrender. They were never that clear on this part.

"We do acknowledge your concerns," he says to Seath, since his own nation once fought for the same right Seath now demands—the right to be known. "But I'll offer nothing until the permanent ceasefire is signed. Our alliance must be certain this time."

"And what does that guarantee me?" Seath responds, tapping the barrel of his rifle. "I've heard Northern promises before, as my grandfather did, and my father. And I've seen the way they turn out for us." He gestures at the mutilated room, at the young Commander. "You think you're different? That you won't betray me for a chance at more? No, I won't sign away my loyalty so easily. I'm a valuable card in this game."

"We *are* different. We've fought the same battle as you," the Commander tries. "We fought to be equal. We wanted something better."

And they had. The Commander believes this, clings to this truth, even as he knows this same honourable intention was swiftly buried beneath the tracks of armoured carriers, squandered before a valuable lie, used to gain a new kind of power that, while never as vain as that of the kings, was still enough to leave endless bodies bleeding out before a wretched cause.

Seath tilts his head. "And I've heard those same words from your father, too."

The Commander waits, perspiring.

He's realizing this game might actually have no end. Honour can't be purchased with blood or sold for lines on a map. His father has tried. Seath has tried.

Now even he has tried.

And he no longer knows why he is here, this place he never wanted to be. He'd give anything to do what's right—but what is right? Feeling so suddenly on his own, at a loss for the next step, he ignores Seath and lifts his gaze to hers.

The lines disappear as he looks into her familiar face at last. Tawny skin, sable eyes, the picture of her Southern mother. She's the one who has known his true heart. The one who begged him to stay alive only long enough so that they could enjoy a new world together—the world that never came.

She's the sky.

She always has been, and something long dead struggles to life in his chest.

He can't know it, not completely, but here at this table, new war hovering on the horizon, it's his eyes that she needs, too. She's been staring since the moment he stepped through the door. Staring, lost, while her fingers grip her rifle, her lips moving over a memory, his name. The cautious glance from him pulls her back to herself.

It keeps her from running.

From screaming.

From simply firing her gun into the broken chandelier above and letting the bullets be wasted in a moment of defiance of everyone who has brought them to this place. The people of the North and the South. From the east and the west. He's too much as she remembers—fair hair stirred by light, grey eyes veiled. But he's also different—wearied, thin, empty—and there's nothing warm left, only a tired shadow of what came before. It breaks her heart. She remembers when his smile burned like the beautiful sun, bright as light on water. No steel in his blood.

She loved him then.

"I'm not my father," the Commander says at last, "and I don't wish to fight you any longer. You've already decimated our ranks. Be our ally and soon you'll have your land back, forever."

"Soon?" Seath repeats.

"You have my word. If you cease targeting us."

"I'll do my best, Commander. But I can promise nothing certain until the last of your guns have disappeared across the sea once and for all."

She's so tired of listening to words—words upon words upon words—and never a single promise with meaning. Never the truth. It's the disease of war, on every side. She has lived two lifetimes in her short years, as a princess, as a sniper, and she's beginning to think there is no place left for hope. Only victory will write the words that matter.

"Then we are at an impasse," the Commander says, "as always."

She brings her fist down on the table, silt sent flying. "Children are suffering, Commander! There's no running water, no electricity. Your rotten shells land on the innocent along with the guilty, can't you see? Fight your war against the North. Do what you will. But if you refuse our terms, then we make no assurances about your army's safety anywhere in the South."

Hot silence.

"Are you threatening me?" the Commander asks her, his shock evident.

But she doesn't back down. Not this time. Dark eyes on faded grey, the night sky and the sea. Opposites who loved, adored.

Betrayed.

Seath conceals amusement, fiddling with the safety on his rifle.

"If I agree to your terms," the Commander says carefully, "then you must promise me you'll put down your gun."

Seath of the Nahir nods. "For now, I do promise."

"I wasn't asking you."

He looks at her, waiting, but she can't agree to this, not in good conscience. The ones who valiantly resist the North are her blood, her family. She's been brought to life among these Southern steppes. The suffering, the laughter, the love. An intricate world of a thousand stories, and it's her home. She will not surrender it to another while there's still breath left in her bones.

She replies in a local tongue, instead. One he won't understand.

The Commander looks to the older man for explanation.

Seath pauses. Hesitates. "She says she'll make no promises to you."

The roof rattles again overhead, propellers snarling in a second pass, and she can see the ruin of her betrayal across the Commander's face. The way he's too young again, overwhelmed by the reality that it's as if they never loved at all.

Strangers and enemies, like everyone else.

She wants to add something to soften this blow, to explain that war is no good for the ones like them, the ones who have held love between their own trembling hands. It's only good for the steel-souled who scrub blood from boots. It's for those who burn unflinchingly with a loyalty forced into their veins from their first breath, a dangerous allegiance that can't be ended or surrendered, not even for all the world, not even for peace.

It's not for them, and yet they've chosen it.

Her lips begin to form the words, but he's already heading for the door, and she's left desperate. She longs to remember him as he once was. With river water on his skin, young and beautiful, the boy she'd have given her whole world to.

She longs for her words to mean something.

She stands. "I was sorry to hear about your brother, Athan!" It's the only thing she can think of.

He stops, staring at the door. "Which one?"

A breath of wind blows through the tattered silk curtains, and Seath frowns.

No one has ever apologized in this war.

It takes too much love.

I

MEMORY

1

❧ ATHAN DAKAR ❧

Savient

3,000 feet.

Darkened earth stretches beneath my plane, endless shadows and sleepy towns, and a thin band of light smirks ahead. Dawn, telling me to hurry the hell up and find the final target. Should have reached it five minutes ago.

I scan the ground again, a bit more purposeful now.

This Night Navigation exercise shouldn't be taking this long. I'm supposed to fly cross-country from objective to objective, using only my instruments, but so far my route has taken me in circles. Somewhere back there was the third target—an illuminated munitions factory at the outskirts of town—and next, in theory, is a rail line running south.

"You were only supposed to fly us three degrees off course," I scold my plane. "Now look what you've done. How am I going to correct for this properly when I can't even see down there?"

She says nothing in reply, propeller thudding in the darkness, its metallic hum a constant tremor through my body, but her wings wobble suddenly as if annoyed I'm trying to pin the miscalculation on her.

Better check my flightbook.

"A good pilot routinely checks his map when flying," Major Torhan likes to say. "A great pilot doesn't need to, because it's already in his head."

Well, it would be in my head if I'd wanted it to be. If I were actually trying here, I'd have memorized the map before take-off, followed my instruments perfectly, and this whole thing would be over and done with ahead of schedule. But unlike my fellow Academy pilots, who march around dreaming of spectacular glory in the squadrons, I'm less than eager about the prospect of an early grave. One lucky shot from the other side and all those push-ups will be for nothing. You're just a bit of finely carved kindling, but no one ever mentions that part. Not to your face, anyway.

And certainly not when you're the General's son.

Since I've seen the way death looks up close—limbs burnt and black, like charred biscuits, ugly as hell—I think I'll forget the final target and just enjoy this moment of perfect sky.

Dawn skies are meant to be gloriously on fire.

I yank the stick back and my plane growls in protest, shaking between my gloved hands. "Come on, you old beast," I mutter. She's not as impressive as the squadron fighters, more a training animal, and impatience nips as her rattling engine gathers strength for the climb. Thick grey cloud surrounds us, slipping over the wings. But light grows above, reaching through, and then . . .

Brilliance.

The sky is ablaze. Sunlight hits the eastern mountains in the distance, peaks cutting between the rays—a wild temptation of endless pine and jagged cliffs. Desire tightens in my chest, the urge to throttle forward and not look back. For my father, those mountains are power. Rich with coal and oil. Heavy with iron ore. They're the lifeblood of his army and the foundation of our nation that even kings envy. But no matter how he tries to break them, carve them, exhaust them, they remain larger and more impressive than anything he can build. And one day I'll crash there. I'll burn up these wings forever and live by my own compass. Life at the Academy is a daily game of charades where I play my part and follow every order, but all I'd like is for just one person to look at me and ask, "Do you even want to join the squadrons, Athan Dakar?"

I fling my plane into a spin.

All of her shudders with a slight stall, all of me weightless for a moment. "Reckless," the instructors would call it. "Save it for battle, son," they'd say. I'm not worried. They've never seen my true instinct in the air, how the plane becomes mine, how it becomes a part of my very soul. Hands on the trim and feet on the rudder. Sky goes over sky, my stomach wheeling with it. Heart pounding with exhilaration. It's like rocking through an invisible swell of waves, a cartwheel of colours, the dawn sea of clouds below, then above, then to the side.

Then sharp orange sun again and I squint, blinded, a large shadow hurtling at me from one o'clock.

I haul back on the stick and throw the plane right.

"Awake now, Athan?" Familiar laughter crackles over the earphone, another plane's engine growling dangerously close above my canopy.

"Damn it, Cyar!"

He's still laughing, circling back around. A perfect attack from the sun, I'll admit that. "And this is why you'll end up shot down one day," he announces. "Too busy daydreaming."

"That was a perfectly executed flick-roll, in fact."

"Perfectly off course too."

"Jealousy," I say. "I've seen your rolls—a little too much slip."

"Yes, and I'm also finished and heading back. Should we expect you around noon?"

"Not if I happen to run out of fuel in those mountains."

There's a sound from him. A snort of laughter if I had to guess. Cyar Hajari's the only one who skims the surface of my discontent, but he'll never get any further. The truth of my charades would hurt him most. They bunked us together when we first arrived here six years ago, both of us wide-eyed and far from

home. He showed up at my door, brown-skinned, black-haired—
exactly the opposite of me—and was from Rahmet, the last
region to join Savient. A place of lizards and lemon trees. I only
knew about it from campaign reports on the wireless radio and
from black-and-white newsreels, and since most boys my age
were too scared to talk to me, being the General's son, I expected the same from him.

And I was right.

He hid in his bunk that first night, silent, but I caught him
crying over his photographs of home. It was the deep hiccup-
ping sort of grief my father would have cuffed me for, and I'd
never seen a boy cry. At least I wasn't the only one feeling alone.

I knew, then, he'd be my friend.

"Just follow me, would you?" Cyar says now, his plane fading
through the layers of smoky cloud.

"If you insist."

We're far enough from Academy airspace that no one's listening to our conversation. Cyar always tries to cover for me up
here, and I try to do the same for him on the ground, fixing his
math calculations when he isn't looking. He's the only person
who knows I'm more than my last name, who understands that,
but still expects my best in the sky. He believes in me. Which
is actually a lot more terrifying than the cold and simple expectation of my father. Expectations can be worked around. Nego-
tiated, if you're clever. But loyalty—and I know this better than
most—is what you die for.

Loyalty is deeper than blood.

We emerge into the brightened world below, motorcars winding down roads, locomotives hissing steam. Cyar quickly finds
the tracks and final objective, an old army depot buried beneath
a crop of trees. I jot down the time in my flightbook. A perfect
twenty-five minutes behind schedule. I can forget being an
officer in Top Flight, or even an enlisted pilot, for that matter.
Which puts me right on target. I'm aiming to fly in transport.

Then I can be stationed at home, and fade from Father's radar, and then—mountains.

I'm still trying to figure out how to talk Cyar into it, too. His noble soul isn't built for deception.

"Start studying your maps better," he instructs. "We've only got five weeks left, and I can't help you on test day."

"I know." I fly above him.

"And we're both making Top Flight. I'm not going to the squadrons without you."

"I'll be there," I say, hating how easy the lie's become.

"Just have to follow the river south." Must be checking his map. "Fifty miles back."

"As long as you know where you're going."

"What are you saying, Dakar?"

I make a tight spin to the left, wings dropping, gaining air-speed so fast my stomach leaps to my throat. Cyar tries to keep up with the wild spiral, but it's too late. I've already swung around behind him. He's in my gunsight.

I grin. "When I'm an ace, I'll need a wingman who knows how to get me home."

Cyar groans. "You're not half-bad when you focus."

"Be sure to write your girlfriend about this one," I say. "Tell her how splendid my flick-rolls are and how I nearly shot you down."

"Sorry, she doesn't like blonds."

That's how it goes, the whole fifty miles back.

Tall lights appear eventually, guiding us to the wide hangars and brick barracks of the Academy. Flags flicker in the dawn breeze, bearing the Safire ensign—a fox between two swords—and runways crisscross along the western side.

Control directs us back onto the circuit and gives clearance to land. Cyar goes first, a perfect show. Wheels kiss the tarmac lightly, then a gradual deceleration. I follow behind and make sure to come down at a ridiculous speed, jolting the plane against

the runway with a rookie's charm. That'll earn some frowns
from the flight instructors.

At rest by the hangars, the propeller spins to a stop and I look
at my crumpled map again. It's a damn mess. Lines here and
there and everywhere. No one's going to believe I found the
proper objectives based on this.

I jump down from the wing to begin post-flight checks. Cyar
settles his plane, then jogs over. "Let's see the nightmare," he
says, gesturing for my flightbook.

"I lost it."

"Right. That will go over—" He freezes, looking past me, eyes
wide.

Alarm grazes my pulse.

Let it be Torhan. Let it be only Torhan. Let it be—

I turn. Oh, God. It's Major Torhan indeed, standing by the
airfield fence, arms crossed. And next to him?

The ruler of Savient.

General Dakar.

My father.

They're discussing something intently, waiting in the silver
light, eyes trained on us. No, on me. Who am I kidding? I move
to climb into the cockpit. "Well, I'm off to get lost again. Mountains, hopefully."

Cyar shoves his map and flight plan at me, hidden by the
shadow of the plane. "Take them."

"No."

"Take them!"

He's going to make a scene. There's no other choice but to
accept his selfless offer. And just in time, too. Torhan waves,
motioning me to them.

I draw a breath and square my shoulders. Here goes. There's
no sense fabricating answers in advance. Father's stare tangles
them up somewhere between the brain and the mouth, and I
can't afford that. Not at this point. If he figures out my mistakes

are not from lack of talent, but deliberate self-sabotage, it'll be the end of me. And he's very good at figuring out lies. Just ask any man who dared betray him during ten years of revolution—I'm sure they were wishing for better answers as the ropes tightened on their wiggling necks.

But I walk towards Father as if it's perfectly normal he's decided to drop by and check on me. Like I have nothing to hide. I haven't seen him in at least three months. He's got a war in bordering Karkev to worry about, a land thick with corruption that's also conveniently a chance to demonstrate his military might to every royal kingdom in the North.

When you're the youngest son, you tend to end up lower on the priority list.

And that's fine with me.

Major Torhan wears a formal smile as I approach. I return it. Father offers nothing, dressed in his grey Safire uniform, green eyes examining close enough I feel them hit my bones. If I wasn't so well practiced with it—his stare—I'd be sweating a hell of a lot more right now.

"A rather rough landing today," Torhan observes.

"Came in too fast, sir. Tailwind."

"You completed the course?"

I nod and hand over Cyar's pages, guilt threatening to swallow me whole. But I don't let it show. I can't let it show. Father watches with brow raised, glancing at the runway. Skeptical?

I rub at my neck. Then stop.

Torhan studies the map. "We've finished our third quarter reviews, Athan, and I'm pleased to say that in academics you have the highest grade here. Nearly a perfect hundred in every subject."

"Thank you, sir."

Mathematics has always come easily to me, since I was a child. For a long time, my mother was the only one who knew about my gift. She said it was our secret. She'd kneel before me, begging me not to tell anyone else the truth. She said he'd take me away.

I knew who He was.

But I didn't know where he'd take me.

She wept when, of course, he did find out, when he finally saw me as more than a useless third son and lured me into the Academy testing with a promise of airplanes. I was too young to understand their war over me. Now I know, and I'm doing my best to honour her plea, to not let him take me any further from her, into those graves that certainly already have my brothers' names on them.

The way I have it, they all think I'm quite clever on the ground, brilliant with numbers and angles, but a lousy pilot in the air.

Tragic.

Torhan clears his throat. "Your flying, however . . ."

Here it comes. I don't dare look at Father.

"Your flying needs a bit more work, and that landing today was proof of it. Careless. You won't make Top Flight with lazy maneuvers."

"I know, sir, but it's difficult to remember everything at once."

"Not a good trait for a fighter pilot." Torhan frowns. "A shame."

"Who's in highest standing for Top Flight?" Father asks, as if he doesn't already know.

"Cyar Hajari," Torhan replies.

"And when Hajari makes Top Flight?"

"He'll be training with the officer corps, of course. We have high hopes for him in the Karkev campaign."

"Very good." Father's gaze returns to me, cool, pointed. "It's unfortunate you won't be joining him on the frontlines. He'll have to find someone else to watch his back."

I nod and shrink a few inches on the inside.

I hate the very idea of it.

A transport plane flies in low, halting our conversation. It glides onto the tarmac, flaps raised, smoke hissing from the wheels.

"Athan might yet pull it together," Torhan suggests once the noise fades. "I've seen it happen. Some pilots take more time before everything clicks in the air." Apparently he's covering for me now. I'd like to be grateful, but it also feels a bit like unasked for pity, which annoys me.

"Then it had better click soon," Father observes, sharp, and I barely stop my hand from rubbing my neck again.

Torhan gives me a thin smile. "I'd best get back to the office."

A convenient excuse, and he departs. We stand in silence. I know Father hoped for a better report. He's been waiting years for one. But he refuses to pull strings for me or my two older brothers. As he likes to say, we're not princes, we're entitled to nothing, and therefore we can very easily lose it all if we don't play our cards right. Which I've been doing an excellent job at.

Father adjusts his cap to block the rising sun, the silver fox emblem on it catching light. "You have leave the rest of the week to join us in Valon," he says. "We're launching the *Impressive* for her first sea trial this afternoon, to coincide with the Victory Week celebrations."

"You want me there, sir?"

"Your mother requested it."

He stresses "mother" to be sure it wounds, but it isn't necessary. Of course he doesn't want me there. He probably thinks I should stay here and practice hard until my piloting skills magically click.

He meets my eye, his steel gaze slightly shadowed by the peak of his cap, and I see the detachment there. It's louder than any spoken word. It holds the weight of continual disappointment, perhaps an edge of bitterness, cutting me raw in a clean, precise line. I wait for him to say more—what, I don't know—but I wait. There's always something like desperation when I'm standing a foot from him. Like maybe he'll finally say the thing I need to hear and life will make sense. Like maybe I'll finally feel like his son.

Like maybe he'll just pull out a gun and shoot me and get it over with.

But all he says is, "The flight leaves at nine. Bring Hajari if you'd like."

Another cruel reminder that I only have my best friend until the day we graduate, and unless things change soon, and drastically, it will be goodbye to the one person in the world who's my true ally.

And Father knows it.

With a curt nod, he turns and strides for the office building beyond.

I walk back for the round hangar, where early morning mechanics are muttering to each other, tools striking metal and ringing off walls, the air smelling like leftover kerosene from night lamps. Cyar waits patiently, pretending not to notice whatever's taken place outside. He's good at that.

I shed my gear—gloves, boots, charcoal-toned flight suit—and place them inside my locker, next to my notebooks about strategy and tactics, beside pencil sketches of birds and airplanes and mountain huts I'd like to construct by hand someday. And in the middle of it, taped to the door, a photograph of me and my two older brothers balancing on a rock by the sea—young and scrawny and somehow smiling all at once. Father gave it to me when he left me here. *"Nothing's gained without sacrifice"* it says on the back.

It's what he said to us during the teeth-rattling nights spent hiding from shells. What he said to us when our encampments gave way to mud like soup in the summer, flies crawling into your nose and into your mouth while you slept. It's what he said to his men before they came back split apart and soaked with blood, skin flayed like fish, bones scattered and buried in graves from one end of Savient to the other.

For a long time, I convinced myself this picture was proof of his love. Some bit of regret when he realized he was leaving his eleven-year-old son alone, five hundred miles away from home in a grey-walled dormitory room with nothing warm or familiar. I wanted to believe he'd miss me. I wanted to believe it meant something else.

But now I'm seventeen and I know it's only ever meant exactly what it says.

Nothing's gained without sacrifice.

That's it. That's all it is, and worse than that, I'm beginning to suspect it's the goddamn truth.

I slam the door shut with a fist.

2

Etania

It's a day for escape, and I'm determined.

My mare, Ivory, is my sole friend in the early morning plot, galloping us hard through royal Northern forest without a flicker of protest. Most horses might balk to be alone, but I'm certain she enjoys our madcap rides as much as I do. She's all curious energy and pricked ears as we veer off onto a forgotten path, her fur warm beneath me since I didn't bother with a saddle. Fallen trees from winter winds litter the trail, their stark branches broken and skeletal, much larger than I should be jumping without proper tack. But I count my strides—one, two, three!—and Ivory, the most darling mare in all the world, forgives when I get it a hair wrong, sailing us over with perfect ease. I wish the jumps were even higher. I'm wild for a thrill, and my heart matches Ivory's eager hoofbeats, sweat soon sticking beneath my braided hair.

Once far enough, I half-halt on the reins and Ivory shifts to an easy trot. A clearing opens ahead, nestled at the foot of the brown peaks, the field thick with winter-yellowed grass trampled by snow and rain, insects flitting between dry stalks of thistle. I dismount and tie Ivory to the narrow trunk of a young chestnut tree.

There.

We're wonderfully alone, just two little specks beneath the towering cliffs.

I'm sure the poor stable boy has gone and paced himself into a grave by now. He's mostly freckles and bits of hay, steady with the horses yet skittish with me, and I talked him into my escape. He knows my mother, his Queen, doesn't much like me adventuring out here alone—riding bareback, no less. And I might have promised her I'd keep to the short, circular trails close to the palace. I promised, yes, but today's a day for broken promises since it's sunny and lovely and also the anniversary of my father's death.

I need to be out in the woods with him.

Setting down my leather bag, I sit on a wide rock and retrieve my paints and paper. The cold seeps through my pale breeches as I mix swirls of yellow and brown together on my palette, then set to work creating the scene before me. A few drops of red are for the new buds gathering in the branches above. Father never liked to paint things as they were, always adding colours where there were none, and today I'll do the same. For him.

In my mother's homeland, Resya, the dead are not to be mourned. It dishonours their memory and disrupts their sleep, and so tonight she'll hold a party instead to celebrate a colonel in our air force, something to pretend today's any other day, but how can I do the same? Father loved her with a bright, burning devotion. He loved her at first glance even though he shouldn't have—a raven-haired noble lady visiting his court, from a kingdom across the sea. Though Resya might be ruled by a king with Northern blood, its people are perched on the edge of violent revolt, the last royal stronghold in the stormy South. She wasn't made for these wet forests of Etania. She was born of a windswept, desert sky, in love with sun.

And yet he adored her.

And he adored me the same, bringing me into the woods, to

the mountains, teaching me to believe in this small and simple kingdom that belongs to us. He said my dark eyes and sandy skin matched the colours of the swirling autumn river. He taught me to read, to paint, to listen to the birds, and I cling to those precious memories of him even as they slip from my fingers with every year that passes.

Ten years gone feels like a lifetime.

Above me, swallows flutter in branches of black pine sheltering the meadow, an aeroplane spinning between thin clouds. A lone fawn slips through the brush, and I keep silent, adding her to my scene.

She waits patiently. No fear, no hurry, nibbling at dry grass.

Father would have loved this place. He'd be here now, and I'm certain he is, made of stars and light and whatever else the soul becomes in the infinite dark.

The fawn twitches, raising her slender head. She looks right at me, and I hold my paintbrush still, waiting.

The little ears swivel.

From the tops of the pine, a dozen birds stir to flight. In the far distance, a faint yelp.

Something unwelcome leaks into our peaceful place, tension rising in Ivory, her head high and still, and I see it in the fawn, who's now entirely uncertain, looking between the woods and me. And since I know what's coming, I have to break our moment of trust.

I leap up, splattering paint, ruining everything, and run towards the fawn with arms flailing like a wild turkey.

It bolts from the clearing—from me—just as a crack shatters the silence.

Ivory trembles on her lead, and a dog yelps again, louder now. Voices call back and forth. I sit down on the rock, feeling miserably evil for chasing the fawn. But I saw Uncle Tanek's hunting dog chew on a baby deer once. I never want to see it again.

On cue with my rotten luck, that same black creature bounds

abruptly from the underbrush, a colourful pheasant caught between its teeth. Six men emerge behind. They each have a rifle
in hand and my uncle, Tanek Lehzar, leads the pack. He removes
his fine-rimmed spectacles and, wiping a gloved palm across his
balding head, speaks firmly to his dog. He bends over and takes
the bird from its obedient jaws. Then he spots me, expression
darkening. "Aurelia, what on earth are you doing out here?"

His question goes in one ear and out the other. My stomach
is too busy twisting at the sight of the tallest hunter.

Ambassador Gref Havis.

Havis trails the group of courtly men, casually reloading his
rifle. He's from Resya, tall and angled with dusky skin, dark hair
pushed back from his handsome face. If he were only a passing
diplomat, a friend of Mother's from long-ago days, I wouldn't
pay him a wink of attention. But as it happens, he's also intent
on being my suitor, and my mother's entertaining his impossible offer—a terrifying prospect.

He's only an ambassador.

And he's also old enough to be my uncle.

My real uncle steps in front of me and says, "We could have
harmed you by accident, child. Does your mother know where
you are?"

"I'm studying for the university exams," I say, still seated on
the rock. "She doesn't mind."

He looks at my glistening paints and frowns.

"I'd bring Renisala with me," I add, "if you didn't keep him
so busy with political things."

Uncle furrows his thick brow. "Political things? Such as
reasoning with your mother's council? Preparing for the Safire
visit? Your brother, Aurelia, is learning to run an entire damn
kingdom."

"Yes," I reply. "Those things."

I say this like it means little, because I know the tone vexes
Uncle, and it's what he expects of me. He thinks I only paint

and sketch and play with horses. That I'm at best useless, and at worst, slightly in the way. It's always been like this. I'm not as interesting to him as Renisala because I'll never sit on the throne. But just because I paint and seem useless doesn't mean I don't listen or have opinions. I listen all the time and know the impending visit of the Safire General from the east—a man with no royal blood, no claim to a throne—is a shock to all. No one else in the North is eager to deal with him, and yet my mother has opened our gates and promised Etania a new and impressive ally with untapped wealth to be shared, an ally who is little better than a rough-handed commoner who patched together a war-torn land with his own gun.

A bloody uniform, Reni says, is no substitute for a God-given crown.

And many in our capital feel the same, passionate enough to even march round the city square in protest.

I know all this, but I only fold my painting carefully. When I look up, Uncle is still frowning at me and Havis waits beside him in a shadow of tan pants and black coat and muddy leather boots. "You're an artist," Havis observes in polished Landori, our common tongue. It's the language of politics and trade in the North, courtesy of the great empire, Landore, and I've been fluent since childhood.

"Do you care?" I ask.

Someone fires two sudden shots, and we all jump. The black dog yelps with renewed excitement.

"Do you shoot, Princess?" Havis asks curiously.

He likes to address me as simply "Princess," like we're friends of sorts, but we're not. And unfortunately, saying *"Your Highness* will do, thank you very much" comes off as rather ungracious in public, so I have to bite my tongue every time.

"Of course not," I reply. "I'd never torture an animal for sport. Nor did my father," I add, louder. I'd like them all to hear this opinion.

The other men of court, dressed in their tweed caps and wool jackets, begin suddenly gazing at the treetops, refusing to meet my eye.

Uncle points down at my face. "You watch your tongue round our guests."

"It's only the truth," I say.

He gives a tight-lipped grimace—the sort he reserves for diplomats he doesn't like and, more often than not, me—then goes to help restrain his miserable creature, leaving me on my own with the Ambassador of Resya.

Havis gazes down at me, amusement in his eyes.

I glance over my shoulder at Ivory and debate escape. How many steps to her? Could I even scramble onto her without a saddle? And how quickly? She's dancing at the end of her lead with all the fuss.

Havis interrupts my vital deliberation. "Found this beauty in the forest," he says, pulling a white flower from his pocket. "Do you know what it's called?"

I glance at the delicate petals and yellow middle. "Bloodroot," I reply warily. "It grows in the early spring."

"Ah, I don't believe we have it in Resya."

"Indeed. It must be too hot for anything beautiful to grow."

He doesn't hesitate, only smiles and says, "Yes, we must import all our flowers from the civilized kingdoms of the North. Though we have little time for gardening, you know. All the fighting and revolts. Who has time for tending petunias?"

His wry edge doesn't evade me. "Who, indeed?"

"Though to be clear, this entire Northern continent spent hundreds of years with kings lopping off heads and people being pulled apart at the bones, and that's conveniently forgotten when summarizing *your* noble history. Can you explain this curiosity, Princess?"

I refuse to take his bait. He thinks I despise him for being Southern, always luring me into political debates I have no time

for, but I couldn't care less about where he comes from. In truth,
I despise him because I know his most shameful secret—I caught
him with one of our ladies late at night in the palace halls, her
giggling stupidly into his muttered words, his hands cornering
her hips beneath the glittering sequins, their kisses bold and
desperate and sinful with the gold ring on her wedded finger.
I saw the truth and I'll never forget it. Havis is a charming
creature who plays noble at dinner, who's convinced my mother
of his honour and fidelity in all things, but who's a rogue to
the very bone—handsome and vain and free as a wild hawk in
the sky.

And he won't trick me.

"I do quite like the outdoors," he continues at my silence,
studying the mountains, "and being alone. I come from a large
family. Six brothers, and I'm the youngest. There's always someone round every corner."

I reach down to gather my paints and paper. He never accepts
defeat in a conversation.

"You must like to escape out here for the same reason, Princess. Your mother's always with her friends, your uncle, your
brother, even the maids. I'd imagine it's a rare occasion to catch
her alone, where curious ears are not nearby . . . away from eyes
that speculate."

I look up. His tone has changed and he's watching me intently.
"She makes time for me," I say, wary again.

I finally stand, because it's not very comfortable having him
tower over me like this, but it brings me closer to his face. He
smells of sweat and cologne, a shadow of black stubble along his
jaw and neck. My traitorous brain imagines the nightmare of
that strange mouth on my skin, those gloved hands on my hips,
and I feel rather sick. Only his desires to satisfy, never my own.
How do you please a man who has tried a dozen lips before yours?
How can that ever be love?

I'm not even sure how a proper kiss is supposed to go.

He swings the gun from his shoulder, extending it towards me. "Have a try," he says. "It might change your opinion of hunting."

"Never."

"One shot, Princess. You can aim at one of those trees."

"She couldn't hit the side of a palace wall," Uncle Tanek mocks, nearing again. "She'd prefer to throw herself in front of a gun and protect our evening dinner."

His friends nearby chuckle.

Havis gives me a look, the sort that says *"Are you going to let him get away with that?"* and offers his weapon again. I want to refuse. Father hated this bloody sport, as I do. Even touching the metal feels like a betrayal. But Uncle's comment stings, spurring me forward. Sometimes I think his cruelty is jealousy— there isn't a drop of royal blood in his veins, and he lives on the charity of his sister, the Queen Regent, while I'm the daughter of a true Northern king. Even if I never inherit the crown like my brother, I'll still have more worth than Uncle ever will.

The thought is selfishly satisfying.

I take the gun from Havis. "I can manage one shot."

Uncle's lips twist incredulously, and Havis moves behind me, showing me where to place my hands on the rifle. It's terrible having him so close, his breath prickling my neck, but at least this skill might come in handy, should he ever try to kidnap me for ransom—or marry me.

"Aim for the birch tree," Havis instructs, stepping back.

The target is a good twenty meters away. I take a deep breath and place my finger on the trigger. A moment goes by, then another. Everyone in the clearing waits.

A tree. It's only a tree.

I can do this.

But then, like a rotten song that won't leave my head, I see once again the slaughtered fawn from years ago, its eyes wide and rolling, fragile breast heaving, bones and meat exposed to teeth. Eaten alive. I remember being skinny and twelve, trying madly to pull Uncle's dog from it, screaming, grabbing at black fur and nearly getting attacked by those vicious jaws myself. Uncle had to beat the dog back with the butt of his rifle. Afterward, he said I was a stupid, thoughtless girl. Mother was horrified at the bite mark on my arm.

I only felt helpless.

I made sure to find out the combination key on Uncle's hunting cabinet and then silently stole his bullets for two years. He's certainly still wondering where they all went.

Now, I let the rifle drop, clicking the safety latch on, and hand it back to Havis. "I'm sure I can make the shot, but Mother wouldn't be pleased." Which is true enough. She doesn't believe in me doing anything that might be deemed improper, and hunting is quite thoroughly a man's sport.

"Sparing yourself embarrassment?" Uncle laughs. "Wise."

"Saving herself the ire of Sinora Lehzar," Havis remarks, and anger tingles in my mouth. I hate how casual he thinks he can be. Being old friends with my mother is far from permission to address her—or me—with such informal candor.

I'm sorry, Father, I whisper in my head. *They've ruined your day.*

Frustrated, I grab my bag and march for Ivory. I untie her and search for a higher rock to stand on, to mount her, but Havis comes to my side. He's tall, over six feet, and I shrink back against her shoulder.

He holds out his arms, his eyes copper in the light.

It's an offer to help, but I'd rather not owe him anything. He smiles at me too quickly, like he knows my thoughts without even trying, so I relent and place my knee in his hand. He hoists me up. Then he grabs the leather reins and tugs Ivory forward, putting her between him and the others nearby. He holds out a letter, using her body to shield it from sight.

"Take this to your mother, Princess. You're her loyal daughter, and since I returned from Resya last month, I'm never allowed a private audience. Your uncle forbids it."

I stare at the paper.

He thrusts the letter into my limp hand, impatient. "Swear that no one will see except her."

I nod, and he releases the reins. "Ride safe, Princess."

"It's *Your Highness*," I say hotly, since no one else can hear.

He grins, cavalier as a devil, and I slide the letter deep into my pocket. I give a last glance round the clearing, then kick Ivory to a furious canter, abandoning them all behind.

3

❧ ATHAN DAKAR ❧

Valon, Savient

The *Impressive* is everything the rumours promised.

She sits in the water proudly, shining like a tethered beast on display, over eight hundred feet in length with four turrets and eight guns. A firing range of twenty-two miles, gleaming anti-aircraft batteries pointed skyward. Her keel was laid here in the capital, inland from the coast, and the narrow canal that links Valon to the Black Sea can barely contain her.

The crew on board—gunners and armourers, radio operators and signalmen, men from every background under the sun—wave from the deck, showing off for the thronging crowds gathered on the docks below. Shouts and whistles rise on the breeze, tangling with a cheerful military song pumped out by drums and trumpets.

It's always cheerful.

Father stands at the front of a podium decorated with red banners and Safire flags, his hands planted on the wooden rail, his uniform grey as the iron monster before us.

"Ten years ago we brought victory," he declares into the metal microphone, his amplified voice silencing the sailors, the docks, most of Valon probably. "Ten years ago, it was you who united these northeastern territories, forging Savient, Brisal, and Rahmet into one shining nation, glorious beneath our flag. Now we possess the most powerful ship in all the world, the greatest army and airplanes and industry. The old kings of the Royal League watch us with envy. The old empires look in awe as Savient becomes the great power in the east. And this greatness is because you knew the truth. You knew that nothing is gained without sacrifice."

The crowd roars with appreciation—soldiers and civilians, their disparate faces a mosaic of our nation, unified by their lack of nobility from the warm flats of Rahmet to the endless farms of Brisal to the true mountainous north of Savient proper.

West of us, Northern kingdoms reign as they have for generations, entrenched in their belief that possessing a crown is the only legitimate way to rule. Never mind that they built their fancy palaces on the blood and sweat of their lowest classes, indulging in a thousand years of violent, oblivious luxury before they grew tired of trying to conquer one another and headed south instead. The Royal League is a vain sort of club for debating the merits and vices of the rest of the world in private. It requires royal blood to belong. Father doesn't have that, but he does have coal and oil and bauxite. While they were busy hunting for treasure in the South, believing gold was power, my father was harnessing an untapped treasure in these mountains and forging something greater.

Motorized vehicles and aluminum airplanes and entire armies don't run on jewels.

They run on petrol.

I'm sure as hell the royals are regretting the fact they wrote off the east as corrupt and useless, but it's their loss, and now my father's going to prove you don't need a crown in order to last a thousand years. We have power.

"Here's what I've written so far," Cyar announces to me once the speechifying is finished and Father has stepped back from the microphone, commiserating with men in uniform. There's a paper between his hands. "This has to be good, you know."

We're hiding at the back of the podium, still in Academy

uniforms, watching two fighters perform show-off stunts in the empty sky. Black swords gleam on the underside of their wings, the mark of the Safire squadrons. Apparently Cyar's girlfriend has a birthday soon and she needs a poem. He claims she's back home in Rahmet, some beauty who's actually agreed to kiss him and all that, but I think it's a fraud, since I've never seen her picture or anything.

I lean on the rail. "Your lips are so sweet and true, your face so perfect, that sometimes I fear you're not real," I suggest.

He squints at me. "I see what you're doing."

"I'm writing poetry."

"What if I worked in how we first met? Can I make a snake romantic?"

"Don't."

"But that's how I won her heart. Haven't I told you?"

The fighter planes do another showy loop. "You said something about a heroic stunt and a lizard and then she was yours."

"I was eight and she was ten. I asked her if she'd like to see my snake."

"You know how terrible that sounds, right?"

He ignores me. "And she said yes, but when I went to pull him from my bag he'd already escaped into the town pool. She thought it was the funniest thing she'd ever seen. Even went and grabbed him for me!" He gives me his triumphant smile that's all gold, the inner amusement of his private, happy Cyar world. "I hope you get half as romantic a tale as that."

"I pray every night." I shade my eyes. "Look at that sway. Trim it up, would you!"

"You're one to talk," he replies, watching the plane too. "You can barely land without bouncing the damn thing from east to west."

He has a point.

The *Impressive* blasts her deep horn, sound shuddering through our feet, and cheers swell from the dock again.

At the front of the podium, Father now has my older brothers, Arrin and Kalt, on either side of him, each in dress uniform and cap, observing the activity below. Mother and my little sister, Leannya, wait in the shade, their blond hair a mix of sun and shadow. Mother looks like one touch might bring her to tears—she hates crowds and heat and machines of war.

But Father wears his elusive half smile, still studying the giant battleship, entirely pleased. "Wait until this one leads our charge," he says, no indication of who the observation is directed at. "Our enemies will certainly bow before forty thousand tons of Savien steel."

And this is why I don't plan to make Top Flight.

When Father looks at you with a smile, it's a sure sign you're in for a terrible fate.

"Or it's a damn waste of money," Arrin offers, arms crossed, a cigarette between his lips, already bored by the display. At least he's sober. At twenty-five, he's the one with the looks—tall and broad, hair the colour of sandy earth. A hero of the campaign by day and a bastard by night.

"As usual," Father replies, "your opinions on naval matters aren't required."

"Then why did you bring me home from Karkev? To stand here and break a perfectly good bottle of wine on a lump of metal? I have a campaign to win."

"Lump of metal?" Kalt, my other brother, repeats. He's offended, a dedicated officer of the Navy, but since his voice never rises above one singular boring octave, it's difficult to say for sure. "She's the most beautiful thing I've seen."

Arrin snorts, trailing smoke. "First time those words have ever left your mouth, isn't it?"

Kalt glares at him.

Yes, Arrin never ceases to disappoint. He's entirely unpredictable, part brilliance and part madness when it comes to both war and women. Kalt's twenty-two and entirely the opposite—

darker-haired, serious, the spitting image of Father. Indifferent to
girls. His interests run the other way. Mother insists they used to
be inseparable, but since it's a claim that lacks any evidence, I'm
fairly certain they'll just end up killing each other someday. Arrin
with his army and Kalt with his boats. It's the one shortsighted
thing Father has ever done, arming the two of them.

In my opinion.

"Karkev is only a sideshow," Father informs Arrin, which is
the best moment of the day. With one sentence, he's dismissed
an entire war and all of Arrin's part in it. "It was a nest of bandits
that needed to be cleaned out, nothing more. The Northern
kingdoms will thank us. But the Southern continent? *That* will
be a real campaign, Commander, and soon we'll have these kings
begging us to reckon with their disaster down there."

Arrin recovers by putting out his cigarette on the railing.
"Except that merry royal bunch will be the last to cheer you
moving into their territory. You know what they say about you
as it is."

Father smiles again, and this time it falls on me, sharpening
with private certainty. "Yes, but I have an ace in the South. One
clever ace that will make all the difference."

I try to go back to watching the show in the sky, but the dam-
age is done. His pointed gaze is lethal, a probing hook that grips
at my excuses and tries to pull them into the light. I'm the useless one. The one who most certainly won't be anywhere near
the frontlines. Transport, please. But suddenly I'm imagining the
airplanes above us spiraling in flames, metallic tombs of charred
limbs and black smoke, and I know, without a doubt, there's a
reckoning coming for me and me alone.

I avoid his gaze.

Mother intervenes, breaking her self-imposed silence. "You
won't take us to the hell of the South," she says. Her hand grips
Father's arm. "And you certainly won't send our children there.
You won't. This is enough."

"Think what you will, Sapphie," is all he offers in reply.

His gaze is still dominated by the *Impressive*, and she casts me the ghost of a disturbed glance behind his back, as if she can see the death in my head. The charred limbs and black smoke. She knows she can't rescue me from this. I think she's always known, and now it's simply becoming more real.

When the *Impressive* is announced ready for the official ceremony, she and Father descend the stairs for the docks.

Arrin and Leannya follow behind, their arms linked, laughing together as they go. Leannya's his tiny golden shadow, always at his side when he's around. She's the only person in the world he thinks of before himself. And for her part, she tries to look after him, too.

When we reach the wharf, the crowd parts, cameras flashing, bulbs shattering.

With a grin, Arrin passes the ceremonial bottle of wine to Leannya.

Father doesn't object, since having his sweet daughter send his new warship off will look rather nice in the papers, perhaps even better than his decorated eldest son.

Leannya maneuvers herself onto the canal railing, refusing every offer of help from a nearby colonel, then stands firmly in her heels and lace-trimmed dress, raising the bottle high above her. She gives a grand smile for the photographers, looking a hell of a lot older than her fourteen years—when was the last time I saw her? Four months ago?

"For the glory of Savient," she proclaims, making it sound entirely charming.

Then she hurls the bottle at the *Impressive*'s hull with all the force and determination worthy of a Dakar, and it shatters into a hundred pieces, iron plates running red.

4

₃ AURELIA ISENDARE ₆

Hathene, Etania

My boots are entirely muddied by the time I reach the familiar honey-coloured walls of home. After depositing Ivory at the stables, I try to dart inconspicuously for the back doors of Hathene Palace, through the still-dreary east gardens, then sprint across the wide lawn and pray my mother won't see from any of the broad windows. Her quiet displeasure looms like a shadow beneath the spiraling grey pinnacles.

I slip in through rear smoky kitchens and nearly run right into a young hall boy carrying a freshly plucked goose. He blushes hard. The kitchen maids standing at the wood table try not to stare as they knead dough for the oven. It's not the first time I've used this route, but thankfully we've an unspoken agreement where I hurry through silently and they pretend they've seen nothing. It's awkward, yes, but it only ever lasts a moment or two. A brief moment of nearly tripping over vegetable crates, smelling spice and flour and sweat, then I'm up the flight of narrow stairs and bursting into the bright marble halls of the main wing.

Home.

The glossy floors shine beneath my dirty boots, arched alcoves on either side displaying oil paintings and colourful tapestries. I hurry down the empty hall—it's still too early for the courtiers to linger about, the ladies in fox furs and the men with waist-

coats and scarves—and bits of mud fall behind me in a convicting trail.

Mother's rooms are in the quiet western wing, a peaceful
place far removed from the dining halls and audience rooms and
state apartments. The place where she can watch her beloved
sun set each evening. But when I come in view of her parlour,
raised voices filter through the oak. My mother and brother. I
approach cautiously. Pillars guard the Queen's parlour doors, the
elk and wolf crest of Etania painted atop, wrapped in our kingdom's motto—*Loyalty binds us.*

I knock.

The voices cease swiftly. After a breath, the door opens and
my brother, Renisala, stands there, handsome and dark-haired,
his hazel eyes at first annoyed, certainly affronted by someone's
nerve to knock so boldly, then changing to relief as he waves
me in.

I'm his ally.

Uncertain what trap I've stepped into, I try a smile at both,
but Mother's gaze is still fixed on Reni, her body very still, her
anger silent as a cat coiled tight. She reminds me of the *si'yah*
leopards of the Southern steppes. Here, they're only painted in
their elegance, silver-striped creatures with russet fur, decorat-
ing the halls. But in Resya . . .

"And what do you know, my son?" she asks sharply, accent
glittering like desert stone. "You who have never stepped a foot
beyond the western Heights?"

Reni raises his hands. "Stars, this isn't my vain opinion,
Mother! It's in the papers! It's reality, being discussed in every
royal council across the North—except ours. This Southern uprising is spreading faster than it can be contained."

"And you think the truth comes from a bit of paper? The page
lies as easily as the tongue."

He frowns at her derision. "Seath is on the move again, rallying these Southern fools to his Nahir cause, and it's only a matter

of time before that ambitious General Dakar spies a new opportunity there. He'll set his army on the things everyone else
in the North can't keep ahold of. He'll stir it up, unite the South
even stronger. And then do you know what happens, Mother?
The world grows desperate. The Nahir, the North. It will be a
nightmare, the precarious balance upset, and we can't entangle
ourselves in that."

Mother's brows are still raised. "The people of the South are
no fools. The fools are those here in the North who insist on
taking what doesn't belong to them, who haven't stopped pushing and taking for a hundred years no matter the nightmare it
has become."

Reni gives me a grimacing glance, as if he can't believe the
things he's hearing. These careless words from her are what he
fears most. The South is her home. A place she understands
while the rest of the world watches in panic. But she can't say
such things aloud. Not here. Not now. Not when our father went
against tradition and gave his crown to her in full, so she might
rule absolutely until Reni was of age.

She already looks too much like a *si'yah* cat in a kingdom of
wolves.

"Isn't Seath dead?" I ask cautiously, because that was certainly
what I read in the papers only a month ago.

A fresh shadow mars Reni's face. "True or not, someone is
masquerading under his name and leading the insurrection."

Mother laughs dismissively, a bold sound in the tension of the
room. "Seath isn't dead. He's never dead."

Before Reni can react to that, I intervene and offer Mother
the hidden letter in my coat pocket, playing for a distraction.

"It's from Ambassador Havis," I say, confident the bait is
strong.

It works—Reni looks as if I've just handed over a suspiciously
decorated dessert.

Mother ignores his curiosity, ripping the seal, and I slip to Reni's side, both of us facing the large map on the wall, giving her the illusion of privacy. His hand brushes mine. It's a reminder of his love—and also a request I stay on his side no matter where this conversation leads, even if it wounds Mother.

I don't commit myself yet. Ignoring his earnest glance, I focus on the map as if it really is of sudden and great concern. Red lines cover the beige shadows of continents, the tiny shape of Etania buried in mountains, surrounded by our neighbouring kingdoms which make up the western Heights, and all of us in turn dwarfed by the oldest Northern empire—Landore. Across the continent are the eastern nations of the North, new and young and violent, demanding to be treated as equals despite their lack of royal rule. Savient dominates the landscape, having swallowed three into one.

And far beneath the Black Sea is the Southern continent, Resya abandoned at the edge. My readings for the university exams say it was the chaos of the South which once worked to our advantage. There were too many groups, each at odds. They say the people of the South don't have a shared history as we in the North do. Mother disagrees, of course, saying there was once a university there—I can't remember where—which was the most advanced in all the world, founded by a Southern queen no less, which seems too much like myth since there aren't even any monarchies in the South. Instead, the possibly dead Seath is uniting many under his Nahir cause, the uprising greater than it has been in over fifty years. Landore is on the cusp of losing control of its territory, Thurn—along with the precious natural resources and any chance of peace.

Truly, how can anyone say what the best path forward is?

"And what does Havis want now?" Reni asks, slicing the silence with his disdain.

Mother says nothing. We turn, as if we haven't been waiting

for her to speak the past minutes. As if we aren't both desperate to know what requests a shifting man like Havis would bring from Resya.

When she remains silent, Reni tosses a newspaper onto the table before her. The headline sits ugly in black ink.

NAHIR AMBUSH LANDORIAN ROYAL 6TH REGIMENT,
EAST OF RESYAN BORDER

"I don't live in a fantasy, Mother," Reni says, "and I see the cards on the table. We can't have anything to do with your homeland, no matter what Havis says. Not when it fails to take decisive action against the insurrection."

She looks at his face, and then mine, certainly seeing the anger in him and the regret in me. She knows I'm on his side in this. But the familiar strength of a challenge brightens her dark eyes. "And what if this 'insurrection' is in fact a great revolution? A necessary change to right the injustice of the past? What then, my son?"

Her implication hangs starkly, uncomfortable. Reni has no answer. If she could—if it wouldn't stain Reni and me forever—she'd stand before the entire North and say this is all a fiction, that the broadcasts lie, that the Nahir are not the absolute reflection of her people, and that one day, soon, the South will rule itself again in honour, free of Northern influence.

She'd say that—but then she'd have every royal against us.

She closes her eyes briefly, and when she speaks again, she speaks in lilting, soft Resyan. "I desire more trust from the both of you. The two of you are my very heart. Truly, your blood of two worlds is a strength, a great power, though it may not seem so yet."

Reni says nothing. He likes to pretend he can't speak her tongue, as if he's Etanian through and through.

But I reply quickly, in kind. "I believe you, Mother. I do."

Reni throws me a frustrated glance, betrayed, but I can't bear to say any other. On quiet evenings when her door is closed, Mother sits with me and talks in Resyan, only the two of us, and she'll remember how the capital city there glows hot in the evening light, colours of ginger and caramel. How the nights are so peaceful you can hear your own heart beat and thoughts turn. How the lingering heat can be tasted on the tongue, warm and citrus-sweet.

In those secret moments we share, I ache for her. Resyan operas playing on the gramophone, our mint tea steaming with lemon rind. I try to believe her stories, but they feel like a fiction, like ghosts of a place that no longer exists.

I know her loneliness.

But she waits, staring at Reni.

Reni shakes his head, his earnest gaze becoming all Father—quiet, firm, diplomatic. He speaks Etanian. "Listen, Mother. I see the new wealth to be gained from Savient and know why you've pursued this alliance. I know how depleted our mountains are better than anyone. Savien petrol might benefit our kingdom. But that doesn't change the truth—General Dakar is out for his own gain, in the North and in the South. And I'm to trust you as you invite him here? Welcome him with open arms even as our people protest? No, Mother. True power is a unified kingdom, and not even you can deny that."

The silence between us aches.

I see the regret on Mother's face. I know she hates to be at odds with Reni, can see how it bruises her heart. And yet her fire is as strong as his, and her stare is both fierce and gentle. It covers us both. "Someday, my children, you will see that to serve the ones you love, you must be bold in action." She looks back to Reni. "But for now, you are not yet twenty. And until that day you take the crown, I am still Queen—and you will remember it."

5

⟩ ATHAN DAKAR ⟨

Valon, Savient

I arrive to the Victory Week gala dressed in my full uniform—
starched jacket, stiff grey wool, and spotless boots. A good half
hour was spent ironing out creases and shining leather, since
that's my job, not the maid's. Father says there's no reason another person should do what you have the time and ability to
do yourself. And though Savient might not have a real court, and
Father might hold most royal customs in disdain, he can still
throw a damn good party. Anything to win new allies and reward loyal friends, and we three sons are the polished reflection
of him. He expects an impressive appearance.

But I still made sure to run a hand through my combed hair,
messing it up just enough a bit falls over my forehead.

Rebellion—or something like it.

The large room before me whirls beneath dimmed chandeliers, revelers marching about, laughing, teetering on the edge
of tipsy. Voices surge above the music, lit by brandy and whisky
and everything else bitter and strong. All of it's barely contained
by the mahogany walls and heavy, angled curtains. Our home
looks too brooding and efficient for this sort of thing, but tonight no one cares. It's ten years of Savient. Ten years of glory.
A reckless sort of pride because the world is suddenly ours to
take.

I resist the urge to wave a white flag and run out again.

As I press through the crowd, predictable discussions spin about the war in neighbouring Karkev. Men in suits boast over their sons in uniform, the latest promotions and honours, he'd with a hundred ideas about why a war against a pack of isolated Northern criminals has dragged on for two years and how he'd end it. Colonels and captains give me approving pats on the shoulder, too many to keep track of.

"Looking forward to seeing you at the front," one says.

"Ready to shoot a few down," I reply, like there's no better pastime than war.

The wives sigh over my uniform and tell me I'm now as handsome as my brother. Which one? Doesn't matter. On and on, none of the conversations lasting more than a minute or two.

I sweep the room and spot Cyar seated near the back. He and a few pilots have secured a table in the corner, hiding as it were. I'm going to make a break for it.

Kalt clears his throat next to me.

Where the hell did he come from?

He nods towards Mother and Arrin, seated in what looks to be an awkward stalemate. Mother's pouring a glass of wine—drunk, judging by the level of concentration required—while Arrin flirts with a pretty brunette on his lap. A new girlfriend, according to Leannya. As of two days ago. Next to him is the red-haired Garrick Carr, his loyal ass of a friend. This evening's off to a galloping start.

Kalt's eyes narrow on me, an order not to abandon him at the brink of conflict. No sign of Father anywhere.

We head for the table.

When we arrive, Mother offers me a radiant smile doused in wine. Kalt gets a formal nod. Garrick grunts a welcome that's neither friendly nor cold. He's a pilot, Captain of the Moonstrike squadron, but far from an ally. He spends too much time with Arrin and treats me like any other kid brother.

And Arrin?

He doesn't give us a glance. Too busy whispering a trail of kisses across his girl's arm. "It's so cold in Karkev," he says, lips against her skin. "I'm never warm, not like now. I think I'll have to take you back with me."

She giggles. "Whatever you wish, Commander."

He plunks his cap on her head.

We sit at the table and wait for him to acknowledge us. The meals are served. Eventually, he does. "Littlest brother of mine!" That's me. "Have a drink—or three!"

"No, just one for him," Mother says, words unsteady. "Don't be a poor influence."

"Mother knows best." Arrin raises his glass.

Shameless, he turns and gives his brunette a full kiss on the mouth.

"Must you do this at the table?" Mother asks sharply.

"You invited me to sit with you," he replies, coming up for air.

"Yes, I invited *you*. Not your friend."

The girl's smile disappears. No woman wants to be on the bad side of Lady Dakar.

Kalt silently creates a fortress of vegetables on his plate. Garrick fiddles with the cuff of his uniform, blending into the background. The brunette's the only one who doesn't know what to make of it and her red lips press together nervously, cherry red even in the low lights.

"Are you from Valon?" I ask, since someone needs to try.

"Yes." She brightens. "And you study at the Air Academy?"

So Arrin does talk about me now and again. Or maybe she just recognizes the uniform. Probably that. "One month left to go."

"You're very young to be a pilot," she replies, genuinely sweet, as Leannya said she was. "You must be nervous." Then she adds, "And you look so very much like your mother."

"Not really," I say, acknowledging the first statement, then stop, because it sounds like I'm denying the second. Which is ridiculous. No one could see me next to Mother and not know we're the same blood and bone. Same fair hair, grey eyes, fine features. Not to mention, a good three inches shorter than both Arrin and Kalt. She used to tell me I'd catch up, but that became wishful thinking about this time last year when I was still barely brushing six feet. I always try to fudge it on physical reports. Who can tell the difference between five-nine and six anyway?

Arrin grins. "Ah, my little brother's brilliant. He'll be an ace, flying in the skies so high above the rest of us." Always such cheerful sarcasm with him. "Not long now until he earns his wings, then it's off to the war with me and we'll see how brave he really is." He tries to top up my glass and I move it out of his reach. "Come on, clever brother. A drink to celebrate your talent."

"Only if he makes Top Flight," Garrick says, not sounding very hopeful of my odds. "Seventh place is a lot of ground to make up."

"Seventh place?" Arrin repeats.

"Yes," Garrick continues casually. "Major Torhan says he has no instinct in the air."

I'd like to remove that pleasant, fake smile from his lips. "You have no right to discuss my scores, Captain."

Garrick shrugs. "It's only your family. And besides, Top Flight isn't everything. Transport pilots are vital too."

Rather disingenuous considering he currently holds the highest record at the Academy and is also wearing two new medals from the front.

Arrin's still studying me, calculating suspicion in his gaze. The kind that wins him battles. "Athan's not a damn transport pilot. With a mind like his, he could outfly any plane in the sky."

"Outthink or outfly?" Garrick asks. "Two different things."

Yes, it would feel damn good to beat his score and not even

try. I imagine some other world where I actually want to make
Top Flight, where I'm on fire for the frontlines, and the first thing
I do is steal Garrick Carr's glorious star from his swaggering,
cocky hands.

It's a nice fantasy.

Arrin turns from me to Garrick. "Well, I suppose you'd know,
wouldn't you?" His smile reappears and he addresses the table.
"This is a hero of the war, everyone—a hero! You heard about
the victory this winter at Ersili, yes?"

We each nod, me the most. Anything to keep Arrin distracted
from whatever direction he was headed.

"Captain Carr here," he gestures at Garrick and then nudges
his girl, encouraging an interested smile from her, "shot down a
hundred planes on his own. It was incredible. I saw the entire
thing."

"You might have added some extra zeros on there," Garrick
says, far from self-effacing.

"That's not the story you tell at home, Captain."

"In that case, I believe it was a hundred planes plus a
bunker."

"And eight tanks!"

Arrin and Garrick are the only two who laugh, because apparently war is funny.

"And how many of your own squadron did you lose, Captain?"
Mother asks.

The laughter dies, and Garrick blinks. Who brings the dead
to a dinner party? Only my mother.

"Well," Garrick begins. "I . . . it was Ersili we're talking about?
That was a daytime assault and I think—"

"You have lost men, haven't you?" Mother presses. She places
a protective hand on mine.

Garrick glances to Arrin, then back. "Yes."

Her hand tightens, hot against my skin. "I don't trust those
airplanes. Imagine what it must be like to fall from the sky in

one, nothing to do but pray the whole way, flames and the rest.
Imagine the terror."

"Yes, imagine it," Arrin agrees, an edge to his voice again.
"Imagine your little favourite in danger. Here he is, finally old
enough to join the rest of us, and there's not a thing you can do
about it."

I try to slide my hand from beneath hers.

She grips my arm instead, pleading. "Arrin, it's your brother
you speak of. He's only seventeen. How could you—"

"You're right. He's so young, isn't he?" Arrin shoots me a poisonous look. "Tell me, Mother, is that how old I was when I
started fighting? Kalt, you'd know. Was I this old? Enlighten
everyone."

My other brother looks up from his plate. "I know you're old
enough to recognize when it's time to stop."

"Old enough to know when to stop? Me?" Arrin dissolves into
laughter, looking at his girl. "Sweetheart, am I old enough?" She's
moved as far across his lap as she can get without touching
Garrick. Arrin points his chin at me. "What about Athan over
there? Is he old enough for this? Would you make a man out of
him? Perhaps you could tonight, if you have the time?"

Both Mother and the girl gasp.

This really is going down on record as one of Arrin's greatest
nights. If only Cyar were here to witness the unraveling. Or better yet, Father. That would be breathtaking.

Arrin raises his hands. "What? I was kidding. It's a joke." He
looks around the table at each of us, like we're all slow-witted.
He helps himself to the blueberry cakes being served. "I'm sure
everything will be fine and Athan will stay perfect as he is now."

Mother ticks her fingernails against the wine glass. "Are you
done?"

"I believe I am." He lights up a cigarette, the sour smell turning my stomach. His gaze meets mine, predatory again, seizing
on whatever he can find. "You don't approve of this?"

"It's not good for you," I say.

"Not good for me?"

"No."

He blows out a strand of smoke. "I had no clue. What would I do without you, littlest brother?"

I stick my fork into the cake and ignore him. I'm not going where he leads.

But that doesn't stop him. "Don't worry, Athan. You'll get your vices too. You know that, don't you, Mother? He'll be like me. One tour on the frontlines and he'll come back entirely bent out of shape. Drinking, smoking, doing whatever else we rotten boys do. Imagine that. Your favourite brought down to earth with the rest of us."

Mother hurls her fist against the table. "Even if he were all those things and more, he'd still turn out a better man than you'll ever hope to be!"

Someone sucks in a breath. Possibly Kalt. Or maybe it was me.

The words flinch across Arrin's face like a physical blow. For a moment, for one solitary sliver of a moment, I almost feel sorry for him. He's always been a mess. But then he grins. "I think that's the drink talking, Mother."

She springs from the table, pale and furious, and her glass spills. Before any of us can react, she's gone. Off across the low-lit room and through the gaping doorway. The guests around pretend not to notice, heads down, carrying on with conversations, though of course they're watching.

Arrin stares at the red wine stain on the tablecloth. "I think it's time we hid the bottles from her, especially when I'm around."

The two-day girlfriend on his lap looks to me for help.

Me?

It's at this moment, uncanny timing, that Father chooses to enter the hall, Admiral Malek and Colonel Evertal following in his wake. They're his closest advisers, comrades since the beginning. Malek's dark brown skin is accented by a granite uniform decorated in medals, his face wielding its usual detached gaze. His son is a captain in the Air Force—a captain I'd give anything to fly with, in that fantasy world where I actually make Top Flight. Captain Malek is everything my brothers are not. Evertal, at Father's left, wears the same crisp uniform as the men, her blonde hair twisted back tight, pulling at harsh lines around her eyes. Arrin is the closest thing she has to a son.

Those in their way move aside, eyes following raptly.

Arrin quickly puts out the cigarette and pushes the girl from his lap. Garrick's wise enough to suddenly be needed elsewhere in the room. By the time Father arrives at our table, we three sons have stood up respectfully, but Arrin teeters against his chair.

Father wastes no time. "Where's your mother?"

Silence.

Evertal slinks to Father's side. She practically raised Arrin in the revolution, when Mother was hiding in terror far behind the frontlines—or so Kalt told me once—and she gives him an unyielding look now. No mercy. Affection is weakness, especially for a woman who holds a rank like hers.

It's Kalt who finally speaks. "There was a disagreement, sir. Mother left."

"Disagreement?"

"Between Athan and Arrin."

Damn it, I'd like to ram my elbow into stupid, self-serving Kalt. Dragging me into this. But he won't mention Mother's drinking. Father doesn't like talking about it, a secret we're all obligated to keep.

And apparently Father's satisfied enough with Kalt's answer. He won't take the time to find Mother and learn the truth. They don't even share the same room anymore. The only thing Father's ever done in her honour was make the chamomile, her

favourite flower, our national flower. He thinks that counts for
something.

Father turns to the brunette, and she stares up at him wide-
eyed. He smiles, greeting her, and if he knows she's just one of
Arrin's many lady friends, that he won't be seeing her past tonight, he doesn't let on.

Evertal, of course, doesn't smile. She just asks Arrin about
some matter in Karkev and he gives a succinct report. Subdued.

I glance over my shoulder at the table where Cyar sits. He
notices and sends a questioning look. I shrug. Only the usual.

I turn back and find Father watching me, expression nebu-
lous. That's unnerving. Kalt carries on with something about the
Impressive and its sea trial, not noticing—or pretending not to
notice—that his helpful words fall on half an ear.

I finish my single glass of wine.

Father's gaze drifts back to Kalt.

Another glance over my shoulder at Cyar. Now he's motioning for the door, quite the temptation.

"You want to leave with Hajari?" Father asks, cutting Kalt off
mid-sentence.

I swing around. "If that's all right, sir."

"You're not needed here." He studies Cyar. "It's a good thing
you have a loyal friend like that. I'm not sure you'd even know
where you were going without him." He smiles vaguely, the kind
that has something dark beneath the surface.

Play along. That's all I can do. "No, sir."

This is permission to leave and I'm taking it.

Cyar and I escape with a hijacked bottle of brandy. We borrow
one of Father's motorcars and drive it through the narrow streets
of Valon like wild idiots, giving an old man on foot a scare. Yes,
it's a bit reckless, but Arrin's right about one thing—we all have

our vices. I'm used to my plane, to flying in smooth arcs and loops, and every bump on the road is a disappointment. I hate the heavy feeling of earth.

We pull up beside the old wall that once protected the city. It's no longer very impressive, remnants left to bleach and crack, but it commands a nice view of Valon, perched on a rise from which you can see for miles. The rocky green plains of northern Savient stretch to the east, forested along the edges. The vague glimmer of sea hangs in the west.

We crawl up the shortest section, still a steep climb, then walk along the top. It's a fifty-foot drop, but I let one of my boots hang off the edge. Up high is where I'm free. Then we lean against the crumbling stone with our brandy and get drunk. Blissful oblivion.

Cyar grips his crumpled poem between shaky hands, trying to read it with a straight face. Something about "eternal" and "sunflower" and "smile."

God, he's a hopeless romantic.

At ten o'clock, fireworks explode above the city, all exciting sounds and swirls. Spectacular colours like a dawn sky on fire. Burning, brightening, here and there and everywhere.

Eleven o'clock.

We're on the grass, laughing about nothing.

"You compared her to a sunflower? Really?"

"It's a metaphor, Athan. She's like my own little flower."

"I got that part."

"Shining in the sun of Rahmet!"

"Now it makes perfect sense."

He lets out a wistful sigh. "You're just jealous. You've never even kissed a girl."

Midnight.

The show's long over and the drink begins to fade. Thoughts steady as city lights waver on the horizon. Cyar sits, legs dangling over the ledge. The moments pass, quiet, and then he says, "Do you know I wouldn't be here without you?"

"Mm." I'm trying to get the last drops out of the bottle.

"I never told you, but they made me take a second exam my first day at the Academy. I guess they didn't think a kid from Rahmet could've scored so high on the entrance tests, and they were right. I knew the numbers, the math. But the Savien words . . . I thought they'd send me home."

"They didn't."

He stares at the cityscape, pensive. "No, because Torhan said 'Put him in room 36. That'll help.' Your room, Athan, because I needed all the help I could get, from the one student who was bound to be the best. They told me who you were and warned me not to say anything stupid or I'd be shot at dawn. That's why I cried the first night. I thought I'd never be good enough." He faces me again. "And when that teacher called on me, and I didn't even know what a nautical mile was, you were sketching the fox—"

"Yeah, I was there."

He holds out a hand. "Wait a minute, this is important. It was a fox, and right there, beside the fox, you wrote the numbers I needed to answer the question. You looked at me and gave permission, and that's when I knew you'd be my friend. You rescued me when it gave you nothing in return." He pauses. "I'd never have made it this far without you, Athan."

Because you're the only brother I have, I want to say, *and I'd give my life for you.*

"And now we're going to make Top Flight. Go wherever they send us next. We'll be the best and I'll tell the story to my children one day, about how I served with the General's own son." His face is inspiring in the darkness. Flickering lights play across his soft features, his black hair merging with shadows. Honesty woven like loyalty in his gaze.

I try a smile and a nod.

I can't speak the lie tonight.

Cyar drives us home later, since I'm still adrift in a sweet haze. We go around back, trying to sneak through the rear gates, and run right into Arrin, Garrick, and the rest of their club of drunken heroes.

Damn it.

"My seventh-place little brother!" Arrin calls, zeroing in. No sign of his lady friend anywhere. He stumbles over to me wearing a jackal's grin. "Come with us tonight. I know a lonely girl who's in love with me. Not very pretty, but she might settle for you. We can celebrate you turning sixteen!"

"I'm seventeen," I say, annoyed that he looks blurry and out of focus. "And it's not my birthday."

He shrugs, wrapping a rough arm around my shoulders. I stagger backwards. "Not so noble now, are you?" he crows. "Walking crooked. What would Mother think?"

"Throw yourself off a pier, Arrin."

It's probably the stupidest insult I've ever hurled, but Garrick whistles, the drunk ass.

Arrin shoves me away. "That was a low point in my life."

At least he remembers. I was fourteen the first time he took me out with him, hauling me around some salty port town in Brisal, the sort of forgotten place, still burnt-out from the war, where he could be reckless without consequence. He tried very hard to get me drunk. It didn't work—I hated the taste. So he got himself drunk instead and then started pining for some red-headed girl in a brandy-fueled monologue of woe, ready to jump off the pier, and I stopped him. Or rather, I grabbed him from the edge in a panic and he was so drunk he fell on top of me. Then his fist gave me a bloody lip, and he said he was going to die in Father's wars anyway and I was a selfish little bastard for not letting him take the easy way out.

Brotherly love.

"Your loss with the girl then," Arrin announces, once he realizes we won't be convinced. He studies Cyar and me with a devilish smirk. "You two are always together, though. Maybe you need advice from Kalt?"

"Shut the hell up, Arrin!"

I'd hit him, but Cyar already has me through the gates. Not worth the effort. Or the bruises. The ground shifts beneath my feet as we walk, like a listing boat, every step uneven somehow. The house suddenly seems a long way off. I'd rather just sleep in the garden. Not a bad idea. It's warm enough tonight, the air feels nice. Cool and fresh. I start to resist Cyar's pull, but voices drift from the narrow alley to the left of our home.

The drunken heroes?

No, they went the other way. Their laughter echoes somewhere beneath the distant street lamps. I listen closer, trying to think through the whirl in my head.

Father's voice. And Admiral Malek's.

Out here?

I walk in their direction, Cyar trailing behind, and a circle of dark figures appears around the corner. We stop abruptly. The world lurches again, and I grab the wall.

"Havis didn't tell me anything else," a desperate man implores, on his knees before Malek. "He only said Sinora Lehzar doesn't know the ones in Etania are false. She believes her people are truly protesting us, and isn't that what you want? She—"

Malek towers over him. "Then why didn't you bring us his message right away?"

"I was going to, I swear! I wouldn't lie."

Sinora Lehzar.

I know it, distantly, in my fog. The woman Father hates. A Southern traitor from long before Savient. Arrin threw her name as a challenge once, when he was sixteen, and Father broke his nose for it. It's the only time I've ever seen Arrin almost cry.

The desperate man turns to Father now, rushing with, "It's complicated. You know this. She's a damn queen, and we're dealing with Seath—"

Father steps close and aims a pistol at the man's head. "You don't ever speak that name aloud."

He cowers. "Of course not."

"Have you?"

"No, no! I swear to God and all things sacred, I haven't!"

The man's panting breath fills the chilly silence. The gun looms at his forehead.

"I believe you," Father says after a moment.

The man's shoulders drop in relief.

"But I don't trust you any longer."

A sharp report echoes, a shower of red scattering on cement along with bits of brain, and Cyar's fingers bite into my arm. I grab the wall again.

Father stares at the body a moment, then glances up, spotting us frozen in the shadows. Cyar's boots scuff backwards. The instinct to flee. I feel it too, but Father's walking for us, pistol in hand, his gaze forbidding me to run. I can't make my feet work.

"Hajari, leave us," he says when he reaches me.

It's the sharp edge that heels even Arrin.

Cyar hesitates for one noble moment, like the idea to wait for me crosses his mind, even if only for a breath, then his boots are hurrying down the path behind. Don't blame him.

I look at the body on the ground. Blood curls around the man's head, dark as oil in the night. "What did he—"

"Traitors must be dealt with," Father says. "He said one thing and did another."

My limbs go weak.

"Tell me you're going to make Top Flight, boy."

Oh God, he's doing this now? With a gun in hand, with a body behind him? And I'm drunk as hell. Maybe that's a good thing. I'm not even sure what's happening.

"Yes, sir."

"I hear you're barely in seventh place."

Damn Arrin. At least Torhan knew how to keep a secret.

"That's not a bad position to be in," I say. "Seventh out of thirty is really quite . . ." My voice dies.

His eyes narrow. "I realized years ago that you do everything halfhearted. I've watched it and let you carry on, because I figured you were just a child and eventually you'd grow out of it. But here you are, five weeks from graduating and no more committed to anything except your own damn self."

"No, sir, that's not—"

"I won't pull strings for you. Fixing odds helps no one, not in war. But things have become more serious"—he shrugs at the body behind—"and I know there's a wealth of talent buried in that head of yours. You can pretend to be different all you want, but you're fighting for something. I know you are because you're my son, and I won't leave you at home." He stabs the pistol at me. Instinctively, I back up. "This is my only warning to you. If you're not headed for the squadrons, then I'll find another way for you to help me."

"Another way?" I sound a bit hoarse.

"Yes. You could be adjutant to Malek, or a translator in my command. You have a perfect grade in linguistics, don't you?"

I knew I should have failed at everything. Why didn't I figure that one out? Why didn't I let myself fade long ago? Is it because of Cyar? What the hell was I thinking?

I'm not as smart as everyone believes. This proves it.

Before I can speak, he grabs my shoulder, his fury so hot I brace for his fist. A broken nose. But it doesn't come. Only his face inches from my own. "You listen and listen close. I didn't sacrifice everything—the *blood* of my men—to have a son who leaves the hard work to others. I've been through hell for you and you would throw it in my face!"

"I never—"

"You have two choices. Top Flight or my command." He pushes me hard. "Now go sleep off the drink. We're flying for Rahmet in the morning and Hajari won't be coming along. If you want to do this on your own, then you'd better get used to a life where he doesn't throw you a goddamn map every time you need it."

He gives me a last contemptuous glare, then holsters his pistol and strides back for the bloody traitor.

I stare after him, bleeding inside. "Father, wait!"

He doesn't turn around.

I don't know why I thought he would. I don't even know what I would have said.

Desperation.

Shaking, I retreat inside and I'm fairly sure the whole world's crumbling beneath me. I head for Mother's room without thinking. I don't even know if she's awake, or sober, but everything's turned off in my head. Thoughts, words, ideas. The entire brilliant creation of my mind is short-circuiting, and by the time I'm standing in front of her, all I want is to feel her warmth.

She doesn't need to ask any questions. I'm sure she heard the shot, too.

She rests her head against mine, her arms around me gently. I'm ashamed by how quickly it stills my panicked heart. Seventeen, damn it.

"Father just—"

"I know," she says, and there's no reaction. Not a flinch or a tremor, only weary acceptance. She's seen a thousand things from him. She's seen worse.

I want to tell her what he said, the threat that now hangs over me, but I don't know where to begin. I don't know whether to lie or tell the truth or find somewhere in the middle, and she pushes me back, still gentle. "Are you going to make Top Flight, my love?"

Her question holds no mystery.

She wants to know whom I'll choose. It's the only question there's ever been.

"I . . . I don't know," I admit. "My flying scores are too low, but perhaps they'll put me here, in transport. I'd be closer to you then."

She silences me with a feather of a finger. "Is that what you truly want?"

The clock on her table ticks away the midnight silence. One, two, three, four. It winds up my brain, ticking it into the stupid knot it always is. *No*, I want to shout at the entire world. *There are a hundred things burning inside me and I don't even know which one is true. I want to be away from here. I don't want this life any more than I want my own body buried in the damn ground! But I also want to fly, every day if I can, because it's the only place that feels right. I want to fly with Cyar, because the thought of him flying alongside some other pilot, some stranger who doesn't even care about him the way I do, who won't keep him safe, makes me feel like I'm kicking at walls and can't get out.*

But I don't say it.

I don't know if I'd be betraying her or myself.

"I know you're confused," she says softly, but firmly. She's been made tiny from years in His shadow, light worn away, but somehow she's still outside of it. "A mother knows the depth of her saddest child. She feels the pain of her most broken one. You were mine, but I gave you up long ago. Please don't leave your brothers alone in this. Don't choose me. I fear for what he will ask of them." She peers up into my face, her grief holding the weight of an entire family.

I look at her helplessly. "But I'm not like them."

"No, you're not. They are earth and sea. They can only go so far until they run up against each other." She touches my cheek. "But you are the sky, my love. You are limitless."

The conviction in her eyes is too much. She thinks I'm better than them. She's always thought that, earned or not, and it's as unfair as Father's threat, an expectation I can't ever live up to. I'm selfish and rotten at the middle. I'm even as drunk as Arrin right now.

I don't want to do what she asks.

I give her the briefest kiss on her cheek, then escape for my room, chased by guilt and frustration. I'm surprised to find Cyar waiting there, still a bit wide-eyed. He's supposed to be in the guest room downstairs. Oh well. Don't want to be alone tonight. I give him my bed and take the floor, and he gives me a torn glance before pulling the covers over himself.

He knows when to say nothing. But he wants to.

In the silence, the walls seem to shrink by the minute, caving, burying me alive. I can't sleep. I can't think. I drift into the wide sea of memories from long ago, with smoldering towns, flashes of bullets, the smell of petrol and ash. I see a mangled corpse lying in a ditch. My brothers stare like it's the carcass of a wild animal—nameless, forgotten—and Arrin kicks at the twisted limbs. He's thirteen, godlike to me. Tall and unafraid. He can talk back to Father and take the punishment without flinching. He can run laps for hours, in the heat, in the mud, with Father cursing him every step. A fierce fire that never dies out. And all I want is for Arrin to look at me. All I want is for him to say my name and—

I close my eyes.

Nothing's gained without sacrifice. Everyone seems to accept that but me.

6

Hathene, Etania

"Ah, you look lovely in blue, Aurelia."

"You say that about every colour I wear."

Heathwyn, my governess, smiles. "Because it's always true."

She pins my dark hair with a maroon feather clip, her aging hands soft and warm, her own hair brown and greying. In the mirror, my silk dress gathers in all the right places. The rich hue illuminates my amber skin, still a bit paler from winter, and silver beading spirals across the bodice like lights and colours in a night sky. I raise my chin, as Mother would, pearl-drop earrings swinging.

I look seventeen already.

"Now please be courteous with the Ambassador tonight," Heathwyn instructs. "I'll not hear of any more impertinent comments. A smile and nothing less."

I turn from the mirror, facing both my governess and the delicate chaos of my room—chiffon and lace dresses strewn across the bed, headbands of gem and pearl scattered, textbooks towering and filled with notes for the university exams. "But I can't smile at him."

"You must."

"I can't."

"But you will."

And she's right—I will. Such rotten luck, but I will.

At the banquet hall doors, I find Reni waiting for me between the marble pillars, dressed in a decorated military coat, though the only place he's ever fired a gun is on a hunt. He offers an arm, and down the velvet promenade steps we go, smiling grandly.

Smiling, smiling, as we should.

Before us, a long table shimmers with crystal pitchers and silver platters, chandeliers casting a golden glow, illuminating the painted ceiling above, where wild elk arch their antlers before the immortalized form of Prince Efan, his resting sword decorated with peaceful pink orchids—the sacred flower of Etania—and a fox crouched loyal at his feet. Each represents an aspect of the man who began our Northern dynasty six hundred years ago, a man who was brave and gentle and clever at once. I'm sure in Landore they have the same glorious painting, except with their own sacred white roses on display. Every kingdom honours Efan.

Mother stands near the head of the table, dressed in a taffeta gown of gold, tiny mauve flowers stitched into the waist and trailing down to the hem, her chin held high despite the tension of the General's impending visit that permeates the court. She shows no fear, sharpened by a crown she never asked to wear and steeped in the patience of a woman forced to navigate the council of men. In Resya, it's custom for friends to greet each other with a kiss, and she places one now on the bearded cheek of her oldest and most loyal advisor, Lord Marcin. She bestows this honour only on family and those she trusts intimately. It's an elusive gift, one the men of our court crave. Anything to prove they're beloved of Boreas Isendare's ruling widow.

And as for Havis?

I spot him standing in a corner by himself, sipping a very full glass of red wine, stifling a yawn. Stars. But I give him a polite nod, the most I can muster, and he raises his brimming drink in my direction.

"Try a bit harder in public, couldn't you?" Reni whispers.

"Not until I find out what's in his rotten letter."

I can't help but wonder if it might be about me, a marriage proposal mixed in with his other more political requests, but my brother only grimaces through his smile. A princely feat.

The ladies of court, dressed in beaded gowns and draped in silken evening shawls, part respectfully when we arrive at the table. Lord Marcin and Uncle Tanek and the rest of Mother's council, all of them in tailcoats, bow from the neck. The retiring Colonel Lyle, whose party this is, stands with his entourage from the Royal 3rd Squadron, each wearing a uniform inlaid with the gold and green of the Etanian flag. It's a pretty picture of harmony, which is a relief considering the war of opinion beyond our palace gates.

"Beautiful darling," Mother says, taking my hand. She kisses my left cheek, then the other, trailing a scent of jasmine. "What a gown this is! Sapphire goes lovely with your dark hair. You're breathtaking, my little star. Is she not, Lord Marcin?"

"Indeed, Your Majesty," he says with a smile.

My dearest friend, Violet Marcin, quickly leaves her father's side and wraps her arms round me. "Ali, my sweetest heart!" Her painted lips press against my cheek enthusiastically. She's adopted the Resyan tradition as her own, partly because it's in her nature to be warm and bold, but also because she fancies affording Reni the same attention.

I kiss her as well, grinning. "I copied you," I admit, touching my feather clip. "It looked too wonderful on you at your recital."

Violet smiles her grand smile, the sort she wears on stage when she sings. "They say in Landore even larger feathers are being worn. It's a demonstration of Northern solidarity, you see. We should certainly show our support."

"I'm not sure how feathers will frighten the Nahir."

"Does it matter? Now, we need a peacock."

"Stars, where does one find that?"

"I hear such exotic creatures are abundant in Resya. . . ."

I cluck my tongue and swat her arm lightly. She has the nerve to find Havis handsome and urbane, a man possibly tied to alluring adventure. But she can afford such fantasies because she's the picture of Etanian beauty—gracefully mannered, with green eyes and auburn hair and curving hips—and she's already caught the affection of our crowned prince, the prince who's only a year from inheriting his throne.

For her, it's all pretend.

Not for me.

As we sit side by side, her clever smile fades, and she reaches her hand under the table, offering me a small folded paper. Carefully, I look down beneath the lace cloth as if I'm smoothing my dress. We've done this many times before. I peel apart the paper and find a somewhat terrible drawing of a wolf. It's lopsided, eyes and ears out of proportion, shading all wrong, but the wolf was my father's favourite animal, a noble creature long since hunted out of our mountains. And she knows it.

Tears prick my lashes.

Violet touches my hand beneath the lace, distracting everyone around us by boldly fluttering her smile at Reni, on my other side. They play their little wordless game while I recover from the sweet gift.

Of course she wouldn't forget what today means.

At the head of the table, a holy man offers his blessing upon the meal, as is tradition, and Mother nods along, though I know she puts not an ounce of faith in the words. She believes in fate and the luck of stars, not divine favour.

But when he finishes, she says, "Peace upon us."

Champagne flutes are raised—"To Colonel Lyle!"—and first sips are taken.

Footmen step forward, serving silver plates laden with gleaming confit of goose and sour cherries, with poached salmon and

butternut squash. I get my single plate of creamed carrots, dev-
iled eggs, and rosemary potatoes.

Ever since the slaughtered fawn, I haven't tasted a morsel of
meat.

Not far from me, Havis leans back in his chair, tight-lipped,
tapping his knife rudely as a thin man next to him, Lord Jerig,
monologues about how he might solve the Southern unrest if
he were actually across the sea, and if he were actually mad
enough to go to the South. Reni says Jerig is the ringleader of
Mother's critics here at court, set against the General's visit and
anything else that might stray us from Etanian interests.

"It's all very tragic," Jerig finishes, dabbing his lips with an
embroidered napkin. "They've no appreciation for the ways
we've benefited the region. And now it seems Resya itself—the
jewel of the South!—is in Nahir crosshairs. When will they
have enough? Will they not stop until they've forced us out
entirely?"

"Now, there's a tragedy," Havis observes with a trace of bored
irony.

"This General Dakar is no different, in my opinion," Jerig
adds. "He means to solve any dispute with a gun. Surely you, as
a man of diplomacy, see the danger in this?"

"I've never met the General, my lord. I prefer to judge every
situation on its own merits, not the opinions from a newspaper."
Havis pauses. "And perhaps you should do the same."

Jerig laughs, spidery moustache wrinkling. "Ah, still the de-
fender of the South, then? I'm not sure such optimistic sentiment will get you what you wish here at court." His fox eyes dart
across the table to me, and I sense the implication acutely, but I
absorb my irritation by smooshing a rosemary potato.

Jerig won't let it alone. "Your Highness," he says to me. "Tell
me, please, do you think the Ambassador is correct?"

"On the General? Or the South?" I ask politely, annoyed to
the bone.

"Take your pick."

"Well then, I think if the ambassadors were doing their jobs properly then perhaps these Southern men wouldn't be so irritable, and then we wouldn't have the trouble to begin with."

"Oh?" Havis asks with a skeptical, raised brow.

Reni bumps my arm rather pointedly on my left, and Violet laughs into her hand on my right.

"Yes, they sit round tables and talk all day," I continue, louder, "but what good has that ever done in the South? We need men of real action in uniform, like the General. I greatly admire anyone who risks his own life for the service of others. *That* is honourable."

"You don't have to be in uniform to do that," Havis offers.

I raise my chin. "No, I suppose not, Ambassador. But you must agree—the uniform's more dashing!"

Violet laughs out loud, as does Jerig, and Havis has the nerve to join in. Then he stares right at me, taking a savouring bite of the roast goose.

I fume into my creamed carrots, resisting thoughts of Havis's hands on my hips, his rough kisses forcing me into shadowy corners, and instead I listen as the young pilot seated on Violet's right seizes my praise of military men as an excuse to begin some tale about landing his aeroplane in the pitch-black of night. Apparently the 3rd Squadron airbase outside Hathene has a windy approach, and he demonstrates by waving his hand about like an overexcited child, his shiny hair slicked to the side. He keeps peering at Violet like he's waiting for her to give him a round of applause. She has that effect on most young men. But of course it doesn't take long for Reni to notice the lavish attention she's receiving, and he interrupts Slick's boasting with the deceptively casual question "And you think you're better than the pilots of Savient?"

Trust Reni to circle us back round to sour milk.

The pilot smiles nobly. "Of course, Your Highness. They're

only good because they fly such fancy aeroplanes. Give me one of those and I could do the same."

"Well, let's hope you're as talented in battle as you are at spinning tales."

"I'm at the top of my class, Your Highness. That's what counts in a dogfight—talent, not machine."

"And how many battles have you won, rookie?"

The pilot blinks, suddenly aware he's walked himself into embarrassment as others at the table overhear the rising debate and tilt their ears to listen, Violet beaming like a pleased circus master. I'm ready to offer both young men a set of pistols so we can get it over with—Reni will debate this boy into tomorrow otherwise, and Uncle's already nodding along like the quiet instigator he is.

But Colonel Lyle comes to the rescue of his airman.

"To be fair," Lyle says, "it's been proved in history that the desire for victory is of far more importance than weaponry."

"And you don't believe Savient has that desire?" Jerig asks dubiously.

The Colonel shrugs. "It's not the same as here, my lord. Here we've been tied to our land for countless generations. Our crown descends from Prince Efan himself. We understand loyalty. But what is Savient? A ten-year-old nation patched together in the midst of strife? Its people are from three different lands, with three different languages, rallied together beneath their Safire flag. How can such a place hold together when strained? Mark my words, Savient will go the way of the South. The General will overestimate his power and it will dissolve back into the chaos from which it sprang."

Others at the table nod.

"And if it doesn't?" Uncle asks, piqued. "What other land now has such resources as Savient? Dakar has taken the bounty of the east for himself. And he doesn't spend it on palaces, my friends. He spends it on steel. When his army began marching for the capital of Karkev two years ago, did anyone think he would be a mere hundred miles from it today? Did anyone think he'd persuade the Royal League to allow his advance? No, we did not, but he did it. He isn't a man to be underestimated."

I can see Mother stiffen, feeling the barbed betrayal. Even her own brother persists in stoking uncertainty.

Reni appears ready to agree with Uncle, but catches Mother's eye and, mercifully, backpedals. "Regardless, I'm confident we'll gain much from our new friends in Savient . . . however long they manage to hold together."

Everyone hides a chuckle, and I feel compelled to raise my glass for good measure. "To our new eastern allies. To a prosperous friendship."

The table agrees to my toast, and Mother observes with evident approval.

Lyle smiles at my brother, and raises his glass in Reni's direction. "And to you, Your Highness. The 3rd Squadron serves you as loyally as we did your father. You will always have the sky."

Havis rolls his eyes slightly at the flowery compliment, an Etanian tradition of poetic affection among the two forces—army and air, the earth and the sky—but Reni accepts it graciously.

The musicians strike a different tune then, and couples stand to waltz on the dance floor while they wait for desserts to be served. A grinning illusionist turns a little magic show, moving from guest to guest, while Slick continues to eye Violet discreetly. I reach for my wine, pretending my hand is a plane bobbing about and nearly take out a servant's arm as he tries to refill Reni's glass.

Violet tugs me up and we hurry a safe distance away before bursting into laughter.

"I think he was about ready to propose marriage," I say between breaths.

"Then let me go back," Violet replies, a girlish glimmer to her voice. "I'd like to see what your brother does then."

"Violet! That's rotten of you."

"Yes, but he does the same," she insists. "Always smiling at other girls, and always when I can see. He's the rotten one." She's still sparkling, though. "As for Ambassador Havis . . ."

I moan. "Please, don't mention that old rat to me."

"He isn't old, Ali. A man of thirty is at his best!"

"You're mad in the head," I say, stroking her hair like she's a kitten. "And so terrible at art."

Violet puts a hand over her heart. "I spent three hours on that wolf creature, darling. It's not my fault it looks more like a bear."

The illusionist twirls between us without warning, dressed all in silver, like a fish. We awkwardly make way while he says nothing, pretending to pull a rose from behind Violet's ear with a toothy, silent smile. I find I don't like the slipperiness of him. He turns to me, hesitating, and I wonder if he'll try one of his tricks or if he's been instructed not to pester the royal family.

His hand snaps before my eyes, quick, and he opens it to reveal a tiny ceramic fox.

A Safire fox—with a bloody rabbit between its teeth.

Violet slaps him on the shoulder. "That's quite uncalled for," she says sharply, the sort of tone one wouldn't expect from her. "Leave us alone."

The man shrugs, the fox disappearing in his hand again, and he moves on to his next audience.

"Must everyone bring their heated opinions even to dinner?" Violet laments, gripping my arm in annoyance.

"It's fine," I say, staring at the back of the silver man. "How far can it truly go?"

"As far as ridiculous tricks, apparently." Her smile warms again. "Can I please give this court a proper show? They deserve to be entertained with—" She stops, her smile broadening further.

"Care for dessert, Princess?"

Havis's sudden presence behind me is like heat on my skin. Spicy cologne and tempered irritation, looming at my neck. "Dessert?" I ask, turning.

He has another full wine glass in his right hand. "I want to finish our earlier conversation."

Violet nudges my arm.

"I thought it was finished, Ambassador."

"No, I've waited all day to hear the end of the story. About the letter?" His dark eyes bore into mine, forbidding me to lie.

Trapped, I try to concoct some excuse, but Violet ruins that by saying, "I'll leave the two of you together. A pleasant evening, Ambassador." The words purr off her tongue, but Havis gives her only the briefest nod.

Alone now, I see Havis has something in his left hand as well. A plate of marzipan sweets. He offers it towards me and I take one, since at least those look inviting.

"Your birthday's at the end of this summer," he says. "Have you planned any celebration?"

The polite angle throws me, and I pause. "A masquerade." I half expect him to seize onto that and say, "Are you going to be sending invitations? Letters? Like the one I gave you this afternoon, which you gave to your mother, didn't you?" But he doesn't. He just waits. "It's a party where everyone wears masks," I add.

"I'm aware," he says with a frown. "But I do find parties a waste of money."

"Well, that's fine." I muster a radiant smile, one Heathwyn couldn't find fault with. "You don't have to come."

Havis drops the dessert plate onto the nearest table with a rude thump. It makes a nearby footman jump in surprise. "And what of the end of the story, Princess? Did your letter reach its destination?"

"Perhaps."

I catch Reni out of the corner of my eye. Surely he'll come rescue me. Surely he'll . . . No, he surely won't. Violet's slender body tilts forward, showing off her necklace and an eyeful of something else, the jeweled end dangling far below her neck, and Reni stares as if all of the world's problems are suddenly there for him to solve on the swell of her chest.

Stars!

A shade of impatience worms into Havis's gaze. "You're a pleasant girl, Princess, but still a child. You can smile pretty and delight these gentlemen, but what do you know of the Safire? The General?" He drains his red wine. "Having him here will be a good lesson for you. You'll find there's little to admire about a man in uniform."

"You know nothing about what I admire," I retort coldly.

"I know there's more at stake here than you can imagine. Which is why that letter had better have reached its intended audience."

"What are you saying?" His words have an unwelcome edge.

"I'm saying," he leans near, voice low, "you have an entire court divided and how long until that spreads to an entire kingdom?"

I try not to show fear at those words. Most days, it's easy to overlook the division between my mother and brother, the rising boldness in Reni. But the General's invitation has dissolved their mirage of unity, and with everything I heard between them earlier today . . .

"My brother will be king in a year," I inform Havis, more confident than I feel. "That's a fact, and nothing to be divided over."

"The sun rises and falls," Havis replies, "a hundred times before spring."

It's a Resyan proverb about fortune, one that's always felt rather pithy until this moment. Now it feels like something dark.

Uncle Tanek materializes at Havis's shoulder, a shadow of anger on his brow, glancing between us. "Gref, that's enough. Let's retire to my study."

Havis frowns, irritated to have been caught by Uncle yet again, and he looks at me like I'll intervene. But there's a sudden shriek.

A feral, high-pitched sound that rises above the violins and voices. Panicked.

Mother!

The room comes to a stunned halt as she jumps back from the table, covered in blood, red running over her hands and down her beautiful taffeta dress. Reni is already at her side, but she raises her wet hands to hold him back and spins on the silver illusionist. "You vile creature!"

The man doesn't grin, his hands raised. "No, you bring the vile creatures here, Majesty. You bring the Safire to our peaceful kingdom and we won't have it. We won't be silent. We won't watch our home become a piece in their new empire!"

"Get him out of here," Mother demands, and it's then I realize, at last, she isn't harmed at all.

Only an illusion.

Guards grip the man's arms, Lord Jerig escorting him from the room, and Uncle watches them leave with a perturbed expression.

"This court grows wild," he mutters, and I'm not sure if it's meant for Havis or me.

Possibly neither of us.

He leaves to assist Mother, who's struggling to cross the marble floor with a gown soaked in red liquid, her skin still marked by false blood.

I stand there, aware of the eyes that flick from Mother to Reni to me, courtiers wondering at what's just occurred, wondering at why a person would do such a thing and how they should feel about it.

"On that note," Havis says after a moment, "have a pleasant evening, Princess."

His voice is pure satisfaction.

I escape from Heathwyn as soon as I can after dinner. I show her the painting from the woods, of the deer and the mountains, and say it's a gift for my mother on this difficult day. It's a bit splattered-looking, since I had to leap up and save the fawn, but she buys the lie and pats my cheek. "You're such a sweet daughter, my lamb."

Yes, a good daughter who's also about to perform necessary subterfuge.

I slip down the dark halls, aware this is a gamble, but I'm counting on Reni and Uncle and everyone else not to let a stunt like the illusionist's go undebated. And I'm right. There's no sound from behind Mother's door, only a maid retreating from the room with a golden tray of empty dishes. Everyone important is meeting in the throne room.

I hurry through the door as soon as the maid disappears.

Mother's parlour greets me with shadows, faint moonlight illuminating the bright colours of her woven rug, a gift from Resya. I flick on the lamp, my painting in hand. The chandelier and finely wrought walls gleam curiously at me.

Determined, I tiptoe for her bedroom, certain she wouldn't tuck the letter away in her mahogany desk. That would be too straightforward. If the letter from Havis is filled with unwelcome secrets, then she'd hide it well, perhaps in her private vanity.

It's what I'd do, in any case.

I approach the beautiful cabinet, glass perfume bottles glinting on a lace runner with familiar scents of her—notes of jasmine and saffron and citrus. Guilt nips inside as I rest my hand on the first cream-coloured drawer.

What sort of daughter rummages through her mother's vanity?

What sort of daughter rummages through her *Queen's* vanity?

Well, I suppose I do, and I have no choice. Before I can talk myself into retreat, I open the drawer. The first two yield only silken scarves and delicate underthings and makeup, but the third drawer holds a tempting painted box. I lift the top, unable to resist.

The face of my father stares back.

Boreas Isendare.

Stunned, I sink to my knees on the wooden floor, box in hand, the sight of his face so unexpected and wrenching that my hand trembles holding the photograph. Mother doesn't allow pictures of him displayed anywhere, only his formal oil portrait in the hall of Etanian kings. Yet here he is—the real him, not in paint, hidden away with dried, sacred orchids. No one is supposed to pick those flowers. It's considered unlucky to do so. But they're here. He's here. In my hand. A playful quirk to his smile, the gentleness I've tried to cling to with all my being, and all I want is to hold him forever.

There are other pictures, too, of Reni and me as children. Mother and Father riding horses together. She never rides, not that I've seen, but she looks confident in the saddle, and wearing pants. Unladylike pants.

Of course she'd keep that from me!

A feather curves along a photograph at the back, vibrant blue, half-covered behind the others, and I pull it free. It's a woman with golden hair, her eyes like the sea. Though the photo is faint with age, her shy gaze meets mine, her head tilted to the side, blonde strands captured and held in place by the beautiful feather. Beyond her, grey water meets a rocky shoreline. A friend of Mother's from long ago? I don't know why else she'd be here, though she's no one I've seen at court, nor does she look Resyan.

The words *"Sapphie elski'han"* are written in cursive along the bottom, and I sound them out beneath my breath.

Sapphie elski'han.

They carry a familiar, lilting Southern tune.

Pulling myself together, I place the photographs back into the box, memorizing the precious details of Father's face, then I yank open the final drawer and discover my instinct is right. My mother and I are too similar. Hidden beneath an underslip, poking out invitingly, is the edge of an envelope.

Who else would dare venture here?

I open it quickly.

Sinora,

Forgive me for coming to you this way, but I have no other choice.

Seath wants more. His plans are not what we thought and he grows impatient. Your brother refuses to discuss terms— I know he doesn't trust me. Please find a way to meet me alone. I'm concerned for what's next, with Dakar, but I have a proposition.

Gref

My breath cartwheels to a halt in my chest. All air leaves my lungs, the names *Seath* and *Dakar* lighting up like electricity, brightening and searing through my brain.

My hand shakes more than when it held my father's face.

I'm ready to be ill.

The whole world feels suddenly hot at my neck, guilt and fear needling my skin, and I refold the letter, shutting the drawer wildly. I rise from my aching knees and stumble for the door, but then remember my ruse.

I drop the painting on my mother's bed.

Then I flee like a caught spy, switching off the lights, returning the room to shadows, and fly out the door.

I run right into Reni.

"Ali?" he asks, arms outstretched to stop me. He stares in surprise. "What are you doing here?"

My head struggles to work properly as I glance right and left down the empty night hall. "I made Mother a painting. That's all."

"A painting?"

"Yes. Because it's been ten years."

He nods. He knows that today is all about forgetting, even though we can't.

But then I realize he's alone as well, no sign of Mother or Uncle. "And what are *you* doing here?"

At this, my ever-confident brother blanches. I've caught him off guard and he has no time to concoct his story. He didn't plan ahead for this, evidently.

"You're here to find the letter, aren't you?" I whisper.

"And you're not?" he hisses back.

"Either way, you're too late. It isn't there."

Reni frowns, peering at me closely, though I've never given him a reason to doubt me. I long to tell him what I've read. The dark words that threaten to tie our own mother to Seath. Seath of the Nahir! Leader of the Southern uprising and the last person a Queen of the North can be associated with. It must be him—how many Southern men go by that one name alone? But I can't tell Reni. Though he carries the blood of kings, though he's the one who will take the throne and continue our line into another generation, he is also my brother, and I know him too well. This letter would spark him to reckless action, and I can't be responsible for dividing our family even further.

"Very well, then," he says. "But we must keep our eyes and ears open—you with Havis, can you do it?"

I nod, since now Havis holds even more danger than a marriage proposal.

He wants more than my hand in this game.

Sighing, Reni leans forward and kisses my forehead briefly, rare affection from him, and I look up, at his tired face. "We'll get through this," he says softly, certainly thinking of the illusionist's stunt tonight. "Tomorrow is for us, isn't it?"

They're the words of our father, the thing he'd say when long meetings kept him away from us, when he had only time to pat our heads and promise us better the next day.

I nod, wanting to savour Father's promise, but I feel dark, dark, dark and void of colour.

The sun, rising and falling.

II

MURDER

7

Rahmet, Savient

The four-hour flight from Valon to Rahmet is as miserable as expected. My family sits tense in the airplane, too small a space for all of us at once, and my hungover head throbs to the beat of propellers. Far below, the land changes from faint green to sparse brown, powerful bluffs rising up amid a swath of red plains and feathered ravines. I try not to think about Cyar. He was desperate to come along, to see his home after months away. He longs for Rahmet the way I long for mountains. This is his earth, his sacred place, and I wish I'd had the courage to stand up for him. To ask Father to bring him along.

But I didn't. And now I'm left weighing the facts of my life alone.

Cyar in Top Flight.

Me not in Top Flight.

Me translating wireless reports for twelve hours a day.

Me exposed as a traitor with my nose broken—or worse.

Father sits across the aisle from me now, working on his speech, his sleeves rolled up, the tattoos from his long-ago rebel life on display—crossed swords with a shrewd fox between them. His pistol is visible against his uniform, its bloodstains left behind on the cement at home, ready to be scrubbed up by some unfortunate bootlicker. And I wait for something. A glance, maybe. Even a flare of anger. Anything. He can't destroy me and then pretend I don't exist.

But I get nothing.

We arrive at the military base in Rahmet's capital mid-afternoon. It's a sprawling complex of sun-browned buildings and tiny gardens, flashes of colour everywhere. Sunflowers and red sage. Trees of purple jacaranda, pink hibiscus, sun-bright lemons. All the sights and flavours Cyar tries to describe when we're huddled together during cold nights of field training. But on the drive from the dusty airfield, we also passed walls pockmarked with the wounds of bullets and mortars. Broken homes and ruined plazas. All of Savient looks like this in places, and even Valon has roads that lead nowhere, neighbourhoods destroyed and left as nothing.

Perhaps it feels wrong to rebuild on old bones.

While we wait by the base steps for our ride to the city square, where Father will give his speech, I study the intricate architecture of the skyline. My hand itches for a pencil, my uniform already wet with sweat against my neck. It's damn hot.

Mother clings to Father's arm, pale, the product of her many sleepless nights. "Don't give your speech today," she pleads. "Let's wait until tomorrow. Only tomorrow."

"I haven't come all the way here to wait," he replies, motioning for a nearby attaché.

"Then I'd like to stay here."

"Sapphie, you know it means a lot to have you at my side."

"Does it?" At her question, he glances back with a knife-sharp gaze, the sort that might make anyone else cower. But she only straightens. "I'm afraid." There's a tremor that belies her boldness. "I don't want to be on those streets today. I want to stay here."

Father doesn't respond to that. A convoy of shiny black mo-

torcars has grumbled to a halt before us, men getting out and
saluting, and Father nods at each. Mother's fear is swept aside
by protocol. We all move to get in the nearest car, but she remains where she is, planted with arms tucked around herself.

Father waves a hand, wearied of her. "I don't need this. If you
wish to stay, fine. Athan will stay with you."

I step back from the car. An indirect order.

"No, let me," Arrin says out of nowhere.

Father turns with a frown. "You?"

Arrin nods.

There's a moment of silence, Father deliberating, and we all
wait for the inevitable dismissal of Arrin's request. If anyone
should be on that podium, it's the decorated eldest son with his
medals. Not to mention, Mother and Arrin left alone together
would probably end in anarchy.

But Father relents. "All right. Athan will stay too."

Kalt gets his little wisp of a smile, the one that's silently
pleased with the outcome of events. Now he's the only son to
be seen with Father. They climb into the car and it's Leannya
who pauses at the door. She looks divided, no doubt regretting
any decision that takes her away from Arrin, tiny gold shadow
that she is. But she offers us an embarrassed wave, an innocent
betrayal, then slides in beside Kalt.

"Don't forget to wear your sun hat," Mother calls.

"I won't," says Leannya's voice from the window.

The convoy springs to life, spitting up thick dust, and the
three of us left behind stand awkwardly. I tug at my sweaty
collar.

"Let's walk in the gardens," Mother says to me.

"Now?" Arrin asks behind her. "At least wait until it cools off."

"It's the only place beautiful here." She's still talking to me.

Arrin opens his mouth, and I cut him off with a sharp look.
He rolls his eyes but stops, surprisingly cooperative today.

"A walk would be nice," I lie, giving Mother a reassuring smile.

She returns it.

In the compound garden, there's not much to see. We loop the fragrant yard on an old dirt path lined with flowers and spiked agave, one fountain sputtering warm water in the middle. Mother clutches her arms to her chest as she goes. She glances up at the apartment buildings beyond the high walls. We follow ten feet behind, giving her space. We both look ridiculous, dressed in our best uniforms—Arrin with his medals—and wandering this trail in uncomfortable silence.

I pluck a tiny lemon and put it in my pocket. For Cyar. Academy food usually tastes like old newspaper, and he's relentless in his attempts to improve it with the dried herbs his sister sends.

Cheers rise from the nearby square, drifting in the heat. Malek's voice echoes over a microphone. He applauds the Rahmeti people for their loyalty and courage during unification. It's always the same shiny words. In my mind, I see a young Cyar, hiding in his basement with soldiers bleeding on the floorboards above his head, an entire town decimated by shells, ripped apart at the seams.

Loyalty and courage.

"Father's rather furious with you," Arrin observes.

"I hadn't noticed," I reply.

Anger's still hot inside me. I'm certain it was Arrin who told Father about my seventh-place standing. Arrin who would have made a deal of it and suggested that maybe I wasn't trying entirely hard enough, whispering my treason.

He shrugs after a moment. "I'm sure it was the same speech we've all heard. How he didn't sacrifice everything to have such a lousy, useless, rotten son. Am I right?" There's a trace of humour in his voice.

"Maybe," I say, annoyed he's right.

Mother sits down on a bench to adjust her sandals. We stop, keeping distance.

"You're carrying the tradition," he continues, "and you had it coming. Don't look at me like that—you did. Trying to flunk out of the squadrons without Father noticing. Are you an idiot?"

"Better than your brand of it."

Father's amplified voice drifts over the walls.

"Some men look to the stars to find their destiny. Some men wait on fate. But Savient leaves stars and fate to lesser men, for we forge our own destiny and shape it to our will. Soon the war in Karkev will be won . . ."

Arrin points at the square. "Are you listening to those words? Are you really hearing them? That's our father. That's what you're up against and you think you can win by playing the fool?"

". . . it will be our victory and ours alone. Not by luck or by chance but because our skill, our strength, and our honour said it would be so. It must be so. And so it is, and so it will always be with the great men of this world, favoured by God. So it will be with the Safire . . ."

"Do you know why I can get away with what I do?" Arrin presses. "It's not because I play a fool. It's not because I do what I want. It's because when I'm on the frontlines, I'm everything he expects me to be. I'm brilliant. And he *needs* me. That's the only thing he'll negotiate with. The only card that wins."

I tear at my sweaty collar, unbuttoning it. Arrin's making too much sense. This isn't right.

"Look at you both," Mother interrupts from down the path. There's a smile in her voice. "You pretend not to care, but I know the two of you are tied together until the very end."

"Lucky for Athan," Arrin says, stepping away.

She has an orange and yellow hibiscus flower in her hand, and she walks to him, bringing it to her nose, breathing in the scent. "Not like you and Kalt, though. You two were my twin terrors, weren't you? Together every moment of the day, searching for mischief. You talked him into all of it, didn't you? Always a leader. He'd have been a good boy if not for you."

Arrin appears wary. "Let's not take a trip down memory lane, Mother."

She fingers the delicate petals. "But you remember the sea, don't you? You were so small then. Only to my knee. We were in the land of my parents and you'd run up and down the cold sand, catching shellfish."

"I can barely remember last week, Mother."

"You'd cling to my neck while I took you to the deeper water. You were scared, but you trusted me. I wouldn't let you fall, and your toes touched the crests. Now do you remember? Before he took you from me?"

Arrin tries to keep space between them, but Mother grasps his hand, like she might just throw herself into his arms if he'd only turn around and invite her. Arrin looks frustrated, vaguely undone. Fighting some invisible battle, and Mother's in tears now.

"I love you, Arrin," she says desperately. "I do."

He shakes his head and pulls from her. He walks down the path alone, stopping beneath the shade of a tree, shoulders hunched.

Mother covers a sob with her hand and stumbles in the opposite direction.

I look back and forth between them.

Stuck.

I pick up the hibiscus she dropped and put it in my pocket, trying not to crush the paper-thin petals. She'll want it later. Then I shut my eyes. In the darkness, the world's vague and warm, my skin prickling with heat. Another cheer rises on the wind. What sort of man can conquer an entire land but let his family come to this? Someone needs to ask that question. Someone needs to save us from ourselves.

A loud crack resounds off the compound walls, and I open my eyes again.

I wince at the bright light.

Another crack follows.

Echoing.

Before I can think, something heavy hurls me down behind the nearby fountain, both of us collapsing against the dirt. "What the hell are you doing?" Arrin growls. "Get some cover!"

I look at him, scrambling to catch up. "Gunshots," I manage. I'm not sure if it's a fact or a question.

"You don't goddamn say!" He hits me on the head, hard, then pulls out his sidearm, scanning the garden, the sky, the apartments. He grunts. "Damn it, I can't see anything."

"Where's Mother?"

He doesn't answer, just glances around again, then hauls me to my feet.

Our boots pound down the path in her direction. She's frozen by a small lemon tree, staring above the walls. We come to a wild halt at her side, and there's another violent snap in the air, close enough my eardrums burn.

Arrin waves us to move again, but Mother begins to faint. I reach out and grab her, sinking with her as she falls. I kneel there, wondering what to do next. Everything's cold with fear. Icy in the noon heat.

Then why are my hands warm?

I hold one up, running with red.

Arrin stares.

I turn back to Mother. An ugly wetness grows on her dress, beneath my fingers, her eyes wide and unfocused. My lifted hand shakes. Something hot trails to my elbow, soaking the fabric.

Arrin drops to his knees beside Mother. He throws off his impressive uniform, pushing it to her wound. "Pressure here," he orders, forcing my hand on it.

Red bleeds through.

I clutch the makeshift bandage while Arrin moves her jaw to open the airway. Fragments of medic training flit through my horror and I want to grab them, but they're too slippery, disappearing in panic.

More boots pound through the garden, soldiers surrounding us, setting a perimeter with weapons raised. I hardly notice. My eyes are on her face. Each breath from her is like a gasp, a sucking from deep within. A horrible sound.

"Get a medic!" Arrin shouts. "Her lung's collapsed!" Then he holds her gaze with his own, his gloved hand steady around hers. "You'll be fine. Father's coming, I know he's coming."

She tries to say something, but it gurgles from her chest, that awful sucking noise. Blood mixes with the dirt beneath us, her skin like snow even beneath the speckled shadow of the tree.

The air smells like blood and citrus.

Sweet and sharp. Sickening.

Arrin slams the ground with a fist. "Where the hell's the goddamn medic?" Then he leans near her, taking off his gloves so his hands are bare around hers. "Please, Mama, please hold on." My right hand is still pressed to the wound, my left arm supporting her head. I stare into her face, and she reaches a bloodied hand for my cheek, unable to close the distance. I bend closer and she touches me. She tries to speak again. I taste salt.

People shout—soldiers and orderlies—but Arrin's the only one I hear. He talks to her, promising her things I can't make out. The doctor finally appears. At last. Father and Evertal and Kalt and—

"Let go, Athan."

I don't know who says it. I'm gripping Mother with both arms and they're trying to put her on a stretcher. I stand up. My knees throb. The group rushes for the base and I trail behind in a blood-stained uniform, hands sticky. I touch my cheek and it comes away red.

Father pales at the sight of me.

I've never seen him pale.

"Take my son," he orders Evertal. "Clean that off."

Evertal nods, gripping my arm, and I try to protest. I need to stay with Mother. She was trying to reach for me. She couldn't. But there's no strength left in me. We step through the doors and Evertal steers me to a sink. She washes my hands, murmuring bits of comfort that don't mean anything. Everything inside me shakes. Blood everywhere, all over me. Mother's blood. It's washing down the drain in ribbons. It's splattered on my face like paint.

The room sways at a strange angle and my stomach lurches.

Evertal grabs me, forcing me to look at her. "Eyes up here. On the horizon." She squeezes my shoulders. "Don't look anywhere else."

I nod in a knee-jerk kind of way.

What the hell's she saying?

This can't be real.

Afternoon turns to evening, the world a strange dream around me. Blurry and unending. Muted words about fear, about horror, about the attackers who haven't even been found. I pray and pray, but God doesn't answer. Father's used up all his divine favour and now there's nothing left for her. Hours have passed when Arrin finally sits down in the hospital chair next to me. He swallows, leg trembling slightly. "We did everything we could, Athan. We did everything right. It didn't work."

His words sound faint. I've been waiting long enough for this and it washes over me vaguely, like someone else's death, someone I don't even know.

Arrin rests a hesitant hand on my shoulder.

I'm too far away.

The hot night sinks down, and I drop into bed, crawling into a long, fitful sleep. It drags me to a strange place where past and present meet and nothing makes sense. She's still alive and begging me to wake her. "Don't let him take you," she weeps.

"Don't let him do this to me." She reaches like she did in my arms, reaching and not finding. "Wake me," she whispers.

Wake up, wake up.

Wake up!

Kalt shakes me with both arms. He's leaning over my bed, alarmed.

My eyes sting with the light. The clock says ten in the morning.

Fifteen hours?

"We're going home," Kalt says, "to bury Mother and have a proper funeral."

No, it's too soon. She needs to be buried in the mountains by the sea, the place she loved best. She doesn't want to sleep forever in that city Father bought with blood. She needs the sea before they shut her away.

But no one listens to me. Or maybe I don't even speak.

Leannya curls against Arrin during the flight, refusing to let go, a tiny white-knuckled fist around his arm. Kalt stares at his boots. Father looks out the window, his spine iron-straight. I want someone to say her name. I need someone to break the numb silence and admit what's happened. I want to fall apart into a thousand sharp little pieces and feel pain.

But nothing comes.

Nothing, nothing, nothing.

Cyar's waiting on the tarmac in Valon, and his arms are around me before I can protest.

"Look at me," he says through his tears. "More of a mess than you. Sorry."

He's rooted in familiar honesty, nothing held back, and I let him hug me. Then I pull the still-fresh lemon from my pocket and give it to him.

They bury her in the evening, everything the wife of the General deserves, the stunned city brought to a standstill. Down the casket goes, into the hollowed-out ground. It looks like a cold and lonely place. Trapped forever. Caged in the suffocating earth.

"Wake me."

But I can't.

She's covered by chamomile and dirt. I offer the crushed hibiscus, the last beautiful thing she held, and Leannya shudders, crumpling back against Father, sobbing. He places a stiff hand on her tiny shoulder.

His silent face holds all the fury of hell.

8

Hathene, Etania

It's morning, the mountains outside still lit with dawn mist, when Uncle Tanek and Havis burst through the parlour doors and interrupt breakfast. Uncle looks like a panicked deer shot in the hind, and Havis like a fellow creature scrambling to keep up and see what happens next. It's almost amusing, the pair of them, until Uncle says, "General Dakar's wife has been murdered! We just received the cable. It's set for the broadcasts this evening."

Mother and Reni freeze with their cutlery mid-air. I do, too.

As Uncle explains how it happened two days ago in a city of southern Savient, and everyone else, including Landore, only received the news this morning, and the General's wife has already been buried in the ground while Savient mourns, Mother grows pale and I feel a sudden panic growing deep inside.

"Who would dare do this?" Reni demands.

"No arrests have been made. The culprits disappeared, but the General says it has the fingerprints of the Nahir upon it," Uncle replies. "Certainly those men know the General is eyeing the South and trying to put his army there. They would take the gamble and make their warning clear."

"And it *was* a gamble," Mother says, an edge of sorrow to her voice. Her red nails are bright against the silver spoon she holds.

The panicky shadow inside me swells further, smothering my heartbeat, drawing the warmth from my cheeks.

"I'm concerned for what's next, with Dakar, but I have a proposition."

Did Havis predict this dark thing?

He's still waiting behind Uncle, his gaze unreadable, a wicked harbour of trouble, and I can't conceal my fury. He meets my eye—and pauses. In that wordless, unnoticed moment, he realizes the truth. Tension flickers along his half-shaven jaw, eyes narrowing.

He knows I read the letter.

I wish I were better at hiding things.

"I suppose the General won't be coming to visit anymore?" I ask, turning from Havis, hiding a tremor by stirring sugar into my tea.

"It seems doubtful," Uncle says.

"We should at least send him a letter of our regrets," I suggest to Mother. "Wouldn't that be proper?"

Uncle huffs a small laugh.

Mother studies me, then addresses Uncle. "Yes, I'll offer the General a letter at once. He's still quite welcome to visit if he chooses."

"But we shouldn't pressure him to—"

She extends her slender hand. "Compose the letter, brother, then I'll sign it. I want it sent by morning."

"Sinora—"

Her night-sea gaze turns quietly fierce, that silent spark that negates her outer calm, and Uncle holds his tongue.

It's not until later in the morning that Havis finds me. The palace halls are bright with sun, yet heavy as nightfall, servants tiptoeing quickly like their heels are being chased. We all know the truth of this murder, and today, perhaps, it's silenced every royal palace. Something dark has reached our shores. The

Nahir have made it into the North. They've murdered an innocent woman and reminded everyone that their uprising will burn and burn, no matter what power rises in the east, threatening to challenge them.

Mother says every person has a reason for why they fight—but what reason could ever justify this terrible act?

I hurry up the grand staircase, feeling Havis's shadow behind me.

Once in the privacy of Mother's quiet wing, I spin to face him. "What do you want, Ambassador?"

His expression holds no mercy. "Don't think I'm stupid, Princess. I saw the way you looked at me. You read my letter."

"That's your own fault, Ambassador. Why did you give it to me anyway?"

"I told you—your uncle forbids me from the Queen. He keeps me at his side from dawn to dusk, invites himself to every meeting. He's a fool grasping for power, but I think you already know that."

"You are a *snake* and a danger to my family."

For one cramped moment, his cruel stare bears down, devouring my certainty. I've pushed too far with the letter. I should never have tried to play his games. Now when he tricks Mother into allowing our marriage, he'll know I betrayed him right from the start, and he'll pretend to adore me all while seething with a vicious hatred, a hatred that could keep me from my family forever, locked in a place on the edge of hell.

He steps back, though, throwing his infuriated gaze onto a nearby painting. There's a tense tremor beneath his stubble, and it takes a moment to lessen, his eyes absorbing the scene—vibrant flowers and narrow green leaves, colours of amber and brick and ginger. In the middle, a young girl sits on a hill. Dark-haired, a hint of a smile on her lips, a sleek cat curled at her feet.

"It's Resya," he says eventually. A statement, not a question.

I don't want to answer. He's distracting me. But he's right, because the painting was a gift from Father, commissioned for Mother's birthday long ago, and it's the only thing in the palace she calls her own with a jealous fervor. Too many times she's stood here, as if she might leap inside and feel the cat's fur. As if she might catch the scent of Southern wind if she waited long enough.

And too many times I've also waited here, wondering, deep down—far away and out of sight, like a shameful secret—if Mother loves that place more than she loves us. Father was her bright sun, her greatest friend. But now he's gone, and the winters here are still bitter, and this kingdom is still an elaborate Northern gown she's never quite fit into properly.

What if she passes the crown to Reni and then quietly retreats home? Why else would she think of giving me to Havis?

I hazard a glance at him. He's still staring at the picture, lost in his secret thoughts. His black shirt is stitched with spirals of gold and red, distinctly foreign, its elegant patterns like the rug on Mother's floor. I realize I don't know him.

Not at all.

He turns, looking down at me with private skepticism. "You know so little of the world, Princess."

Our brief stalemate dissolves to fury. I know enough. "You're wrong, Ambassador. I've seen your letter and we'll never do what you ask. You can tell that to Seath. You can tell him I said it myself!"

Havis seizes my arm, and the thought of screaming comes to mind, but the cold alarm in his gaze silences me. "Don't you dare say his name aloud," he hisses. "You don't talk about that man, not here! Not after the dark events of today."

"Do we have trouble with the Nahir? Tell me. I demand to—"

"Hush!" His grip tightens, pinching skin. "After what's happened in Savient, I don't think my letter much matters anymore. Nothing can stop what will happen next. Though if you're so insistent on meddling where you shouldn't, ask your mother

yourself. Are you brave enough for that?" Sudden, twisted pleasure appears on his face. "Yes, you should ask her everything that
burns inside you, Princess. Ask her about me. About the wedding
in Resya she's already spoken of. She wishes it when you're of
age. Seventeen, isn't that right? At the end of the summer?"

"She doesn't!"

He brings his face too close to mine. "The truth is, Aurelia,
I'm on your side. I'm headed back to Resya for a month, but
when the Safire arrive, remember—"

"You're lying! Mother doesn't want me to marry you. You've
nothing you could ever offer us." I pull out of his grip desperately, panicked. "You humiliate yourself here. I'll have a duke,
a prince even, and everyone knows this except you!"

For one horrid moment, I'm sure he'll spit at me or kiss me, but
instead he says, "Too bad I'm only an ambassador, isn't that it? We
sit round tables and talk, and what good does that ever do?"

"I'm asking my mother for the truth," I declare, spinning from
him, "and then I'll tell her to send you back where you came
from."

"She won't."

"Wait and see."

"She's not your father, and in days like these, that's a very good
thing."

I stop.

"Boreas Isendare was a romantic," Havis says. "He couldn't see
things as they were, only as he wished. He never deserved such
a woman as Sinora Lehzar."

His words sear me with the sharpest sense of loss and sorrow.
For a moment, I think I'll surrender to misery right there, in
front of Havis. But I rally whatever part of my mother is in my
blood. I turn to face him. "Don't you *ever* mention my father's
name again, Ambassador."

A shameful tear still warms my eye.

I don't wait long enough for him to see it.

9

❧ ATHAN ❧

Valon, Savient

On the third afternoon after Mother's death, I sit alone folding bits of paper. It's a stupid game. Make some little shape—a plane, an animal, whatever—then try to repeat the whole thing with eyes closed. A pointless challenge for my brain. A way to pass time. I've already emptied and smashed enough brandy bottles, and Cyar's forbidden me from drinking any more. He says I'll become Arrin.

Mangled papers surround me when Kalt appears in the doorway.

"Pull yourself together," he orders. "Father's got something to say."

I stand, unsteady. "To me?"

"Don't be a selfish ass. It's bigger than that. I've been looking everywhere for you." I stare at him and his bland face. Nothing visible, no grief. That same stupid, monotonous voice. He takes a long breath. "Just come. It's not my order."

Of course it isn't. It never is. It's always going to be Father saying and us doing and never mind how we feel about it. And now that Mother's gone, there's no one left to question his sanity in our defense. No one left to plead our case after too much wine and promise things that can't be.

She's gone.

It's gone.

We're all gone, burned up with the dreams and the hope and the rest of it.

I crush a paper plane between my hands and follow after Kalt.

Father's council room—windowless and encircled by heavy oaken walls, like a buried ship—is a place I've never been allowed before. The carpet is stitched with the Safire crest, large beneath our feet, and a square fireplace sits cold and grey, its mantel bearing framed portraits of Arrin and Kalt in uniform. They look like strangers in photograph, stiff and serious. Vacant.

Father stands at the long table, hunched over it in the low lights, while six top officers in Safire uniform sit waiting, clearly on edge. Silence with Father is always terrifying. Maybe especially for these men, since they're not even blood, and if he needs to pull his pistol on someone—which I know he's done before, on the frontlines—it's more likely to be them than Arrin.

Probably.

Arrin is opposite us, leaning back in his chair, arms crossed and face perturbed. His left hand ticks away like it's on a trigger.

"Keep your mouth shut," Kalt mutters to me.

I don't think I'm the one who needs that warning.

When Father clears his throat, everyone straightens, Malek and Evertal the quickest. "The murderer who committed this heinous act has been waiting a long time to pounce," he says. "I swear to God and each of you here today that when I've finished with her, she will wish for hell." He raises his eyes, darkened by exhaustion and fury. "Sinora Lehzar is the devil I will crush. She is a viper. A liar. A cheat. She's everything despised in the North, a false queen, and I won't stop until she burns before the world."

Of course.

Blood and fireworks. The woman he hates.

A queen?

Arrin's still ticking.

"It's early," Malek says carefully. "More investigation might be needed."

"More investigation?" Father snarls. "It was an assassination in broad daylight, practically on the anniversary of Boreas's death! She never made her shots in the dark. She was brash. By God, I gave her that first rifle! She always said—" He stops abruptly. His gaze sharp, reckless. "That wretched woman has burned a long time for her revenge, but this won't end here. I will destroy her."

The Admiral pauses. "Yes, but Sinora would have targeted you, not Sapphie."

Father laughs, a cracked sound. "She said she'd never kill me, only bury my heart. One of her damn Rummayan proverbs. Well she hasn't buried mine yet, and I'll have hers between my fist."

"Of course," Malek says, wisely retreating.

"The traitorous bitch deserves to hang," Evertal offers, "for more crimes than this."

Something unsettling lurches me back into the present, out of the fog of grief in my head. Father's hatred of Sinora Lehzar has always been a whispered fact. An indistinct rage that stretches back long before I was ever born. A name never spoken—unless you want a nose shattered, or a bullet in the brain.

But no one ever mentioned she was a queen.

That sounds infinitely more complicated.

Arrin shakes his head. "Suspicion around our small table doesn't equal tangible proof. Without actual evidence against Lehzar, we can't make a move. It's stupid to even think of it."

No one breathes. Now is about the moment when a pistol might appear. If it's going to happen, this would be it, and everyone at the table looks terrified except for Arrin.

Father glares at him. "Evidence? She's from the dirt, and that's where I'll put her again."

"She's a goddamn queen of the North, Father."

Father gives a derisive snort. "Far from it."

Beside me, Kalt looks impassive to the dangerous revenge brewing in front of us, nodding along with everything Father says. Evertal, too. Her lips hold a wicked smile. So Arrin's our only hope for reason? That's alarming. If we go after a ruling royal, and we fail, it will be Savient burning instead of Sinora Lehzar. She has a crown.

How does only Arrin see this?

"We should trust Father's judgment," Kalt puts in. He addresses Father. "I'd support a strike against her, sir."

Arrin rolls his eyes. "Of course you would."

"We're bringing justice to our murdered mother," Kalt says sharply. "Why are you being difficult?"

He's not being difficult, I want to snap. *For the first time in his life, he's being smarter than anyone in this damn room.*

But all that comes out is, "He sure as hell isn't, Kalt!"

Everyone turns in their seats, stunned, Kalt the most. Arrin raises a brow at me. He waits for more, sensing an ally. But Father's looking at me too, and my throat constricts.

Arrin strikes on alone. "Father, I'm not saying I won't bring her down. Believe me, I will. But Mother's murder is a charge no one in the North will buy. They want to believe it's the Nahir, not one of their own. How would we ever convince the Royal League of her guilt?"

Father circles Arrin, hawk-like. "Do you think I got to where I am by being as foolish as you're suggesting? When I finish Sinora off, every royal will applaud my good work. The League itself will carry out the verdict. I swear it."

Arrin finally stops his ticking. "What I thought. And that's the problem, Father. You want to do it by their rules. You want their approval for it. But we don't have the luxury of time. We need something better than this impossible murder charge. Something irrefutable. And we need it before we reach the South— God knows her camp will be waiting there to pounce."

"You're scared of fighting a real war?" Kalt taunts.

Arrin throws up his hands. "Yes, that's it, Kalt. You've caught me. Though I suppose I'll have to hide back here with you, since your boat won't be very helpful in a landlocked kingdom like Etania."

"I was talking about the South," Kalt clarifies indignantly.

Father slams a fist on the table. Everyone jumps. Malek, Evertal, and the rest drop their eyes. Arrin and Kalt shut up. Father's anger has built like a storm, and suddenly, for some horrible reason that doesn't even make sense, he jabs a finger at me. "*You.* Let's hear what you think about all this. Clearly you have an opinion. Won't you say it to my face?" He waits a fraction of a second—hardly enough time to answer—then snorts. "No, of course you won't. You never do. You just carry on and avoid the real work."

Heat creeps along my neck. All six officers are gaping at me now, the seventeen-year-old kid no one ever thinks about much but who apparently has earned himself an entire dressing-down in the council room. The humiliation scalds.

"Father, this isn't the time," Arrin intervenes, a slightly pitying move, which only makes things worse.

Father raises his hands. "Isn't it? They say he's very smart. Brilliant, even." His smile is cruel. "So what do you think I should do? Come on, boy. For once in your life say something useful!"

His mockery is too much on top of everything else. I stand abruptly. "I think she'd hate you for this," I spit. "She'd never want her death used for more war. She'd weep in her grave, and you know it."

Kalt gasps. His hand starts to move, like he's going to yank me back down, as if that will undo what I've just said, but I don't care. I stare at Father and he stares at me and I wait for the gun, the one that certainly has my name on it now. It feels damn good to say the words and not even think.

For a long moment, Father doesn't move, dangerously still. I watch his hand, terrified. The pistol is an inch from his fist, the trigger a moment from my head. Blood on the floor like oil. Just like the traitor, but this time it's going to be mine. This is it. Then he says, "You're dismissed."

I'm turning before he's finished the order.

I don't look at Arrin or Kalt or anyone else and their stupid pity.

I march out the door, blistering with anger, overwhelmed by fear, every emotion crackling through the numbness in a glorious rage, and nearly trip right over something small and blonde. I catch myself against the wall as the door slams shut.

Leannya scurries back, quick as a mouse, but there's no guilt in her eyes. No regret at having been caught spying. Only an equally furious rage in her eyes. "How could you?" she demands in a whisper. "You and Arrin both!"

Her words are spoken so delicately it's like they might dissolve between her mouth and my ears, but they slap me still. "Leannya, it's not—"

"How dare you speak for Mother! You don't know what she'd want. None of you do. You were never here, but I was, and she'd have done anything in the goddamn world for you!" Her fury is almost as shocking as her language. She's every bit as dogged as Arrin. "I hate the way you all sit around and talk. Baiting each other, like it's a game. I *hate* your talk. I hate you!" She shoves me with more force than I expect.

Then she darts down the hall. A fleeing gold shadow.

I stand there, trying to figure out what's just taken place between us, the fact that my own sister hates me—hates all of us— and it's completely illogical, then realize I might be doing the exact thing she despises and chase after her. Through the main foyer, up the stairs, to our family quarters. I find her in Mother's parlour. She screams as perfume bottles shatter against the wall. Glass splintering, like the brandy bottles. She hurls each and every one until there's nothing left but a thousand useless shards and the stench of perfume—rose and vanilla and lilac, rotten when flung together in a mess.

She stops. Trembling.

Then she drops to her knees, whispering, "No, no, no," pale hands trying to pick up the broken pieces, cutting herself on sharp edges. "These were mine. She said I could have them. She said I could. Why did I do it!"

I don't dare touch her.

She lets the hurricane unleash, in tears, in fists. Then it subsides, and she stands again, swiping the tears from her face. Her eyes accuse me. "You gave in to them. You're supposed to be better than that."

"Better?"

"Yes. I used to tell Mother how scared I was for Arrin, because I know when he goes to the front he doesn't think of anyone else, not even me. He just wants to win. I can't watch over him there. And Kalt would hang his own neck if it pleased Father. But she said I shouldn't worry, because we'd always have you. She said you're better than that and you'll always come home."

God in heaven. Mother's finding a way to speak to me from the grave. Leannya waits for me to contest her words, and a new kind of ache throbs beneath my ribs. Mountains. That's what I've wanted forever. The escape I've always craved. The nobler life. But it's not more noble—it's only more easy, away from here and these impossible decisions, away from expectations. If I go, if I trap every weakness, kill all the guilt, and do what I want, then I'm exactly the same as Arrin and Kalt and Father.

I'm a Dakar.

The truth startles me with its sudden, shameful intensity.

Leannya waits. I reach for her hands, now pricked with blood, and hold them gently. I try not to think. "Mother was right," I say. "You'll always have me." It might be the worst promise I've ever made, an impossible vow to keep with whatever the hell's going on in Father's council room, but in this moment, it's the one thing I know I want to be true. The thing that needs to be true. "I'm here for you. I swear it. I'll fight for you."

She studies me a long moment. Tear marks on her face, blood on her hands. Her stare is careful and searching, scouring my bones, looking for lies like a true Dakar, then she reaches a verdict and throws her desperate arms around me.

She believes me.

And maybe I do, too.

I go to Father's room in the evening.

I'm not exactly sure why. It's a terrifying decision, one I go back and forth on, but the words I hurled at him in front of his men were rotten. I'm old enough to admit it. I need to be better, for Mother at least. For Leannya. I won't let this family become a stalemate of battle lines.

I swallow my wounded pride, my fear, and when I reach the door, I knock once. The quick kind that's not very committed.

Gathering courage, I try a bit harder.

Then again.

Well, he has to be in there. Haven't seen him since the meeting, and Arrin was complaining that someone else was complaining that he never showed up for a later briefing. Which means he's there. Father doesn't disappear. He makes other people feel like disappearing, but he never does it himself. Before I can shrink away from the door, like my feet want to, I just go ahead and open it.

A narrow hall greets me, hollow and devoid of colour.

To the left is Father's study, books and maps on each shelf, desk covered in files, scent of cigarettes and leather. No sign of him. Cautiously, I walk through, my boots creaking against the wood floor as I near the desk. I glance down at the photographs spread in a haphazard array. There's Malek holding a weathered Safire flag, triumphant. Another with Mother sitting by the sea, a child in her arms, her face too young. She was only my age when she had Arrin. They say the marriage came first, but I suspect it was the other way around. The last photograph is of Father leaning against an elaborate sandstone building with Southern roundels. Next to him is a short, unsmiling woman. Her black hair swallows light, a rifle across her shoulder, expression fierce.

A long-ago ally turned into his worst enemy.

Lehzar.

It's scrawled right there, in dark ink, and though I have no idea what went sour between them—Sinora and my father and Malek and Evertal—it doesn't matter. Blood runs down my hands again, sticking to my skin. Mother struggling for every ragged breath in my arms. That gasping wet sound.

I grab the knife sitting on his desk, the slender one for opening letters, and thrust it into Sinora's heart.

Weak laughter reaches my ears.

I turn with a start and find Father watching from the adjoining room, half-hidden by a leather chair. He's slumped on the floor against the wall, legs bent at the knee, bottle in hand.

"You want to kill her?" His voice wavers. "It'll take more than that. She's clever as sin."

My squashed terror springs back to life. I'm not sure if it's in response to being caught, or seeing him drunk. Probably both. And I'm ready to run. Get away from the bullet that's been waiting for my selfish face. Get away from the inebriated General of Savient who despised me even before I insulted him publicly.

But he holds out a hand, palm towards me, like he's cautioning an animal. "Stay."

I don't move.

"You've already trespassed here," he says. "Might as well have a drink for it."

"I came here to apologize for today, sir. I shouldn't have said it. I was upset and—"

"Sit down, Athan."

Athan.

He says it like it's nothing. Like it's easy, meaningful. But I can't remember the last time he addressed me by name, and familiar desperation rises inside. The wanting of something I can't explain. That place in me only he can reach. He looks uncomfortably alone there, smoking his cigarette. He never smokes. Not like Arrin and Kalt, who always have the things in hand, but he sucks it down now, fingers shaking slightly against the flimsy paper, expression disturbed.

Slowly, I walk over and sit on the floor next to him.

He hands me the whiskey. "Have the rest. You're not as noble as you pretend."

He's right, but Cyar's warning is still in my head, so I place it on the floor beside me, untouched. He doesn't seem to notice my decision, staring at the wall, smoking. Moments pass. I can feel my pulse scattering.

Finally he says, "Everything happens as God wills."

He's never said that out loud. Everyone else prays for war, prays for peace, prays for this and that and whatever else, but Father makes it happen. He's always made it happen.

I rest my arms on my knees. "I guess."

"Are you ever going to be more committal?"

I shrug.

"Ah, you're too good at this." He picks up a pen, flicking it between his stumbling fingers. "By the time I was fifteen, Athan, I'd already learned how to survive alone. Desert fever took my mother. My father was cut down by Landorian bullets in Thurn. He never knew how to win, only how to fight. Fighting forever and gaining nothing."

I listen, seeing Mother's coffin, the way the cold earth took it completely.

Nothing's gained without sacrifice.

"But Sinora. She was outside the game, outside the rules," he continues, more to himself, "and that's why I made her my ally. We had both been stolen from. She believed in my desire for justice, before she . . ."

He trails off, burying the secret he almost revealed.

"You knew her in the South?" I venture.

Father's head falls back against the hard wall. "Yes. We saw the disaster that was Thurn, the crimes there that no one remembers. The way these Northern kings took land that wasn't theirs and tried to make an entire people think and be as they preferred. And now they're surprised by unrest? They believe they have the right to own others, to force loyalty. But you can't, Athan. Loyalty is in the heart. It must be earned." He closes his eyes. "It was supposed to be me, not your mother."

His words stick on one another, slurred, and a tremor of pity kicks me in the gut. I don't want to give it to him. Not now, not like this, but I say, "I believe you, Father." I think he needs to hear it.

Father shifts, looking at me. His boots nearly touch mine. "You were right about her today. She hated war. She hated what I did, and she'd hate what I will do next. But the world doesn't care how noble you are, son. It only cares about strength."

I feel myself nod.

"And yet I trusted her." He tilts his head, studying me. "Arrin's barely controllable, and Kalt craves everything I have, but you . . ." He takes a drag, exhales smoke. "Would you believe she never wanted you? Your mother, I mean. She didn't want to give me another son. When she realized she was carrying you, she tried to beat you out of her own womb, but I stopped her. I wouldn't let her do it."

His words don't register. They hover between us, everything suddenly turned upside down. My past. My present. Mother desperate and fighting to shield me from his ambition in the only way she could. He, in the end, offering me life. I don't want to believe it, it's backwards, but he nods and says, "It's the truth, ask Arrin."

I realize my hand is a fist, biting into my own skin.

"But I have always believed in you, Athan, and I want to trust you. Can I?"

His question finally sinks in. He wants my loyalty. He always has, and it's not just because of my scores. It's deeper than that, something I owe my life to him for, and the possibility is like a tailspin, gaining momentum as reality blurs. Every one of his words is from a bottle. That has to be it. But I crave them, savouring them despite the whiskey on his breath. I've been waiting every day of my life for even a fraction of this. I've waited without even realizing it. Watching him come back from campaigns and hoping that he might offer me more than a cuff on the head. Waiting for a glance that wasn't cut on a knife point.

Waiting for a reason to try.

"Yes," I say. "You can."

It's not a lie, and I hate that it isn't.

He leans near, a secret for me alone. "The truth is I gave Sinora that first rifle, but she was the one creating chaos. She studied the Landorians so closely she could always spot an officer no matter how they tried to hide. She knew their tricks. She'd pick them off one by one until the rest didn't know where to turn or what order to follow. A silent, shrewd war." He points his pen at me. "But I have a way to stop her, Athan. And if we stop her, stop this chaos she thrives on, then the world will be better for it—in the North, in the South. This doesn't have to last forever. This can end. We'll have peace."

I nod, overwhelmed by that impossible offer.

An end.

Enough.

Home.

He's never said that before.

I'm desperate to believe, and he smiles very slightly, half-hidden. Then we sit like that, sprawled together, quiet.

After a while, I get up.

I leave Father in his study, the knife still stuck in Sinora Lehzar.

10

Hathene, Etania

It's midnight, and the maidservant is clearly startled to see me when I knock on Mother's door. Her mouth hangs slightly open, glancing at the clock, at the late hour, but I have a plan for that. My eyes well up, my body shivers and shakes, and the girl switches to horrified. I've never played this card before, and it works well.

She escorts me inside quickly and through the audience chamber, through the private withdrawing parlour, right to Mother's bedroom. I don't wait for any further permission. I push through the heavy door and the maidservant makes a squeak-like sound. I close it on her gaping face.

Mother turns in evident surprise.

I stare at her, also surprised.

Soft, Resyan lyrics sigh from her gramophone:

> *In the open air, I call to you.*
> *In the heat, I sing my song.*
> *I am a mountain, a song you remember,*
> *and my feet are roots fed with blood,*
> *with old dreams.*

She stands at the vanity with its glass bottles, wearing only her lace nightgown and silken robe, her black hair unbound, face

free of powder and rouge, skin a deep shade of russet beneath
the lamp. Everything queenly has been stripped away. She's herself, vulnerable before me. Eyes glittering with what might be
tears. And suddenly, she looks so much like a mother—warm
and glowing in the light—that resentment stings. I wish I could
run right to her and bury my head in her shoulder and breathe
in her jasmine scent and hear her tell me everything will be all
right, that there's nothing to worry about and Havis is banished forever. I want that so badly I can feel it trembling in my
breath.

But she's the one dealing these dark cards.

She's the one with secrets.

"You can't send me to Resya, Mother. Please don't do it!"

It's not what I intended to lead with. My emotions are swirled
and tangled inside, and that's what comes out.

She looks at me as if perplexed. It's too dark to tell. "I'm sending
you nowhere," she says after a moment. "You're only sixteen."

"But almost seventeen," I say helplessly. At seventeen, everything can change for a girl. Marriage. Death. It all looks the same
to me now. "I have to go to the University, as Father would want.
You can't send me away yet."

Mother laughs shortly. "Oh, come now, Aurelia. Don't make
that your excuse."

The ease with which she bats away my plea wounds me further. Of course it means little to her, she who was never properly educated, whose own father adored her for being clever and
quick even though she couldn't read a book. But this is all I have
as escape. She doesn't understand. Perhaps if I study hard, if I
speak many languages and can debate economic policies, then
Reni and his council and everyone else here will consider me too
useful to send away. Perhaps I can make it a waste to marry me
even into another Northern kingdom. I can make them want to
keep me here. This place I love with every beat of my heart, this
place my father believed in.

My home.

My mountains.

Mother's elegant brows draw together, studying my desperation. "Resya is freedom, Aurelia. Do you want to be cooped up forever in a palace? Bound to some spoiled duke? I'm offering you a way out, with a man who will let you do what you please."

"He's a snake," I choke out. "And I'm going to the University. I have to go!"

Her eyes narrow, colour rising on her cheeks. "Tell me this, Aurelia—is life learned behind those high university walls? Can you learn there how to mourn your husband's death? How to be handed a crown and expected to rule? How to start a new life in a strange land far from home? No, I learned these things by living, and believe me, the lessons of life are far harsher than my words to you now."

A hot and reckless bitterness pounds through my veins, sparking me. "And was it life that told you to negotiate with the likes of Seath?"

Mother grips the edge of the vanity. Silence swallows us, the song ended, and she doesn't move, staring at me. After a long and empty moment, she comes closer and I see stark weariness in her eyes. "You read the letter, did you?"

"Yes."

"Did you tell your brother?"

"Never."

She sighs, her hand reaching for mine. The gentle touch softens my raging anguish. She leads me to the vanity bench and we sit together on the velvet cushion, a heaviness in the silence. She wears no jewelry, but her wedding band glimmers on her finger, the one thing she never removes.

"Listen, then. I will tell you the truth about your father. You are my own heart, my bright star, yet you see precious little of the true world beyond these walls. I will show you. I will show you why you must trust me in these matters." She holds my gaze. Steady. Then she speaks in Resyan. "The truth, Aurelia, is your father died because of a lie. A few men in our kingdom questioned his right to this throne. They said he was never a son of Prince Efan, but rather the great-grandson of a farrier. They're the ones who killed him."

I blink at her. Her words don't make sense. Everyone has always said Father's heart gave out suddenly, that there was nothing anyone could do, he died too young and—

"They were foolish men," Mother continues plainly, "and I have no pity for the foolish. They believed what they wished, no matter the impossibility of it. But your father . . . Your father didn't think it honourable to punish others for ideas. He thought the whispers against him would pass." She drops her eyes. "That rumour in the night found a way to steal the light of my life."

The pain in her voice can't be hidden. It's raw and vulnerable, and a horrible pain seizes my chest. All of his warmth, his gentleness. Taken for a lie. I didn't think it was possible for his death to be any more painful.

Murder.

"Why doesn't Reni know the truth?" I whisper, afraid of the answer.

She grips my hand, endless sorrow in her eyes. "How I long to tell him, my star. I know his bitterness. I see his anger towards me. And if I told him the truth, perhaps he'd trust me again. But if anyone should ever ask him about his right to this throne, his answer must be 'yes' and it must be held with all the conviction in the world. He can never doubt. He must be blameless." She looks sadder than I've ever seen her, a mother who can't ally with her own son. "Death was your father's fate and he let it be so," she continues, "but know that I didn't let it go unpunished. Those foolish men paid for their crime, in secret. The rumour was cut at the roots." She draws a line across her neck, a Resyan gesture that not only reflects death but also deep necessity. Something that can't be undone. "We are safe, and your brother will never rule in fear."

A shiver treads along my skin. I should hate the idea of it, the idea of an execution without trial. But I don't. No one should be allowed to hurt a gentle man like my father and get away with it. They deserved what she did.

"And what about Seath?" I ask.

She touches my cheek. "We have no trouble with him. He may be violent now, but many years ago, he was a reasonable man, studying to be a doctor at the university in Resya. Your uncle did business with him. Unfortunately, your uncle was left in his debt." She shakes her head. "I have a way to settle the matter. The Havis family has great influence. But you must never speak of Seath, do you understand? Certainly not here."

I nod quickly. They're a mirror of the words Havis spoke, and I understand now. Rumours in the night can steal everything, and my mother already walks a fine line between worlds. This rumour of her brother dealing with Seath—even innocently, years ago—could ruin her if placed in the wrong hands. The sort of crime that might cost our kingdom everything.

Long ago, I watched a newsreel of a Landorian traitor being executed before the Royal League, before all the representatives of the Northern kingdoms. An officer accused of aiding their enemies in Thurn. They read the verdict, put the noose round his neck, and then the film ended. Reni said it was an honourable death, but I can still see the man's panicked face. The reality of impending death, before a thousand cold eyes, and it still haunts my midnight thoughts. He was only a common soldier.

What would they do to a traitorous queen?

"These are two quite different things," Mother continues, seeming to sense my fear, "but only one matters. Paying off Seath? That can be done. The South is not so fickle as your Northern textbooks would have you believe. But protecting your brother from a lie against our throne? That is a more dangerous game. I know he longs for a happy kingdom, but I won't allow the dissenters in our square to gain influence. I have seen what these ideas can rouse, and I will use my fist. I will frighten them with the General's alliance. Anything to make sure they understand the order of things, and your brother's right to rule is never questioned."

"But what if they—"

"There is nothing to fear," she says firmly. "Everything will be made right."

She's as confident as if she were dealing with a pebble in her shoe, as if she had already reached down to flick it away, and something shifts inside me. Something important. Like the sun rising above the mountains, beginning as a shiver of light, then changing to a glow, and then appearing in bright brilliance, this mysterious thing suddenly makes sense. Of course she wishes to welcome General Dakar. Of course she wishes to show the North he can be brought into alliance. He has a chance of saving the South. He could ruin the Nahir and therefore Uncle's lingering debt, rescue the world from madness and remind Etania what the strength of this new age looks like.

His victory is our victory.

A man who creates peace from chaos.

And Mother knows this. She's always had a plan in motion, always, even in spite of the ire of Lord Jerig and Uncle Tanek and Reni. The world looks darkly different now. Filled with necessary secrets. Stories upon stories that never appear on paper or in ink.

Is this what Reni thinks about late at night? Does he wonder about the things he can't see?

Can I even keep a secret like this from him?

But I must, because Mother's right. He'd never stop running. If he knew our father was murdered for a lie, he'd fight his way into the very past to make things right, rousing a long-dead rumour, breathing new life into something dangerous in his efforts for justice.

"Perhaps you could let Reni give a speech," I suggest, trying to help his cause, the least I can do while she's listening so closely. "The ones protesting in the square don't know any better, but perhaps there's a middle ground to be reached? A way he could appeal to them to trust you?"

She cocks her head, studying my face and the mouth that spoke the words. A long moment passes, then she says, "If life has taught me one thing it is this—never negotiate with your enemy. Stay one step ahead instead. Now, you write that in your books and put it in ink, my dear heart. We women must always have our secrets."

III

LOYALTY

Leannya,

I'm writing in the hope of this reaching you before you head to Brisal for summer classes. Can you send me an address once you're there? I'll keep it close.

As you might have heard, I managed to get myself into Top Flight after all—even took first place and smashed the record set by that ass Garrick Carr (don't tell Arrin I called him that, but you know it's accurate). Everyone's thrilled about my success—meaning everyone in a rank above me, Torhan and the rest—since it seems they were betting on me all along, but I feel suspiciously like a new thing for them to play with. That's unsettling, given what they can now order me to do. But the actual flying on test day? I wish you could have seen it! It had nothing to do with any of them—just the familiar raw adrenaline, the energy shivering through the metal and into my skin, light glinting on glass and wings in bright flashes, an infinite and endless sky, high high high above the madness.

All of that joy has made me an official Lieutenant, in line for my own squadron. (Cyar got second place, an officer pinned with wings, but I'm still the superior rank. I hope this means he has to pack my bags if I ask.)

Since I won't be seeing you when I'm briefly home in Valon, here's my official hurrah for Arrin. I'm sure winning

the war in Karkev has humbled him entirely, given that his
name is now the one on everyone's lips, all those fireworks and
such every night in his glorious honour. Is he even sleeping at
home? (Don't answer that. Yes, you're supposed to be watching him, but let's not expect too much.) I'm grateful our oldest
brother has managed to win the war, and now he'll win the
next one (in theory), and if I'm lucky it will be before I ever get
the orders to join in.

Oh, I forgot. I already have orders. Father's taking me
with him to Landore—so much for sitting it out. Something
about wooing a king into letting us put a base in one of their
colonies . . . Does that sound suspicious to you? I'm optimistic still.

Either way, I promise to write from wherever they (he)
send me next. I'm praying to train under Captain Malek in
the 4th. Wish me luck on that front. You know how great the
captain is!

With all my affection,
Athan

11

⚔ ATHAN ⚔

Norvenne, Landore

I've never seen anything like it.

A vast harbour glimmers before us, teeming with ships from
every kingdom in the North, the busy seaways of the Black Sea
converging and rallying at the steps of the world's greatest empire. Merchant vessels and passenger liners break through waves,
colourful flags snapping in the wind, and two battle cruisers of
the Imperial Navy of Landore prowl among them, monstrous.
Beyond the water's edge, domed buildings of white-stone spread
as far as the eye can see. Each one looks elaborate and frivolous,
and lounging on the highest hill, overseeing its grand domain, is
the vainly glorious royal palace.

Our Safire contingent is picked up by motorcar from the airfield outside the city, escorted onto the long, wide avenues of
Norvenne. Father's been here before. So has Arrin. But Cyar and
I stare out the windows, entirely overwhelmed by the beauty
and opulence. No scars of battle anywhere. Not a single pockmarked wall. It's a place that doesn't remember war, and couples
stroll beneath linden trees, laughing as they toss coins for musicians and fountains.

The radiant centre of the Northern world. An empire of seven
hundred years.

It's making Valon seem rather rustic.

Garrick spends most of the trip reading a briefing in his lap, but even his mouth hangs slightly open when we pass between the towering pillars of the palace gates. They're inlaid with jewels and solid gold.

Real jewels and gold—on a damn gate!

Acres of buildings open up before us. Gardens with fancy sculptures and glassy lakes. A vast central courtyard is hemmed in by aureate walls and rows upon rows of windows, while an elegant statue of their long-ago ancestor, Prince Efan, perched astride a stallion sits in the centre.

"Why doesn't your family have a place like this?" Cyar jokes, turning circles as we walk for the huge entrance.

"We have the *Impressive*," I reply.

When we step through doors and into the entrance hall, we're greeted by unexpected chaos. Well-dressed lords surge by, calling for their stewards, panicked like a bunch of colourful fish out of water.

"Thank God you're here!" one exclaims, his only greeting to Father. He's heavyset, stuffed into ridiculous velvet pants, and I don't dare look at Cyar. We'll both laugh. "The news arrived an hour before you, General. They've seized Hady! The Nahir. Overwhelmed us, caught us by surprise, and then"—the man looks like someone's squeezing him from the inside out—"and then they hung the city consul and two of his advisors. God in heaven!"

Amusement about the velvet pants disappears.

Father glances at Arrin, then back. "Hady? The port city?"

"Yes," the man moans. "They've access to the river and canal now. To the sea! How could they have organized such an attack?"

"How indeed?" Father shakes his head.

"Please, General. His Majesty is already in discussion with the council, and awaits your contribution to the matter. General Windom is also here. An old friend of yours, I hear."

"Yes." Father smiles. "It has been a while."

I remember Windom from the years when we first moved to Valon. He was the first Landorian official to consider Father's rule legitimate. He came in the summer with his daughter, touring the factories where the Safire airplanes and tanks were being produced at record speed, watching the impressive wealth steaming in on trains from the mountains. He was the first to see Savient's promise—and believe in it. Now, apparently, the two of them are conspiring together over the South.

Father never forgets an ally.

The velvet-man brightens. "I'm confident the pair of you can concoct a grand strategy." He glances to Arrin. "And bring your son. Certainly the hero of Karkev will have much to offer."

God, they're worshipping Arrin here, too?

But my brother pales slightly at the request. I give a questioning look, and he turns his back on me, which he can do now. Father ordered me to adopt Mother's long-forgotten surname, Erelis, for the time being, as a safety measure.

"You're young and untried," Father said, "and I don't want you in any crosshairs."

So far, Arrin's doing a great job of pretending I'm nothing but a speck of a junior officer to him.

They stride off to meet with General Windom, and Kalt stares after them, left behind.

Cyar glances at me. "A bunch of Southern rebels have overrun the Landorian army and taken an entire city hostage?" he asks in Savien, so none of the lingering footmen understand. "I hope the King doesn't expect us to get it back for him."

"My father can only hope," I reply.

Cyar gives a short laugh. Reality must finally be dawning on him.

I offer him my bag. "Officer Hajari, could you carry this to my quarters?"

"Don't get any ideas, Lieutenant."

"That's insubordination, Hajari. A punishable off—"

The nearby footman takes my bag quickly, then Cyar's, and says, "Right this way, gentlemen," politely waving us to follow.

We both gape like he's offered to carry us, too.

"Dear God," Kalt says, brushing me on the way by. "It's like you came off a farm."

But apparently this is real, and men are here to serve us—actually serve us—so we shrug and follow them, grinning, into the maze of gilded halls.

King Gawain hosts a reception in our honour that night. It's held in a marble pavilion overlooking the sea, a more casual affair which is probably out of consideration for Father's disdain of court formality, but still feels a bit like being talked down to. Like we can't quite handle the full spectacle of a royal feast—the manners and the servants and the fifty silver forks to choose from. Violins mix with the stir of the evening tide, and brass tables—most with spirals of Southern flair, an exotic novelty—overflow with food and wine while courtiers, ambassadors, and military elite clink glasses in the salty breeze.

I find myself sympathizing with the exotic tables. Everyone's staring at us in our Safire uniforms, like we're foreign creatures that don't quite fit. The Landorian officers chuckle behind glasses of brandy, dressed in their deep blue tailcoats and gold sashes. They all look the same—fair-skinned and well-bred and haughty. I can see the curiosity in their eyes as they study Admiral Malek, with his dark skin and many medals, every Safire uniform paying him deference. In their world, leadership looks only one way. I'm sure they'd question even Cyar—if they cared about two young pilots—for not fitting their ideal mold. I'm suddenly very proud of Savient. We might not have a palace the size of a city, but we do have a military where respect is earned and given on nothing but actual merit.

The girls in silk dresses aren't much better.

"That one seems to have her eye on you," Cyar observes, nodding discreetly at a blonde with a feathered wrap in her hair. She's clearly appraising my value, the feather large enough she looks like she might topple.

I flick an olive into the air and catch it in my mouth. "You think?"

"Yes—and don't do that."

"Why not?"

"You'll just prove everyone right."

I don't care. If I'm going to be a novelty, I may as well make it worthwhile.

Gawain sweeps among his guests, large and formidable in a suit covered with emblems and medals. I'm not sure where he'd have won anything—certainly not on a battlefield—but he's still striking in his own way. As tall as Father, with a grey beard kept trim, his face tan and soft from years of being well fed. He's like the rounded lions carved into the arches of this pavilion. He also has three daughters, the eldest of whom possesses wide brown eyes and ample curves. Arrin's predictably intrigued. He offers her wine, escorts her to a table with gallant flourish, but she rebuffs every attempt like he's some mutt-dog getting under her feet. When he nabs the seat beside her, her polite disinterest flashes to temper.

Not a good game to play. Not with our base in the South depending on Gawain's seal of approval.

"Keep an eye on him," Father mutters to me, before moving on.

What am I supposed to do? Swat Arrin's hand? I'm only an Erelis here.

I take the seat across from them and give a clear warning look, but Arrin pretends not to see. He's busy bragging about his exploits in Karkev, routing the enemy and all that. She keeps her eyes on the food before her, stoic, but eventually her resolve weakens.

Arrin Dakar always wins a stalemate.

"Congratulations, Commander," she says, adjusting a string of jewels around her neck. "You won a war in some backwater kingdom. I hope those farmers didn't give too much of a fight." She has a porcelain doll's pout, entirely the opposite of Arrin's normal red-lipped finds. She's like something made of air or glass, perfect from every angle, and I like watching her. It's enjoyable in a strange, frustrating sort of way.

"Those farmers with field guns, Your Highness?" Arrin grins. "No, we hardly broke a sweat. The only reason it took two years was because we quite liked the cold and didn't want to leave so soon. The mountains in Karkev are stunning. Have you been?"

"I've no interest in visiting a corrupt place like that."

"You'd prefer the heat? Then how about Thurn? There's a rumour we're headed there next."

She fidgets with her fork. Even that's graceful. "Thurn is a wild place, Commander."

"Then let me tame it, Your Highness. I'll do it for you, in your name, because you deserve nothing less. I'll make that hell into a paradise, fit for both your crown and mine."

She rounds on him. "You aren't a prince! You're a uniform and little else!"

Of course. That's all we are in this room, to these people.

But Arrin tilts closer. "That's not what most ladies say, not once they get beneath this uniform."

She gasps.

It's a damn good thing no one else heard that.

"Ignore him," I say quickly. "He's drunk."

She looks across the table, noticing me for the first time. "He had one glass of port."

A servant scuttles over to refill the Princess's glass, and he's nearly trembling with nerves. He won't look her in the eye. I begin to wonder if we missed a lesson on protocol somewhere. How do I even address a royal? Do they still cut off people's heads here for looking at a king the wrong way? Someone should have been a bit clearer with us before this moment, seated at this elaborate table, Arrin about to sink his own ship in the usual spectacular fashion.

But he finally deigns to acknowledge my presence. "I'm not drunk, Lieutenant *Erelis*. But you should be, because you're clearly not a winning personality when sober." He turns back to the ample curves. "Your Highness, the Lieutenant's still a rookie in the ways of war. He doesn't yet realize that all of this"—Arrin gestures at himself—"could be buried and forgotten tomorrow."

Good God, is that one of his lines?

"And as a matter of fact," he continues, "what are you doing here anyway, Lieutenant? Go sit with your own kind." He gestures at Garrick and Cyar and the rest. "That's an order."

"Sir," I say with a submissive nod, standing.

It nearly burns my whole tongue off.

"And good evening, Your Highness," I add to the Princess, attempting to recover some manners, but she doesn't even hear me.

Oh well.

I try to scout out Father in the sea of uniforms. There's a bump against my shoulder, a Landorian colonel giving me an annoyed look as he passes. I don't apologize.

Why should it be me?

After wandering a bit more, I find Father leaning against the farthest balcony of the pavilion, the sunset sea behind him. He's standing with a man who doesn't look local. Brown-skinned, with sharp, lean features. Southern? The man laughs and tells some story, clutching a wine glass in each hand, his arms linked around the same number of women. Father listens carefully.

When I near, the man urges the ladies away. He looks me up and down. "Who's this?"

"My youngest," Father says, which is suspicious. If Father's introducing me honestly, then this man is in on the game, and this isn't idle conversation.

Then again, Father's conversations are never idle.

"Stars, another son? They don't end. Ah, what are you? Fifteen? I know exactly how it is to be the youngest. I bet you're only here to smile and serve the food."

I narrow my eyes. "I'm almost eighteen, actually, and—"

"Yes, just here to serve the food," Father interrupts. He hands me an empty plate. "Get Ambassador Havis more of the dessert pastries. Those women left nothing. Bring another glass of red wine, too."

Me?

"Do I need to ask again, Lieutenant?" There's an edge of impatience in Father's voice.

I shake my head and turn.

"They can be quite temperamental at this age," the Ambassador says, vaguely smirking.

I clench the plate in my fist and resist the urge to hurl it back at him.

Fifteen? That's just insulting.

At the dessert table, I grab small cakes and stack them haphazardly. As many as can fit, crumbling beneath my fingers. I fill a wine glass with cranberry juice. It all looks the same anyway. My mistake.

I swing from the table and stop in my tracks.

There's Arrin and the Princess, leaning close enough now he's got a very fine view of the ample assets. And she's lit with a smile, her hair rich with the sun's glow, listening as he demonstrates some trick with a coin, leaning closer every second.

How the hell does he do that?

Kalt materializes from the crowd beside me, also watching. "Quite a gift, isn't it?"

"The gift of having the face of a god and the morals of a portside sailor?"

"Yes, well, if it gets her to sing our praises to Gawain, then who gives a damn?" He crosses his arms. "No matter how much people want to strangle Arrin, they still want to claim him as their own. Father. Evertal. Even this Windom."

"I mostly just want to strangle him."

That earns me a slight smile. "Did you know one of the rebel militia units in Karkev asked to shake his hand after they surrendered? They were that impressed by his fight. God, it's almost mythological."

There's sincerity in his voice. Genuine, bittersweet. At least I don't care about living in Arrin's shadow. In or out makes no difference to me, but it's not the same for Kalt.

I offer him a pastry. "If only Gawain had a prince, right?"

It takes a moment, the joke seemingly lost, or perhaps an inch too far, but then he begins to chuckle. Both of us do. It feels good to laugh, for real, in this overstuffed circus.

"Not enough servants are there, Lieutenant?" Garrick says on his way by, stealing from my plate. He's outfitted in his full dress uniform, armed with medals from Karkev. On a mission for fancy Landorian beds, no doubt. "Thanks for the dessert, rookie."

His first officer, Ollie Helsun, follows behind, giving a snort. Ollie's the very best wingman. He'll laugh at any unfunny quip if it's made by Garrick.

"Your arm looks rather lonely tonight, Captain," I observe.

"Haven't found a lady yet worth my stamina," Garrick replies in Savien. He sounds charming, like we're sharing bawdy humour, pilot to pilot, but the fact that I beat his Academy record simmers between us. It's going to for a while.

"Perhaps you can take a lesson from the Commander," I say, equally charming.

He glances at Arrin, absorbing the scene—the porcelain girl of perfection tracing medals on my brother's chest. His expression sours. In Savient, being a captain counts for something. Here, he's just another one of us.

Another meaningless Safire uniform.

He marches off, Ollie trailing after, and I want to call, *"There are some targets too high for even you, including my score!"*

But I don't. Because I'm a lieutenant now.

"Pilots are cocky bastards," Kalt observes. "If you'd like, I can shoot him out of the sky with my ship. Friendly fire happens."

"Please. By the way, do I look fifteen?"

"What? No."

I leave my brother, continuing back for Father and Havis. They're deep in conversation, alone. Father's presence has a magnificent way of discouraging anyone not invited.

The Ambassador grins when I offer the desserts. "Very well trained, aren't you?"

I bite my tongue, and Father waves the plate away. I set it on the balcony beside us.

"As I was saying," Havis continues, "I quite miss the years based here in Landore, but my reassignment has proved invaluable."

Father nods. "Etania."

"It was an unexpected change, but a welcome one."

I raise my brow. "From the greatest empire in the North to that little kingdom?"

"Your point?"

"It sounds like a demotion, Ambassador."

"It was a reassignment," Havis repeats.

"Then congratulations. I'm sure you've earned it."

Father gives me a warning glance.

"You must know, General," Havis continues, like I'm not worth his time, "I was truly shocked by the news of your tragic loss."

"It was the act of a coward," Father says tightly.

"Indeed. It has stunned the world, felt by everyone in the North, even in the little kingdoms."

"Yes," Father agrees, "there does seem to be much regret and fear, what with the condolences sent to me." Father lowers his voice. "But of course I don't quite believe this could happen to just anyone. I believe my wife was a carefully chosen target."

"It's possible."

"And I believe your enemy is the same as mine."

"Also possible."

They're dancing around the name they won't say out loud.

Sinora Lehzar.

It's not time to speak it, not yet, but the danger of even discussing the possibility here makes my palms sweat. Maybe that's why they're doing it.

Who plots regicide at a royal gala?

Havis smiles faintly. "You needn't tell me these things. You know what I've lived through."

"Yes. Your brother was a good man, a loyal fighter, before—"

"My family hasn't been as lucky as yours, General."

"It's not about luck, Havis. What happened could have been avoided, and you know it."

"Perhaps, perhaps not." The Ambassador drifts back to me, unhurried. "When my brother went to war, he was like this one. Too young to know any better." I narrow my eyes again, because he has no idea what I've been through or why I do what I do, but he shrugs. "I've since made my own way. Free of that madness."

"And you're ready to work for justice?"

There's a long pause. The tide chugs in and out, thumping below us, and the Resyan man smiles, lifting his wine glass. "I'm from the house of Havis, General. I do anything for the highest bid."

He sips the juice, then makes a face.

12

⫷ AURELIA ⫸

Hathene, Etania

The loss of Hady arrives in a panicked tremor of rumours, gaining momentum and infecting the court with a vicious sense of persecution.

"Took the consul of the city himself, can you believe it? Hung him along with the officers. Left them bloating in the sun for three days."

"I heard the entire week. My cousin serves with the Landorian forces, you know. He fled in time."

"Truly, how could a pack of rebels pull such a thing off!"

"Outside help, I'm certain, but from where?"

They glance at my Resyan mother with an unspoken question in their eyes, and while she hardly seems to notice, I'm terrified they might somehow peer inside her head, see the words "great revolution" and "necessary change" there, and find their unwelcome answer.

Which is why I decide to host a Royal Chase.

"Stars, no one wants a frivolous thing like that right now," Uncle complains when he learns of my idea, and that Mother's supportive of it. "The world's on the brink of boiling over again, and you think a horse race through the woods will distract our people from it?"

But I do, and Mother agrees. Even Reni gets a perky smile over it, because secretly he loves a good competition, especially a public one. And since his stallion is without a doubt the most magnificent in the field, of course he'll win.

My brother needs a victory, and I'd like to give him one.

Race day brings the first truly hot day of summer. People flock from Hathene to the palace grounds, lured by the chance to make a gamble, and I think it's very convenient that men are so moved by money. They stroll paths normally forbidden, admiring from afar the gardens, the royal airfield, the stables. Palace guards in green livery herd hundreds of commoners to a viewing point on a hill overlooking the lawn, while Mother and her court are escorted close to the course and the finish line, where a small podium has been raised. Cheerful enthusiasm grows as bets are placed and debated amid colourful parasols and caps.

"It's good for the spirit to be outside," Mother says to me, a tad wistful. She holds a wine-coloured folding fan in one hand, and with the other reaches out for the light, like she's grasping a tangible thing. "I've missed the sun."

It's rare she steps outside like this, especially in summer. It burnishes her amber skin to a deeper shade that, no matter how lovely, only sets her apart further.

It does for me, too, but they'll never keep me indoors, no matter what the court might think of my Southern hue.

Behind us, Uncle follows with the occasional long-suffering sigh. The Chase used to involve guns, but when I first learned that a fox would be released to die for the sport of it, I sobbed an entire night and Father changed the traditional rules to make it only a race. Uncle finds the whole thing rather pointless now.

Lord Jerig is waiting near the podium, pinched per usual, and Mother suggests we invite him to stand with us. "Sometimes the wisest move is to invite the enemy to your table," she explains, striding for him with a diplomatic smile.

Well, if she thinks so.

Lord Marcin and Violet follow behind, Violet wearing a gigantic feather and clutching the arm of a boy I recognize—Slick, from the retirement party. She laughs with him, apparently not at all concerned the Prince will soon see her flaunting this clever-mouthed pilot boy, but her gaze darts often to the stables beyond, her laughter not entirely real.

Uncle pretends to be gracious and offers me a hand when we reach the podium steps.

I shake my head and follow Mother and Jerig up.

Then I stand before the crowd of courtiers, a circular brown microphone level with my mouth, and the group seems suddenly much larger. A lot of faces, familiar and unfamiliar, all staring expectantly at me, the host of the race. Waiting for me to give a pretty little speech. Even Violet hushes Slick soundly, his face wincing like a scolded puppy. But since I've seen Mother do this enough, I know how it should go, and I give a diplomatic smile.

"Welcome, dear friends, to our day of sport. We are honoured by your presence, each and every one of you." I make sure to nod in the direction of the nearby hill, to the city folk listening to my echoing voice from a distance. "I hope you will enjoy this competition in the spirit from which it was born—for the love of our steeds, for the joy of these woods, and out of respect for excellent sportsmanship. This day is for all of us."

I think my cheeks are a little pink, but otherwise my voice sounds steady.

The courtiers clap—Violet extra vibrantly, as if I've just juggled a dozen eggs at once—and a loud trumpet rings silvery across the lawn. Seven horses appear by the eastern gardens, Reni leading the group. He's dressed in a leather coat and tall riding boots, astride his bay stallion, Liberty, who is mostly royalty himself—a gleaming mahogany creature with black points reaching to his knees and hocks, a giant among the other horses. He prances beneath my brother's half-halts. Sweaty froth already slicks his neck and chest.

They're trotting to the start line, waving at the eager specta-tors, and nearly to us, when there's a sudden shout. Then another.

I shade my eyes from the sun, trying to see.

A strange tide erupts from within the crowd on the hill, emerging like furious ants onto the green before the horses.

"No Safire boots in Etania!" a man shouts, throwing himself down, arms spread.

Others shout the same, and the crowd silences in confusion. The courtiers before me clutch hats and parasols, gaping. Moth-er's hand grips my arm like a vice as a mob of men in dark coats surround the horses and flail their arms at Liberty. Reni strug-gles to keep the stallion from rearing up. Liberty hops to the side instead and tosses his head, whinny mixing with the chants.

I break free of Mother's grasp and hurry down the podium steps, sprinting for Liberty as best I can in a dress. Someone needs to take hold of the panicked stallion before he throws Reni off completely!

Guards have surrounded the men when I arrive, cuffing them behind the head, a commotion of shouts and fists and struggling limbs. Reni is still aboard, hollering at the men. "Your voices are heard! Her Majesty will listen. See, she comes now. Make your case and you will not be ignored."

He sounds older addressing them, and he looks like some sort of knight, reining in his trembling, glorious stallion in circles.

I turn and find Mother close on my heels, but she's glaring at Reni in fury. The look on her face is frightening. "Get these criminals from my sight," she orders the guards. "Hold them until we have answers, is that understood?"

One of the men struggles between his captors. He has a grey mustache, his cleft chin blunt and square, intimidating even with a guard gripping either arm. "No Safire boots in Etania!" he shouts again into the wind. "We don't want those bloody tracks here!"

"A *Resyan* woman doesn't speak for us!" another cries.

Mother draws all of her fierce and catlike elegance into one single, dark-eyed gaze. "Your Queen speaks for you, *traitor*."

"They've harmed no one!" Reni declares roughly from atop Liberty.

The harsh tone sends his stallion lurching backwards, nearly slamming into the horse behind him, and I seize the bridle. The moment my fingers are gripping the reins, Liberty stills. My hands stroke the arch of his lathered neck. His breath continues to come like a dragon snorting, sides heaving, but he respects my touch.

Reni doesn't even seem to notice, his gaze fixed on the protesters. "What is it you wish to say? Your Queen listens."

Mother snaps her fan in anger. Sweat brightens her face. "I do *not*."

"Then if you won't," Reni announces, "I will."

Stars!

I clutch the reins tighter, but a strange silence falls, a long moment where no one moves, not the courtiers gathered in their finery, nor the crowds in their tweed and cotton, nor the guards in their green livery. Even the wicked men in dark coats look stunned. It's as if we're all waiting for some balance to shift. Some weight to move one way or another and make it clear how to feel about this unexpected confrontation.

Perhaps that thing is me.

I release Liberty with a last stroke on his shoulder, then step out where all can see. "My Royal Chase is no place for this kind of display," I say to Reni alone, but loud enough everyone else can hear, too. "This isn't how we settle things in Etania, is it?"

Reni's silent gaze begs me to be his ally.

But I can't. My father, and now Reni, may have allowed such opinions, and perhaps these men have the right to believe them, but it can't be like this, not now.

I have to stand by Mother.

"No," I continue louder, "Her Majesty is right. This isn't the way to express a concern. They won't ruin our day with incivility. The General is our honourable ally now, a man committed to encouraging peace, and these men seek their own vain attention."

Everyone stares.

I motion at the guards. "Don't just stand there. Do as your queen orders!"

They pale at such a blunt order, from me of all people, but lead the men from the lawn quickly. The lords and ladies nod their heads, murmuring agreement, and Reni is wounded. It's only in his eyes. He still sits proudly on Liberty, shoulders squared, but thick betrayal hangs between us.

How I wish I could explain.

How I wish he knew the truth of Father's death, of all the things unseen.

But Reni doesn't even glance at me on his way to the start line, denying me the chance to kiss Liberty's nose for good luck, to wish him a safe race. He doesn't even notice Violet and Slick.

I stand bereft beneath the sweltering sun until Mother kisses my cheek. "Thank you, my heart," she says in Resyan, so no one else will know the depth of her gratitude.

Please, Father, tell me I did the right thing.

But there's no reply, only a hush falling as seven riders take position at the start.

A gun fires, echoing, and the horses leap forward, earth flying behind. They gallop the lawn at a blistering pace and the first hurdle—a four-foot hedge with ditches on either side—is taken at full tilt. Only one horse refuses to follow through. The rest are up and over, sweeping past us with Reni in the lead. A heart-lurching jump into the river is next, and he doesn't slow down. Of course he doesn't. I hear Mother make a tiny, terrified noise as Liberty launches himself over the drop. Two horses follow behind. The crowd gasps, thrilled, and the animals are nearly on top of one another in the water, struggling to find footing and reach the opposite bank. Reni storms up the far side of the river and disappears into the woods. The rest follow in pursuit.

We can see nothing for a few heated moments, only hear the sound of hooves echoing among the oak and chestnut and pine.

No one speaks, waiting.

Then Liberty bursts out of the woods and into the river again like a hurtling star. There's a gasp from the crowd around us. He's quickly up the riverbank in a spray of water and sweat, Reni atop with a soaked leather coat. They're both nearly neck-deep in splattered mud. Liberty reaches forward to stretch into the gallop of the straightaway, breaking for the finish line, but his hoof hits the slop of wet dirt and slips beneath him. He falls forward, shoulder hurling into the earth, and Mother cries out beside me.

My breath disappears.

But Reni hangs on, kicking with his heels. Like an awkward baby deer struggling to stand, Liberty scrambles up just as another horse crashes through the water behind them. Reni senses competition and whacks Liberty with his crop on one heaving flank. The stallion pushes forward, but there's a limp in his front-right leg. He gallops slightly off-kilter, favouring the injury.

"No," I whisper. "No, no, no."

My brother continues with that wicked sting of his crop. Once, twice. Again and again, Liberty trying so hard to give Reni what he demands. Destroying himself to obey. His ears twist in frustration, in pain. And I did this. I've given my brother a reason to push beyond what's right and win something for himself. I want to run and throw myself in front of him, like those men, and beg him to stop.

But I can only watch as Liberty fights, brutally, for the lead.

He crosses the finish line first.

The trumpet sounds, and everyone claps brightly, congratulating Mother, the spectators on the hill celebrating with loud whistles and applause. My brother doesn't lift his hand in triumph, though. He pulls Liberty to a halt and swings wildly off, dropping to the ground, kneeling before anyone can stop him, feeling Liberty's injured leg with desperate hands.

I blink back tears.

No one else seems concerned about the stallion's state, only watching curiously as the head groom jogs over and joins Reni, the freckled stable boy now holding Liberty's reins and looking wide-eyed. They walk Liberty forward a few steps and he staggers.

"Might mean a bullet for that one," Slick observes matter-of-factly to Violet.

Violet covers her mouth and turns away.

I draw closer, shaking with anger and horror. I have to know.

"We'll need to give him a few days' rest, Your Highness," the groom says to Reni, unable to disguise his grief. "We won't make any decisions until we see what we can do."

Reni nods, silent, and removes his helmet. His dark hair is matted and wet. I want to hit him and hug him at the same time, the selfish, selfish boy. He's destroyed his beautiful horse. He did it to win, and yet here he is now, trembling with regret.

They lead Liberty away at an awkward hobble, and I place my hand on Reni's arm.

He pushes me off. There's a glimmer in his eyes. "Don't say it."

Then he's striding for the palace, mud-splattered and defeated, and I curse this lovely summer day for being so rotten on the inside.

13

Norvenne, Landore

After eight days of negotiations, Landore approves our base in Thurn.

Father had me record their hours of debate. A discreet way to bring me into the thick of things. I sat silently in the back of their meetings with another young translator, writing down the Landori discussions as Savien words. Every day that the tragedies mounted—first the loss of Hady, then a slaughtered unit outside the city of Beraya, and after that an attack on a Landorian merchant ship off the coast—was a strike against Gawain. His council couldn't hide their panic. They resented the stalling, and Father's steady optimism won him allies.

The morning after his victory, Father orders Arrin, Kalt, and me to an early briefing. For the first few minutes, only Kalt and I are present. The clock on the wall ticks the awkward silence. It bears the crest of the Landorian forces—a crowned lion, flames in its growling mouth. I trace the design on my thigh with a finger. Waiting.

The door swings open, and Arrin stumbles through still buttoning his collar.

"Late night?" Father asks, the barest thread of humour in his voice. The dangerous kind.

Arrin's undeterred. "Entertaining Gawain's daughter with a

trip to the opera. She rather likes me, in case you haven't noticed. I'm sure that's been helpful to you."

"Entertain?"

Arrin appears offended. "I wouldn't mess around with a princess. I'm not that stupid."

Kalt raises a brow, silent, and Arrin whacks his shoulder, then
slumps into the vacant seat on his left.

The lion clock keeps ticking.

Quarter after seven. Could I be out of this in ten minutes?
What are the odds of that?

"The coming weeks will be strategic ones for us," Father
continues, "and unfortunately, I can't be everywhere at once.
Arrin, you'll go to Thurn with Windom, to investigate the situation firsthand."

Arrin slaps the table. "I get to be the first one of us to visit
Thurn's welcoming locals? Fun."

Father looks at Kalt. I love when he ignores Arrin completely.
"You'll return to Valon. Evertal's conducting our summit with
the new Karkevite leadership, and I need someone as my voice
there."

"How about I take the summit?" Arrin asks. "I won that war.
Send Kalt and his sailboat to visit the friendly Nahir."

"You're well aware that Windom is grateful for your expertise," Father replies.

Arrin grimaces, drumming his fingers on the chair. "He's the
one who's been in Thurn as long as I've been alive. He and the
rest have made a damn mess of it, and now I'm expected to clean
it up *and* tame the rebels? These aren't the kind who'll shake
my hand at the end of the day."

"You're quite right," Father agrees, "and if they cut out your
tongue, they'd be doing me a favour."

I laugh. Can't help it. Kalt suppresses his behind a cough.

Father turns to me. "And you're coming to Etania."

Laughter dies on my lips. "Sir?"

"Yes, what?" Arrin echoes.

"I'm not going alone," Father says. "I'll have Malek there, but he'll be with me every moment. I need someone to watch where I'm not."

My mouth hangs open. It's only been six weeks since Mother's death, and if Sinora Lehzar did it, then I can't face her. I can fake a lot of things, but I can't look into that woman's face and smile.

I can't.

Arrin beats me to the protest. "This is absurd, Father! We don't know what Sinora's capable of. You'll give her a perfect target."

"No, *you* would be a perfect target," Father says. "You're worth something in this game. Athan counts for nothing."

I'm too stunned to be offended by that.

"Then take me," Arrin says. "Let's see how far she's willing to go."

Father frowns. "Your bold instinct doesn't always translate well in politics." He turns back to me. "She has two children about your age. You can get them to talk, can't you?"

Now this has to be a joke. "They're royals," I say. "They'll never talk to me."

"Arrin found a way here."

"I'm not entirely sure that's the way you want, sir," Kalt offers.

Arrin whacks him again, then leans on the table, motioning at me. "That bitch will know exactly who he is, hidden behind the name Erelis or not. She knew Mother. She knows more about us than anyone else in the North, and that's a bad enough card as it is. Don't shove Athan into it."

Is Arrin still defending me? That might be the most surprising thing here.

Father smiles. "Of course. But I have Sinora up a tree. She'll play innocent, anything to avoid suspicion, for as long as it takes. If she doesn't play by my rules, I'll simply let the noose tighten quicker."

Only my father can smile while talking about a noose.

"You'll come to Etania," he says firmly, "and then, Lieutenant, you begin your training in Thurn. I've just received word that the remodeled fighters are on their way. New twelve-cylinder engine. Twin cannons along with the machine guns. Squadron officers are getting them first, but I've requested some for certain officers-in-training."

And there it is—the hook. I sink back in my seat, the glint of new metal before me. A fresh fighter. A real one with the black swords of the Safire beneath the wings and more firepower than whatever the rest are flying with. Any advantage in the sky is worth it, especially from the man who said he'd never pull strings.

"Air Force command will be curious about how they handle," Father continues. He knows he's angled me into position. "You'll give them a full report."

"One for Hajari as well?" I ask, since this is key.

"Naturally."

Father holds my gaze, waiting.

I nod. "Thank you, sir."

"He bought you with a plane," Arrin mutters. "Everyone's gone mad."

Father ignores him again. "Any questions?"

We shake our heads.

"Very good."

He goes back to signing his papers, clock still ticking, and I wonder what I've just agreed to.

The gleam of new metal disappears the night before we leave Norvenne. I lie there, memories of Mother covered in blood sabotaging my sleep, eating away the early morning hours. When it's time to get up, I glance in the mirror and find a pale-looking kid with shadowed eyes and a hint of weary desperation. It's not very attractive. The only thing I want right now is to fly. It's been two weeks since I was in a cockpit and there's a terrible impatience building, like I'm holding my breath, drowning underwater until I'm in the sky again.

But it's Garrick and Ollie who get to pilot the two new fighters from Landore to Etania. As dawn touches the east, the large airbase on the outskirts of Norvenne hums with activity. The Landorians have the busy east runway, their blue uniforms darting around the tarmac in the distance. Most of their airplanes are bound for the South, military transports loaded with supplies and weaponry for their forces there. We have the quiet west circuit. Father's plane is fueled, and an unmarked transport sits beside it, smaller and older.

Father's with me on the dispersal hut balcony, watching impatiently.

"Why aren't our fighters on their way?" he demands.

"Nearly ready, sir," says a crewman with a nervous salute.

"That's what someone said fifteen minutes ago. Her Majesty expects us by morning."

The crewman nods and scurries off, hollering orders over the radio in his hand.

On the tarmac, Garrick and Ollie are dressed in flight suits and waiting to climb into their cockpits. The two new fighters—complete with twin cannons—appear ghostlike in the low light, grey wings the colour of the sky.

"Damn engines. They'll need to refuel twice as much," Father says to me.

I stifle a yawn. "Bringing them along is a headache."

"I need to make the proper impression. These new planes will do just that."

"I meant Captain Carr and Officer Helsun."

Father pins me with a look. "You'd better learn to have a more optimistic view of Captain Carr. You and Hajari are being placed with the Moonstrike squadron for the summer. Carr is one of the best in the air, and he knows how to run a successful squadron. He'll show you what it means to be decisive."

I'm in the middle of another yawn, my stunned hand gripping the metal rail.

Before us, Garrick climbs into the cockpit, waving to ground crew, a stupid grin on his face like he's putting on some kind of death-defying show. The engine starts with a piercing growl.

"I can't train with him," I say above the racket. The noise feels a bit like protection, emboldening me. "Let me fly with another squadron. Captain Malek would be—"

"No, it's a good test, as Arrin suggested." Father's facing the tarmac again, but he glances sideways at me. "If you're going to be a leader, you'll have to learn to deal with your opposite."

Of course Arrin was behind this. I can feel exhausted anger ready to leap out, but Father halts it with a sharp look. "I'd hate," he says, "for Officer Hajari to go into battle without those cannons. I think it's up to you to prove he needs that new fighter. Perhaps he'd even do better in another squadron, away from you? Separation is good for growth."

With that brutal threat, he strides down the steps onto the tarmac. I'm left behind, horrified, envisioning Cyar with some slower, obsolete plane in a war-torn sky where I can't even help him.

The two new fighters hurtle down the runway and break for the western horizon.

Fast. Deadly.

Cyar taps my shoulder. "You look miserable."

"I couldn't sleep."

"And?"

"We're training with Garrick Carr."

He gapes like I've just kissed his girlfriend. "How the hell did that happen?"

"Apparently I need to learn to deal with my opposite."

I can't tell him the whole truth. That's something he doesn't need to know. He doesn't need to know that he'll always be the vulnerable piece of my life Father can manipulate on a whim. I never thought how far that might go.

We walk, depressed now, for Father's plane as the sun appears in the east, washing the base in bright light. The familiar stench of kerosene and the clang of idling metal, the oil-stained tarmac beneath our boots.

Kalt is planted by the neighbouring, unmarked plane, ticking off a list with a pencil, dressed in his heavy wool overcoat. He closes the book when I approach, and Cyar goes on ahead.

"Presents for Thurn?" I ask, watching the men load crates of rifles, handguns, even a few ancient bayonets. The sort of weapons Father's men used twenty years ago to make Savient. "You know, if we're going to help the Landorians, they might prefer something a bit more useful. Like actual machine guns. Maybe some mortars?"

Kalt gives me an annoyed look. "It's for the Etanians. They like the old-guard look for their mounted military parades, so we're gifting them some Safire vintage. Apparently that's a thing royals do. Shows unity. And you'd better not act this fresh in front of . . ." His mouth sets, unwilling to say Sinora's name out loud.

"I'll be good," I say, imagining Cyar in a cannonless plane. I hand him a small blue box. "Please make sure Leannya gets this when you're home." He inspects the box, giving a shake. "Careful, Kalt! It's breakable."

"What is it?"

"Perfume. Just make sure she gets it."

He nods and footsteps pound behind, coming near. Someone calling my name.

Arrin.

I ignore him, turning from Kalt and heading for Father's plane, but he catches up just as I reach the steps. He grips me by the shoulder before I can ascend and forces me to face him.

"You be careful," he orders. "I begged Father to take me instead, but he won't listen."

I've spent too many sleepless hours thinking about this. I don't even care anymore. But one emotion remains. "You've got a lot of damn nerve, Arrin," I say, stepping close. "There are twelve squadrons and you made sure I'd have to salute Garrick!"

Arrin opens his arms. "I've seen what he can do in battle. You'll learn a lot from him."

"Don't make this sound like a favour."

"This has nothing to do with me, Athan. If you don't learn to separate what you want from the job that needs to be done, then you're headed for a fall. Why do you think I'm still here? It's not because I do what I want."

That makes me laugh. "Right."

"Bite your tongue. You think I want to spend the summer as Windom's pet? It's about as close to a personal hell as I can imagine."

"Why?"

"None of your damn business." He grabs me by the shoulder again. "Don't trust anyone there."

I throw him off and head up the stairs.

"I mean it, Athan! You watch your back."

I stop at the door and face him. My voice is slick with sarcasm. "Like you watched mine?"

He stands down there, glaring all hell at me, hands balled like he'd rather they were around my neck, and then I do the one thing I want to do, the thing I've always wanted to do—I give him the one-fingered salute.

Then I disappear into the plane and there's not a damn thing he can do about it.

IV

SEA AND SKY

14

❦ AURELIA ❦

Hathene, Etania

A tremor of anticipation wakes me before dawn. The eastern mountains have only just begun to glow, bringing with it the Safire arrival, and I sit in my bay window, silent, sketching the familiar view with lazy strokes of charcoal against blank paper. I feel mostly calm. Ready. But my stomach still feels like a knot, and I sing to myself in Resyan, distracting my nerves best I can.

"I am a mountain," I whisper, "a song you remember."

Invariably, my sketch changes to Liberty. The leafy branches become his mane and his eyes have hawks in them, wings spread. The poor stallion is still trapped in his stall, injured leg wrapped and splinted, and subtle despair tinges the groom's reports. They're leaving the decision up to Reni, the very worst idea. Reni won't even speak of it. He pretends it never happened, refusing to visit the stables, and now the General is coming and everyone will forget suffering Liberty altogether.

I shade hard enough my pencil splinters.

Yesterday evening, Heathwyn lectured me on the protocol of this visit, rattling off the things to remember while a maid carefully manicured my nails, another one softening my hands with lavender-scented oil.

"All discussion with our visitors will be conducted in Landori, and you're always to be pleasant and welcoming, no matter the attitude your brother adopts. And you be sure to offer the General the greatest respect. No commentary on Karkev or Thurn or anything contentious. Divert the conversation with a smile if you must, because your smile will be your greatest credit to this visit."

I made sure to smile extra wide at that, and she clucked her tongue.

"Please, Aurelia, remember you will be watched every moment and your words and actions will reflect entirely on your mother. Reflect well, is that understood?"

She doesn't know how well I understand that, how the weight of this visit feels like an entire secret world on my shoulders, one that no one else sees, and I promise to smile, smile, smile. Now, the morning sun shines fully and I strain my ears to listen for the sound of aeroplanes in the sky.

A slight impatience pricks inside.

Heathwyn arrives with warm bread and marmalade in hand, a nervous set to her lips, and I pick at the breakfast while she and another maidservant fuss with me—braiding my hair and pinning flowers, dabbing red on my lips and buttoning me into a sea-blue gown with ivory pearls—but in the end, it turns out well.

"The Safire won't know where to look first," Heathwyn says, studying me in the mirror, pleased. "You or your mother."

"I'm sure it will be Violet's breasts," I reply with a grin.

Heathwyn clucks her tongue yet again, but she hasn't seen Violet's chosen gown for today. I have, and so has Reni, and it certainly leaves only the most critical things to the imagination.

"Aurelia, such comments won't—"

Her rebuttal is cut off by a growl that rattles the very windowpanes. It's a fierce sound, echoing harshly off the mountains, passing close overhead. I rush for the window and press my face to the glass, trying to peer up, and Heathwyn tells me to stop because I'll rub the pink off my cheeks. But there they are! Two Safire fighter planes circling low, flashing brilliant silver in the morning sun. They're all sharp angles and grey metal compared to the smooth curves of our green Etanian planes, their ferocious noise carrying, surrounding us, seeming to grow with each moment like there are at least ten more hidden out of sight. One loops higher, playful in the morning sky. Black swords wink from the underside of the wings as he spins. Easy and graceful, like a falcon, before diving low again and rejoining his friend. Together, they arc towards the western airfield.

"Stars," Reni says, appearing suddenly behind me. I step back, giving him space to look as well. "They're moving at quite a speed, aren't they?" He cranes his neck as they disappear from sight.

"Have you ever seen anything like it?" I ask.

"I have. It was at a circus, and everyone was dressed in ridiculous colours and acting like fools."

I swipe at his arm. "I hope those aren't your opening remarks to the General." I notice, then, that nestled against his elegant green coat is a ceremonial pistol. "And I hope you're planning to take that off."

"It's custom," Reni replies. "Father wore his to every diplomatic function."

"But we're insisting the Safire remove theirs. It doesn't look right if we refuse to do the same!"

Reni shrugs. "Dogs are muzzled, not royalty."

On that vain note, he marches back for the hall, waving for me, and I say a quick, fervent prayer to my father that Reni doesn't begin a whole war in one day.

Outside, the west entrance of the palace is bright with sun, its honey-coloured walls almost a glare. Etanian and Safire flags dance in the thick mountain wind, displayed in hopeful unity, and courtiers wait along the wide stone steps with chiffon skirts blowing, music sparkling amid the excitement. All eyes are on the long runway before us.

Reni and I stand on either side of Mother as she waits quietly, regally, at the top of the open-air steps in a maroon gown trimmed with gold, her chin raised and my father's crown glimmering on her black hair. It's a rare occasion for her to wear it. But today it gleams, luminous as she, a glorious reminder to the kingdom that there is nothing to fear and she rules in splendour. But there's still a tiny tremor nearly hidden. She fingers the lace detailing of her skirt, and I wish I could squeeze her hand in reassurance.

On the tarmac, the two Safire fighters have landed, silver pipes along their nose trailing exhaust. The wind smells strongly of petrol and smoke. In the distant sky, a larger aeroplane appears, wide-winged and imposing. We watch it lower, hitting the runway with a high-pitched screech. It's very large, propellers on either side, and the wings rattle as it brakes, swaying side to side slightly. There's a fox-and-crossed-swords crest painted on the flank, and everyone lining the steps ceases their chatter, tilting their heads, whispering now as if their words might already be heard by the General himself.

One of the Safire pilots leaps down from his now idle fighter. His red hair is ablaze in the sun. The second pilot walks over, and they light up their cigarettes without even a glance at the royal court waiting nearby. Etanian ground crew attempt to speak to them, but they ignore it, striding for the large plane, trailing smoke like their fighters.

Mother flicks her hand. The royal guards on the tarmac come to attention.

Safire uniforms emerge from the General's plane as the metallic creature hisses in the sun, steel and aluminum pieces settling. They march down the stairs, appearing confident, but none of them look quite like General Dakar—at least, not as far as I know. I've only ever seen a few distant photographs in the newspapers. It's not until the two Safire pilots stamp out their cigarettes and straighten that I think we must be nearly to him. A man with dark skin appears at the top of the stairs. His uniform's richly medaled, his head swiveling round to take in the runway and palace.

"Admiral Malek," I hear one lord say knowingly to a nearby friend.

Then the Admiral is down the stairs and another tall, grey-clad figure looms in the door of the plane.

The General, at last.

He pauses there for a long, weighted moment, surveying the world before him. His gaze moves from the line of royal guards to the stone steps and then on up to Mother beneath the arched facade. He smiles.

Descending the stairs, he greets Lord Marcin and Lord Jerig with handshakes. They both put on a good show, thank the stars, then Admiral Malek and the General walk across the tarmac together, the General offering those he passes a formal, yet affable, nod.

When they stride up the palace steps, he's still wearing his polite smile, and Mother returns it. It's her polished one that radiates certainty. The General drops into a short bow before us. The rest of his Safire party, following behind, do the same.

"Your Majesty," he says. "At last we've arrived. We're honoured to be your guests."

Mother dips her chin in respect. "You're most welcome in Etania, General. The honour is ours."

I can't help but stare at him, now only a few feet from me. He towers over her, his face angled and weatherworn, dark chestnut hair greying, and he speaks Landori with a pleasant accent, his voice low and graveled.

He turns to Reni. "This must be your prince. Nearly a man grown, I see."

Reni conjures a sudden smile. "Welcome to our kingdom, General."

"Thank you, Your Highness."

"I must say," Reni continues, "your remarkable reputation precedes you, and we have enjoyed following all you do with an attentive eye, particularly in Karkev."

Stars, I'd like to slap Reni for that, but the General simply tilts his head and says, "Is that so? Well, I hope you're learning something."

Reni's expression tightens, and Mother laughs, the kind that makes everything seem light, motioning me forward. "And this is my star, my daughter."

"Ah, yes." He glances at me. "Pretty as your mother. They must say that often."

"It's truly an honour to meet you," I say. "We're grateful you're willing to grace us with your distinguished presence."

"You are kind."

His green eyes study me, as if waiting, and I'd rather not disappoint, not after Reni's jab. I nod at his fighter planes nearby. "It's been said, General, your aeroplanes are the most impressive in all the world. Perhaps while you're here, you might be willing to give us a demonstration. We'd be quite thrilled."

Reni looks at me like I've sprouted a second head.

The General turns to Mother, smiling. "I think I like your girl best."

He offers me no further reply, nor any acknowledgment of my compliment. He even turns his back slightly so our conversation is clearly ended, and my cheeks sting a bit. The Admiral beside him looks me up and down, a cursory appraisal, detached, and it feels like the entire world has just witnessed my rebuffed attempt at diplomacy.

The entire world except for one.

Violet's standing a few steps away in her tempting emerald gown, beautiful, lit by sun, and oblivious to my miserable exchange with the General of Savient. She's happily occupied with something else—the red-haired Safire pilot. He's gulping her in without shame, confident as a strutting cock, and she blushes with that breathless delight that makes him try even harder.

"Let's move inside," Mother says. "This wind is strong, isn't it?" She smiles again. Always smiling, no longer a tremor to be seen. "In the mountains, weather can change with the moment. We'll be sure to safekeep your planes inside our hangar."

She motions Reni and me to her, and we head through the tall doorway for the cooler halls of Hathene Palace. Marching boots echo in the quiet. The music's long since ceased. Palace guards approach when we reach the grand staircase of the main foyer, decorated now with large porcelain vases of Etanian orchids and Savien chamomile. The tender white flower with its sunny yellow middle seems entirely dissonant alongside the men it represents.

Mother addresses the Safire. "As was agreed upon prior to your arrival, I will now ask each of you to lay down your sidearm. This is a peaceful meeting and I wouldn't wish to invite any opportunity for mistrust."

No one mentions the fact that the Prince of Etania has a pistol strapped to his hip. The General simply nods and hands his over first, then waves his men forward. They go, one by one, Mother scrutinizing each with great attention, as if memorizing their details will keep them from entertaining trouble. The last to surrender their weapons are a younger pair, fresh-faced and lean. One with copper skin, and after him, a fair-haired boy.

Up close, they can't be older than Reni, and Mother stares longest, a strange expression on her face.

"You're starting them quite young these days," she says to Dakar.

"We don't spoil our boys in Savient," he replies, glancing at Reni, which seems vaguely rude.

Mother raises one arched brow. "Indeed."

"The proposals are ready to be discussed," Uncle intervenes. "Perhaps we shouldn't let these moments go to waste?"

The General turns, pausing. He reminds me of Mother, unlikely to say or do anything that isn't precisely necessary. "We've only just arrived, Lord Lehzar, and my men are tired. After a day of travel, surely you wouldn't begrudge us some rest?"

Uncle steps back. "As you wish then, General."

"Please, make yourselves welcome," Mother says to the gathered group of Safire. "A private dinner will be prepared for you, and tonight, it would please me to have you attend a music concert, in honour of this great visit."

"Thank you, Your Majesty," the General says.

He addresses his party in Savien, and it's not quite beautiful, slightly jarring at times. There's a brief discussion, the Admiral expressing some concern and the red-haired Cock asking a question, but the General responds with a few firm words and then they're gone down the hallway, escorted by footmen to their quarters.

By afternoon, the Safire soldiers are wandering the palace at a leisurely, unarmed pace. Though their stiff grey uniforms and tall leather boots feel entirely military, all structured patterns and battle-hardened medals, they smile casually, laughing together, lighting their foul-scented cigarettes inside, young and easy and striking. Our Etanian soldiers keep their short hair properly gelled from forehead to nape. I expected the same from the Safire, perhaps even more so. But instead, these foreign boys keep theirs longer along the top, barely slicked back. A romantic sort of look that suits the old oil paintings they stand before, smoke curling about them with serpentine trails.

The lords don't bother to hide their judgment. They pronounce their opinions in Landori, not Etanian, so as to be sure they're very much understood, subtly critiquing the General's victory in Karkev, the new agreements in Landore, anything to prove they won't be won over by such young warriors.

The Safire soldiers ignore the barbed comments, uninterested in anyone but themselves. If anything, they appear mostly bored.

Violet and I watch from a safe distance. A smile plays on her lips. "They're very handsome in those uniforms."

I don't confirm or deny this. "They seem arrogant," I say, not wanting to admit it out loud yet, but I think to Violet it's all right. She needs the tempering.

"There's nothing wrong with a bit of boldness. It will certainly help in the South."

"They have no manners, Violet. Smoking indoors, even! Who raised these boys?"

"Then we'll have to teach them better," she says, giggling suddenly.

The Cock has materialized on the second floor, gazing down at us from over the marble railing. He gives a cavalier salute, and Violet, rather impetuously, waves back. He's much older than us. Far from a boy, broad-shouldered and tall, and his ranking shows.

"Do you think the men in Savient know how to dance proper, or shall we have to teach them that too?" Violet whispers in my ear.

A nearby lord frowns, observing us, and I'm afraid I'll be implicated in this indecency. What frightens me more, though, is her genuine intrigue. It feels different from Slick, who was simply her chess piece for a single dinner. I won't let her do this to Reni.

I grasp her arm and pull her from Cock's attention. She follows, feet dragging, glancing behind like she's abandoning happiness altogether. I'm not sure where I'm taking her. There's little escape, since the Safire seem to be everywhere, but she's quick to protest once we're on our own.

"It's not wrong to indulge them," she says.

"They're getting enough attention as it is."

"From lords mocking them behind their hands? By God, Ali, we need to do our part and make them feel welcome!"

She's grinning, and I'd like to shake her for it. I'm annoyed by her delight, annoyed further by the Safire and how utterly uncaring they seem about the gracious welcome we've given. Perhaps they're exactly what Reni predicted—rough-handed men who care nothing for the order of things.

I march Violet down the hall, round the far corner, then halt abruptly, Violet bumping into me. We've nearly run headlong into two Safire uniforms. They blink at us, startled as we are.

It's the younger pair.

Surprise changes to a quick smile on the fair-haired boy's face. "Princess Aurelia," he says, as though he's said my name a hundred times before and has any right to greet me without introduction. "How are you?"

His hair falls in a mess over his forehead, like he never bothered to do better when he woke this morning, or when he got off the aeroplane here, and the casual appearance accentuates the informal greeting.

I really don't know who raised them.

I lift my chin, waiting, and it takes a moment. Understanding dawns and both boys step swiftly to the side, one right and the other left. Violet and I walk straight through the middle. We continue down the hall and I don't look behind.

"Regardless of manners, the handsome pilot was quite taken by me on the steps," Violet insists. "Did you see how he smiled at me?"

"No," I say, because I'm sure he was staring more at her breasts.

The sun's lowering behind the mountains by the time I have a moment alone with Reni. He's been in meeting with Uncle, and refuses to admit any details of it to me, which only sparks my

irritation hotter. I don't trust either of them. And that realization, the feeling of something unspoken between us, like we're
on opposite sides of a divide, leaves us both sullen and silent as
we cross the lawn to the quiet edge of the forest. There's only
the distant sound of engine noise, one of our Etanian aeroplanes
rattling down the runway and rising into the golden sky.

Reni leans against an elm, his arms tucked under each other.
"Well, I'm beginning to see how they got Karkev under their
belt."

"It's true," I agree. "I don't think the Safire care much for pre-
cedents."

Reni snorts.

The Etanian plane spins high above us, a glinting bit of green
in the reddening sky.

"And now Mother's decided I'm not to be a part of the negotiations with the General," Reni continues, his frustration clearly
chafing. "Uncle says she thinks I'll do something rash. But we
need to bring up Karkev. Dakar needs to acknowledge the truth.
He said he'd secure his own borders, no further, and now he's
taken the whole thing! He claims nothing was written down, but
does a man's honour need to be in ink?"

The plane does another sudden spin, impressively quick.

"Yes . . . ," I say, watching.

"Yes?"

"I mean, no."

The plane drops into a steep dive and disappears from sight.
I've never seen a pilot practice tactics near the palace. I don't
think it's allowed, but perhaps they've been inspired by the
Safire show this morning.

"I suppose you'd be applauding these things, Ali, being the
fan of the Safire you've suddenly become this spring. Are you
still in awe?"

His words light the match, and I glare at him. "You want to
know why Mother won't invite you to these negotiations? It's

because you aren't even strong enough to handle the fate of your own horse!"

He flinches visibly and the drone grows louder again, gathering strength.

"That's a rotten thing to say," he whispers.

It is, and I mean it. "Don't you dare leave Liberty like this. If you don't have the nerve to put him out of his misery, then I will. *I'll* give the order to pull the—"

Propellers erupt above us, drowning me out as the Etanian plane charges over our heads, rolling wildly across the tree line like it's coming down in flames.

"What's that mad pilot doing?" I gasp.

Reni scowls. "About to get himself in a lot of trouble, that's what."

He turns on his heel, sprinting for the airbase, certainly glad to have a sudden and tangible mission. I chase after him, eyes to the sky. The plane attempts an even higher loop, fighting the strong mountain wind, wings trembling. It's nearly terrifying. I half expect the little plane to come to pieces.

A man in Etanian uniform rushes over when we reach the tarmac. "Forgive me, Your Highness. I wasn't aware of this." He waves down the runway to where three young men stand in the shade, including Slick. "I'll deal with it right away."

Recognition darkens Reni's face. "No, Captain. I'll deal with this myself."

Now the mission has taken a very personal turn, and I have to hurry to keep up with Reni's ever-lengthening stride. But my eyes are still stuck to the display above. The three boys also peer at the sky, unaware of our approach. One's in Safire uniform.

"What is happening here?" Reni demands imperiously when we arrive.

All three whirl to face him.

Slick swallows, going pale as a daisy petal. "The Safire wished to test one of our aeroplanes, Your Highness."

Reni looks incredulous. "That's a Safire pilot up there?"

No one answers, so the Safire boy nods. It's the young one with black hair. He seems embarrassed.

"They made us do it," Slick insists, "and we were afraid to say no."

"Made you?" Reni repeats.

"You know how they are, Your Highness."

This earns him a resentful glance from the Safire boy.

"Regardless," Reni says, "I'd expect better resolve and loyalty from one of Her Majesty's pilots."

Slick flushes, and the plane hurtles past, performing an upside-down roll.

We all stare.

"This doesn't look safe," Reni announces.

The Safire boy shades his eyes from the sun. "Don't worry. He's very good. But today there's a lot of—how do you call it in Landori? Wind from the side?"

"Crosswind," the other Etanian pilot supplies.

"Yes, crosswind." A smile splits the boy's face.

Reni brushes him aside. "Bring that plane down now," he orders.

For a moment, the foreign boy appears confused, since we're nowhere near the airbase and have no way to communicate with the reckless pilot above. But Reni just scowls further and the boy does the only thing he can—he jogs onto the runway, flapping his arms at the sky. It takes a few moments, no indication that he's successful, before the plane circles lower and waggles its wings in response. It's caught on strong gusts, bucking from side to side. A mad show from any angle. But despite the fight, it lands on the runway without a jolt, gentle and smooth, and the Etanian pilots glance at each other, evidently impressed. Brakes hiss as it screeches down the tarmac. The nose swings round when it comes to an abrupt halt not far off, oil dripping down the wheels and propeller whirring. The three pilots go to meet the daredevil.

I snatch my brother's arm. "Don't be too harsh, Reni. The plane is still in one piece."

He glowers in disgust.

This is it, then. The first battle of the visit and I can't even call for support. Who's going to come? The ground crew?

I simply watch, helpless, as the propeller silences, and the glass cockpit slides open. The fair-haired boy from the hall stretches out, wearing a triumphant smile and a pair of flying goggles, his hair even more a mess now. He doesn't notice us standing in the shadow of the elms. "How was that for a show?" he calls to the pilots, words tinged with the Savien accent.

They say nothing, as if they weren't at all impressed only moments before, and the other Safire boy motions in our direction.

The one in the plane turns. His sunlit smile fades. He hops down from the wing, pulling off the goggles, then lopes over to us, hair all askew.

"Your Highness," he says, giving a short bow to Reni. There's a streak of black oil on his cheek. "How are—"

"What the hell do you think you're doing?" my brother asks.

The pilot glances over his shoulder. "Flying, I think."

"Yes, I can see that. Do I look stupid to you?"

The blond boy stares. "No," he says, though he really shouldn't have hesitated.

"Then give me an honest answer."

"I was comparing your airplanes to ours."

Reni crosses his arms. "Comparing? To test maneuverability, I assume? Airspeed and thrust?"

The Safire boy smiles. "I didn't know you were a pilot."

"I'm not."

"It sounds like you are."

"No, it sounds like you're *spying*."

The boy begins to laugh, but it dies on his lips when Reni takes a step closer. The boy puts his hands in the air.

"Our aeroplanes aren't to be used for your amusement," Reni says. "You Safire think you can run around the world and do what you like, but not here."

"Please forgive me, Your Highness. I wasn't trying to cause trouble." He sounds honest enough.

Reni waves him off. "Save your excuses for the Royal League when you and your General are tried for war crimes."

The boy frowns at that, Reni stepping round him for the other pilots, and then he gives me a shrug, hands still raised. I'm not sure what it means. If he's embarrassed or apologetic or uncaring. "I haven't been in the sky for weeks," he says after a moment, as if the whole thing can be redeemed with this reasoning. "And your pilots said it would be fine."

"It's not fine," I say.

"I see that now, Princess. But I only wanted to fly."

Again, he uses that informal address on me, as if only Reni deserves a proper title. It's exactly what Havis does.

I face the other way, partly annoyed, partly not wanting to be swayed by the honesty in his gaze.

"I'll be reporting your leniency to the Queen this evening," Reni informs the Etanians, relishing the traumatized look on Slick's face. "I doubt she'll be very pleased to hear of this." Then he walks back and tugs at my arm. "Let's go," he says, giving Slick, then the Safire, a last stern glare.

The blond boy sighs, rubbing the oil splotch from his cheek. He looks rather defeated standing there—long Safire hair tousled with sweat, hand gripping his flying goggles, all of him made more romantic by the pretty aeroplane and sunset mountains beyond.

But since he's now set the precedent for foreign spies in our

aeroplanes, I suppose he'll have to deal with the inevitable consequences.

I shrug at his last hopeful glance, more a plea, then follow my
brother back for the palace.

In the evening, Mother holds a music recital to welcome our
guests. The old palace theatre, with its mahogany walls and
carved stage, brims with the upper class of Hathene, everyone
eager to observe the Safire from a comfortable and close prox-
imity. They sit in their velvet seats, talking behind hands and
stealing glances at the General and the Queen, then hush when
the draping curtains are drawn back.

Instrumentalists perform first, a duet between violin and vi-
ola, followed by a troupe of dancers in traditional dress. After
that is Violet, ready to share her beautiful voice. She glides to
the front of the stage in yet another alluring gown. This one covers up more, thankfully, but the lace along the arms is still thin
and delicate. A mauve ribbon sparkles in her auburn curls, and
in her hands she holds an entire fan of peacock feathers.

I hope to the stars Havis isn't in any way responsible.

As everyone sighs along at just the right notes, her voice pure
crystal, the kind that belongs crooning on the wireless, Reni sits
next to me, mesmerized. Perhaps he didn't notice what happened on the steps with Cock, a fact which makes me feel guilty,
like I should warn him or protect him from the truth. But then
I remember Liberty and I feel less charitable.

Wondering how her new admirer is enjoying the show, I peek
over my left shoulder to where the Safire soldiers are seated
across the aisle. Cock leans forward in his chair, his captivated
gaze on Violet. Beside Cock is the pilot who flew the second
fighter plane, the one with jet-black hair and high, handsome
cheekbones. There's a weary weight to his head. I follow the line

of Safire and realize they each appear quite bored—or perhaps quite tired—with the exception of Cock.

Movement at the end of the row catches my attention. I peer harder in the low lights, realizing it's the blond boy, the daredevil, discreetly waving at me. He makes a spinning motion with his hand, kept low behind the seat, then places it to his chest, face something like regretful.

I give him a confused shake of my head. At least his hair's finally combed.

He tries again, a bit more dramatic, though still low enough not to be seen by those around him. It's the worst kind of charades, and I stare at him, baffled.

Reni nudges me sharply. "Violet's singing," he whispers.

I face forward again as she reaches her highest note. The violins swell, and she lifts a hand, like she's the star of the North. Rousing applause greets her. Then the lights lower, instruments shifting hands, a horn sounding in the darkness, and she begins a song in Savien.

Both Reni and I turn to each other, stunned.

When did she learn this?

The strange words sound sharp along the edges, but the melody is haunting. A beautiful song that brings the room to perfect stillness.

I glance over my shoulder at the daredevil again. I can't resist. He's still watching me, but there's an annoyed look on his face now, like I've offended him somehow. I've no clue what he's getting at. I try to convey that in the faint light, try to shrug at him without being noticed, and then, as if frustrated by me and the theatre and even this beautiful song in his own language, he gets up and marches down the aisle and abandons the show.

Just like that.

15

The music show is the end of my endurance and I can't listen to another word of that miserable song.

Sinora picked it on purpose.

I know it.

The familiar words fade behind me as I escape the theatre, desperate to shut them out. Words about soaring hawks and sea-weed fish and waves crashing on white cliffs. It's a folk song from Mother's home. The north of Savient, where mountain and water meet. She used to sing this same song to me during the revolution, drowning out the night gunfire, promising me over and over that the flashing lights on the horizon were too far away to hurt us.

Grief twists my anger, aching.

I'll never hear her voice again. Not now or any day until I die.

And it's because of Sinora Lehzar. Sinora, who knew who I was the moment she looked at me, a razor question in her gaze. She's the face from the photograph on Father's desk, beautiful and hard, wielding something far more formidable than a gun—a gold crown.

"Slow down," Cyar calls at my back.

"I'm not listening to that poison."

"It's just a song, Athan."

From anyone else, the comment would snap the thin restraint inside me. But it's him. And he says it in his usual honest way, calling a spade a spade, and maybe it is too ridiculous to think Sinora could have known this song, this one song, was mine.

I slow my stride.

At least he's talking to me again. Up until now, he hasn't said more than one full sentence. For Cyar Hajari, that's approaching merciless. He blames me for giving in to the Etanian pilots and their obnoxious goading, and now we're both marked spies. That's a bit true, since I could have turned back when they suggested Safire pilots are only able to fly with fancy machines. But how could I let that go? And how was I supposed to know aerobatics are forbidden this close to the palace? They should have mentioned it. Cyar says I should have asked.

Yes, because my family always asks before acting.

"I just want to sleep," I admit to him, rubbing at my raw headache. The long day of travel, the time adjustment—it's ruined us all. Well, all of us except Garrick, since that girl on stage might as well have been singing for him alone. "When are we up for watch?"

"Three in the morning," Cyar says with his own look of woe. He's as excited as I am about the prospect of babysitting airplanes in a cold hangar.

Together, we walk the silent halls for our guest rooms. Everyone important is still perched in their theatre chairs, and I think of the Princess watching me with her perplexed little look, pretty eyes and full lips ruined by the same disease of Norvenne. That displeased, royal frown. Reminding us we're strange foreign creatures, baffling and base, to be endured only until no longer needed.

We turn the corner for the Safire apartments and find two figures standing together in the low evening lights. It's Malek and a rich-looking Etanian man.

"The shipment went to your eastern airbase," Malek says quietly, "so it should be easy to unload. I trust you have the proper way to disperse it?"

"Indeed," the man replies, sounding pleased. "I'm well-connected, I assure you. On paper we have it bound for the Queen's Mounted Regiment."

It takes my distracted brain this long to realize I understand them not because they're speaking Landori but because they're speaking Savien, and I stare at the mustached man.

An Etanian lord knows Savien?

Malek spots us walking towards them, and steps away.

"The show over, Lieutenant?" he asks me.

"We left early."

Malek gives me an examining look, like I'm the one discussing logistics with one of Sinora's men. But I remember the lord now. He was at her side when we arrived. He didn't look so friendly then. A bit hateful, actually.

Now the man offers me a meaningful smile on his way by, the sort that implies we're in on the same secret. I'm the wrong person for that. But I give him the same smile in return, because I've learned it's always best that people at least *think* you know the secrets.

"Good evening, Lord Jerig," Malek says.

"Pleasant evening, Admiral."

The man disappears down the hall.

Then Malek nods at me. "Lieutenant," he says simply, and since I find the man intimidating even on a normal day, I say, "Admiral," and keep walking for our room.

Cyar shuts the door once we're inside and turns on me.

"Tell me what you know, Athan."

"Nothing," I say quickly, but his glare is still suspicious.

I wave my hands in surrender. "All right. There was a shipment of vintage weapons. It's a royal tradition to share these things. They use them in parade." The excuse sounds even worse now that I'm saying it out loud. I must have been really tired when Kalt used it on me.

Cyar looks at me hard, clearly deciding whether to let it go or force the discussion further. Then he shakes his head and begins unbuttoning his uniform, shedding it quickly and dropping into bed.

I make it as far as my shirt. "I swear I don't know anything else, Cyar. I'd tell you."

He says nothing, dark hair buried in the pillow.

Guilt leaves me standing there, half-dressed, because I do know more. I know that if I don't get the royal siblings to talk to me, if I don't show up with something useful at the end of this week, it will be Cyar facing enemy planes without any kind of tactical advantage. Possibly in an entirely different squadron from mine.

Sinora's supposed to burn—I want that.

But Cyar is a different matter, and holding this secret feels like uncomfortable power.

I strip off the rest of my uniform, hating the feel of satin sheets on my bare skin, hating how it smells like Sinora's lair all around me. And then I force myself to close my eyes.

There's a knock at the door within moments. Or at least that's how it feels.

"Get up bootlickers," Garrick orders. "Your turn to watch the birds."

I push from bed, groggy, and everything feels stiff. I'd like to ignore him and say to hell with the fighters. Who'd touch them, anyway? But Cyar's already standing, pulling on his shirt. Can't let him go alone.

By the time we're creeping down the midnight halls and across the wet grass, weariness gives way to unease. Sinora could be crouched anywhere.

We relieve those on duty and hunker down against the wheels of a fighter, cement floor cold beneath us. Have to find a distraction. Anything to keep me from looking at my watch, or into the darkness beyond. Shadows shiver along the walls, sinister patterns with teeth for ends. They grow in size, twisting, coming closer, and I keep reminding myself I count for nothing in this game.

Never thought that would be a relief.

"Vintage weapons for parade," Cyar muses eventually. "Did one of your brothers tell you that?"

I don't confirm or deny.

"Do you think he'll actually try something now?"

The *he* in this doesn't need to be explained. Cyar never calls him my father. He's always the General. Or *he*. Or *him*. Vague things that keep it distant.

I shrug, fighting a yawn. "Doubtful. He doesn't rush things."

Cyar is silent a moment. "I don't think it's the whole kingdom's fault what Sinora did."

His observation sits uncomfortably between us in the chilly air. Cyar and his honesty.

"Then Sinora better cooperate," I say, covering my own uncertainty. "Hopefully she cares about Etania as much as you."

Cyar sighs. He doesn't like that answer, but he says, "Either way, no more airplane stunts. Don't crash yourself before you're off the runway."

"I won't."

And I won't, for his sake.

The cement numbs my legs and we shift closer for warmth—it stopped being awkward long ago, after nights of field training. The hours drift by, indistinct. A grey haze appears above the mountains. They're not jagged and snowcapped like the ones in northern Savient. These are round and welcoming, green and full of life. What I've always hungered for. I walk to the wide hangar doors, and the air smells like wet cedar in the dawn mist.

I want to disappear into those woods and never come back.

On the far hill, the gardens hold pinpricks of colour. Bright on dark, like the ruby pins in the Princess's hair. Thoughtless flecks of wealth. How can I smile at her? I don't want to, and maybe that's my problem. She gets this beauty, every day spent in ease, no struggle from beginning to end, and all while her mother's a devil gambling with lives. A traitor who tried to hurt my father by taking my innocent mother.

I lean on the cool door.

A devil who gambles with lives.

All right, perhaps we have that one sliver of a thing in common.

16

The stables are my escape in the morning. It smells like grain and leather and mud, the most beautiful scents in all the world. But today I'm here to face my guilt—Liberty. I force myself to peer into his stall, to see him standing there and hobbled on three legs. Those lovely, strong legs. They're meant for galloping, for leaping obstacles, and the sight of him confined to this cramped space, riddled with pain, breaks my heart. I offer him an apple, and he nudges it with a soft nose, then turns away.

His heart is broken, too.

An hour passes quietly with Ivory, currying and brushing her, then feeding her the apple that Liberty refused. I step out of the stall, latching the metal tight, and spot a yellow-eyed barn cat skulking through the grass outside. It's crouched with tail twitching, hunting some poor little animal. Vicious thing. I run over, hissing, and it bounds away. The baby sparrow on the ground makes no effort to move, so I kneel down and nudge it lightly once. Then twice. On the third push, it flutters up and away for the forest beyond.

The cat barrels after it.

Stars, maybe it's *me* that's cursed.

"Princess," a familiar voice calls.

I turn on my knees in surprise.

The fair-haired daredevil is suddenly standing there, looking down at me curiously.

I hurry to my feet, embarrassed, and we're very alone, no sign of the stable boy with his pails of grain. The pilot wears the same peculiar expression as the night before, watching, waiting, but what's he waiting for? He approaches me.

"Yes?" I ask, attempting an air of authority.

He nods to the trees beyond. "I'd like to explore the woods. Which way do you recommend?"

This must be a lie. Some kind of game, though it makes no sense. He can't think it's fine to just walk up and ask me this, like I'm a footman with directions. But he's still standing there, expectant, so I think he does. "There are many trails," I say. "Five hundred acres of them. You'll certainly get lost if you go on your own."

"Oh."

"And you wouldn't want to get left behind after dark. We have wolves."

"Wolves?" He sounds intrigued. "Here?"

It's my own invented lie, hoping to strike some sort of fear into a Safire heart, but it seems that has failed, too. I stride past him, in the direction of the palace. Best to leave while I can.

I hear footsteps on the grass behind me.

Is he actually following me?

"Princess, I was dishonest. I didn't wish to only ask directions. I wanted to apologize."

His Landori is polished and gently accented, not what I expected from a lowly pilot. It's like the tide along the seashore, rising and falling on different words.

"Apologize?" I ask over my shoulder.

"Yes, for yesterday. I shouldn't have flown without permission. I was hoping you might be willing to overlook it. Or better yet, perhaps you might ask your mother to overlook it?"

I stop and turn. We've reached the eastern gardens. "You should have thought of that before you climbed into the plane."

His eyes are an earnest grey, surrounded by dark lashes. "I

know. But I'd rather not die for a crime I didn't commit. I'm only seventeen."

"Die?"

"Yes, doesn't the Queen hang foreign spies? Or is it the firing squad? If it's something worse than that, please don't tell me."

Amusement lurks behind his words, but I won't give in. "If you weren't spying, then what were you doing?"

"Flying. That's it. Those pilots of yours, they insulted our reputation, said we wouldn't be able to do a single maneuver in this mountain wind." He steps closer. He smells like something warm from the runway. Petrol, maybe. "And that isn't true. I had to prove it."

"That's a terrible excuse for recklessness."

He smiles, near enough now I could touch his arm. "You're right. Can I try again?"

"No," I say, but it's a bit less forceful.

He reaches down and plucks an orchid from the garden. He holds it out to me, the russet-coloured watch on his wrist flashing in the sun. "I'm truly sorry for what I've done. It was thoughtless."

I stare at the flower, at the soft pink petals, then at his chest, the simple stitching on a less formal uniform, the unbuttoned collar, and then again into his face. Blond hair brushes his forehead, more windblown than messy, his fair skin sprinkled with a few faint freckles across the nose. Again the grey eyes and dark lashes. He's all the colours of the seashore. Elegant, but in a shadowed sort of way, like he's seen most of life and knows already how it goes.

It doesn't match his sweet smile.

"What's your name?" I ask.

"Lieutenant Erelis."

I take the orchid from him. "I'll admit that was some fancy flying yesterday, Lieutenant Erelis."

"I graduated at the top of my class, Princess."

"Ah, I've heard that before. But the real test comes in battle, I think."

"You're very right," he agrees. "But since I've already shot down three enemy planes . . ."

Three! I take him in from head to toe again. Perhaps that explains the shadows.

"Possibly four," he amends. "The last one wasn't proven, but I like to count it. The fuselage was smoking. I'm certain the pilot had to bail."

"Does your friend fly, too?"

"Yes. Which is another reason why you can't let them execute me. I've made a solemn promise to Cyar—Officer Hajari, I mean—that I'll only die in flames and at his side. It would be a waste to hang here, for an offense I didn't intend."

Amusement continues to slip between his words, that subtle certainty like he's watching me from another world, set apart and pleased with his story. I'd like to dislike him for it. But he's not so distant as the others in Safire uniform, closer and not much older than me. Seventeen, he said. And at least I haven't seen him holding a filthy cigarette.

"I'll see what I can do, Lieutenant."

I resume my march down the garden path, because this is where our conversation should end, but there's a clip of boots on the stone behind me.

Heathwyn's voice chirps in my head. *"Divert with a smile."*

I turn again, doing just that. "Yes, Lieutenant?"

He appears perplexed. "Was I dismissed?"

"Yes."

"You didn't say anything."

"Did I need to?"

He steps back, returning my smile of diversion. "Sorry. I'm accustomed to more direct orders."

"You're dismissed, Lieutenant."

He nods and gives a salute, then turns and walks back in the opposite direction, straight for the woods.

"Please don't get lost," I call without thinking. "I've done it myself, and it isn't fun wandering in circles for hours."

He spins and walks backwards. "I have a compass."

"Even so, you shouldn't go far." I raise the flower in my hand. "And this is bad luck."

"Bad luck?"

"Yes, to pick our orchids."

"For you or for me?"

"Oh . . ." No one's ever explained the logistics of it to me. It's superstition. "I'm not sure."

He's ahead of me, though, already grinning. "Then let's pray we each get half of the bad luck. An even share of it."

I toss the flower into the nearest fountain. "No, I think I'd rather pray that you get all of it, Lieutenant, as I'm the innocent one in this. Which is too bad. You'll be needing good luck for your next dogfight."

The Safire boy laughs, a bright sound.

I hear myself laugh, too, then quickly stop before anyone sees.

A flustered and urgent Heathwyn greets me at my room. She says I've been summoned for lunch with Mother and Havis, and where have I been? And why am I covered in dust? And now I just need to go and make up some excuse. I hurry regretfully for Mother's parlour. Lunch with the newly returned Havis certainly isn't my first choice of things, but in the interest of pleasing Mother during this critical week, I'll do it.

When I arrive, however, I'm surprised to find Uncle with her as well. The three of them are sitting round a table set with china and lace, ladling from a bowl that smells like tomatoes and cinnamon.

"Aurelia," Mother says. "Where have you been?"

"Grooming Ivory," I reply, going to her side. "Reni won't be joining us?"

She pours steaming water into her cup. "He's reviewing agendas with Lord Marcin."

How on earth did Reni talk himself into that one? "You'd better not let him bring up Karkev. His opinions on that won't be appreciated by anyone Safire."

"He knows his boundaries," Mother says.

"Does he?" I venture, and I think it's a legitimate question after the Chase.

"He knows his boundaries," Mother repeats, sharper, "and you know yours."

Havis sips his soup silently, playing uninterested in the conversation, and I'm about to ask if Violet's feathers came from him when Uncle says, "You should avoid affairs you've no experience with, Aurelia."

I turn to him, annoyed. "I never said I agreed with Reni. In fact, I even met one of the Safire today, and I'm thinking to invite him to sit at our table this evening. It would look good for the court to see us welcoming them as friends."

"You're inviting the General to our table, then?" Uncle asks dubiously. His eyes look extra birdlike through his spectacles.

"No, but I would if you thought he might accept."

"Please do."

"I would!"

Mother raises a hand between us. "Tell me, Aurelia, who exactly are you inviting?"

It seems I'm now stuck. I said it mostly to silence Uncle, but they're all watching me, awaiting an explanation. Havis butters a slice of bread. "It's like you said at the Chase, Mother. Sometimes inviting the enemy to your table can smooth things over."

"The Safire aren't our enemy," she points out.

"No, but Reni believes he caught one of them spying on our

aeroplanes yesterday. He made a horrible deal out of it, and may have offended them. We should make amends before word of it gets to the General."

Havis looks up.

Mother frowns. "Spying on our aeroplanes?"

"Not really, Mother. He only wanted to fly. He's a pilot, and a very good one."

"I'm sure it was spying," Uncle mutters.

"It wasn't," I insist.

"It wasn't," Mother agrees, giving Uncle a pointed glance. "And Reni was aggressive with him?"

"You know Reni. You'd think the Safire pilot tried to start a war."

Mother clucks her tongue.

"Did he speak with you alone?" Uncle presses. "Did you get a name?"

I divert the first question with an impressive smile. "Lieutenant Erelis."

"God in heaven," Havis coughs into his soup.

"Lieutenant *Erelis*." Mother draws out his last name, thoughtful, then looks again to Uncle. "I've no issue bringing an officer to my table. Aurelia's right. It would give the right impression to the court, and General Dakar."

Uncle throws his napkin to the table. "It's a pointless gesture. A low-ranking officer means nothing to anyone. And not only that, he's a spy. There's only one reason one of them would try to talk their way into our aeroplanes."

"You weren't there," I say, "and it's best to avoid affairs you've no experience with."

Perfect silence envelops the table. Uncle's cheeks turn a fierce shade of pink, and no one moves. Then a sound escapes Mother. Her lips twitch, widening. Soon she's laughing enough tears sparkle in her eyes.

Uncle and Havis sit staring at her.

"Thank you," Mother says to me, chuckling over the words. "I needed that."

"Then I should invite the Lieutenant?" The full implication of this is suddenly dawning on me.

"Please," she says.

Neither Uncle nor Havis looks so happy about it, and I wonder what I've done. Certainly the Lieutenant won't accept such an offer. He'll say no. He must. Reni will hate the idea, and Havis will slink his way to my side. Instead of doing good, it will do the opposite, and the entire thing will be terrible, from beginning to end, with me trapped right in the middle of it.

"I suppose I'll invite him, then, Mother."

"Splendid," she replies. "I look forward to seeing him up close."

I hope to all the stars he says no.

17

"Do you think she'd poison my wine?"

I ask Cyar the question in Savien as we stand at the edge of the bustling, golden reception. The ballroom around us vibrates with voices and violins, the air stinking of perfume and fresh-cut flowers wound around large pillars. Above us are bright facades of mountain scenes and elk, chandeliers twinkling like obnoxious stars. Food and wine glistening. Sinora's elaborate production of fake generosity.

"In front of everyone?" Cyar asks, eyeing the lengthy table of appetizers. "All these foreign visitors?"

I shrug. "She killed my mother in broad daylight."

"I don't think she'd waste the poison on you."

I'm about to question that, but he's already investigating what's on offer, a plate in hand and a pleased look on his face. If there's one thing we learned from Norvenne, it's that royals serve good food. I pretend to study it as well, but my survey leads my eyes away from the table and onto the Princess, speaking with her brother. She's small in the swirl of courtiers and dignitaries. A glimmer in the unfamiliar crowd.

Should I approach her again? It's difficult to tell how today went. She laughed at the end, but maybe it's all a ploy, pretending she doesn't know who I am. Maybe Sinora gave her the same mission Father gave me. A chance to rout out secrets and discover exactly who's making what move, and where, and when. It's possible.

The Princess tilts her head now, whispering to her brother. They're a matching pair—dark-haired with the hint of Southern features, glittering in their fancy clothes.

"I'm surprised to see you here, Lieutenant." The voice has a suspiciously familiar serpent quality, and I turn to find Ambassador Havis. "You don't seem very useful in a place like this," he adds, as if it's up for debate.

"You're right," I say. I take the plate of glazed-something from Cyar's hands—Cyar making a little noise of annoyance—and hand it to Havis. "I'm the youngest. I believe I'm here to smile and serve the food."

Havis doesn't smile at my joke, nor does he accept my offer. There's nothing pleasant between us, and that hasn't changed since Norvenne. He stares hard, and I just wait, because I think he thrives on watching people squirm, and unfortunately for him, I've got a lifetime of experience with that type. Eventually, his eyes drift to the royal table, to the Princess, and I follow.

She's glaring a black storm of fury at me.

I almost take a step back from it, my stomach doing a giant leap into oblivion. She knows who I am. Of course she knows, because she's Sinora's daughter, and now I'll never get her to speak with me, or even look at me, and it's goodbye to Cyar's twenty-millimeter cannons. Goodbye to serving together. He'll be pushed into the hell of battle and I won't even be there to cover his wing.

I feel sick.

Unaware of my impending horror, Havis mutters, "Watch yourself," and brushes past.

I wait a moment, steeling myself, then hazard a glance back to the Princess.

Thank God and everything holy! Her furious gaze has followed

Havis—not for me, after all. Her eyes return, softer, more hesi-tant, studying me from head to toe. We've been instructed to show up in full dress uniform. Polished with leather gloves on. I never feel entirely like me in it, which I guess is fitting for to-night. Did I tell her it was three planes or four? Five? Need to keep my story straight.

She motions me to come.

Me? I check to see who else is around, but we've put ourselves in a corner, our normal strategy for these kinds of parties, and there's no one except Cyar. This must be what it's like in the gunsight of an enemy plane. Time to act, whether you're ready or not.

She waves again, an encouraging impatience to the gesture.

"That's for me, isn't it?" I ask Cyar.

"Certainly isn't for me." He snatches his plate of food back. "Get yourself off the runway, Lieutenant."

He's right. Unfortunately, I have no idea what the sky looks like beyond the runway, if there's a storm of vintage weapons brewing. But since Father's only ten feet away, encircled by a cap-tive audience and certainly keeping an eye on me, I'd better act.

I straighten my shoulders and walk for Sinora's table.

"Good evening, Lieutenant," the Princess says when I arrive, chin raised.

"Good evening," I say, suddenly wondering if I need to bow or not.

"I hope you'll sit with us for the evening."

Yes, this feels like a trap somehow. There's a flicker of polite anxiety on her face, the way Kalt looks when Arrin and Father are going at it in public, and why else would she invite me here? I try to think of a way around the offer, but she beats me to it.

"I told my mother about your apology and she was happy to have you join us tonight. The entire misunderstanding is for-gotten, all that business with the aeroplane. It's fine now." She smiles again.

If only it were that simple.

The Prince, standing nearby, appears less forgiving.

"You want me to sit with you?" I clarify, looking at him.

She clasps her hands. "Only if you'd like to, of course."

"I'm sure the Lieutenant would be happy to honour us with his presence," Havis contributes, swooping to her side with a relishing grin. He sounds far too enthusiastic about it.

She darkens again, that little storm breaking through the politeness, and steps away from him. "You don't have to, Lieutenant. We'd understand if you have other obligations."

I really can't tell if she wants me to stay or go.

"I suppose . . ." I glance over my shoulder at Father's table, but he's working his crowd. Uninterested in my predicament. "I suppose, yes. Why not?"

"Wonderful. Take that seat there," Havis says. "I'll request another glass of wine and—"

"First, my mother wishes to meet you, Lieutenant," the Princess interjects, and my pulse picks up hard. I'm in the gunsight now. There's a shadow on my wings, no going back.

We walk for the head of the long, narrow table, my thoughts bolting in a hundred directions, and the Princess stays at my side, heady jasmine filling my nose. Sinora greets us with an inclined head. She's dressed in gold, seated like a lounging cat beside one of her lords.

I bow to her. It hurts my bones.

"Ah, Lieutenant," she says. "I heard a rumour today about you and one of my aeroplanes." Her red lips purse with what might be amusement.

I force a smile. "Only a bit of fun, Your Majesty."

"Fun? I didn't know the young men of Savient were allowed that indulgence."

"Only when we're certain not to be caught." I nod towards Father, then lower my voice. "So please don't tell on me."

She chuckles, sharp lines appearing around her eyes and

mouth. "Your secret is safe with me." Then she regards me, taking her time. I'm sure she sees all of Mother in my face, lit like
a spotlight in the dark, maybe even a trace of Father. "You seem
familiar, Lieutenant. I can't put my finger on it, but you remind
me of someone I once knew."

My blood prickles hot. "I hear that a lot, Your Majesty."

"Oh?" Her lids are lined in black, feline. There's a question
in her eyes, like perhaps I'll admit the truth to her.

I manage a laugh. "No, not really."

She stares, her face changing from surprise, and then she
laughs as well, loudly, though no one else at this table besides
Havis would ever get the joke. "Be welcome here," she says with
a sweep of her hand, jewels on every finger.

"Thank you, Your Majesty."

I turn and nearly run into the Princess. Forgot she was standing behind me. Her face is upturned to mine, eyes wide and
velvet, relief there, like I've passed a test.

"Lieutenant," Sinora calls, "perhaps you're unaware, but it's
customary to bow when departing my presence as well."

She's making me do it again. She's reminding me of my place,
and all of me burns with hatred as I oblige.

The Princess escorts me back to our seats, putting me at an
empty spot between two lords, and a fresh glass of red wine
awaits. She sits beside her brother, across from me, and Havis
lounges on her other side, flicking a steak knife against his
plate.

"We're delighted you decided to join us," she says once I'm
seated.

"Yes, thrilled," the Prince echoes, sounding rather the opposite. "We're eager to learn more of your exploits, Lieutenant . . . ?"

"Athan Erelis."

"Mm." The Prince sips at his wine, analyzing me.

"Athan," the Princess repeats under her breath.

Servants set steaming plates before us. "Lamb in mint sauce," they announce, but the Princess gets her own little creation. All greens and potatoes.

"You don't eat meat?" I ask.

She gives a delicate shrug. "No creature should die for me to live."

Apparently she doesn't see the irony of that, surrounded as we are by all this indulgent grandeur, but I let it be. I try to search for any guilt or nerves or angle to her face, but she only smiles, looking mostly pleased with me. Curious and waiting. At my hand, my wine taunts like a viper. The fear is illogical, since this entire visit is perched on the illusion of alliance, and harming one of us, even a rookie officer, would only unleash a nightmare of diplomacy.

Still . . .

The Princess gestures at my glass. "It's the best wine we have in Etania. My favourite." Her lips part with pretty expectation. "It's very sweet. You'll like it."

Would they send me to my death in such a tempting way?

The Prince drums fingers against his glass. "Perhaps we should toast to something," he suggests, raising it in my direction. "To the new agreements between Savient and Landore."

His words are edged with sarcasm, more of a challenge, but I raise my glass anyway.

The Princess joins in, then takes a sip, and her brother adds, "Or should I call them concessions? I'd like this to be accurate."

She chokes slightly on her wine, and I send my glass flying.

Better to be careful.

There's a collective gasp as red liquid runs between silverware and candelabras. "God, I'm sorry," I exclaim. I grab a cloth napkin and cover the red splotches with it.

The Prince extracts his glass from the mess, unimpressed. Servants reach around me, removing forks and soiled napkins, and everyone at the table looks perturbed. Sinora watches from her seat with a frown, like I'm trying to ruin her evening on purpose.

The lord on my left gives a sniff of disapproval.

"Sorry," I say, turning, and realize it's the Savien-speaking lord from last night.

"Indeed," he replies, icy. "You Safire do bring chaos, don't you?"

We're no longer friends again, and I try to figure out how this benefits either of us. Is he helping Father by stirring sentiment against Sinora? By hating us? It's the sort of convoluted plan Father would concoct, so I guess it's possible. Anything to make sure the trail never leads clearly back to him. But I hate not being sure.

I'm on my own here.

"It was an accident, Lord Jerig," the Princess says on my behalf.

Havis sips his wine with a sly smile. "Was it, Lieutenant?"

I have the sudden strong urge to kick him under the table. I'm now on everyone's nerves, the idiot who spilled his drink, and I can tell the Princess feels sorry for me. If Arrin were here right now, he sure as hell wouldn't have people feeling sorry for him. He'd have a hundred stories from the war, distracting everyone until they forgot he was Safire, until they were desperate to have him on their side.

At least until he pulled a gun and just shot Sinora point-blank.

"Here, try mine," the Princess offers, extending her glass to me. "Though I already took a sip."

She's earnest about it, and I suppose if she's tried it, then it can't be poisoned. The plan would have to be pretty elaborate if it was going to go like this. I test the drink. Rich, with a pleasant aftertaste.

"Yes, very sweet," I say, but I'm looking at her face.

She smiles again, her polite interest transformed to something warmer.

A bit of confidence restored, I turn to the Prince. "Concessions?"

"I don't think I need to explain myself," he says, cutting his meat with precision. "Your military base in Thurn is a curious development."

"They asked for our help, Your Highness, after what happened in Hady." I pause. "You do know what happened at Hady, don't you?"

"Of course I do," he replies sharply. "I'm well-informed, Lieutenant."

"Of course you are. But you seem confused on the nature of our agreements, which is understandable, since you weren't there."

The Prince pins me with a sour look, and I wonder if I've stepped too far. But he has no right to be sniping like this. We're supposed to be allies here, and whether he knows the truth or not, he should be better at playing along. He's Sinora's son, after all. He should be smarter.

"Perhaps, Lieutenant," Havis says, pointing his steak knife at me, "you could further explain your *personal* position on the matter?"

I'd really like to kick him now.

"I don't have one," I say. "I trust the decisions of my superiors."

"Will you go to Thurn, then?" the Prince asks.

"In a few weeks, yes. King Gawain is intent on moving our forces to the region as quickly as possible. Hady is a vital point to have lost, but we'll reclaim it."

"But why is it so important?" the Princess asks. "It's terrible what happened, of course, but it must have some other consequence to rally such fuss over it. The papers tell us only so much." She seems genuinely curious, setting down her cutlery to listen to my answer.

"It's a gateway city," I explain, glad for a chance to wield the conversation. I had to translate all of this in Norvenne. I know infinitely more than the ridiculous prince. "It lies at the mouth of the Izahar River, the longest flowing river in the South. The rebels are calling the area they now control Free Thurn, and they've no interest in negotiating around a table. The Nahir want to establish their own government, you see, claim the region as their own, but hopefully a Safire base will make them think twice before they attempt anything else."

"Free Thurn," the Princess repeats, considering the idea of it. Then she nods at me with a pleased expression. "You're doing a very brave thing, protecting our noble Northern empire." She turns to her brother. "We should be grateful to Savient."

"That wasn't quite what I was trying to suggest," I say, a bit uncomfortable now.

"It's very brave of you to take this daunting task upon yourself," she finishes generously.

"Hear, hear," Havis says with a false, knowing grin.

"But you must be careful," she continues, leaning forward slightly. "It's very dangerous down there, and seventeen is much too young to die."

I feel my lips twitch. "Is it?"

"So I've heard."

She smiles, just for me, and the Prince rolls his eyes slightly. Such royal manners.

We eat our meals in a bit of a truce while Lord Jerig talks at the woman on his left about how anyone with Southern blood really can't be trusted, not even the ones from Resya, and my suspicions are confirmed. He's here to slander Sinora. He seems to be doing it well.

A more familiar voice carries on from near the foot of the table, filtering through the noise of conversation.

Garrick.

When did he get here?

"Strafing runs are the most nerve-racking," he shares between bites. "You have to bring your plane dangerously close to the ground, avoid the flak and try to hit whatever target presents itself. I tell you, life seems precious in moments like that."

The singing girl, beside him, hangs off every word.

"And what was it like to engage the Karkevite pilots?" a bearded lord asks. "I've heard they proved to be more of a challenge than expected."

"You've heard right, my lord. Many of their planes were Landorian models, hijacked from the northern borders. But we did what needed to be done. We gave their supply lines hell and kept them running for the hills."

"I can't imagine!" the girl says, thrilled.

The Prince makes a sound close to a growl, his glare zeroed in on Garrick and the singing girl, and now I might see how this is.

Good luck, Captain.

The Princess tries to whisper something to her brother, but he ignores it and stands abruptly. "This show's become old," he says to no one in particular, and then he's gone.

A servant scurries after him, carrying the plate of half-eaten food.

"Captain Carr brought down two planes entirely on his own," the singing girl reveals with pride, as if she's accomplished it herself. "Pilot to pilot."

"In the pitch-dark," Garrick adds, and everyone chuckles.

The Princess raises her chin. "Only two?" she says to the girl. "Lieutenant Erelis has brought down three, possibly four."

My hand freezes on my fork.

Garrick sets down his glass, leaning forward in his seat to peer down the table at me. "That's right, Lieutenant. I always forget that last plane. How did it happen again? A direct shot to the undercarriage? God, it's a good story, I can just never remember the details."

He has no sense of camaraderie, the ass. "It's really not that exciting, Captain, not compared to—"

"Don't be bashful, Erelis. Everyone would love to hear about it firsthand." He smiles like a bastard. "Including me."

"I don't think it's important what I accomplished," I say. "What matters is we won."

"The Lieutenant is very modest," an older lady says, pleased.

Garrick frowns. "Yes, he's extraordinarily good at flying under the radar."

The bearded lord raises his hand. "I must say, though, I saw one of our pilots practicing yesterday near the palace and what a splendid display it was! Perfect talent. Why, if our boys had your magnificent aeroplanes, they'd be unstoppable."

The Princess meets my eye, secret amusement quivering between us, and I make a slight face.

"Congratulations, Princess," Havis says. "You seem to have found yourself a man in uniform who's humble about it."

She doesn't look at him. "Please go bother someone else for a while, Ambassador."

"As you'd like, but don't let him off the hook too easily."

"Something I should have thought of long ago with you."

He appears amused. "Enjoy the evening, Princess. Lieutenant."

I nod, wondering what, exactly, he's up to. If he's on our side, then he's as much of a bastard about it as Garrick, and I suddenly feel very alone at the table. I don't even have Cyar.

I pick up a cloth napkin and get to work.

"What are you doing?" the Princess says after a moment.

"Folding."

"Folding?"

"It's fun to do." I finish, then hand her the little swan I've made.

She studies it, holding it like it's made of glass, looking between me and the swan like there's some invisible thing to be discovered there.

Then she squashes it.

"You killed it," I say.

She smiles again. Her fingers work quickly, reassembling the cloth, tying this way and that, then she hands it back. A flower. "This one won't be bad luck."

She looks friendly between the flickering candelabras, and I can feel her reaching across the divide, trying to offer something real. Against my better judgment, I reach back. She can't know who I am. Or if she does, she's better at this game than I ever want to be. "I'm still sad you killed my swan."

She laughs. "So, what else do you do, Lieutenant? I mean, when you're not at war and all that."

I shrug. "Paperwork."

"And?"

"More paperwork."

"Oh."

"Are you disappointed?"

"Not at all! I just thought . . ."

"Go on."

"Well, you're Safire. You must do something special."

"Such as?"

"I don't know. Flying blindfolded, maybe."

I snap my fingers. "Yes, I completely forgot to mention that part."

A giggle's hidden behind her palm. "I assume that's how you won Karkev?"

"That and our talent with wine toasting."

She laughs out loud now, bright and honest, and I almost do the same. Hers is contagious. But she coughs it away just as suddenly, casting a glance to Sinora, who's watching us both with a bemused expression.

The Princess contains herself quickly, fiddling with her cutlery and lining them up on her empty plate. She avoids my gaze, our moment of solidarity gone.

"Dance with me," I say.

It's one of those times when I surprise even myself.

"Dance?" she repeats.

I nod to where others have begun to waltz, violins and cellos and the rest of it. "Yes. I'm not very good, I admit, but . . . well . . ."

She waits.

"I've never danced with a royal. And maybe you'd be willing to give me the honour?"

A faint blush of pink appears across her nose. "I . . ." She glances at the head of the table again.

"Come with me, Princess, or I'll have to pick someone else."

I push from the table and leave her behind.

Please don't come. Please don't come.

Then why did I say it? Was it for Sinora or for me? I don't know, and I wait at the edge of the dance floor, wondering what I've done, afraid of this girl I barely know.

The scent of jasmine appears at my side.

"Thank God you came," I lie. "I was worried I'd have to ask your brother."

She laughs, but it's a bit hesitant again, like she senses my fiction.

I hold out my gloved hand—I think that's what I should do—and she takes it. We skirt the group to a less crowded corner, eyes following us the entire way, and I'm not sure how to begin. "I have another confession to make, Princess. I only know how to waltz in theory."

"You've lured me out here and you don't know how to dance?"

"I assumed you'd be the expert."

She makes a little exasperated noise, like the one Cyar made earlier, then puts my arm around her waist. "Violet was right, then. You'll have to be the woman and follow my lead."

She presses closer, apparently comfortable with this, and I suddenly realize that this might be the most of a girl I've ever held at once. "Should I find this insulting?" I ask, trying a joke. My breath's coming a bit shorter. I hope she can't tell.

"No, though everyone in the room will think you dance like a lady."

With that grinning jab, she begins the waltz, taking evident pleasure in pushing me here and there, coaching our steps and counting the beats. I'm terrible. Truly miserable. I run us right into another couple by accident and they mutter something about the damn Safire getting in the way.

That's just unfair.

The Princess gives me another pitying look. "You're really not very good at this."

"It's not as easy as flying blindfolded. My feet keep getting in the way. I don't know what they're doing."

She laughs freely, too close, thin blue fabric against my arms. I can feel the heat from her, the gentle curves. Her skin's the colour of sun-washed sand, a softly scented warmth that I feel through my uniform, through my own skin and muscle and bone. I feel it everywhere. And I wonder what she thinks of me. She can't know the truth. She wouldn't look at me like this if she did. And I like the way she's looking.

"Princess Aurelia," Father calls.

I nearly put us into another couple pushing her from me. She spins around.

He's standing at the edge of the floor, Malek at his side. Malek's lips rise on one end.

"Your mother has outdone herself," Father says. "I hardly feel worthy of such a reception."

The Princess smiles. "You deserve all of it, General."

He nods, watching, certainly noting her hand still half around my arm. "You're a gracious host yourself, " he says after a moment. "But you needn't humour us too far." He smiles, glancing at me. "I didn't know you could dance, Lieutenant."

I'm not sure why, but guilt has me by the throat. There's nothing to be guilty about. I'm doing exactly what he wanted. It's the worst time and place to lose words around him.

"I was teaching Lieutenant Erelis how to waltz," the Princess says, rescuing me. "No one's ever shown him."

"Evidently," Father says, amused.

Malek laughs, a rare thing, and they both turn, moving on in the direction of Sinora's table. I'm not sure if I'll be hearing about this later. Since I'm not his son here, there's not much he can do in the immediate future. Though there is Garrick. . . .

"Will you get in trouble for this?" the Princess asks me.

"No, I don't think so." I spot Cyar at the mostly empty Safire table, playing with a wine glass, bored. My escape. "Though I should head back. It looks like I've left him on his own long enough, doesn't it?"

"Yes, I think you're right," she says, studying Cyar with careful consideration. Then she releases my arm and gives a cheeky smile. "You're dismissed, Lieutenant."

Another bit of laughter escapes me. "Thank you, Princess. And thank you for dancing with me. It was an honour."

"No, the honour was mine."

She seems to mean it, and I want to tell her, "*No, it isn't and you don't know what you're saying.*"

Instead, I say, "I'll try not to forget what you've taught me."

I walk away while I still can, threading between the chatter and music, and Cyar sighs when I drop into the seat beside him. "Your table sounded far more exciting than mine," he says.

"I'm never doing that again."

"Your father seemed pleased."

"He'd better damn be."

I rub at my forehead. It's a relief to speak Savien. Familiar, easy words. An hour of fast and formal Landori has my brain knotted.

"That bad?" Cyar asks.

"Garrick certainly didn't do me any favours."

"But you ended up waltzing with a princess."

I rub some more, then raise my head and look at him. "Do

you know what she was doing this morning, Cyar? Rescuing a bird."

He stares at me. "A bird?"

"Yes."

"And?"

How do I explain this thing that makes no sense?

"And so I'm not going to drag her into this mess. It's better to let her stay out of it, right? I'll keep working on the Prince. He's stupid enough he'll admit things without even realizing it. But I'm not going to talk with her anymore. That's it. No more. Don't let me do it."

"I won't."

"That's an order, Hajari."

"Yes, sir."

There. I feel better saying it out loud.

I take off the restricting gloves finally, the scent of jasmine coming with them, and lean back in my seat. The music continues to play, laughter drifting, the fancy room strange and dreamlike. I've done everything Father wanted. I have one of Sinora's children speaking with me, willing to get closer, and she might actually see me as a person, not a uniform. Someone to trust.

But it doesn't feel like success.

"I would have been completely on my own at that table if not for her," I say, more to myself.

"At least you weren't poisoned with the wine," Cyar replies.

18

The morning after my dance with the Safire pilot, Heathwyn's less than pleased. She says such intimacy doesn't look proper in front of the court and he should be politely discouraged away. I try to explain that I'm only doing my small part in diplomacy, since it's not as if I'll be invited to any formal negotiations, and Heathwyn replies that the negotiations are behind closed doors, for good reason, and the footmen will be far more interested in gossiping about the things they can actually see in broad daylight—like royals flirting with young men of no standing.

"Do you want all of Etania to hear whispers of their princess charming an upstart?"

"He's not an upstart," I reply. "He simply can't dance."

And then I have to bite back a little smile when I think of the Lieutenant fumbling over his own feet with such helpless charm. It's not fair that a no-name officer should be so interesting. He's like a half-finished painting, and I want to see how it ends.

Trying to be productive for the exams, I take my history book and settle myself on a wrought-iron bench hidden beneath the trees, just in view of the hangar. I won't go out of my way to find him. But sitting here, studying, might at least offer a glimpse of him or a chance to wave hello. I can't dance with him and then ignore him completely. That would be rude. I might even offend him, and I won't be responsible for such a hitch in Safire-Etanian relations.

I read a few pages, about the Wars of Discontent a hundred years ago, about my own great-grandfather who helped usher peace in the Heights, then peek over the top.

No sign of anyone Safire.

It's not until I've made it another six pages, through the peace treaties and reconciliations that kept our region of the North civil for subsequent generations, that Lieutenant Erelis and his friend appear. They're both dressed casual, still in grey-tone attire but now short-sleeved and relaxed. It's reassuring. He seemed very different in the impressive uniform last night, more imposing, but now he's a boy again, and he glances my way.

I busy myself with treaties. I won't encourage anything.

An hour goes by—an entire endless hour—and they remain by the hangar doors. They don't look like they're doing much. Two Etanian pilots approach for a short conversation, there's some poking round one of the planes, then it's quiet again. Still he won't come. He glances at me, then talks with his friend, gradually becoming more animated, and then they both look at me. The Lieutenant shrugs and walks across the grass.

I hide my victory behind the book. When he arrives, I pretend to be surprised. "Yes?"

"Are you spying on us, Princess?"

"I believe that's your job. I'm studying for an exam."

"Oh? Well, never mind, then." His hair looks a bright beautiful colour in the sun.

"Never mind what, Lieutenant?"

"Nothing. You need to study."

"Tell me."

He nods at the hangar. "I was going to let you look at our planes, since you were so interested in a demonstration. But I can see you're very dedicated to your studies and I won't interrupt."

I shut the book. "I'm not dedicated enough to pass up an offer like that, Lieutenant."

"Please," he says after a moment. "Just call me Athan." Then he smiles, the kind of smile that ruins any lingering objections.

I apologize to Heathwyn in my head and stand, tossing the book behind.

We walk for the wide metal doors, side by side. The other pilot is waiting for us, his expression like that of someone who's just learned he was accidentally right. He glances at Athan, perhaps waiting for an explanation, but when none comes he extends a cautious hand to me. "I'm Cyar," he says, then withdraws it awkwardly. "Sorry. I suppose princesses don't shake hands."

I reach out my hand. "It's a pleasure, Cyar."

He accepts the offer, relieved, his eyes warm. They're as dark as mine. It makes him feel familiar and safe for some reason, an unexpected connection.

Turning, I step into the cool of the hangar, drinking in the beautiful aeroplanes resting on the concrete floor. I touch the grey steel, the smooth lengths and sharp edges, then trace the symbol on the flank—a faded moon and stars crossed with swords, words written round it.

"That's the Captain's squadron symbol," Athan explains. "Moonstrike."

"And this?" I point at the words.

"*First into the fray.* His squadron motto."

I test out the Savien sounds on my tongue, studying the gleaming wings closer. "He's very good at telling his stories."

"Which your friend quite likes," Athan observes, "but not your brother."

His bold speculation halts me a moment, but then again, this seems to be the trend with the Safire. "She has a lot of confidence," I admit. "So perhaps she's a good match for your captain." I turn. "And where is your aeroplane? In Savient?"

He shifts. "No. I don't actually have one of these yet."

"Yes, you do," I say, catching him with a smile.

"I do?"

"You can't shoot down three without your own."

He looks to the ceiling briefly. "Can I confess another thing, Princess?"

"Yes?"

"I might have made that up. The three planes, possibly four."

I blink, stunned, and turn to Cyar, who's now busily occupied with his boots.

"You mean you've never been to war?" I ask.

Athan looks sheepish. "Well, not yet. But I will. And I'm sure I'll get at least three."

"Why on earth would you make that up?"

"So you'd talk to me," he says with fervor. "You're a princess. I had to make myself interesting somehow or else you'd never bother to notice me."

Stars! The explanation is heartfelt enough that it begins to feel unfair questioning him. How does he manage that?

I cross my arms. "Well done, Lieutenant. Now you're not only boring, you're also a liar."

He holds up a hand. "But I did get top score when I graduated. That part was true."

"By cheating, I'm sure."

Cyar chuckles, and Athan's shoulders drop. "Are you going to dismiss me from your presence now?" Athan asks me. It's the same sad expression from when I killed his swan, which makes me think he isn't taking this seriously.

"I'm considering it," I say regally. "I don't like dishonest people. And I'm sure Cyar could show me the planes well enough on his own, couldn't you?"

Cyar glances between us. "Yes. Maybe. Well, I think . . ."

"Perfect. Which one do we—"

"All right, let's be honest," Athan interjects. "Ask me anything. No more stories, now that we're friends. Anything."

"You have a lot of nerve, Lieutenant."

"I've learned from the best." There's a feather of a smile on his face.

"I'd like to hear about Savient," I say. "What makes it special, how you've come this far from nothing, and why you think you can make things right in the South."

The smile on his face grows. "That, Princess, I can do."

And he does. They both do, in fact. We sit on the grass outside the hangar, hidden from palace sight, Cyar passing round candies from Norvenne while they share their history with me. They swap the tale easily back and forth, the pieces of their story connecting, overlapping, and I try to picture a world where someone could find electricity and running water a fascination. But Athan does. As a child, he had neither. And Cyar thought it was normal for abandoned bodies to simply show up, mutilated, in the morning rubbish pile on the street. It's unfathomable. That these three rival lands, each ruled by vicious men, abandoned by everyone else in the North, could slowly unite beneath the General's Safire flag and choose peace is almost mythic.

But the General did it. He gave them something larger and grander to believe in.

"Then if peace hadn't come," I say, thinking aloud, "you two would be enemies now. You might have had to shoot your best friend and you'd never even know it."

"He could be my possible fourth plane," Athan agrees.

"Although with his sense of direction," Cyar says, "he'd never make it home after."

Athan fires a candy at Cyar, who tries to dodge but it hits him squarely on the chest, and Athan smirks. "See? This is why he was second place in our testing. Not quite quick enough to be the best."

"Think what you'd like, Erelis, but you'd better not land on the wrong runway in Thurn. The Nahir would like your neck."

"More than yours, I'll bet."

They both laugh like that's a funny thing, but my stomach turns. It's easy to forget what they're trained for, where they're headed, when lounging here with palms against summer grass. "What's it like in your capital city?" I ask, trying to reclaim the conversation. "Does it look like Hathene?"

"I don't know," Athan says. "I grew up in the countryside on a farm. I've never been to Valon."

"You're a farm boy?" I laugh.

"Is that funny?"

"I don't know. I've never met a farmer before."

"Good God, Princess." He glances to Cyar. "Can you believe this?"

"No, I can't," Cyar replies, "but please tell her more about your farm."

"I have a better idea." Athan jumps to his feet and points at me. "Let's get you in a plane. Isn't that how I lured you here?"

"You lured me here to see them," I clarify, "not to get in one."

But he's already gone, excited by the new idea, so I trail after him into the hangar. Two Etanian mechanics are working in the corner, and certainly they'll watch what we do with interest.

"Won't you get in trouble?" I ask, hanging on to his arm, like that might stop us both.

"No." There never seems to be any hesitation with him.

"But the General—"

"The General's in negotiations with your mother. I doubt he has time to worry about whether or not a princess is sitting in one of our planes. Unless you plan on flying it, of course. Because I've learned the hard way that might come off badly."

He gives that resistance-ruining grin again, and the next thing I know I'm climbing onto the wing. I take his offered hand, this time feeling his warm skin free of gloves, and step gingerly into the open cockpit. Both of them climb up after me, leaning against either edge to point out the switches for landing lights and oxygen supply, the elaborate system of instruments that indicate everything from altitude to fuel temperature. It's dizzying.

Cyar taps the control panel. "It's easy to lose track of the horizon when performing fast maneuvers. Good pilots trust their instruments as much as their instinct."

I peer round the narrow space, at the endless buttons and knobs and numbers. "But how do you remember it all when someone's shooting at you?"

"I'll let you know when I find out." Cyar gives a little shrug. It's an endearing reaction, like he didn't know what to do with himself and so his shoulders went up of their own accord.

"Why aren't you a lieutenant as well?" I ask curiously.

"Me? I'm not the sort to order others around."

"But you're an officer."

"Yes, but Lieutenant Erelis was good enough to get promoted right away. A future captain. You have to be quite extraordinary for that honour."

Athan makes a face, propped on the other wing. "The honour of being first into battle, you mean."

Cyar salutes him glibly.

They lecture some more about aeroplane things that make little sense—pitch and yaw and something-magnetos—and then the tale circles back to Savient, and how Athan would like me to sign a letter for his sister so he can prove he met a real princess, and Cyar talks about how he joined the Safire army so his family could show their loyalty to the new nation, and how he had to travel on a train for three days, all by himself at age eleven, to reach the Air Academy. I look between the two of them, and suddenly feel very small.

They've lived an entire life already.

"Flattering the Safire with more of your compliments, Ali?" a scornful voice interrupts.

We turn in surprise.

Reni prowls towards the plane, frowning.

"I was learning how to fly, in fact," I say, gesturing at the cockpit. "It's more complex than it looks."

"And I'm sure you've also been enjoying their luminous tales of heroic victories. I hope they didn't forget to mention the innocent people murdered by its bullets."

Athan's on the wing closest to Reni. "I'm sorry?"

"Don't deny it, Lieutenant. Many questionable things took place in Karkev, things your General is now trying to hide."

Athan drops down onto the floor. "I wasn't there, Your Highness. Can you enlighten me with your own personal experience on the matter?"

Reni grimaces. "On second thought, you keep quiet. I don't trust a word that comes out of your mouth as it is."

"That's not—"

"I said keep quiet."

"No," I object from the plane. "Keep talking, Lieutenant. You say what you'd like."

Athan glances between us. "Two royal commands at once. Who's the higher rank?"

"Me," Reni snaps.

"Oh." Athan steps back and gives me an apologetic look.

I pin my brother with a glare, hoping he'll take the hint to quit before he makes a fool of us, but he doesn't. "Ali, the Safire forces committed crimes in Karkev that are sickening. I've tried to keep these dark things from you, but evidently you need to know before you start waving this fox flag yourself." I roll my eyes at that. He ignores it. "The General himself accepted the surrender of a town only to send these very aeroplanes after the people he promised to make peace with. A land may be filled with criminals, but it doesn't mean the honourable way of fighting can be forgotten."

"Wait," Athan says. "None of that's true. Those are lies spread by the Karkevite rebels."

"Is that so?"

"Yes. Did you read it in the papers?"

Reni pauses. "Well, no. But I have reliable sources."

"Here in Etania? Halfway across the world?" Athan gives a skeptical look, then glances at me. "I promise it isn't true."

Reni narrows his eyes. "Were you there, Lieutenant?"

"No."

"Then your opinion counts for little."

"But my brother served in the campaign, and I can assure you he never said anything about murdering anyone."

Reni stalks closer. "Your brother was in Karkev?"

"He was . . . *involved*, yes."

"Then he's complicit in the crimes carried out. He's a blind fool who follows without question."

Athan grins. "Yes, he is."

"Is this a game to you?" Reni asks fiercely. "Your General reneged on every promise made. He swore left and right that he'd stabilize his own borders and push no further. And now, two years later, where's your army? In the damn capital of Karkev! It makes one wonder how Savient came about, doesn't it? Perhaps it's time the Royal League heard how he actually built his 'new nation.' It's rather convenient, I think, that he found such support there and suddenly there's no one left to object. Not a single protester to the Safire cause."

The amusement vanishes from Athan's face, like a cloud over sun. Sudden and sharp. "You forget to mention, Your Highness, that the rulers of Karkev let brigands run wild and terrorize their people, as the old leaders did in Savient. Why? Because the corruption kept their pockets full of gold. If you'd like to applaud them for that, please do, but being a royal yourself, I suppose you'd be better acquainted with those who feast than those who suffer."

Reni flushes. "How dare you . . ."

"I'm not going to stand here and listen to you speak lies about us, not when you yourself have more to answer for."

Colour drains from my cheeks, and Cyar appears equally stunned, still beside me. No one speaks.

"I don't need to answer to anyone, least of all you, Lieutenant," Reni says at last.

Athan draws a breath and steps away. "This is pointless. You believe whatever they tell you."

Reni snorts. "I'm not the one who runs to fetch when the General whistles."

"At least I've seen enough to know why I'm running."

"I'm not as ignorant as you think," Reni bites, voice rising again. "I know far more about the politics of these negotiations than you."

"Then why are you standing out here with me?"

"Watch your mouth! This palace is mine."

"Funny, because I thought it belonged to your mother."

I gasp, a slightly strangled sound.

Reni's face darkens with fury. "Might I remind you that you're not in those negotiations either."

"Which is fine with me," Athan replies hotly. "I'm a youngest son. I don't expect much else. But if I were you, I might be a bit more insulted."

"There's an order to things, Lieutenant, and unlike you Safire, I accept it!"

"Perhaps that's why you're losing your girl to an upstart Safire captain with no crown at all."

Reni's fist strikes Athan dead in the face, horribly perfect aim. Athan keels over, and Cyar leaps down from the wing.

I stand in shock. "Reni!"

My brother appears stunned by his own reaction, staring at his fist like it isn't a part of him. The two Etanian mechanics gape in the corner.

Athan groans and raises an arm to keep Reni back. "God, I didn't see that coming."

"You didn't?" Cyar asks, already at his side.

"I . . ." Reni begins, then stops.

Athan winces. "Do you feel better now?"

My brother swallows, his mouth opening like he might say something further, then he closes it yet again.

I crawl down out of the plane and run for the pilots' icebox near the mechanics. They quickly pretend to be working again. I fish some ice from inside, wrap it in a nearby rag, then hurry back to Athan. He's sprawled on the floor, leaning against the wheel of the plane.

"I'm terribly sorry," I say, hand trembling as I pass him the compress.

He rests it on his eye. "Why are you apologizing?"

"I don't know," I fret, kneeling before him, reaching to make sure he has the ice in a good position.

"I've got this," he says.

"I feel terrible."

"It isn't your fault."

We sit there, him wincing and me feeling useless. I knew it. I knew Reni would start a war, I just didn't see it happening quite like this. Not that Athan's words weren't entirely out of line either, but he's Safire, and what else would anyone expect? Reni shouldn't have provoked him.

"How can we make it up to you?" I ask.

"Please don't worry."

"Anything at all."

"I'm fine."

"There must be something."

"Well, I suppose there's one thing." As usual, no hesitation. Here or there. Never in between. "I'd really like to climb that," he says, pointing out the hangar door, to one of the higher peaks nearby. "But I might need someone to show me the way. I've heard the trails are confusing."

I look at the mountain. "Climb the entire thing? With me?"

"I was thinking your brother."

"You're joking."

"Princess, we Safire never make jokes. But if you're willing to go with me instead, that would be fine, and I'll lie about where this injury came from." He flinches, head crooked as he balances the ice.

It takes a moment, but I realize he's teasing, something playful in his good eye.

"All right," I say, voice lowered. "But it will take the entire day."

"I have ways to make it happen if you do."

I nod.

He salutes.

I turn from him and find Reni still watching us. Cyar's trying to show him the fighter plane—a noble but futile distraction—and my brother ignores it, walking towards us with a frown, the sort that means he's unfurling knots in his head.

"For a junior lieutenant," he says to Athan coldly, "you do have a lot of gall."

Athan shrinks slightly back against the wheel, ice perched on his face, and Reni leaves the hangar.

19

Our third night in Etania, we're off the hook for watch. A full seven hours of sleep that feels decadent. Cyar and I wake up, yawn our way through some calisthenics, and I throw on some sunglasses to hide my left eye. It's rather swollen and ugly. Somehow, though, Father finds me at breakfast in the Safire lounge—a common area with games and cabinets of expensive liquor—and the next thing I know he's pulled the glasses from my face and snapped them in two. I'm sure he's heard about the illegal stunt with the plane, and maybe even my run-in with royalty, and there's a brilliant threat in his glare.

Then he's gone.

Garrick sits smoldering across the room, a cup of coffee clenched between his hands. He's looking at me now with a face that says, *"You do one more thing wrong, it's my neck on the line, and I swear to God I'll kill you for it."*

I give him a smile that says not to worry.

"You really had that fist coming," Cyar offers.

"You're right." I remove the cherries from his plate.

"But I know you don't regret it."

I toss a cherry into my mouth. He hates them, I love them. "That stubborn ass of a prince couldn't survive a single day outside this palace." I grin, and regret it.

Pain.

"This might not be a good idea," Cyar observes. "The hike."

"You think a sixteen-year-old girl is going to murder me in the woods?"

Cyar pauses, then shakes his head. "Never mind."

Bad idea or not, my bag is quickly packed and I'm off. Yes, it's going against my own rules, but if I have to die, it might not be such a terrible way to go. Murdered in the mountains, or executed for it later. At least it'll be an enjoyable last few hours.

"Where are you off to this early?"

Havis catches up to me in the hall, pacing alongside, and I don't look at him. "A hike with a local."

"Who?"

"The Prince was happy to volunteer his time."

"I find that difficult to believe, Lieutenant, considering the rather fantastic rumour going around."

"Is there?"

Havis grips my arm, halting me. "Yes. One of Sinora's lords heard—from a major in the auxiliary air force, no less—that the Prince was seen sparring with an impudent Safire boy in the hangar, and won. He was quite impressed."

"Hardly a fight," I clarify, since it's not like I could swing back.

"Well, either way, it's a good thing the Queen's son seemed the victor, otherwise the story might not have been so charming." His voice lowers. "And Sinora won't be pleased to find you sporting in the woods with her daughter."

"There are lots of things she wouldn't be pleased about." I wrinkle my nose. "And that's an unfair angle to assume."

"You undermine your Father's mission."

"What if I said I was acting on his orders?"

"And what if I said I'm marrying the girl?"

I step back as far as his grip allows. "Marrying her?"

"Yes, when she's old enough." He smirks at my skepticism. "Listen, Lieutenant, the tree may be corrupt, but the apple still looks fine to me. Don't bruise my apple."

That's rather disgusting. But I saw him in Norvenne "sporting" with his lady friends as it were, so it's not a surprise he'd find some kind of reward in this mess. When Sinora's brought down, where else would the Princess go?

Something guilty nips inside.

"She'd never choose you," I say.

"She'd never have a choice."

I yank my arm out of his grip. "Good thing I don't like apples, Ambassador."

"Yes, good thing." He turns and stalks off, but not before adding over his shoulder, "Nice eye, Lieutenant."

The Princess is waiting for me outside on the garden walkway, bag in hand and looking entirely different. Gone are the fussy gowns, replaced by brown pants and plain shirt, her hair pulled into a simple braid. Not a jewel or a pearl in sight.

She waves me over anxiously, glancing at the palace. "Hurry. Before anyone sees."

"We're doing this in secret?" I figured she'd tell at least one person.

She stares at me a moment, at my eye, then darts her gaze away. "Would you prefer I invited my brother?"

Her sarcasm is music to my ears. "Lead the way."

She ducks behind the bushes of the gardens, motioning me to follow, and we slink to the stables, heads down, like there's a sniper on the loose, but really it's our parents that we're terrified of. The whole thing is comical enough I almost laugh.

Almost.

She stops at a split-rail fence just beyond the horse pasture. The mossy woods are alive with sounds—snaps and rustles and feathers taking flight—and far above us the tree line gives way to rocky bluffs, sunlit and surrounded by a spotless sky. The definition of an inviting horizon.

"Here, we have to climb it," she says, gesturing at the fence.

"Is this a trail?"

"Not officially, but you wanted to climb that mountain, so here we are. And there's less chance of running into anyone this way." She removes her bag from her shoulder. "I'll go over first."

"No, let me." That's what a gentleman does. "In case there are wolves on the other side."

She smiles finally, a bit of tension disappearing from her brow.

I hand her my bag and hop the wooden rails. She struggles to pass it to me over the top, then gives me hers and crawls up and over.

I weigh her pack in my hand. "This is rather light."

"Yours is rather heavy. How much water did you bring?"

"Enough."

"How much is enough?"

"Three bottles." Her face colours slightly and I point at her bag. "You do have water in there, right?"

"Yes."

"And?"

She shrugs. "A sketchbook."

"And?"

"Paint."

"And?"

"Stop interrogating me, Lieutenant."

"I'm not interrogating," I say. "I just want to make sure if we get stuck up on that mountain we survive."

"Then what did you bring?"

I shoulder my pack again. "Water, matches, food, a warm jacket. Thank God you brought the sketchbooks, though. I don't know where we'd find anything else to burn in the middle of the woods."

For half a second, she looks ready to give me another black eye, but I grin and it throbs.

A pleased smile appears on her lips. "If we get stranded, I trust you'll share, Lieutenant."

"That's a large assumption, considering you hardly know me."

"I've a good feeling."

"Well, if it's a risk you're willing to take, let's go."

She waves in assent and leads me onward. We cut over fallen logs, through the brush, and the conversation stays polite while she follows her map in hand. She's good at coming up with pointless topics that mean nothing—weather and palace history and the quality of my previous night's sleep. Years at those stuffy dinners must teach you something about small talk.

"Be honest," she says eventually, looking over her shoulder. "Did you really take top score when you graduated?"

"You're never going to trust me again, are you?"

"No."

I nod and raise a finger. First place. The best.

"You must be very smart," she says with a bit of awe.

"Not very." I point to my left eye.

She laughs. "You're lucky to have such a gift, Athan."

I like when she says my name. I feel like she's really seeing me. Maybe that's why I hear myself say, "No, I'm not lucky." She throws a questioning look, and now I'm stuck. The real answer would take an hour-long explanation and wind up in places we can't go. Places where she'd realize I'm not a friend at all. So I shrug. "If I were ordinary and forgettable, then I could do whatever I wanted. But like this . . . well, other people get ideas for you. Expectations, you know?"

She looks at me a long moment, puzzling, like she's trying to figure me out, then she nods and studies her map again. I'd like to see what's inside her head. A clue about what she thinks of all this would be nice. But just as quick she's marching ahead, pushing branches out of the way while I try to avoid them on the return swing.

We've gone for a good ways and the earth rises sharply, the forest dense and the trail thin. Sweat begins to tickle the back of my neck.

DARK OF THE WEST

"You're sure you know where you're going?" I ask.

"It's an old hunting route. Reni and I used to explore here, but I've never gone the whole way."

"And you're sure you can get us back? Because that's usually Cyar's job."

She smiles. "If you give me some of your food at the top, I'll take his place."

"Fair enough. You're actually quite good at this, Princess. We could use you in the army." A branch flings with impressive force and grazes my face. "Great aim, too."

Her laughter echoes in the silent woods. It's a fun game, making her laugh. It always sounds like an accident, like she meant to keep it in but couldn't resist the opportunity, and that makes me feel funnier than I am.

Up we go, higher into the splendid wild. Pine and fir and sprawling chestnuts tower around us. When we reach the open slopes, the sun is bright but the air chillier. A strong wind stings my face, fills my ears. It's like being in an airplane, but without the metal and glass to protect. Sea swells of air tugging and pushing.

Long strands of dark hair escape from the Princess's braid, brushing her face while she tells her stories. "They say there are wild horses in these mountains," she shares, pointing out at the peaks that stretch north. "Descendants of Prince Efan's stallion, the one he rode when he won his battle for the North."

"You should get one for yourself," I say. "Royal horses."

"I wish! But they're impossible to catch. If they sense danger, they'll run for days. They'll run until their hooves and nostrils bleed. In the olden days, they say men would capture them and ride them into battle because they'd never stop. Loyal even to death." A sliver of sadness appears on her face, and she turns from me.

"What's wrong?"

For a moment, it's only the wind in my ears and on my face. That steady rush.

Then she says, "Nothing. They might not even exist. But I saw something this summer that makes me think they do."

I wait.

Her velvet eyes meet mine again. "I think my brother might have a horse with that blood in him. Loyal to death."

I don't understand, but I don't press any further. She's filled with something sad and strong. It's a wholly different experience seeing her here—perched on a rock, overlooking the view, no gown, only mud on her boots. I like how the mountains bring her alive. Opening her up, even the sorrow. How I suddenly feel I have a chance at touching her skin to know she's real as me. I remember the curves of her body beneath my hands during our dance, the heat, and find myself staring at her.

"Should we keep climbing?" she asks.

"Oh, right. Let's go."

I sound stupid, even to my own ears.

She shifts from foot to foot, aware of my stare. "I must look awful right now." Her forehead is smudged with sweat and dust.

I try to think of a compliment, but I've never done this before. What's too forward? What's proper? She looks terribly pretty even like this, but saying it now feels wrong and not saying it feels even worse. I still don't know what she thinks of me.

"Not as bad as me." I grin, pointing again at my bruise.

The dark eyes falter with disappointment, and then I feel disappointed, too.

"Come on." I nod up the trail. "We must be nearly there."

⊰ AURELIA ⊱

The open-face ridge appears just as I think my legs will fail me. I've made a good show of keeping up with Athan, but this is farther than I've ever hiked and my lungs ache like stones in my chest. Far below is the palace, surrounded by the rolling valley, and in the distance, the spiraled roofs of Hathene, the city cream-coloured against the green. I pause to admire it. An excuse to take in a few more greedy breaths.

Athan hops onto a nearby rock, balancing on one foot. He's been doing these silly things the entire way up—hanging off branches, scaling outcrops. I consider pushing him off the rock when he's not looking, but motion him closer instead. "I've remembered something very important."

He tips forward, still balancing. "Which is?"

"First to the top of the ridge wins."

Before his genius mind can comprehend the challenge, I sprint across the hard ground. The wind-roughed summit glitters ahead in the sun.

He races after me, but I crest the rise first.

"That was cheating," he complains, hands on his knees.

I grin, equally exhausted. "That was quick thinking."

We plunk down in a spot sheltered from the wind, stretching out our legs and retrieving lunch from our bags. Mine's rather meagre, and Athan dangles his fresh bread and meat in front of me.

"Do you want to get down from here later?" I ask.

"No," he says with a smile, but he surrenders some to me anyway.

While we eat, he tells me about flying in an aeroplane, what it's like to explore the cloudy realms above. I close my eyes and imagine the feeling. He makes it sound very lovely, like the plane is alive and a friend, the world a much better place at 15,000 feet. After a while, I pull some paper and a pencil from my bag, and, to my surprise, he produces a sketchbook.

He gives me a sly look. "You don't think the Safire enjoy art?"

"I suppose you have the creativity for it," I say, "if your lies are any indication."

But it's a good feeling that spreads inside me, the sense we've found common ground at last.

We work in silence. He understands the quiet, the peace, and his hand moves without pausing, eyes focused on the paper. I outline the palace below. When we share our pages at the end, my heart does a little trip. It's me. He's drawn me—my face turned towards Hathene, hair tossed in the breeze. He hardly glanced my way once.

"You don't like it?" he asks hesitantly, trying to cover it with his book.

"No one's ever made a sketch of me before," I say.

"Really? You don't make your servants do that in their spare time or something?"

I reach over and snatch it from him with a grin. "You have such a terrible impression of us. But did you do this from memory?"

He shrugs. "Everything in my life moves quickly, there and gone. I've learned to remember well."

"But not directions," I tease.

"I remember what I want to remember," he says honestly, and there's a tingle of warmth on my nose.

I hide it by studying the way his lines are soft and shadowed, more an impression. "You draw like my father did."

"Your father was an artist?"

"Yes. He died when I was young, but I remember watching him paint. He'd sit in the garden for hours."

"You're more like him than your mother, then?"

It's yet another bold question, but I'm not even surprised by it this time. There's a sense of refuge high up in this secret place, away from the world and its usual patterns. "I'm not sure," I admit. "I know him mostly through the stories told by others, things I think I remember about him. But then I never know if I'm making those memories up. If I just want them to be true." I pick at the charcoal pencil. "And my mother's an equal mystery. She's from Resya, you know. She never talks of her life before she came here, since she can't, really. You know how it is these days. And . . . Well, sometimes I feel torn between the two. My mother and father. I want to honour them both equally and I'm not sure I know how. Does that make sense?"

His grey eyes watch me. "You might be surprised."

I don't mention the protesters who question my mother's loyalties, who hate her and long for the days of my father. I don't mention this, because Athan's uniform is the source of their contention, and I don't want to go there. "Tell me about your family," I say, deflecting the attention away. "You said you have a brother?"

"Oh God, I have two."

I laugh at the face he makes. "And your father's a farmer?"

He erases a smudge from the portrait. "Yes."

"What does he think of you off round the world in uniform?"

"He's very proud. It's a more noble life than that of a farmer, don't you agree, Princess?" He grins. He has a way of saying things with such candor, so effortlessly, and yet his eyes tell a different story. That shadow that looks older than it should on seventeen years.

"And what does your mother think?" I ask.

His eraser stops, but it seems a logical question. I wait. I need to see the full picture of him.

"I don't know. She . . . she's dead."

"Oh, I'm sorry. I didn't—"

He waves it off, eyes on the rocks at our feet. "How could you have known?" He waits a moment, then says, "And I don't know what she thought. She never expressed herself well."

This, I believe.

"It's been ten years for me," I say. "It still feels like yesterday sometimes. How long for you?"

"Two months."

I bring a hand to my mouth. "Stars! I should never have brought it up."

"No, it's fine. It doesn't matter." But he looks scattered, and now I know why. It's too fresh. It's still raw inside him. "I should be the one apologizing," he says. "The other night, that girl—your friend—she sang one of my mother's favourite songs. I couldn't bear it. It was as if someone chose it just for me, and I had to leave. It was rude of me."

Something guilty lurches in my stomach. I don't want to accidentally hurt this boy I hardly know. He already has a dark bruise left behind from yesterday, the weariness of a life already lived, and this unintentional wound from the song feels even deeper.

I want to take it away.

I want him to trust me.

"My father was murdered," I say, the first time I've ever spoken the words aloud, certain he won't judge. He looks up sharply, and I add, "But it's a secret. I didn't even know until this spring."

His eyes flick over me, like he's seeing for the first time. "That's terrible. Why?"

It's another logical question, one I should have seen coming, but the words still fumble off my tongue. "I . . . I don't know. They never found who did it. I suppose if the kingdom knew that, the fear would spread." That's close enough to the truth.

Athan frowns. "No one was brought to justice?"

"No."

"Then you *should* tell someone. Let the world know. It's not right what happened."

His certainty catches me off guard. Also the awareness that he won't just accept my reasoning. He's too stubborn and Safire for that, so I raise my chin. "It's not right to frighten an entire kingdom and chase revenge your whole life," I tell him. "What happened was my father's fate."

He leans back on his hands. "Well, that's an interesting perspective."

"You don't agree with me."

"I think it's quite a luxury to be able to sit around and wait for fate."

I face him on the rock, arms crossed. "I'm not saying it was easy losing my father."

He faces me, too. "But what about everyone else's father? And mother? You don't care about them since they never had a chance to begin with? Since at least you have a fancy horse and a glass of wine?"

I recoil, unsure how we ended up here and what fire I've lit in him. I'm the one who needs sympathy, not him. "What are you saying?"

"I'm saying it's not much of a life, lounging around with power but doing nothing."

A bitter laugh escapes me. "And what you're doing—running across the world with a gun—is better?"

"Yes, because I know what guns can accomplish. My home was built with bullets. I'm doing what's in my power, and while it will never be the same as yours, at least it's something."

I think of the protesters and realize they have something infuriatingly in common with the General's bold men. I point a finger. "And that's exactly what's wrong with you Safire. You think anyone has the right to rule and change the world, but that's not the way it is."

"Why not?"

"Because there's an order to things! God put leaders in place, kings who know how to rule and guide properly. It's how it's always been and—"

I realize he's laughing at me. He's laughing at me like I've just told a marvelous joke.

"My God, you actually believe all this, don't you?" he exclaims.

I turn from him, furious now. I could slap him for being so cruel, right at the moment when I thought to trust him. I want to yell at him and say, *"People like you are the ones who took my father! People like you who are rotten enough to think you know bet-ter!"* I want to yell at him until my voice is hoarse, not because it's him, but because I can. Because he has no idea what the truth is, and what I'm fighting for, and how miserably afraid I am of what might happen if Seath isn't defeated. If the protesters keep growing in numbers, and if they discover some way to connect Mother to the trouble in the South.

I have to think about all of these things, and all he has to do is follow a damn order.

It's not fair.

He waves at the palace. "Tell me, Princess, how does some-one born inside there ever learn to rule? I'm genuinely curious. What brilliant thing is your brother going to teach the world when he sits on that throne? What does he know that no one else does?"

I sit silently. I hate that I have no answer.

"That's not how leaders are made," Athan finishes. "You go through something horrible, you prove yourself, and then you're a leader. Those are the ones who change the world."

"Stars!" I stand up suddenly, just so I can stare down at him. It's vainly cathartic. "You think we can't rule? Who are *you* to talk? Look at your arrogant general! Controlling you with his orders, starting wars wherever he wishes. Did you hear nothing my brother said the other day, or do you refuse to even think of it? At least our monarchies are peaceful!"

"Peaceful?" He laughs unkindly, glaring up at me. "Really? Is that why all those grateful people in Thurn are revolting?"

I glare back to him. "What are you implying?"

"What do you think? You have no idea what goes on there! You can't own people, Princess. You can't force loyalty and expect them to thank you for it. No one will take that forever. Believe me, eventually it has to end. They're going to do some-thing about it."

"Then go fight for the damn Nahir!" I snap. "You'd suit their revolution."

It takes a breath, but the fierce fire in his eyes slowly fades. He stares at me, and stares at me, then gives up and settles against the rock, arms crossed on his knees, looking more like a dejected boy than a soldier.

I think I've won, but strange guilt snakes inside me. Carefully, I sit down again as if too much noise might annoy him further. There's only the sound of crickets in the thin grass. I realize he makes no sense to me. At times, he's easy as a cat in the sun, and at other times, so boiling with hidden passion that I'm left startled and bewildered. I saw it in the hangar. I see it now. I want to peer inside his mad little Safire head and find out what's there. But I can't.

We sit like that, not speaking, for a long while.

Then he gets up and goes to the ledge of the rock face, dragging his boot over the edge, stretching his arms wide. The air is turning golden, the sun lowering, and he looks over his shoulder and says, "If I were you, I wouldn't leave here either."

He sounds apologetic. Wistful.

I want to tell him he's right and he's wrong, but I just nod.

When he comes to gather his things, he looks at his watch. "We should head back. Wouldn't want to be stuck here in the dark." He gives a cautious smile. "Wolves and all."

Warmth returns between us, comforting.

There's a sharp drop from where we've been sitting back onto the ridge. It was easy to climb in my hurry, but more precarious-looking now. Athan navigates down, then reaches up a hand.

"Thank you." I'm glad for an excuse to touch his skin again.

"You're welcome, Princess."

"Ali," I say, and he smiles.

20

⇥ ATHAN ⇤

Daylight's almost gone by the time we're snaking through the palace gardens, just as we did earlier, our faces tinged by sun and dirty from head to toe. Aurelia still looks like perfection—windswept and warm. She was silent for most of the hike down, distracted by quiet thoughts, and I really shouldn't have said what I said at the top. I think she's forgiven me, but it's hard to tell. I suspect she's very good at playing diplomatic. When she means to, anyway.

Cleverly, she sneaks us in through the kitchens. We're greeted by the curious faces of servants holding crates and hoisting vegetables, and we step through the chaos, then weave down the narrow halls and up a flight of stairs. We must be in the clear.

The Prince and Havis appear at the top, and I collide right into her.

There's a moment of awkward nothing before the Prince says, "I saw you both from the window. God knows who else did."

Aurelia goes a bit pale. "Does Mother know?"

"I told her you were out on Ivory. She's been busy enough that she believes the story."

"She'd like to see you now, though," Havis says. "Shall we go to her parlour?"

Aurelia darkens beside me, the glorious little storm that

Havis brings out. I'm fairly certain she knows this man views her as an apple. "I'm showing the Lieutenant to his quarters," she says.

It's a nice excuse, but also unhelpful, because it puts me into the "sporting" category again.

The look on the Prince's face suggests the same. "I'll show him the way. And you can go with the Ambassador to see Mother as you should."

Yes, this is definitely an ambush.

Aurelia and I look at each other, a silent exchange of *"Good luck,"* then climb the stairs and pick our poison. She and Havis disappear one way, the Prince hurrying me off the other. A bit of fear finally quickens inside. We're alone and hostility radiates from him like pulsing flak. I feel very unarmed.

"You're having a pleasant stay?" he asks, once we're alone.

"I am."

He grunts, either approval or annoyance, and stops. I'm forced to do the same. "Your father as well?" he asks.

Blood careens to a halt in my veins. The truth finally spoken. But I yank my mask into place and we size each other up. Time to play by his rules.

"You'll have to ask him that," I reply casually.

He steps close. "I'm sure my mother would love to know the truth about you."

He thinks she doesn't know? Then he's in over his head. "Perhaps."

"Why are you showing such interest in my sister?"

"You can see her pretty face plain as me. Why do you think?"

He growls, breath hot on my face. "If you touch her, there will be hell to pay."

"Then why don't you tell her who I am?"

"Why don't you?"

His question bites more than I'd like. I shove it aside. "I'm under direct orders not to reveal myself to anyone, under any circumstance. Things are tense in Thurn. And we've already had one member of our family made an unjust target."

"Convenient," he says.

"Necessary," I say.

We're still nose to nose in the empty hallway, tempers smoking. But he starts walking again. I follow warily.

When we reach the entrance to our Safire floor, he gestures. "Here you are, Lieutenant."

"Thank you. I don't know how I'd have made it without the help."

He gives a sour glare, then blanches.

I turn just in time to see Garrick disappear around a corner with a brunette on his lips.

The singing girl.

For a moment, the Prince looks ready to hunt them both down, the blackest kind of fury in his gaze, but I'm the only one within reach. The highest target there is. "Hell to pay," he says, seizing my arm tight enough to leave another bruise, "do you understand?"

I nod and he departs. My heart continues stammering away. I don't like being afraid of him, but he knows. He's aware there's a larger game afoot, and if he hasn't told anyone else by now, then maybe he's actually smart enough to know what moves to make. Damn him. I liked it better when he was an idiot. I don't think he'll rat me out to Aurelia. He's too much like Kalt—hiding behind his pride, happy to have important secrets. But Havis? Sinora? I thought for sure they'd tell her. Now I wonder if they see the truth I'm beginning to see—that even if they told her who I was, my real name, she wouldn't hate me. She has no reason to. In fact, she might even try to get closer, earnest in her interest, and they can't afford that. She'd only ask too many questions. They can't make her despise me without opening up a darker, hidden truth, and for all her noble talk about fate and acceptance, Aurelia's got a fire that refuses to be written off. Maybe that's why no one shares the things they should.

Or even the things they shouldn't.

Guilt creeps into my throat again, dry and scratchy.

Murder.

Why did she have to tell me that?

⇥ AURELIA ⇤

When Havis and I reach Mother's parlour, the sun has fully set and the halls are deepening to midnight blue in the low light. She's posted guards outside her doors for the duration of the Safire visit, and they give us both a strange look, a touch nervous.

This makes me suspicious, and I turn to Havis. "Why does she want to see me?"

He blinks a moment, like he's considering a lie, then tosses it aside. "She doesn't. But I need you to call on her for me. She's in meeting with the General and I dare not interrupt. For you, she'd be more forgiving."

"No," I say. "I won't."

"Then I'll be sure to explain how I found the Lieutenant cornering you in an unseemly way. He might not wriggle out of that one as easily as he did spying."

Fury burns away my reluctance. I knock on the door lightly, and nothing happens. Havis reaches over and raps on the wood with a fist. The guards nearly perspire.

"If she's angry," I say, "I'm blaming this on you."

"She won't be angry."

Stars, how does he survive life with such smug conviction?

A maid-servant opens the door, peering at us like a twitching bird.

"The Princess needs to see her mother," Havis says for me. "Now."

She nods, overwhelmed by the blunt order, and allows me into the room. We cross the parlour to Mother's private drawing room, but she hesitates with knuckles to the closed door, eyes on the Resyan rug beneath her feet, unwilling to proceed further.

I do the knocking myself.

After a long moment, it opens. Mother's face quickly switches from annoyance to surprise. "Aurelia, what are you doing here?"

Behind her, General Dakar is seated at the small table, no sign of Uncle or Admiral Malek. It's only the two of them and a half-eaten meal.

I swallow, a tremor of uncertainty rippling. "Ambassador Havis would like to speak with you."

Agitation shadows her face, her hand on the knob of the door, but the General appears unhurried. "Go on, Your Majesty," he says. "I'll wait."

Her eyes dance to me.

Dakar smiles. "And I'd enjoy a chance to become better acquainted with your daughter."

Now my palms are sweating. The prospect of being two feet from the General of Savient, alone, is more than I bargained for.

Mother seems to feel the same way, shifting on her feet in hesitation, but she nods. "Very well. I'll return shortly."

The maid-servant hurries after her to open the main door, and I attempt to compose myself. My brain runs through a hasty checklist of politics not to be mentioned—Karkev, Thurn, the Nahir.

"Please, sit down," he says, gesturing to the seat my mother abandoned. "Would you like a drink?"

"Yes, thank you."

I settle before him as he pours tea from the pot, an unexpected thing to see the General do, and I feel like a curious child pretending not to stare. His harsh face, littered with lines, speaks to a life lived on the edge of something awful, yet I can't help but notice he might have been quite handsome once upon a time. There's an elegance to his long nose and strong jaw.

He sets the pot down and studies me. I glance away.

"You look . . . ," he begins, then stops. "Well, you look like your mother, Princess."

It's an odd time for that observation, because I feel as far from Mother as a muddy stick from a star. I'm still covered in dust, hair a mess—and wearing pants, no less.

"Thank you," I say, though.

"And we'll have to make plans for the air demonstration you requested."

I glance into his face fully, now, out of surprise. "The air demonstration?"

"Of course. Your compliment the day we met isn't forgotten. I wouldn't wish to disappoint you."

He sounds much kinder about it now than he did on the steps. Perhaps here, away from public view, he can afford to be more generous. "We'd be most honoured, General."

"I'd offer one this week, but you can't have a proper demonstration with only two planes. We'll need to bring more."

"I suppose so," I say, though I really don't know any better. Two planes would be exciting enough for me, and perhaps for most of Etania. And it would be particularly exciting if Athan Erelis were to be flying one of them.

He continues to watch me, hand resting on his cup.

"It's truly wonderful of you to visit Etania," I say. "We're very grateful for your willingness. They say there's no other place like Savient in all the world."

He nods.

I want to go further, to fill the silence, but I only know about Savient from the papers—things about his aeroplanes and monstrous battleships and the fact his eldest son is said to be more

ingenious than all the Landorian colonels combined. These
things sound too formal and detached, things he certainly hears
everywhere he goes. Things he'll only nod at me about.

But since I now know Athan's perspective of things, perhaps
that's the best place to start. "No one understands yet, General,
but truly, I don't think leadership can be learned only in a palace. You've been through such terrible things, and you bring the
experience and wisdom that most of us long for."

He raises a hand. "Princess, I'm not a man who enjoys flat-
tery. I prefer honesty, from everyone."

"Oh." I pause. "Well, I did mean it. I believe you'll settle the
South and make the world a better place." I swallow, awkwardly.
"For us . . . and for them."

I'm not sure exactly what I intend with the last point, but if
others in Savient believe, as Athan does, that the people in Thurn
are unhappy for good reason, then I'm willing to show my acknowledgment of it.

Interest flickers on his face, and he offers me a bowl of summer cherries.

"My favourite," I say, taking one.

"I have those in my family who feel the same. My youngest
son could eat them with every meal. And my daughter." He
smiles. "You remind me of her, in fact. Not in appearance, but
you possess similar charm."

"You have a daughter?"

"I have four children. Does this surprise you?"

"No," I say, but it certainly does.

I only know of the brilliant eldest son, since he's mentioned
in the papers a lot—mostly for his battles, but also because he
was photographed at the opera with the King of Landore's most
beautiful daughter. But what would Dakar's girl be like? I picture her as tall, with perfect posture and no smile. Maybe handy
with a gun. I wonder if she's happy. She must be, to have such
an impressive father at her side.

Then I remember the news from this spring.

"I'm sorry about your wife," I say carefully. "It was tragic."

His smile lessens. "It's kind of you to offer your sympathies."

"I hope you can bring her justice."

"I will."

It feels like I've taken a misstep, touched on something tender. I backpedal and say, "Your daughter's very fortunate to have such a brave man for her father."

He tilts his head. "Why do you say that?"

Here we go, treading feelings still fresh and new, but at least they're honest and certainly he'll appreciate that. "I loved my father, but he wasn't a warrior," I say, sifting through the thoughts I had on the way down the mountain. "That's why he died."

"You believe that?"

I bite my lip. This isn't territory I should go into, yet it's the truth, because I'm certain the General of Savient would never allow himself to be murdered. It would have happened by now. My father, however, didn't think about such things. He painted pictures and ignored the whispers, as Mother said, and fate took him. I wish that thought wasn't in my head, but it is.

People like my mother and the General don't wait for fate.

They play a step ahead.

I'm silent and the General finally says, "I know nothing about the circumstances of your loss, but I do know that being a warrior isn't what matters in the end. What matters is playing your cards better than the rest—and with the right side." He leans closer, chair creaking. "Take that from one who's spent his life cheating death."

His face is still hard, all intense certainty—I'm not sure he knows how to look pleasant—but his words only affirm what Mother said to me in secret, and I'm beginning to see why the two of them get along well.

"Do you really intend on giving me an air demonstration, General?"

"I never lie, Princess."

"Then might I make a request?"

He's still leaning forward. "Whatever you'd like."

"I'd love if you brought Lieutenant Erelis and Officer Hajari. Between you and me, I find them both quite charming. They're good ambassadors for you. You might even give them a promotion."

His brief smile appears. "Princess, promotions are given for acts of valour, not social graces."

"I'm sure they'll manage those too."

"Indeed." He appears satisfied. "I'll see what I can do."

Heels click on the parlour floor, coming near, and he leans back in his seat.

Mother appears in the doorway. "I apologize, General, for the delay." She looks between us, expression clouding. "But it's taken care of now."

"Nothing to apologize for, Your Majesty," he says.

And then he looks across at me, like we have an honest understanding.

The General leaves not long after, and Mother orders me into her bedroom the moment he's gone. She closes the door firmly. "What did he talk about with you?" she asks. There's new tension in her face, along her shoulders.

Havis has managed to ruin her day—or perhaps it was me.

"He told me about his daughter. He said I reminded him of her. And he offered me an air demonstration, but I doubt that will happen. I'm sure he's too busy."

"Hm." She studies me a long moment, then strides to her vanity, searching for something. "He seemed in a good mood when he left."

"And what did you talk about with him, Mother?"

I know it's bold, but the General has that lingering effect.

She stops searching. "Me?"

The quick reply, almost off guard, makes me even more curious. I want to see what she'll say. She's the only person in Etania to entertain a private audience with the General—other than me now, apparently.

A strange look crosses her face, something I can't read, and she says, "There were things that needed to be discussed away from the official record. Not every state agreement is meant for the papers."

Stories upon stories that never appear in ink. It seems the world is full of them now.

"Is he pleased with us?" I ask.

"Of course."

"And Ambassador Havis?"

"Ah, he's requested a return to Resya on urgent family business."

"He interrupted your meeting for *that*?"

Mother turns with a sharp look. "Mind yourself, Aurelia. His mother's quite ill." She runs a brush through her hair, tossing it over her shoulder. "It seems the General might have found new supporters in Classit and beyond," she continues. "He wishes to tour the Heights and has requested that I accompany him. He'll return in ten days to retrieve the rest of his contingent here."

"You're going with him?" I ask, stunned.

"To mediate the discussions. He needs a local ally. These small kingdoms are still cautious about entering negotiations with a man such as him, and I've proven it can be done."

"Then who will oversee things while you're gone?"

She rarely leaves, and the idea of the palace without her is a bit frightening. She's the gravity that keeps life in tune.

She allows a smile. "Have you such little faith in your brother?"

My eyes widen.

"Reni can manage ten days on his own. It's time for him to

assume these responsibilities." She pauses. "Though you will let me know what business he entertains?"

The question, again, is so casual it almost blends to nothing, but it carries too much weight, something like betrayal. Like spying.

"I'll try," I say, "but he doesn't let me anywhere near his business."

"Of course. I wouldn't want him to feel mistrusted, yet . . ."

She doesn't say it aloud, but she knows what Reni did to Athan, since Uncle was quick to pass it along as an amusing tale—the Prince putting the Safire in their place—and she admonished Reni strongly for it. She wasn't happy. Now she draws me to her, pushing the windblown hair from my face, and I feel again like a muddy little stick.

"I trust you can be a welcoming host to the Safire while I'm gone?"

"Always," I say.

"Soon things will be as they should. I've done an impressive thing bringing the General to our side, and everyone will see it in time. They'll applaud me. They will."

"They will," I agree.

She has no choice but to be right.

∌ ATHAN ∈

At midnight, a fist sounds on the door.

I know before opening it I'll find Garrick on the other side. I went looking for him earlier in the evening, suspicious, but Ollie was outside their room, telling me some story about Garrick being sick and how he couldn't be disturbed, and that's when I knew what was up.

Ollie's a faithful wingman on the ground, too.

"Get dressed," Garrick says, glaring at me when I open the door. "You're on watch until dawn."

I stand there, shirtless, exhausted from the mountain and craving sleep, but he's determined to punish me for my investigation. To remind me to keep my mouth shut. "You're feeling better now, Captain?"

He ignores it. "The General is headed to Classit tomorrow, for further negotiations, and while he's gone you're entirely under my leadership."

Father's leaving me on my own? A warning might have been nice, but I suppose this is how it's going to be from now on. Everything trickling down through goddamn Garrick.

I think that's what I'll call him.

"And I require that every report be filed," goddamn Garrick continues, "every watch observed, every button polished and bootlace tied, do you follow me?"

"I follow, sir. Though I don't think you'll need to worry about any laces untied with me."

I regret the words the moment I say them, right as they're leaving my tongue, but it's too late to call them back and there they are.

He shoves a furious finger in my face. "The next time you speak to me like that, I'll punish Hajari for it. I doubt you'd be so bold if you had to watch him run fifty laps at midnight."

Cyar looks up from where he's been cleaning his boots, alarmed.

He has no idea how mild this threat really is, comparatively.

But I nod. Garrick disappears back out the door, perhaps off to grope his fancy girl some more, the girl who certainly won't bother to remember him after this week, and I give Cyar a repentant look. "Sorry."

"Don't apologize yet. But please don't let it get to the point where you need to."

Reluctantly, I pull on my shirt again, then my uniform, then my muddy boots. A cold, lonely hangar. Until dawn. I gather my sketchbook pages, then realize Cyar's dressing as well. I give him a dismissive wave, but he pulls on his gloves anyway.

"I'm not letting Sinora murder you without me there. I couldn't live with that." He glances at the page in my hand. "Is that the Princess?"

I hide it quickly. "No."

"Yes, it is. I just saw it."

"So?"

He sighs. "You shouldn't be spending time with her. She doesn't seem to have anything useful to offer, and you're not very good at separating how you feel from the job that needs to be done. You know that."

I haven't told him about the murder confession. Maybe I'm hoping I'll forget.

"True, but I need to learn," I say. "Otherwise I'll never get a squadron. And then I'll have to take orders from goddamn Garrick the rest of my life."

He doesn't smile. "Be careful, Athan. There's no talking yourself out of this one if it goes bad."

"I can talk my way out of anything."

"But can she?"

I don't like that question. I don't like it because it reminds me there's another person involved in this. I like having my own things to control, my own problems and solutions. The prospect of flying with Cyar is stressful enough, having to worry about him when the sky's on fire. I don't want to worry about this girl a world away whose mother is destined to burn.

But I do.

21

The next day I hide in our lounge. I'm not exactly worried about the Prince, but I'm also far from inclined to take any undue risks, now that he knows the truth. Besides, I have Thurnian lessons to catch up on. We're supposed to be studying the local language before we sail south. I busy myself conjugating verbs, trying not to think anything undignified about Aurelia, and then suddenly, like magic, she's right there in front of my desk in the Safire lounge, inviting me to tour the palace.

I don't know what to do.

I need to follow Cyar's advice, and I try to look to him for help, but he's pretending to read a book on the nearby couch. So much for his noble lecturing last night.

He's officially useless.

She continues to press, and I tell her I need to finish the assignment, but she just says, "I'm sure Officer Hajari would finish it for you. Wouldn't you, Cyar?"

He looks up, surprised. As if he hasn't been listening to everything. "Yes, I suppose I could." He catches my look. "Or no. I don't know . . . I mean . . . there's a Landori word for this, but I can't remember—"

And that's that. I stand and announce, yes, we should do the tour, and she beams at me, all bright and warm and smelling too damn wonderful, and I make sure to hurl a dictionary at Cyar on the way by.

"I hope you find that word you're thinking of."

"Thank you, Lieutenant," he calls with a guilty smile.

The palace is a friendlier place now that it's free of Sinora and Father and Malek. The court has decided that without the promise of speeches and good food, there's little point to being here, and the halls are empty and echoing. As long as we stay ahead of the Prince, we should be fine.

Aurelia takes us from statue to tapestry, explaining each one, the story and significance, how it fits into the five hundred years of Etanian glory, and it's a little overwhelming how one tiny kingdom can have this much history. She's particularly proud of her great-grandfather, showing off a marble bust of his bearded face.

"He helped end the Wars of Discontent in the Heights," she explains. "Drafted the peace treaty, in fact. They were awful wars, went on for twenty years. I think two hundred thousand soldiers were killed?"

"Battles in mountains aren't advised," I say.

"Truly, how can anyone fight for twenty years? In any case, we learned our lesson. War is no good. We've no interest in a repeat."

She tugs me along, pulling me by the arm—which I pretend doesn't affect me but is actually the best part of the tour—and we enter the grand ballroom. Without the din of music and laughter, without the tables and silks and steaming dishes, it's like a hollow golden shell. Our steps sound lonely on the marble floor. Their royal ancestor, Prince Efan, gazes down from above, a sword in his hand and a fox at his feet.

"I like the fox," I say with a grin.

She replies with her own smile. "We're going to hold my birthday masquerade in here," she announces, stretching out her arms. "You should come, Athan. It's at the end of the summer. Surely you could get leave?" Her voice is teasing, but there's a genuine question in her eyes.

"I don't think you know how the military works," I say, teasing back. "Or war in the South."

We exit through narrow corner doors on the far side, presumably where servants scurry in and out, then make our way, stealthy, down some narrow stairs, down another hall, and into a library. This room's smaller, with shelves of colourful books. The carpet on the floor bears the woven crest of Etania, and the windows stretch from floor to ceiling, letting in light and a beautiful view of the mountainscape beyond.

"My father's library," Aurelia says with another grand sweep of her arms. "His favourite place." Dust particles shimmer around her like a halo. "Want to see my favourite painting?"

She has that secret look, just for me, a perfect hook.

"Of course, Princess."

"Please, call me Ali."

But I can't. I really can't, not when she's already this close under my skin. Cyar's right—people have a way of lodging themselves into my heart, and once it's done, it's done. I'll lose all sight of Father's mission. Maybe I already have.

"Or at least Aurelia," she pleads, coming near, gold earrings shivering with the movement.

I give in. "Whatever you'd like. . . ."

She waits.

". . . Aurelia."

Victory brightens her face, settling on her lips in a mischievous quirk. I can't win against that. She takes my arm again— my reward for weakness—and tows me into an adjacent room. On the far wall hangs an oil painting of a dragon and unicorn, the two creatures crouched together on a sunset cliff.

"My father painted this one for me," she says. "The fable I love best—Elinga, the unicorn of the mountains, and her friend, Elois. I'm dressing as Elinga for my masquerade. I've designed a gown and matching mask!"

"Delightful," I say with exaggerated interest.

She hauls me to another painting. This one's a battle scene, with swords flashing and horses rampant. Three suns blazing. A black steed in the centre, tail in flames, its eyes charged with flickers of orange. "More to your liking, Safire boy?" she asks wryly. "That's Prince Efan winning his battle. Remember the one I told you about yesterday, with his horse?"

"Prince Efan. The man every king in the North claims to descend from."

She looks surprised. "You know the story?"

"Believe it or not, we do have history books in Savient. Though I am wondering—why's the horse on fire?"

"They say he was a gift from God to win the battle."

I grin. "Fate happened, and you wound up with a crown on your head. Not bad."

She doesn't laugh, and it makes me feel bad for saying it. We study the painting, wordless.

She pushes the thick hair off her neck, over her slender shoulder, and I'm caught by the urge to trace stray strands from her skin. To feel her warmth, to run my fingers along her arm and around her waist again.

The sudden grief on her face spoils the idea. "They say," she says softly, "that nothing can harm a descendant of Efan. They say we have divine blood in our veins and that God will watch over his chosen line. You must think that's strange."

Of course I do, but she looks at me now, all of her heart on display, trembling in front of me, and suddenly I see it very clearly. Her father wasn't kept safe—he was murdered, and the idea of it haunts her. The certainty that something wrong happened at the very heartbeat of her existence, something ruined before she ever had any say or stake in the matter. Something that could ruin her, too.

I know. Because it's the same fear in me.

"I don't think God plays favourites," I admit, afraid she'll think I'm callous and unbelieving. "I think we have to watch out for each other."

She looks at me a long moment. Not scrutinizing or searching, simply looking, like I'm oil on canvas. Like she's memorizing the colours of my soul. "Is that why you wear this uniform, then? You truly believe it's the best way to do good?"

"Yes," I say, "and no."

I can't help being honest. She turns my thoughts grey again, that in-between fog of doubt.

Her eyes linger on my face, and I want her to like what she sees. I want her to find what she's hoping for. In this moment, all I want is to tell her the truth, to be honest and see what she thinks of it, to see if she'd still laugh at my stupid jokes even knowing who I am. If I played it right, she'd still forgive me at this point. I'm not my father. She's not her mother. I could get her on my side before the war breaks.

The idea grows like a trap, luring the words into my mouth.

A sudden noise saves me from myself.

Both of us jump. I hold out a hand, keeping Ali back, and walk carefully around the tall bookshelf behind us.

Long-lashed green eyes stare back at me, caught.

"Sorry, Lieutenant. I was looking for . . . books," the singing girl says, glancing rapidly from shelf to shelf, proving to me she's as mindless as she seems.

Ali's quickly at my side, expression firm. "Lieutenant, please excuse us. I'd like to have a word with my friend alone."

Thank God.

It's the escape I need, before I do something stupid.

I take it and run.

⇥ AURELIA ⇤

Athan obeys without a question, a nice perk of his being military-bred and conditioned to orders. I need offer no explanation. Once he's disappeared out the library door, I cross my arms at Violet. "Were you following us?" I demand.

"I was attempting it," she replies airily. "The two of you are like mice. Here and there and everywhere."

"Who put you up to it?"

She doesn't answer, creamy cheeks pinkening.

"It was the peacock feathers, wasn't it?" I hiss.

Violet clutches my arms gently. "Now wait, Ali. Just listen. Havis was worried about you. He didn't want you running into any trouble this week with strange men from foreign countries."

"Havis *is* a strange man from a foreign country," I say. "And what does it matter to him what I do?"

"He's protective of you, of course. He considers you dear to him."

Trust Violet to make it sound romantic! But this has nothing to do with his false affection towards me. This has everything to do with the fact that I know too many of his secrets, that I read his letter, and he doesn't trust me with any of it. I actually wish he were here right now, to confront him properly.

"Violet, you can't tell him a thing."

I refuse to give Havis a reason to slander Athan's reputation—and I know he would, at first chance, to keep me under his rein. I've been alone with Athan all day. Scandals can grow in any direction with fertile whispers like that.

"Oh, there's nothing to share," Violet says with a clever smile. "I see no strange men. It seems, instead, you've found an attractive lieutenant from an allied nation, which has nothing to do with his stipulations."

I realize what she means, her cheerful deception pulling

a grin from me. She's too clever for Havis. "You're the dear-est," I say gratefully, then pause. "You think the Lieutenant is attractive?"

I'm a bit afraid of the answer. Not that I'd deny it, but saying it aloud feels too official. Like I'm committing myself to some-thing I don't yet understand.

And then what could I ever do about that?

"Certainly," Violet replies. "Too young for me, of course, but he has a refined grace that's delightfully boyish, yet still conveys a hint of something deeper."

"He does," I say, pleased by her analysis.

"I'm a rather quick judge of character," she reveals, "and I think he's a sweet match for the sweetest heart I know."

I kiss her cheek. "Oh, thank you, Violet! I'm sorry Havis tried to bring you into this."

"Well, I got a fan from it. And don't worry, I never intended to tell him a thing. I'm here simply because I've never seen you flirting so madly with a boy—the show's been irresistible! Though I have a lot to teach you, darling. You're going to kill him with all these depressing facts about war."

I laugh and kiss her again, once, twice, then quickly on the lips.

22

The days of quiet halls are everything. Wonderfully every-thing.

Reni is happy to be king of an empty castle, spending his hours in the council room with Uncle, pulling in the sour Lord Jerig from time to time, and as I predicted to Mother, he refuses to let me anywhere near his business. He's polite to the remain-ing Safire and little more.

Heathwyn is my only deterrent to spending time with Athan. "Polite discouragement," she reminds me.

But since I can't fulfill Mother's first duty, with Reni, I have no choice but to fulfill the second, with the Safire, and so I aban-don polite discouragement—really, I abandoned it days ago—and spend every quiet hour that I can with Athan and Cyar.

I've never loved quiet this much.

We hide in the hangar as rain stammers on the metal roof, playing card games. They teach me words of Savien, and I teach them Etanian. I know, now, that when Cyar arrived at their Academy, the Savien language was new and unfamiliar to him, his mother tongue being Rahmi, and that Athan was the one who coached him through it and then helped him tackle Land-ori afterwards. I know that Cyar has a girlfriend, a year older, with black hair and dark eyes, and that he sees her only in the summers, though with his training ahead in Thurn this will be the first one away, and that makes him sad. He misses her. They write letters and she talks about helping his mother with gardening back home and she particularly loves sunflowers.

I know a lot of things about Cyar.

But Athan remains a step ahead. He dodges questions and latches on to whatever Cyar says. He always has something to add. Languages come easy to him, and to prove it, he tells a story about his brother trying to jump off a pier, switching from Savien to Rahmi to Landori and then even to a few words of freshly learnt Etanian. I don't know the point of the story. Then I compliment him on his leather watch, and he says it was a special gift from his pier-jumping brother long ago. Then, a few moments of conversation later, he circles back to the topic, grinning, and says, "Or maybe I stole it from him. I don't remember."

Always stories within stories.

I know he says these things to make me laugh, and perhaps that's why I sometimes don't. I like watching him try. I'm sure that deep down this entire show is because he's only a farm boy and what else does he have to brag about? Certainly not the crescent moon of purple lingering ugly beneath his eye. I'd like to grab him and make him slow down for just a moment. I want to look at him and really see. But he's too quick.

Confusing and quick and captivating.

When the sun arrives again, we visit the stables and I show off Ivory and the other horses. Cyar is in love with each one, complimenting them from withers to fetlock. Athan hangs back. He pats Ivory in her stall once, then retreats again to a safe distance in the alleyway.

"Come on," I tease, "you fly an aeroplane. You're not allowed to be scared of this."

"My plane doesn't get moody when it's hungry," he replies, serious.

Cyar rolls his eyes and scratches Ivory's neck. She relaxes into his touch. "You'd like Rahmet, Princess. Everyone has a horse. In the spring, we celebrate the change in season with a festival,

the best horses on display. They hold riding contests that anyone can enter, even the girls—and the girls usually win."

I must have a dreamy look on my face, because Athan shakes
his head and says, "Don't let him fool you. Rahmet's full of
snakes and spiders the size of your hand. Far from magical."

"Ah, but when the sun sets on the red rocks?" Cyar brushes
Ivory's forelock to the side. "Everything turns to gold. The only
thing more beautiful is my girl."

That earns him my romantic sigh.

Athan nudges my shoulder. "He even writes poetry."

Cyar grins. "Only when I'm drunk."

"Little sunflower, shining in the light—"

"Shut up, Erelis."

I laugh and drag Athan closer to Ivory again. I like the excuse
to touch him. "See? She won't hurt you, I promise."

He rests a hand on her back. "Good enough?"

"No. You have to pat her neck."

He obliges awkwardly, uncertain, and Cyar leaves us in the
stall alone. I step closer to Athan. The air shimmers with dust,
smelling like mud and hay and that special scent unique to
horses. It's everything I love. Hesitantly, I rest my hand on his,
helping him settle into a more certain rhythm.

"She's soft," he admits quietly.

"She is," I say.

His skin feels warm beneath mine, and even though I know I
can let go, let him do this on his own, I don't. His hands are
gentle. Like he's touching a baby bird. I think of them operat-
ing one of those beautiful aeroplanes, through the reaches of sky
I'll never see, and it seems breathtaking in its beauty. Something
godlike that shouldn't exist. I remember the way his hands felt
around my waist when we danced, warm and weakening. If only
he'd touch me again. I want to savour it more completely. His
hands choosing me, for a moment, above anything else.

Hands that will kill or be killed in a place far from here.

I pull myself from him.

"Are you all right?" he asks.

"Yes," I say, rubbing my arms. "Shall we see the other horses?"

He nods, looking a bit confused, disappointed even, and we step into the alley, latching Ivory's door.

Cyar's halted at another stall down the way. He looks sad, staring through the iron bars, and I know whose stall it is.

Liberty.

Cyar's hand grips the bars. "What happened to him?"

"He was injured in a race," I say. "They hose the leg down every day but it's still swelling. He's stopped eating." I can't hide my grief.

"Bring him out," Cyar says. It's the closest thing to an order I've heard from him yet.

But I do it, and Liberty stumbles into the alley, favouring the injury. Cyar drops down, feeling the swollen tendons, careful and quick. "Do you have rosemary oil?"

"I'm sure we do."

"Your groom should put that directly on the leg. It will ease the pain." He considers a moment, still on one knee. "There's a flower we have at home, it's called *jurica*. I don't know what it would be called here. It grows near rivers. Has a red spiked top."

"A spiked top . . ." I try to think of everything I've seen out in the woods. "Like a star with a yellow middle?"

"Yes. Exactly."

"I've seen that." A bit of excitement rises. "Can it help?"

"It can bring back the appetite," Cyar says, standing quickly. "Show me where you think it is."

I nod and thrust Liberty's lead at Athan. "Hold him. We'll be back!"

Athan stares at us, then at Liberty's giant head, then back at us. "Hang on, I don't—"

Cyar and I are already running down the alleyway and out into the warm sun.

We gallop for the river, diving into the wet grass along the ditches, finding ourselves ankle-deep in mud. My shoe nearly comes off, and despite Liberty's miserable state, we can't help but laugh. I really didn't ever expect to be mucking through the river with a Safire soldier. What would Heathwyn think? But I spot the desired plant first, raising it triumphantly.

"Water-willow," I say.

"*Jurica*," Cyar corrects, and we both grin.

When we burst back into the shade of the stable, I dissolve into laughter all over again. Cyar, too. There's Athan, cornered by Liberty's huge, curious frame at the back of the alley. Athan has the lead by the absolute farthest end, entirely useless, hands raised. "It's attacking me!" he exclaims.

"He'll never survive Thurn," Cyar says to me.

"Please take care of him," I reply.

Then we go smiling into the grain room together and mix a paste with the *jurica* plant, and I hope to the stars the people of Rahmet have discovered the miracle to save my brother's horse.

❧ ATHAN ❧

With each passing day, my mission loses its relevance at a re-markable pace. Aurelia reveals no fatal secrets about her mother, not even when I try to press her about the protests I've caught rumour of. She navigates around the issue quickly, and the only secrets she hints at are the ones that have meaning for me alone—half-hidden looks and little smiles. Tempting things. When Father asks me what I did for a week, I'm not going to have any kind of answer he'll appreciate hearing.

"*I mostly thought about kissing her*" won't go over well.

That would only put me in league with Arrin.

But now we're sitting here, wet with river water, basking in the sun, and I just don't care. The Prince showed up right as we launched our narrow rowboats into the river. He was trying a new strategy. Smiling and acting cheerful. Clever, because Aurelia adores him for it. She thinks he's coming around. He even opted to row with Cyar, leaving Aurelia with me, and the whole thing quickly became a race—with three boys, it was inevitable. We would have won, too, if Aurelia hadn't put her paddle into a half-submerged tree. She scrambled, using far too much force, yanking, and then we were sidelong into the rough current. Capsized in a moment.

Cyar, the traitor, paddled on with the Prince, both caught up in the competition of it.

We chose the sunny shore.

"I think you've lost your best friend," Aurelia says as they disappear from sight, stretching herself out on the grass. She's clearly pleased to have her brother playing with the Safire.

"Or perhaps you've just lost an heir to the throne."

"Is that a threat, Lieutenant?" She doesn't sound a bit suspicious, which proves how wrongly I've tangled this up. Or rightly. I can't tell.

"You know, you look pretty even half-drowned," I offer, trying distraction.

She smiles and shrugs, hands plucking dandelions, as if I'm saying something inconsequential. She does that well. One little turn of her cheek and whatever I've said becomes nothing. It wouldn't bother me so much if I weren't trying.

But I am.

She leans over and rubs a dandelion against my bare arm, leaving a yellow mark behind.

"What was that for?" I ask.

"I don't know." She does it again, hand brushing my skin. "Come on, show me how you think under pressure, pilot boy," she teases.

I pretend not to care, as if I'm not bothered enough to move, but all I can think about is her touch. Her dark eyes are brighter in the light, like dark honey.

A large drop of rain lands on her cheek, and she wrinkles her nose in an endearing way, glancing at the sky. "Stars, what's this?"

"I believe in Landori those are called clouds."

"Ah, you're quite brilliant, Athan."

"Thank you, Ali."

A sudden smile lights her face, drops falling around us faster. "You used my nickname."

It's a surprise for me, too.

She stands, motioning me to my feet, and I do as she asks. Helpless. "Dance with me, Lieutenant," she says, her left hand taking mine, her right on my shoulder. "Dance with me in the rain and we'll see what you remember." I almost protest, but she's already against me. Her half-dried hair tickles my arm, her bare skin against mine. My heart pounds wilder than it ever has. Temptation burning. Just one moment. One moment like this, all alone on the rainy shore, the mountains right there, so close I could touch them.

Her so close, to touch.

To kiss.

"I kissed her, Father," I imagine myself saying.

I imagine her in my arms and everything else burning around us and then I push her from me, terrified, like she's something that might shatter between my hands. The Prince and Cyar have appeared again, paddling their craft closer, and her brother's fury is a siren at the edge of my vision. "We need to untie our boat, Ali."

"We have a moment," she says, hurt evident. Something fragile I have power over.

"This will only get worse."

The rain falls harder, proving my point, and she lets her hands drop from me. Her disappointment hammers at my resolve.

"Perhaps later," I say, even though it's a promise I shouldn't make.

"Perhaps."

She's already walking for the river.

23

The afternoon the General and my mother are to return, Athan and I are alone together. We wander the halls, buying time, even though he's said three times now that he really must go ready his things to leave. I can't bring myself to agree to it. He eventually just invites me to join him while he packs.

The small guest room has a single window overlooking the woods. Cyar's bed has been neatly made, his bag already gone. Athan tells a laughing monologue as he folds and sorts, some tale about Cyar and a snake and a pool, but I'm adrift. I'm caught between two currents of certainty—one, that I'll never be able to forgive myself if I let him go thinking I don't care, and the other, that this evening he'll be gone and no matter how we pretend, we'll likely never see each other again.

What's the point in speaking my thoughts if they can't become anything?

"You have to picture this, Ali—a giant snake loose in a pool while mothers run in fear. Cyar may seem like the mature one now, but he was a little tyrant back in the day. Says his mother was relieved to ship him to the Academy to be straightened out." His laughter stops. "You don't find this as funny as I do?"

"It's very funny." I'm tired of stories about Cyar.

Silence stretches a long moment, then he tosses something at me. "Here."

I catch it between my palms, startled to interest. A coin from

Savient. One side bears the familiar fox in swords, the other a ship with banners.

"Save it, Ali. When you visit, we'll go to Valon and spend a night there, maybe drink too much. Bring out the rebel in you."

"And what would your girlfriend think of that?" I ask.

I need the truth. I'm sure she's there, some girl who knows what he knows, who lived through the bullets and the revolution and who understands the strange things that make him tick.

His smile fades. "Girlfriend?"

"Yes. I assume you have one. Like Cyar."

He stares at me, then shakes his head. "I don't."

"No?" Relief warms.

"I've spent five years at an academy full of men. We had two female pilots, but they graduated ahead of me. There's a reason I can't dance." He pauses. "Besides, I don't think it matters much anyway. I'm going to war and I'll probably die, so then what?"

"Don't say things like that," I whisper.

He shifts, perhaps embarrassed. "I suppose I've never been very good at this," he admits.

"Would you come to my birthday masquerade?"

Regret softens his discomfort. "I'm not sure you know what you're asking."

"It's one night, Athan. You have leave, don't you?"

"Not to come halfway around the world."

"I promise it would be worth it." It's silly even to my own ears. I'm asking for the impossible, but I'm desperate for him to pretend along with me, to pretend he'd try for me.

With a sigh, he motions for the coin. "Let's do this your way. We'll let fate decide." I hand it over and he makes a fist, resting the coin on his index finger. "If it's a fox, I come."

I nod.

He flicks it and it spins into the air, then lands on his outstretched palm, results swiftly shielded by his left hand. "What do you think it is?"

"A fox," I say with certainty.

Instead of revealing the coin, he tosses it back at me without warning. I'm not quick enough and it falls to the floor, spinning on wood. "Why did you do that? Now we'll never know!"

"Sometimes it's better not knowing." He looks at me, grey eyes rueful. "I'd prefer to dream."

Stars, I'm so frustrated by the distance soon between us, the distance even here and now. It's all new and frightening. "Then it's a good thing you don't believe in fate. You'll have to make it happen, won't you?" I move closer. "We should practice our dance, Lieutenant. The one we didn't have time for at the river."

"Here?" He starts to look round the room, but he's quickly drawn back to me, my face.

"Yes. You said later. It's later, isn't it?"

"Let me check my watch."

I grab his hand before he can tease his way out of this, placing it on my waist. "Dance with me."

"Anything to see you smile," he says, the humour in his voice lessened, replaced by a gaze that makes me hot from head to toe.

I'm so close now, and he doesn't back away, nor does he come near. He stares like he's forgotten how to breathe. It's easier than I expected. There's nothing to distract him from me, and as we dance, I can't keep track of the steps. He's no longer the strange and distant boy from the dinner twelve days ago. Now his touch is meaningful, because it belongs to him, Athan Erelis, and desire for something I can't explain sparks wild inside.

"Please come," I say into his ear. "Ask the General for special permission."

His shoulders shift beneath my hands. "I'll write you."

It's a middle ground, the only thing he can offer, and I accept it gratefully, clinging to his warmth and the sensation of him here and now, on the earth, with me, far from the clouds above. His breath against my forehead. I look up, at his lips, his perfect lips, and I know they're meant for me. A taste I long for. He leans down. His warm mouth almost to mine.

A tall shadow appears at the open doorway.

Stars!

We jump away from each other.

It's General Dakar, Admiral Malek behind him, and both appear stunned. New heat surges across my cheeks.

The silence is terrifying.

The General cocks his head. "What social graces indeed, Lieutenant."

Athan doesn't speak, eyes on the floor.

This is all my fault and guilt pulses beneath the mortification. "Your tour went well, General?" I'm grasping for an escape.

"Yes. Your mother was a most beneficial ally. I'm appreciative of her efforts. Likewise, your willingness to be such a . . . generous host."

The Admiral appears faintly amused behind him.

The General turns to Athan. "Gather your things, Lieutenant. You're late as it is."

"Yes, sir." He grabs his bags and heads out the door, no farewell offered in my direction. Not even a glance.

It hurts.

"You must forgive our sudden departure, Princess," the General says. "There are new and pressing matters in Thurn, and we simply can't afford to stay longer. This has been a happy visit for us all, but the South doesn't wait on such things." He tilts his cap to me. "Thank you, again."

He and the Admiral turn down the hall, and I'm left alone—so terribly alone—in the empty room with its solitary view of the woods.

There's a golden glow behind the western mountains as the Safire planes are fueled, the placid evening interrupted by urgent

shouts and propellers spinning. Men smoke last cigarettes before a long flight. Within the palace, heated words whisper of a
new uprising, panicked fears about the Southern troubles that
only seem to be getting worse, a storm that hasn't been this dangerous for half a century.

Seath of the Nahir—the man who came back from the dead.

I watch from the window, afraid to go outside to the wide steps
with Mother and Reni and the other courtiers gathered. That
would make this real, inescapable. There's no last chance to give a
proper goodbye to Athan, or Cyar. Gone, like cool water drying
from my skin on a bright day, disappearing. As if they'd never
come.

Engines stammer to a start and catch in the breeze.

Is he looking for me out there? Is he searching for my face
beside Mother?

The thought of him hoping, and not finding, spurs me from
the window. I hurry down the hall with desperation rising, out
onto the steps, afraid I've missed my chance.

Far below on the tarmac, the General gives Mother a final nod
while he stands near his impressive aeroplane.

I search the grey figures. There he is, illuminated by the western
glow. Athan. His face is turned to the steps, waiting, and our eyes
meet from a distance. He waves quickly. Even from here I can read
the regret. Then he turns and retreats into the large plane, gone.

Gone.

The planes rise up into the burnt-ember sky, dark against light,
towards the mountains, and I watch until they've disappeared,
until I'm sure my sorrow will wrench my heart inside out.

I turn for the doors, and stop.

Havis stands in the entrance, leaning casually. A young man
with sun-burnished skin waits beside him.

"Goodbyes are difficult, aren't they?" Havis says. There's a
cigar in his hand.

I bury my grief and step round them without a word.

V

BLOOD TIES

24

⊰ ATHAN ⊱

Norvenne, Landore

Rebellion.

Revolt.

The words are thrown around the airplane as we fly for Norvenne. A failed uprising in the Thurnian city of Beraya, and the Nahir hung three Landorian officials just as they did in Hady. Then they burned a Safire flag on the city wall. It's a taunt that won't be ignored, and anger is palpable in the cramped air of 20,000 feet.

We stop to refuel.

We take off again.

But I have my own fear. The looks from Father gnaw at my certainty, the creeping exhaustion of two lengthy flights delivering the final blow. This past week was a spectacular mistake. I began with the upper hand, but somehow, now, I'm the one admitting defeat.

I miss her.

God, I do. My life is grey, straight-lined, an inevitable path of compass points and marching orders. All charcoal. But she's spiraling colour. She's fireworks. Sunsets. Dawn skies in flame. She could scatter like light and end up anywhere. My fitful sleep is broken by the image of her on that balcony, gold as sun.

Beautiful in a world of steel.

When we land outside Norvenne, the mountains are gone,

only a distant cityscape beginning to wake as day appears. The runway is still lit by lamps, and Kalt's standing by the narrow doors of the airbase. He looks tired. There's a very good chance he's been waiting there all night. Waiting for the moment of Father's arrival so he can get another order and say another "Yes, sir."

But Father only nods to him, cursory, then motions for me. Here we go.

"What did you do?" Kalt mutters on my way by.

"Nothing," I say. And everything.

Like a guilty dog, I follow Father into the airbase. This conversation won't be pleasant. I have little to show for a week's effort, only the purple around my left eye, but I have to be quicker than him. I have to talk my way out of this somehow. Words hover like fog in my mind, wavering.

I'm too exhausted for an interrogation.

Father claims a small office, locking the door behind us. We sit down across from each other in two brown leather chairs and he flicks the blinds open. Harsh light floods the window. I squint.

"That was an interesting predicament I found you in," he says, the implication like a razor.

"It was nothing, sir."

"Not according to Captain Carr."

"Captain Carr," I say, "spent every day with an Etanian girl in his bed."

"And you didn't?"

I blink for a moment, offended. "Me? No, Father, I've never even—" Then I stop, about to admit the one thing no almost-eighteen-year-old son should ever admit out loud. "I'm not Arrin," I finish instead.

Father waves, like he doesn't want to hear any more either. The earlier disgust on his face said enough. Not because of what I might have done, but because of who I might have done it with. Sinora's daughter. A gross betrayal in his eyes.

"Then what's your report, Lieutenant?"

I steady my hands on my knees. I have to make this good. "I'm certain Sinora's lying to her children, sir. She's protecting them from the stain of her crime. They know nothing."

"The Princess isn't aware of who you are?"

"Not as far as I can tell. I don't think Sinora wants to answer those questions."

He nods. "Sinora's mastered her act well, hasn't she? But she can't play innocent forever. I always warned her not to get ahead of herself." He crosses his arms and looks out the window. "Nothing else from the Princess, then?" I hesitate and he continues, "I must say, I did find Aurelia charming. Quite like Leannya. She doesn't seem like the others."

A sliver of hope squirms inside. He used her name. "No, she doesn't."

He looks back at me. "But she *is* like them. Nothing changes her blood ties, as I'm sure you know."

The hope dissolves. "Of course, Father." His stare pierces, scraping my soul, searching for treason or weakness, but I'm better at hiding. "She told me something interesting, actually," I say, stifling a fake yawn. "She told me her father was murdered."

It works, and I relish the satisfaction of seeing my father, the General of Savient, recover from obvious surprise. He leans forward, examining me like he thinks I'm lying. "She said this?"

"It was more of a confession, since she only just learned the truth this spring. No one else in Etania knows. It's been hidden."

"Murder," he repeats.

"Or so they've told her." I struggle to keep afloat. The almost-kiss he saw was convicting enough. But if I can make my connection to her purposeful, then he'll tell me to continue it and he'll never know the truth, and then I can protect her.

It's a miserable logic, but all I have.

He cocks his head. "That explains what she told me."

"You spoke with her?"

"Oh yes." His lips twitch. "She had some impressive praise for you, in fact. And she told me her father died because he wasn't a warrior."

I wait. I don't know where this is going.

"She sees him as weak," he explains. "I'd wager she admires ambition more than Sinora would like. I'd also wager she listens more intently to their words than they believe. Perhaps you can continue to nudge her in the right direction?"

He means towards him, towards his army and ambition and the glorious sun of the Safire. An unknowing traitor in Sinora's own home.

"I doubt that," I say, trying to apply the brakes without stalling. "She'll forget about me after this week."

"You believe that?"

"I told you. I'm not Arrin."

"I've never seen any girl look at Arrin the way she was looking at you," he points out, and panic rises in my chest, but I've created this. "The Prince is a lost cause," Father says. "He's already set in his ways. Bought by Tanek Lehzar. But the Princess? She's outside of it. Inconsequential to them, and the most perfect gambit for us."

I shake my head. "She doesn't know what they know, not like we need." I'm not even sure what that means. Weariness and guilt have made a mess of my head.

"She knows enough to say how the winds are blowing. And if she likes you as well as it seems, enough to reveal a thing like murder, then it wouldn't take much on your part to encourage her to share more." He nods with approval. "You've done better than I hoped."

No choice now. Have to finish the act. "I want Sinora brought down," I say, as if it's as simple as that. It used to be.

"Then we can't let this opportunity go to waste. I promised

the Princess an air demonstration at the end of summer, but until then—"

"I said I'd write."

"You did?"

"I had to keep my foot in the door somehow. I spoke with her governess before I left. I talked her into it."

Again, he appears pleased. "I think I've underestimated you. Though there's still the chance of Sinora laying eyes on the letters. You can't write down anything that might be useful to her."

"Never. And imagining her face when she discovers them is entirely worth the trouble."

Father laughs. A real laugh. "I'll give you rein to do what you think best." He pauses. "But stay out of that girl's bed." Then he stands before I can remind him that's impossible, since I'll be thousands of miles away. "With this new revolt in Beraya, I'm advancing my schedule for the region. Arrin and Windom return tonight, and they'll brief us on the situation. You leave for Thurn tomorrow. Your reward sails with you, Lieutenant."

The suddenness of war startles me. Then again, maybe it's better this way. No time to think.

"Twin cannons for Hajari?" I ask, like I'm not afraid.

He nods. "The fastest planes in the sky. For both of you."

I manage a smile. Cyar safe, for now. But what about her?

By morning, the *Impressive* paces like a wolf in the waters near Norvenne. She arrived in the night, a silent ghost churning up the harbour, red banners colourful against grey iron. She easily puts the Landorian flagships to shame. Everyone on shore gapes, overwhelmed by her sheer size and strength. Kalt tells me not even Gawain's most lethal ship, the *Northern Star*, can match her for speed or weaponry, and nothing but a shot from God to the magazine could ever destroy her beauty.

It's the most excited I think I've ever seen him.

Shadowing the *Impressive* are three Safire battle cruisers, two destroyers, and a large transport. The beginnings of our sea cavalry, chomping at the bit to head south across the Black.

We're given a briefing along with the other squadron pilots being deployed, and General Windom tells us this new rebellion in Beraya, near the Resyan border, has put the entire western region in flames. The victories of the Nahir are luring more to their cause, rallying greater numbers.

"Nahir power has never stretched this far," Windom explains. He's a burly fellow, balding, more like a bear in his pristine blue uniform. He glances at Arrin more than Father. "But with Landore and Savient united, we'll bring them to their knees. Our army extracted their secrets in Beraya. We have the upper hand, I assure you."

"Taught them a damn good lesson, too," Arrin mutters beside me.

I mutter back, "What the hell does that mean?" But he looks the other way.

Father speaks next, giving directives for his squadrons. Nightfox—led by Admiral Malek's son, the captain I'd be flying under if there was any sense of fairness in the world—is headed for Beraya to patrol army supply routes. Lightstorm gets the prize, Hady, and will be waiting on the forefront of strikes to reclaim it. As for Garrick and his Moonstrike pilots . . . we get Havenspur. The seaside capital isolated from the recent violence. It's out of consideration for us, the rookies. A place to break us in that's not about to explode. But there's no glory for Garrick there, and I can see the frustration in him. For once I understand it. I wouldn't want to babysit Cyar and me either. Not when Father saves all his praise for Lightstorm and Nightfox, bound for the frontlines.

Garrick gets nothing but an order.

At noon, Cyar and I stand on the wooden docks, bags in hand, controlled chaos everywhere. Supplies are loaded—trucks and ammunition and fighter planes. Voices ring across the water. Smells of salt and seaweed and that rancid fish scent that hangs over every wharf. We'll be on the *Pursuit*, a destroyer, smaller than the battleships but still fearsome. It's also the vessel Kalt serves on, and I'm a bit suspicious that Father arranged it this way.

Kalt's overseeing activity from the deck above. Garrick's younger brother, Folco, leans on the rail beside him, equally red-haired but infinitely more likable. He and Kalt have been friends for many years. Both wear the formal overcoats of the Safire Navy, striped with maroon on the shoulders and made for thick sea winds.

I'm admiring the colourful barnacles on the hull when a crushing arm wraps itself around my shoulder.

"Ready to sail, littlest brother?" Arrin asks, pushing me along. "I know you can't handle the waves and it's been rotten weather lately."

I halt us. "Sounds like clear sailing from the reports."

He shrugs. "That can change in a moment. Just like the South. You sure you're ready for this?"

Cyar slinks to the farthest end of the dock, well-trained about when to give my family space, and I remove myself from Arrin's grip. "What did you mean this morning in the briefing room? When you said they were taught a damn good lesson in Beraya?"

He frowns. He's tanned from his days in the sun, faded red along his forehead. "I meant they won't be trying another stunt like that again."

"The Nahir, you mean?"

"I meant what I said and let's just leave it at that."

He turns with a shake of his head, and something dark kicks inside me, something I wish I could ignore. "Sinora's son accused us of crimes in Karkev," I say at his back. "He said Father accepted the surrender of a town, then strafed it. I told him they were lies."

Arrin stops.

"Tell me they were lies, Arrin."

He spins and strides back. "Listen to me, Athan, I don't know what world your noble little brain lives in, but you're going to learn very quickly that those who seem like the enemy might not be, and those who don't seem to be very much are. Garrick told me what you did in Etania—playing with Sinora's daughter like she's any other girl to be had, even after I told you not to trust them."

"What did we do in Karkev?" He won't divert me out of this.

"We won a war."

"How?"

"Goddamn you," he says.

"I defended us, Arrin! I swore they were lies, and I deserve to know the truth."

"You've done nothing to deserve anything. You flirted with a pretty girl and ate fancy food for twelve days. Ask me again when you've lived under barrage for an entire night."

"I have," I say. That was my entire childhood.

Arrin sticks his face right in mine, breath stinking of tobacco. "All right. Fine. But first, do you want to know what those lovely rebels in Karkev did to us? To our soldiers? They tied them to trees and threw grenades at their heads for fun. They dug holes in the snow and dropped them in naked, to die slow or let the wolves do it. When men fight like that, I don't give a damn how we win. And I won't apologize for anything."

I take a step back, realization dawning. "Father didn't strafe that town. You did."

"So you're brilliant, after all."

I lower my voice, unable to hide my sudden desperation. "What are you planning for Etania?"

His fingers bite my arm. "Why? So you can warn your new girlfriend?" Before I can protest, he hits me on the head. Hard. Like the day of Mother's murder, when I didn't even realize we were under attack. "You idiot! Don't you see what's happening here? Father wants to do this the slow way. He cares what these royal bastards in Landore think. But if we're going to do it, then to hell with the rules. We don't have time. Sinora has a gun at our heads and we have one at hers. It's only a question of who shoots first." He shoves me away. "It *will* be us."

The *Impressive* blasts her horn, and the people on shore cheer, delighted by the prospect of vengeance in Thurn.

Arrin gives me a mocking salute. "Goodbye, Lieutenant. Watch your neck down there."

With that, he's across the dock and over the ropes.

The dark thing gnaws at my stomach hard. Suddenly, I don't want to get on this damn ship, not with Arrin left here to plot behind my back. I don't trust him. He's no longer the pragmatist from the council room, though I knew that had to be a sham. Arrin is Arrin. He either thinks too much or doesn't think at all. He'll never see that Ali is innocent in this.

The dock moves beneath my feet, and I shut my eyes, feeling the shift and creak and stir of the world around me. Waves. Ships. Wind.

"Ready, Lieutenant?"

Father's voice.

My eyes open, and he's striding near, boots heavy on the wood.

"Yes, sir."

He stops, giving me the usual quick scrutiny. Checking for hidden messages. "Now that you're in service, you'll be earning your own pay. Don't be like Arrin and spend it in one place."

"No, sir." It's not like I even go out most nights.

"And you always be ready to fight, even in Havenspur. Anytime I've been told a sector is quiet, it soon enough becomes hell on earth. You remember that. You always be ready to fight."

I nod.

He looks up at Kalt and Folco, still on the deck. His eyes

narrow, dissecting them. "And watch those two. Kalt will be stationed nearby. I want a report on what you find."

"Find?"

He turns. "Goodbye, son."

I swallow, unsure what I'm supposed to be reporting. "Goodbye, sir."

I feel like there's more to say, but he's already turned away. What would I have said? I never know. A hundred voices circle around, and suddenly all I want is to turn and hightail it for the mountains. One last shot at freedom.

"You waiting for the footman?"

Cyar's question snaps me back. He's by the gangplank.

"I think that's you, Officer Hajari." I pretend to toss my bag at him. "Why else would I keep you as my right hand?"

He smiles and says, "For the cherries," then nods at the ship. "Let's go. Before we both have second thoughts."

Gripping the rails, we walk the creaky ramp, and the *Pursuit* groans deep within, the water below churning to furious life.

25

ᴥ AURELIA ᴥ

Hathene, Etania

The days following the Safire departure are empty and colour-less. The strange beautiful accents have disappeared, along with the clipping leather boots, the lingering scent of cedar and cigar smoke that trailed their officers. The familiar now seems too tame and predictable. Only delicate silk on marble and hushed laughter in the halls.

The silence leaves room for misery.

Despondent, I open my atlas to a map of the world, tracing the patchwork colours, the faraway shapes, and on these pages, the distance doesn't seem so miserably vast. The space between Savient and Etania spans the stretch of my hand. Across knuckles and palm and the length of fingers. Across mountains and valleys and an expanse of deep sea. Athan doesn't seem so far away on paper, the memory of his smile still making me warm and deliri-ous. It's all I can do to hold back laughter and tears. I feel I'm be-ing broken into terrible, wonderful little pieces on the inside, and Heathwyn is kind enough to pretend she notices nothing.

If I had wings, I'd be gone.

The third morning after the Safire departure, Havis and his new guest host a lunch for Mother, Uncle, Reni, and me. Their table is rich with foods from Resya—olives and tomatoes driz-zled in currant and cinnamon, fried eggplants with onion and garlic and sea salt. The air smells like delicious spice. But Mother

appears hardly wooed. She and Uncle have already met with
the two of them, no doubt thanks to the recent events in Thurn,
and our new guest invites suspicion. He's quiet and sharp, his
collared shirt unbuttoned at the neck, cream against brown skin.

His gaze strays everywhere but our faces.

"This is Lark Gazhirem," Havis explains as we wait to be
seated. "A dear friend from King Rahian's court."

The introduction encourages a smile from the young man—
he can't be much older than Reni. "I'm honoured, Your Highness." He bows to Reni, then to me, finally revealing his eyes to
mine. They're a bright copper.

We sit, and Mother waves the footman out. Discussion begins
with routine things, like the splendid weather in the mountains and Havis's mother's continued illness. He's grateful he
was given the brief leave to see her, and we each offer appropri-
ate condolences.

Lark says nothing, sipping at mint tea and fidgeting with his
fork.

Reni watches his restless hand.

"Ambassador Gazhirem, have you been to the North before?"
my brother asks suddenly.

The copper eyes glance up, caught off guard by this direct
address. "I haven't. It's my first visit and I'm quite impressed."
He speaks Landori with confidence, his accent as refined as
Havis's.

"Indeed," Reni continues, "and please forgive the intrusion
into matters that might not concern me, but may I ask the purpose of this first visit?"

The words are mildly caustic, since the crown prince should
certainly be concerned with all matters, and Mother casts Reni
a warning glance. His eyes remain on Lark, intent.

Lark sets down his glass. "I have a proposal, Your Highness.
From Resya. Perhaps I might share the details with you in a private meeting?"

"That won't be necessary," Mother says. "I've heard enough already."

Lark frowns. "I was referring to the Prince, and he deserves—"

"No," Uncle intervenes. "We've had our deliberations and made a decision."

"Discussed what?" Reni asks, chagrined. "I have a right to hear it."

"We'll discuss later," Uncle says.

"No. No, I insist on hearing."

It's the first time Reni's ever not deferred to Uncle, and uncomfortable tension prickles the air. Lark appears vaguely amused, gaze darting round at the key players in this standoff. It's as if he is waiting to see who will say what and when. Sensing a stalemate, he leans towards Reni across the table. "My father works for King Rahian. He has a proposal that could bring us all peace."

Peace.

I sit straighter.

"Why didn't your father come himself?" Reni asks.

"In the South," Havis offers, "it's a gesture of trust to send your child to dialogue on your behalf. It displays faith in the goodwill of another."

Mother raises her hand. "Enough of this. Years ago, I had much respect for King Rahian, but he has turned himself into a bitter isolationist, ruined by drink. I won't entangle myself there."

I can see Reni's expression brighten slightly, a bit of pleasure in his eyes to hear Mother say this. It's what he has longed for from her, a blatant refusal to get involved with her homeland—and to hear it out loud, to the face of an ambassador from Resya, is victory to him.

But Lark won't be hindered. "It isn't Rahian's fault. His crown descends from Efan, as yours does, and yet he's rejected at every turn simply because he was born into a kingdom on the Southern continent. I thought you, at least, might understand the injustice of that."

"It isn't injustice," she replies. "It's politics, and my hands are tied. I've plenty before me with the General. I won't push my people to accept the entire world at once."

"Ah, yes," Lark says darkly, "you'd pick that man over us."

His boldness is astonishing, and Reni's anger flashes. "You'd best watch your tongue and remember to whom you speak," he says. "You've no right to address her in such a manner!"

"I have every right," Lark replies. "I'm the same as you at this table."

Reni and I gasp. No one else looks so surprised. Havis only rubs his head.

"Blood ties," Lark explains curtly. "Cousins, to be exact. My father is your uncle."

Mother drops her cutlery. "Thank you, Lark, for choosing such an inopportune time to make this announcement."

"They should know the truth, since you've never bothered to share it. Are we so embarrassing to you?"

I stare at Lark Gazhirem, at his agitated fingers and youthful shoulders and obstinate face, and try to reconcile the fact that he is actually family. Mother doesn't speak of those in Resya. I never imagined she might have more brothers and sisters there, cousins and in-laws, but here he is.

Reni appears equally confounded by the revelation. "Cousins? But you aren't a Lehzar."

"I have my mother's name," he explains, as if it's of no great importance. "Listen, I know your dislike of the General. You don't want another to interfere in your affairs, but this is exactly what everyone in the North wants for the South. They don't give us a chance to defend ourselves. They don't let us speak—"

Mother's fist falls on the table. "I said this matter is closed!"

"—but I have a proposal that could save us all from war."

Havis puts a swift hand on Lark's arm, pushing him back. "Now certainly isn't the time or place. Let's not ruin this meal with useless debate."

Mother's expression is still tight. "Thank you, Ambassador."

There's silence, then Lark says, "Though it is rather odd that despite your disdain of Resya, you plan to marry your daughter to one of ours. What on earth will your proper Northern friends think?"

For an awkward moment, the words don't register. Then suddenly the air has disappeared from the room and my breath catches. I look from Havis to Reni to Mother—all of them staring at me—and she leans forward, like she's going to reassure me, but I don't give her the chance.

"What does he mean, Mother?"

"My star, he spoke out of turn, as he has since the moment he sat at this table. I didn't wish to tell you this way. I wanted—"

"What does he mean, though? What does he mean?" Panic has me fighting for coherence.

"You've always been aware of the Ambassador's intentions. This isn't a surprise."

I turn to Reni, but he won't meet my eye. There's evident pity on Uncle's face. A touch of regret on Havis's, even.

It's true. It's true and everyone at this table knew it except for me.

"Is this a proposal?" I ask Havis, terrified of the answer.

"Not yet." He looks oddly addled. "We're going to announce it at the end of the summer when—"

"Not until you're seventeen," Mother explains.

Seventeen. Marriage.

Death.

I should have seen it coming. Havis warned me and I didn't believe him. I convinced myself Mother trusted me, that she needed me here with her, an ally, and that Reni might find a way to intervene. I let myself get distracted by Athan Erelis, let myself believe I could have his warm kiss, that there was a chance at something more, and it was a lie of my own making.

I've tricked myself.

"You see, then?" Lark persists, raising his hands. "You would give your daughter to this man, you would send her to a kingdom with a drunken king, and yet you make me look the fool here?"

Mother turns on him. "Yes! Because your father's schemes threaten to undo everything I've worked for. I brought the Safire into alliance. I made this happen with my own two hands. The world isn't in a state for you to plot games and win profit for yourself. You're up against players too large for that."

"This is about *peace*," Lark declares. "This is about the peace our ancestors dreamt of. Or have you forgotten where you come from?"

Mother points a finger at him. "I do not answer to you or your father, Lark Gazhirem. You shame your mother's name with this."

"You don't even know what I'm asking," he replies, vaguely hurt. "You won't even listen!"

I sit in the midst of the hurled words, splintering, wounded, and only Reni's hand on mine reminds me to breathe.

I stand from the table.

I want to cry, I want Mother to see my pain, but there's nothing in me except fury. She reaches a hand towards me. Her eyes beg understanding. But I leave them all and their rotten betrayal behind.

I spend the entire day in my room, refusing every knock. The first few times it's Heathwyn, speaking softly, and then after that it's Mother, imploring me to open the door and let her in for only a moment.

I sit by the window, temper burning.

The colourless world has become a heated red. I can't even soothe myself with thoughts of Athan's arms round me. Instead, I imagine lying beneath Havis, his heavy, hot breath on my face.

His beard against my naked flesh. Everything of mine taken by him. Trapped in Resya, learning to kiss his lips, forced to please him while Reni rules Etania, and Athan flies in a faraway sky, and the world burns up in flames.

I want to scream until the palace shatters round me.

There's another knock at the door.

"Please let me in," Reni says. "It's nearly midnight and you've eaten nothing all day."

I glance at the clock.

Midnight? It feels like it's been only an hour, or maybe an eternity.

"I have a meal, Ali. And some pastries."

Surrendering, I rise from my chair and unlock the door. Reni takes a cautious step inside. He holds a tray bearing the promised desserts. We sit on the bed together and divide the food between us, picking at it silently, and I'm afraid to speak. I might just tell him everything, even the unbearable desire I hold for a boy I can't have.

"I'm sorry I didn't warn you," he says, guilt in his hazel eyes. "I knew."

It isn't a surprise. He knows many things, keeps them from me, locked away behind closed doors with Uncle. But this one thing he should have told me. This thing that might ruin my life. And now I also know something, and I'm prepared to use it. I have no choice.

"Father was murdered," I say, picking out my next pastry.

Silence.

I study each one, the different designs of frosting and fruit, the spirals of dusted sugar. I say nothing and make my choice, then look up into the shocked and wounded face of my brother, see the way even horror makes his handsome features harden into something regal.

"It's the truth," I say. "Mother told me. He was poisoned by his enemies. She doesn't wish you to know, because she's afraid it will make you a reckless king, but now you know. I've told you. I've given you this card to hold. Now you have to do the same for me."

His hand trembles as he reaches for mine, hoarse pain in his question. "How can this be?"

I explain as much as I can, about Father allowing ideas to flourish, how he didn't wish to punish those who spoke against him in secret, but I don't mention the buried rumour of Father not being royal. I won't give Reni a reason to doubt. I won't let any poison fester.

The truth breaks over him, my revelations hitting like stones, heavy, and his shoulders droop. Perhaps he's feeling foolish for ever entertaining the protesters' concerns, for speaking against Mother.

Perhaps I've shown him his own shame.

"Thank you for telling me," he says, voice thin with grief. His hand squeezes mine. "And in return, I'm to stall this engagement?"

"Any way that you can, Reni."

"Of course."

And I believe him. I wrap my arms round him tightly, forever in love with his firm and gentle nature. He puts on a good show of being ironclad, of being proud, but inside he's all Father, too earnest for this shifting world. Wanting it to be better and more orderly. More kind.

There's a soft knock on the door and Heathwyn's troubled face appears.

Reni deposits his sorrow somewhere deep inside, hidden, and stands quickly, bidding me good night.

Tonight will not be an easy one for him.

Alone with Heathwyn, I await a lecture, something about how I am too old to be abandoning my mother's table so childishly, then locking myself away, but instead her lips purse. "I may regret giving this to you, lamb, but I haven't the heart to keep it on me any longer."

She produces an opened envelope and hands it over. *"Aurelia"* is written on the front in small, rushed letters, no address anywhere, no other name.

I tug out the paper and unfold it. My heart flips. "It's from the Lieutenant."

"Yes. He gave it to me before he left. He asked if he could write you and I was thoughtless enough to hesitate." She sighs. "He did look very hopeful."

My exhaustion gives way to pure joy spiraling like lights. "He says he misses me, Heathwyn, and that he'll try to write me, even from Thurn! He says he'll never forget the way my smile—"

"Yes, I've read it, though I quite wish I hadn't. I should have thrown it away."

"But you didn't," I say, tracing the paper with a finger.

"I didn't," she replies, frowning at her own charity.

"You can't tell Mother. Please don't, Heathwyn."

She gives a deep sigh. "You have everything, but I think you deserve one thing all your own. Don't give me a reason to regret it, sweet girl."

I'm already rereading the letter, the words written in wavering cursive, endearing in their sloppiness. "He's going to send me an address as soon as he can. Hand me some paper, please! And a pen. I need to have a letter ready to go. I hope he doesn't think I've forgotten him. I wonder if he's already left across the sea?" I look up. "Tell me, Heathwyn. Do you believe the General can make the Nahir agree to peace? Do you think they might see his army and give up before there's even a fight?"

She kisses my head, handing me a pen. "This war is young and doesn't yet know what it wants. There's time for all things hopeful."

I'm determined to believe her.

I'll believe it until the very day the earth opens up and swallows me whole.

26

⊰ ATHAN ⊱

Havenspur, Thurn

During our four days at sea, I've scoured every level of the *Pursuit*, an obsession born of claustrophobia. I have to know where it all goes. The ship's a maze of narrow passageways, leading up and down with ladders and railways and metal steps, salt clinging to the dank air, the whole thing rolling side to side in the large waves. There's not much else to do. Cyar writes love sonnets to his girlfriend when he thinks I'm not looking, and the other Moonstrike pilots mostly ignore us. They served in Karkev together and have their own inside jokes. Their own private camaraderie. The only moment of excitement is when a flare appears in the inky night, the *Impressive* discovering the bloody aftermath of an arms exchange gone badly. We don't see anything of it. But it's still a pleasant welcome to the South.

When Thurn materializes on the horizon, the frayed coast is a damn relief. Waves crash on broken rocks, a brilliant gold sun lowering beyond. The *Impressive* blasts her horn as we enter Havenspur's harbour. Promenades meander along the shore, shaded by long-leafed trees, buildings of cream and sienna rising up, towers twisted and roofs decorated with broad arches. The *Pursuit* is quickly moored at a dock closer to the city. Next to her waits a local supply ship, the sailors on board the smaller vessel watching us disembark with vacant eyes. They rest against metal boxes, unhurried, tanned faces shining in the sun.

As we stand on the humid wharf, waiting for our hosts, an armed Landorian soldier orders something at them in Thurnian.

They shrug, bang the containers, then shrug again.

The Landorian looks chagrined.

Unsure what to do, we pretend not to notice. Sweat pools quickly on my neck and tiny bugs try for my ears. Ollie removes his officer's cap, fanning his face with it, and the other Moon-strike pilots group around him, their backs to us, as usual.

"I wonder what sort of snakes they've got here," Cyar says to me curiously, analyzing the strange, lush world just off the dock.

"Please don't go looking."

"Oh, don't worry." He grins. "They'll find us."

Right when Cyar's about to go for a search anyway, three mo-torcars cut their engines on the road, and a short, stocky fellow steps out of the first. He's dressed in uniform, fair cheeks burnt from the sun. He attempts pacing grandly down the dock to us, though he doesn't quite have the build for it. "Gentlemen, I'm Major Wick. Welcome to Havenspur."

He shakes Garrick's hand and the two of them discuss the logistics of our fighters' arrival, further along the coast, close to the airbase, then they motion us to the cars.

Kalt's up on the *Pursuit*'s forward deck, and I wave goodbye. He nods with what might be a smile. It's difficult to tell from below. Then again, sometimes it's difficult to tell with Kalt up close.

We're soon rolling into the downtown sprawl of Havenspur. It's larger than it looked from the water, unfurling itself slowly as we rumble over patchy cobblestone and deeper into a warm maze of large colonnades, fancy motorcars, and women in wide-brimmed hats. Graceful buildings line the road, flecked with scaling paint—teal and coral and bronze—their bruises concealed by bright flowers. Ornate brass fences shelter billowing orange trees and patios for tea. It would almost be Norvenne if not for the many soldiers easing among the crowds, rifles slung

over their shoulders, observing the late afternoon current with
discreet precision.

Ollie rolls the front window down. Hot, fragrant air seeps into
the car. "The girls here are quite pretty," he observes, nodding
appreciatively at one with a dress almost above her knees. He
throws his officer's cap back on.

The Landorian orderly behind the wheel chuckles. "Havenspur's one perk, isn't it? The ladies in this city come from good
stock. Nobility, even. Did you know General Windom is a second cousin of His Majesty? His family was one of the first to
settle here. He's a good man, knows the land well."

Ollie's still tossing suggestive smiles out the window, distracted.

"Do the people here consider themselves Landorian, then?" I
ask from the backseat.

"Yes and no." The man brakes to let soldiers pass. "Somewhere in the middle, I suppose. But they're loyal to the crown,
of course."

"Then why all the rifles?"

The man catches my eye in the rearview mirror. "Some are
less in the middle."

When we pull through the metal gates of the airbase, guards
salute from their posts. A large flag above parades a winged lion
with a crown between its teeth. We're now on a flat, open ridge
above the city, dusty with few trees, everything orange in the
setting sun. Four wooden barracks, three curved hangars, and
one long runway oscillate in the heat. A lone stone building, elegant but still bleached and weathered, sits apart from the rest,
encircled by rosebushes.

"Welcome," Wick says with pride, "to the centre of my fighter
command, home of the 10th Squadron Lion's Paw. Captain Carr,
you and your first officer will come with me to HQ." He waves
at the elegant place. "The rest of your men may settle in the west
barracks. Hard to get lost here, but if there's any confusion,

check with the pilots." He points at a group of men sitting in rickety chairs by the nearest hangar, playing cards.

"You heard him, then," Garrick says to Moonstrike. "Get everything in order before dinner."

He and Ollie follow after the Major. The other Safire pilots shoulder their packs, wipe their sweaty foreheads, and head off. No invitation offered to us.

I turn in a circle. Faded green hills stretch east and south, nothing on them but a few smudges that might be little buildings or villages or maybe just barren patches of earth. Beyond that—who knows?

Cyar shades his eyes. "I think we should make some friends," he observes, studying the men playing cards. "Otherwise it might get lonely here."

He's right. It's doubtful Moonstrike will even look at us until we've shot down an enemy plane. And in Havenspur, that might take a while.

We march across the deserted runway for the lounging pilots. No airplanes out. No mechanics in sight. Faint music drifts from one of the hangars, a girl singing, so it's probably on the wireless.

The pilots don't notice our approach. One looks about Arrin's age, his feet stretched out before him, a black cat resting on his shoulders. It watches us arrive with yellow-moon eyes.

"You fellows the 10th?" I ask brightly in Landori.

They turn, cigarettes smoking in their hands.

I motion at Cyar. "Officer Hajari and I just arrived. We're wondering where the west barracks are?"

Wind whips through the thirsty grass at our feet. They continue to stare, like I'm speaking Savien.

"Need a compass?" one finally asks.

"Already have one," I say.

"Then you see that setting sun? Follow it."

They chuckle behind cards.

After the cramped days at sea, this is too much. "Listen, we—"

"I'm Baron," a square-jawed pilot interrupts. "You are?"

"Lieutenant Erelis."

"A little officer, hm?" He stands, analyzing me. "Are you with the unnecessary Safire contingent sent to give us the help we don't need?"

I glance at my uniform. "No, I'm with the rebel Nahir unit sent to give you more headache."

Baron steps near, nasty stink of sweat smothering me. "Listen, son, we've done well enough on our own without you fellows. Soon this matter will be back under control, then you and your fancy aeroplanes can turn round and head home."

"I'd be fine with that."

"Of course you would." He pauses, thick brows drawing together. "But since they've sent you over here anyway, might as well borrow some of your brandy. How much have you got?"

"I'm sorry?"

"Dear God, your General better not have sent only bullets. Tell me you brought the important things too!"

Amusement twists his lips, and I look around at the seated pilots and realize they're all hiding laughter. One snorts out loud.

"I'll see what I can do," I say, unsure what's going on.

Baron slaps my arm, grinning. "Glad at least two of you fools were brave enough to come over. Sit down. Do you play?"

"Baron, they were looking for the barracks," says a much younger pilot with brown skin and matching eyes. "Someone should be friendly and show them the way."

"I'm about to win this round. I'm not leaving until it's finished."

The one with the cat around his shoulders stands, and it lands gracefully, slinking beneath the metal chair. "I'm Captain Efan Merlant," he says to me. "Welcome, Headache."

Damn, he's the captain? I salute quickly, as does Cyar, but he waves us off. "We'll get you settled, Lieutenant. Greycap, you sounded the most concerned. Show them the way."

The young one, Greycap, jumps up. "Yes, sir."

"Don't let anyone around here give you more trouble than this," Merlant tells us. "They'll answer to me if they do."

"Thank you, sir," I say.

He nods, blue eyes looking me over, and I wonder if he knows the sort of headache I really am. The Dakar sort.

But Greycap is waving us across the compound, so we follow after him. He's our age and enthusiastic, his mouth and feet moving rapidly, cheerfully revealing he's one of the best pilots here. For some reason, it doesn't sound like bragging from him. He says he's called Greycap because they all go by call-signs. No one uses his real name, Nazem La'hile. His family is from Thurn, and his grandfather joined the Landorian forces sixty years ago. They've been loyal to the crown ever since. Local Thurnian recruits, he says, used to wear grey caps to distinguish them. Hence his call-sign.

"What are yours?" he asks eagerly.

"Don't have any yet," Cyar replies, with equal enthusiasm. He's already won over.

Greycap appears incredulous for a moment, hopping up the barrack steps. "That better change soon. Otherwise we'll just have to call you Safire One and Safire Two." He laughs, like the idea is incredibly funny and we should be laughing, too.

Cyar obliges.

Inside, our new friend points out the recreation room, the small mess, then the showers and latrine. "I hope you've been taking those pills from the medic. Otherwise you might end up spending a lot more time in here, on your knees." He smirks. "Don't drink the water. You're not as hardy as me."

Then he marches us to the tiny room we'll share. One bunk and a closet. It's not much bigger than the one on the boat. After he leaves, taking the force of his energy with him, we settle quietly into yet another new room, the wind creaking lazily through wooden frames. I throw my bag on the top bunk, then make sure to check every corner for snakes.

"They like warm places," Cyar reveals cryptically, a towel around his shoulders as he disappears into the hall with a grin.

I know he's lying. I think.

I pull out the two letters I wrote while at sea and sit by the window, keeping my feet off the floor, safe from the shadows beneath the bed. I wonder if the governess gave Ali my first letter, and if she'll give her these. Perhaps it's all for nothing. Ali's dark eyes tease my thoughts, luring me to that last moment of our dance. Her mouth close and tempting, begging me to be weak for just a moment. So close.

I thud my head against the dusty window.

I hate regrets.

I look out at the South, at the unfamiliar world waiting for me, and even though I'm used to strange streets and sharp corners, grey places I don't want to be, now that I've tasted Ali and those mountains and the whisper of freedom, all of this leaves me dissatisfied. More than usual.

All I see is wasted years stretching into an unknown horizon.

Our first dinner's a tense affair. The mess is divided down the middle, Landorians on one side, Safire on the other, with the officers dining separately. Since Cyar and I don't actually have our own squadron yet, we're left with the rest.

In the name of diplomacy, we head for the Landorians.

"This is Safire One and Safire Two," Greycap announces as we sit.

Baron raises his brow. "That might get confusing in the air."

"How about Light and Dark?" a wiry blond suggests, giving us a sly glance.

Greycap frowns. "Be respectful, Spider. They're officers."

The other pilots chuckle behind mugs of ale. They're at least five years our senior, if not more. I might need to start telling the Landorians I'm twenty-one. Could probably get away with that, and I'm certain the Safire pilots won't rat me out. They're already not supposed to admit my real name under pain of the firing squad.

We eat while conversation bounces around like nonstop flick-rolls. They all idolize Captain Merlant, or Knight, as he's known in the air. Then they share their signs with us—Runyan, Gallop, Prince—and though I press for information on what it's like down here, the sort of action they've seen, they all dance around the topic and try to get me drunk instead. They start listing the things they miss most back home. Spider roars with laughter as Baron continues to take his crude answers a notch seedier, voices getting louder with every swig of drink. The Safire pilots ten feet away glare, so the Landorian pilots call to them, which they ignore, which only makes the Landorians try harder. Then the door to the mess opens and Merlant steps through.

"What's this noise about, boys?" he asks his pilots. "I can hear you well across the compound."

Baron has a sheepish smile. "Talking about home, sir."

"It's more than that, Baron. Don't play me here."

"Women. Just women."

"All poetry, I'm sure."

"What do you miss most about home, sir?"

The Captain picks up Baron's mug and takes a swallow. He's distinguished now in his silk neckerchief and dress coat embroidered with the royal crest. Far from the relaxed pilot stretched out earlier. "I miss rainstorms when the sun shines through. For a few moments, everything's vibrant and alive with colour. Two worlds meeting. Then gone again." He pauses. "Also my wife. And many other things."

"See what a lover he is?" Baron jokes, but there's admiration in his voice.

Merlant smiles. His gaze drifts around the table, stopping on me. I'm sure he knows who I am. Wick must have told him. But his stare is different from most. There's no scrutiny, no expectation. The blue eyes are faintly curious. He gives Baron the mug back. "Try not to drive our new friends away." Then he offers a respectful nod to the Safire pilots.

Just as quietly as he came, he goes back through the door. I ignore protocol and follow after him. Bold, perhaps, but it's what I've learned. Outside, it's still warm in the darkness, and he's stopped at the top of the wooden stoop, as if waiting for me. The two of us stand beneath the ghostly compound lights.

"You do look like trouble, Headache," he says, gesturing at my eye. There's still a faint mark there.

I debate lying, but figure the truth is absurd enough to sound like a lie. "A prince gave me that. You know how they are."

He chuckles, lighting a cigarette and passing it to me. I wave it away. We're facing southwest, inland, and there's a hazy smattering of lights on the horizon. The limits of Havenspur and then darkness.

"Your name's Efan," I observe. "Like the famous prince?"

"The very one. My father's quite a proud monarchist."

"Then please don't hold it against me, because mine is quite the opposite." It's a test, a hesitant one, to see what he'll say, but he only smiles, eyes still focused ahead. Reassured, I continue. "Tell me, Captain. What are we up against down here? No one seems eager to lay it out for us."

"We'd rather not frighten you fresh from the ship."

"I've already built this up in my head to be miserable. You might as well tell me how it is."

He turns. "Why these questions now? Your squadron will be briefed in the morning."

"Because I want to hear the things you won't tell them."

The statement's presumptuous. Arrogant, even. But again, it's what I've learned, so I wait, and he considers me a moment before nodding. He sweeps a hand towards the darkness. Brass lion cuff links glint on his wrists. "Out there is them. In here is us. That's how it's always been, and perhaps how it always will be. But we won't give up Thurn. It belongs to us."

"If it's that simple, Captain, then Hady should be back in your hands. The Nahir are armed, but surely not enough to keep the Imperial Navy at bay? One siege and it would be over."

"Isn't that the question?" He gives a grim smile. "Let me tell you my story first, Lieutenant. Four years ago, our squadron was deployed here to support ground patrols—reconnaissance, flyovers, that sort of thing. The occasional rebel pilots we encountered were easy victories for us. Miserable aircraft, poorly trained. The Nahir didn't have any support. The South is divided, you see. The nations around Thurn are isolationists. Keep to their own interests." He flicks the cigarette. "But things have changed as of late. We've been attacked by planes with no colours on the wings, and they've downed some of ours. The squadron nearest Hady captured a pilot alive last week. Didn't speak a word of Thurnian."

I frown. "Where was he from?"

"Who knows? Wouldn't admit a damn thing, only spoke in Landori when he was . . . well, when he was pressed for answers."

Neither of us speaks. "Where do you believe he was from, Captain?"

I know I'm pushing too far, but I'm afraid I already know the answer.

"With such splendid aircraft and skill?" He swallows, cigarette forgotten. "There's only one place here that can even begin to rival us, Lieutenant. The one place that has shared in our wealth and our history."

Resya.

He doesn't say it aloud, but it's the only thing that makes sense. The one kingdom here with the resources to wage real war. A solid infrastructure, a functioning air force. A king with Northern blood, who swears he'd never aid Seath, who claims to be on our side . . . And then I remember that Sinora is Resyan, and I feel a deep chill in the heat.

This whole thing might be far bigger than even I thought.

"You ask why we're waiting," Merlant says eventually, "and the truth is, I don't know. I think only your father can answer that. If you find out . . ."

I manage a grin. "I sure as hell won't be the one he tells."

Merlant laughs. "Not easy being youngest, is it?"

"Better than eldest."

Somewhere out in the barren hills, an eerie cry echoes, high-pitched, then lowering to a haunting trill. I take a step towards the door.

"*Si'yah* cats," Merlant explains. "You'll get used to the sound."

"They don't attack, do they?"

"Not if you're pure of heart."

I give a questioning look.

"It's local tradition," he says, amused. "But I carry a gun."

"I think I will too."

"Wise." He smiles. "Good night, Lieutenant."

"Good night, Captain."

Merlant goes down the wooden steps, then stops at the bottom. "I've heard you can fly, Lieutenant."

"With no one shooting at me, yes."

"Well, I'm sure you'll do fine. It's a simple trick—always know where your enemy is and always be quicker than him. I'm sure you've learned that well enough in your life."

His words are what I need. Quiet and certain.

We share a final smile before he saunters into the heated dark, and I decide I might just have found someone worth following.

27

Hathene, Etania

The first moment I can, I seek out Lark Gazhirem and catch him alone.

I have a perfect opportunity now, since Reni and Uncle have left for a diplomatic tour of our neighbouring kingdoms, the sort of thing Reni has dreamt of for years but has never been allowed. Mother always felt it was unnecessary. A waste of precious petrol when the Heights have lived in harmony ever since my great-grandfather's treaty. But with this spring of protests, and the General conducting his own profitable tour, Reni convinced the council to put it to a vote. A gracious way of doing it, Uncle said. Something Boreas Isendare would have done.

Opinion was split evenly, until Lord Jerig voted in favour—and asked if he could come along.

Now, they're off for a month on their mission round the Heights, and though Lark's presence clearly needles Mother—and puts the young ladies of court into a curious flutter—he is family, and she won't go against her deeply ingrained sense of Resyan hospitality, even offering the customary kiss on his cheek each time she sees him—all of which means he won't be banished anytime soon.

With Reni doing his part to make us look entirely Northern, I seize this chance to investigate our new cousin and find out exactly what he knows. If Lark holds the possibility of peace, real peace, when Athan's already bound for Thurn, then I have to explore it or else I'll never forgive myself.

I find Lark hiding in the parlour of his guest room, a map spread on the table before him, a bottle of Etanian wine open and mostly consumed. He's wearing his usual white buttoned shirt. It's open casually at the neck, the way a student of the university might dress. He has the clever ability to look very refined and intelligent and earthy.

He stands when I enter.

"Cousin," he greets, forgoing formality.

I shake off irritation, determined to play my role well. Yes, there's a sullen arrogance to him, a restlessness, but he's also now my blood, and that's rather fascinating. It must count for something.

"Tell me about your proposal," I say, conveying as much diplomacy as I can. "I want to understand it and how it might bring peace."

He raises his brow, fingers twirling a pen. His face isn't unappealing—it's actually rather handsome and slender, catlike, like Mother's. "You?"

"Of course."

The dark brow rises higher. I think he sees me as a princess with no thoughts in her head, the same way Athan believed I spend my days getting servants to paint my picture, and it irritates me further.

It's so far from the truth.

"Listen," I say, "you can believe me or not, but I'm the only one my mother will listen to. If you wish her to be convinced of it, you'd best tell me."

He finally looks intrigued, motioning me to the table.

I oblige, immediately suffocated by gingery musk.

"I'll try to make this as clear for you as I can," he says. "Stop me if I get ahead of myself."

"I think I can manage."

His glance is a subtle challenge, and he gestures to the South on his map. "Tell me, then, why everyone wants to call this place their own."

He hardly waits for an answer before opening his mouth again, apparently expecting me to say nothing, but I cut him off. "It's the Harosh," I say, pointing at the territory far down the meandering line of the Izahar River, deep into what's nearly the ends of the earth. "That's where the treasure is said to be found. Gold and copper. Iron and cobalt and diamonds. All kinds of wealth, the things many Northern men have chased but never succeeded in reaching."

Lark appears impressed. "You read your books."

"I'm studying for the exams. There's also a rather depressing aria my friend likes to sing about ill-fated lovers long ago, where the girl was killed by her father and the boy, a knight, was banished to fight there. It seems we find it both a terrible and wonderful place."

"It is," Lark agrees.

In truth, this is all I know of the Harosh. No one mentions it. It's more a myth.

"But what does this have to do with peace?" I ask.

"Nothing immediate," he says, still pleased, "I simply wanted to hear your answer to that question."

I narrow my eyes at him. "I'm not here to play games with you. If you'd like a history lesson, I can bring my textbooks next time."

"I'd be curious to see what's there."

"Lark, what is your father's proposal for peace?"

He pauses, fiddling with the edge of the map. "Tell me about Resya first."

I suck in a breath, trying to save patience, but he seems bent on historical and geographical discussion, circling whatever hope-filled idea he's dangling. "Resya? It's the jewel of the South. Lush in the north, filled with mountains, and trickling to desert in the south. It has gardens and arid steppes and grand operas."

"And does our king fight the Nahir? Does he love the North?"
I hesitate, unsure if this is a trap or not.

Lark lowers his voice. "The answer, Cousin, is he does not. He won't help his royal friends. He's been betrayed by both North and South, left to fend for himself, and he will bleed for neither cause."

The truth of this statement is blunt and startling. I know Resya has been, at best, tolerated as a fellow royal kingdom, and at worst, suspect of being too weak, with the unhelpful sentiment growing round it. But now Lark is telling me these alarming facts with no pretense. No mystery or question about it.

King Rahian is refusing to fight the Nahir cause.

"Are you telling the truth?" I ask. "If so, you cannot speak a word of it here. I beg of you!"

Something melancholy settles on Lark's face, a tad sympathetic. "You are my blood, Cousin. I only tell you the truth. But sooner or later, the North will figure out the game. Rahian has refused to allow Northern armies to launch from his borders. Instead, they're forced to sail all the way to Havenspur, here." He indicates on the map. "From there they have protected routes to transport supplies inland. A narrow point of advance. It's been generations since a large enough force amassed to attempt further south. But now there are aeroplanes and armoured carriers. In this new war, swift armies will bring victory, and using Resya's wide border as a staging ground could make the difference."

"And your father's proposal?"

"To sway Rahian's neutrality. To allow the Safire and Northern armies into his realm and bring about a shorter conflict. Your mother could do this."

Realizing he still means to implement war, I sigh at the map in frustration. "You lured me here with a different promise," I say. "You said there was a way to peace."

A long pause quiets the room. "There is."

I glance up, hungry for hope.

"Negotiation," he explains.

"Negotiate?" I ask, now confused. "With who?"

He hesitates. "The Nahir."

"The *Nahir*!"

I'm gaping at him as his warm hand finds my arm, gripping firmly. "Yes, Cousin. Listen to me. Seath has never been allowed to make his case to the Royal League. No one from our cause has ever been allowed to speak the truth of what's happening. But if they could share their side, perhaps then the North—all of you, so far away—would see our dark reality. You'd see what I have seen."

His dogged gaze is terrible bait. "And what, exactly, have you seen?"

"Those ridiculous feathers being worn in Landore? They're from the golden pheasants of Thurn. Beautiful birds with a long, scarlet plume. The Landorians have taken to slaughtering them and sticking them in their hair, simply because they can. Soon there won't be a single one left." He leans closer, ginger scent curling round us. "And how much else has been taken these past hundred years? Our land? Our traditions? What are bullets in birds next to bullets in people?"

Something sickens within me, alongside disbelief. "How on earth do you know all this?"

He holds his tongue, his earnest gaze struggling between fear and defiance—though of what, I don't know. And then it dawns on me. The passing words he spoke. I feel a deeper horror settling cold on my skin, his hand still gripping my arm like he might convince me by simply not letting go.

"You said Seath has never been allowed to speak to the League," I whisper. "You said no one from *our* cause has ever been allowed."

His brown eyes flicker. "Yes."

"Stars, you're—"

"Nahir."

He says it so quickly, like a fired bullet, that for a moment it's as if he hadn't spoken at all. I stare at him. The roundness of his face, a pink blush creeping beneath the olive tone of his skin. The way he swallows tightly, uncertainty beneath the defiance. I sit there, stunned, and realize he's as stunned and bewildered as am I.

I'm not sure he meant to say that out loud.

"You . . . ," And I trail off. I have no words, no framework for a confession like this.

He offers me the bottle of wine lamely.

"But you're—"

"I simply am," he interrupts, glancing at the closed door, his voice lowering again. "And you can't tell anyone, Cousin. No one knows, not even Havis, but you and I—we're family. I know you'll keep my secret. I want to help you . . . and perhaps you can help me."

"Help how?" I repeat, my overwhelmed voice sounding only half-formed.

The Nahir were not supposed to look like Lark Gazhirem.

"You don't want war, and neither do I," he insists, quietly earnest again. "No one truly does. What I want is a negotiation. The world's finally taking notice of us, desperate to avoid what will come, and now at last is the time. But I can't do this on my own. No one here will listen to me—certainly not your mother. I see that now. But you—"

I shake my head wildly. "I don't understand, Lark. Why the stars would you tell me this?"

"Because you have power! You're young, yes, but I learned how to resist at your age, how to fight. You can, too. The old want to wage war, but we aren't like them, Cousin. We can do better."

"What could I possibly give you?"

"A voice," he says with certainty, like he's perfectly aware of how the world sees him—how *I* see him—and he's fine with it, since he is only himself. His energy becomes his honesty. "Your mother's voice, in particular. It could be the one we need, someone who comes from both worlds, who has allies on every side. Not everyone needs to pick up a rifle to fight. Not every battle looks the same. She could plead our case if you showed her the truth. You said she'd listen to you." He swallows again. "I know you want to protect your family's reputation, and yourself, but what about the rest of us? What about everyone beyond this palace?"

It's too familiar, an echo of Athan yet again, asking me on the mountaintop if I'd think only of myself. Live forever behind these walls and do nothing. I stare at the map on the table before us, where the world looks wonderfully safe and simple. Divided with lines and colours, the soft, small hearts entirely invisible.

Lark clears his throat. "There's also the matter of your uncle's debt. . . ." I freeze, and he looks equally uncertain, which does nothing to reassure me. "I know he still owes Seath money, and you should understand that Seath doesn't let betrayals go, not when there is so much to gain. A Northern royal family is valuable leverage."

He offers no hope, only the truth.

I close my eyes to the devastating reality before me, this world with too much at stake. We're ensnared either way. In debt not only to the Nahir but with a family member in its ranks. And if Lark is one, then what about Lark's father? And his siblings? And everyone else? If this truth spread on the wind—Sinora Lehzar, Queen of Etania, blood to Nahir fighters—it would be far worse than any feeble connection to Resya's questionable loyalties.

This would ruin her. Forever.

Unless . . .

"Let me simply talk with you," Lark says urgently. "You want to talk. That's why you found me here. So I'll tell you what I know, and at the end, you can decide if it's worth your neck on the line to speak on my behalf. Our behalf," he adds, and I'm

not sure if he means the two of us, or the Nahir, or all of the
South itself. He pauses. "Not all of us can be like your father,
Cousin. Not all of us can choose to hide from the world. We
have to live with it, darkness and all."

I let out a trembling, terrified breath.

"Do you truly believe this, Lark? That Seath would speak to
my mother? To the North?"

It sounds too impossible.

But Lark nods fervently. "I do, Aurelia. I do. Your mother is
one of us. And Seath . . . he's old. He's weary. Everyone's tired
down there, even the Landorians, and Seath is ready to take any
gamble he must. Let a truce be reached. But the Safire? They
are young. They'll bring fresh air to the flames, stir the South
far beyond Thurn, and how can anyone escape that alive? The
North will suffer as much as any. Their General is a tyrant. Too
good at war and too ambitious to stop."

It's a mirror of what Reni said months ago. To hear it repeated,
from one on the other side, only frightens me more, solidifying
itself into an inevitable truth. But then that fact frustrates me
further. I'm tired of anticipating the worst, of bracing for our
family's condemnation. Of never acting and always despairing.
This can't be all there is to life—surrendering to terror, allowing a few desperate men to dictate who lives and dies, dictate
when there should be war and when peace. What if they all sat
down for only a moment? What if they stopped long enough to
hear one another out? Couldn't my mother undo the wrong by
negotiating good?

Perhaps my wayward cousin is actually right. Perhaps there's
another move to make.

"Talk to me then," I say. "I can at least listen."

28

❧ ATHAN ❦

Havenspur, Thurn

Major Wick gives a briefing in the ops room before our first flight up. Pacing before a map of the South, he carries on for an hour about land grabs, city divisions, broken treaties, and stalemates. It's a complex situation. A lot of names punctuated with swearing. Resya is an erstwhile ally—isolationist, now, and refusing to allow Landorian army boots into the kingdom. Myar was once under Landore's control, but they lost it during their retreat north fifty years ago. Masrah was Thurn's neutral neighbour—quiet and ambivalent—until it wasn't. And Thurn itself has four different territories, each in various states of upheaval.

"The people round Havenspur are quite likable," Wick says. "They appreciate our hard work, what we've done for them. It's the ones farther out." He waves his hand, sweeping east to west. "They can't be trusted."

Generally speaking, he's just pointed at the entire map.

"And Seath?" a Safire pilot asks. "Does he have any sympathy near Havenspur?"

"Seath," Wick responds darkly, "could talk a prince into trading his own crown for a bloody rifle. So yes, I'd imagine he does have sympathy here. I always plan for the worst, gentlemen. I trust no one."

I can't help feeling a bit bad for Greycap. He's seated next to me and Cyar, and didn't need to be in this briefing, since it's all

.for the Safire. But he came anyway, showing us to the mugs of coffee, poking us into the right chairs, and now he has to sit and listen to someone disparage most of his countrymen.

"It's not that bad," he assures Cyar and me under his breath. "Wait until you taste *mezra*!"

We all grin—Greycap because he's excited, Cyar because he's always intrigued by new food, and me because the whole thing's contagious—then Wick growls at us to pay attention, the older pilots giving us unimpressed looks, and we shut our mouths and straighten quickly.

A board near the door has the Moonstrike squadron divided into different groups, call-signs written in chalk, and we walk over with our nearly empty coffee mugs. Garrick and Ollie are at the top—Falcon and Hawk. Never anything subtle with them. The other pilots locate their names, laughing about who's going up with who.

Two extra names are scrawled at the bottom of the first flight—Charm and Fox. That must be us.

Garrick claps a hand on my shoulder. "Ready, Charm?"

"I thought for sure I was the Fox," I reply.

"No, too obvious. If we want the enemy to go after a plane, we have to make sure it's Hajari's."

I turn to object, then realize he's laughing behind us. "Arrin picked the name for you," he explains. "He said you'd be my little good luck charm in the skies. I sure as hell hope he's right."

I ignore that. Probably a taunt rather than a compliment, coming from Arrin.

He motions gamely for the door. "Let's go meet the ladies."

We march outside and the morning heat's already brewed full force. Garrick directs me to the nearest hangar, then takes Cyar across the runway to another. The Moonstrike pilots have already found their fighters, and only one remains lonely, shining in the light, calling to me. I zip my flight suit, excitement kicking into gear. Also some nerves.

A middle-aged man with blond hair waits by the nose. His pants have oil stains, the Safire crest stitched to his grey shirt. "A nice day for flying, Lieutenant," he calls.

I nod, confused by his familiar address.

"I'm Filton," he says, "your chief mechanic. Arrived last night from Brisal." He jabs his thumb at a thin, freckled boy behind him. "And that's Kif, your rigger."

Right, my new ground crew. The perks of being in a squadron even though it hardly feels earned yet.

I extend a hand, trying to seem confident, older. "Pleasure to meet you, Chief."

He responds with a firm grip. "No, pleasure to meet you, sir. I'm only here to keep the engine running smooth so you don't have to worry at 10,000 feet." He winks.

"Appreciate it," I say, laying a reverent hand on the sun-warmed metal. The underside of each wing is painted with a large black sword. Machine guns point from the nose, twin cannons mounted on either wing, and the thick armoured plating from nose to tail inspires courage. This isn't the tame plane I learned to fly on. This is a weapon.

"Charm, quit daydreaming and get your ass inside," Garrick hollers on his way by.

As always, he's a joy to train with.

I run through my rituals quickly—tightening the flight boots, pulling on leather gloves, buckling the life vest—and Filton works his way around the plane, testing each flap with approving comments. Kif follows and nods.

"Everything good, Chief?" It seems like a question I should ask.

He pats the fuselage. "Ready, sir. We tested her earlier, and she gave a little growl of protest after her days at sea. Purring soon enough. I'll be sure to shine her when you get back. She'll be the prettiest plane in the sky, I promise."

His enthusiasm further bolsters my confidence. I've really got my own ground crew—two of them, even.

Not bad!

He helps me buckle the heavy parachute, then I climb into the cockpit and settle myself. Everything's in order. I pump the primer, flick the engine, and she comes to snarling life with a slight jump, the propeller spinning to a blur on the nose. Filton gives a thumbs-up. Then he and Kif place a hand on either wing, guiding me onto the open tarmac. They let go and offer a last salute.

On my own now.

Garrick orders a check-in over the radio. Six pilots altogether in the first flight. We're flying in formations of three, one plane leading each, and I'm playing right wingman to Ollie for the day. The flank of his plane has three black strikes on it. Three shot down in Karkev.

"We're first," Ollie announces.

"Copy that, Leader," says the other pilot, Sailor, on his left side.

I grip the throttle, ready to release. "Copy that, Leader."

Control gives clearance and we open up. The planes leap forward, engines roaring, and I barely hang on as my plane hurtles down the runway and fights to be airborne. No choice but to let her have her way. She storms up into the blue like a wild grey horse, streaming smoky wake.

Goddamn, this plane's fast!

My pulse races and I struggle to keep her flying straight in the wind, wobbling a bit as I adjust to her whims. We climb rapidly. Already at 2,000 feet. The earth below changes to the blue of the sea, naval ships appearing like little toys playing games on the waves.

"Don't let her push you around too much, Charm," Ollie says from ahead.

I hear his laughter, which only fuels my determination. Might as well try a quick roll to the right. It's been too long since my last time in the sky and the glory of it's overwhelming. Addicting. I spin away from Sailor, my plane wing over wing before I've barely finished the thought.

Incredible!

She's a creature designed for battle. Cunning and fast, no hesitation anywhere. I'm grinning ear to ear.

"Charm, quit those maneuvers without permission," Ollie orders. "This isn't a damn circus."

"Sorry, Leader." I swing her back into position off his right side, but not before waggling the wings, just to see how she handles.

Perfection.

9,000 feet. 10,000 feet.

I've got her steady now, confidence growing.

"Careful in the wind up here," Ollie says. "Keep close to me, Charm."

"Will do, Leader."

"And watch your slip while you're at it."

My slip? I frown behind the oxygen mask. I've been accounting for the crosswind just fine, adjusting the rudders. I clench the stick and follow after him.

For our first authorized maneuver, we do a curving dive, one after the other. Sailor escapes critique, but I'm not so lucky.

"Trim yourself, Charm. Airspeed increased too much on that bank."

It sure as hell did not. I was steady the entire way through, no sideslip to right or left, but I bite my tongue. "Understood, Leader."

Next a roll at 1,000 feet. Low enough to leave no room for error.

Again, I fail.

"A little late coming off it, Charm. You trying to go for a swim?"

God, I could shoot Ollie out of the damn sky right now!

The formations of three spread out, running through mock

fights in rapid succession. I spot Cyar pulling out of the same inverted roll.

"Nicely done, Fox," Garrick says over the radio. "Speed well-maintained."

I grind my teeth in frustration. All my moves are perfect. Easy in, quick out. No room for complaint. But the Moonstrike pilots pretend not to see, accusing me of whatever flaws they can find, telling me to get it right or get out of the way. Too much thrust, not enough altitude, light on the trim.

I give up and start doing my own maneuvers. To hell with Ollie's "no circus" rule.

On my final wingover, I lower my flaps abruptly, slowing and dropping, cutting far too close to him.

Ollie brakes hard. "Good God, Charm! I'm not the damn enemy. Stay clear, would you!"

Serves him right.

We land and I roll to a halt near the hangar.

Filton waves eagerly. "That was a fine display, sir! The squadron's in top form, isn't it?"

I jump down from the wing without a word. Across the tarmac, one of the Moonstrike pilots is giving Cyar an encouraging clap on the shoulder, and jealousy burns.

Filton coughs. "I'll just settle her in, then." He motions to Kif.

The two of them scurry off and my eyes fix on Garrick and Merlant. They're conferring together by the base, glancing at us two rookies, then Garrick waves me over.

Watch your mouth, Erelis.

God, not only am I talking to myself, I'm referring to myself as the phantom who doesn't exist. This is bad.

"What was that flying about?" Garrick asks when I arrive. "You sure you won Top Flight?"

I restrain anger, barely. "There wasn't anything wrong with it, Captain."

"That's not what it looked like from Ollie's perspective."

"He's blind!"

"So you decide to go off and do your own thing?" Garrick shakes his head, rubbing sweat from his red hair. "You going to act like this when you're frustrated in a dogfight?"

There are a lot of very irreverent things I'd like to say to him right now. They almost snarl free, but Merlant's silent, steady gaze stops me.

"This is exactly what I said would happen," Garrick declares. "There's too much of that pride in him."

Merlant gives a slight nod.

That pride.

That Dakar pride is what he means, and the conclusion stings.

Garrick stalks off towards HQ, leaving the two of us alone, and Merlant adjusts his red and blue silk neck scarf. "I wondered what would happen if I told them to give you hell," he explains.

I swallow, throat suddenly parched. "You asked them to do this?"

"An experiment."

The realization stifles my anger, giving way to shame. "I wasn't trying to cause trouble, Captain. I was just . . ." There are no words, no excuses. Merlant has a way of making it seem unnecessary. He's like Father, but for different reasons.

He shrugs. "You're just very much seventeen," he finishes.

"I'm better than this."

He nods. "I believe you, Lieutenant. And I look forward to seeing it." He pauses. "And that was nice flying up there. Though that last stunt where you nearly took out your own leader? Save it for battle next time." He allows a smile, then heads back the way Garrick went.

I stand alone, wondering what they'll write about me in today's flight report. "Very much seventeen," they'll say, and Father's fiery displeasure will radiate from across the entire sea. Now it really does feel like I've made the wrong move. Loss of

airspeed, late off the roll, and smoking on the ground for everyone to see.

That pride.

Those two words burn worst. I have to do better.

At the end of our first week, Moonstrike is ordered on a trip to
the edge of Havenspur, to gain a better feel for the area. Another piece of our Thurnian education. It's a half-hour drive by
vehicle, reinforcing how deceptively large the city is, the swelling mansions of the promenade giving way to skinny streets and
tight alleys, mostly inhabited by exuberant kids and bored cats.
We're deposited, armed and perspiring, in an open market. The
faint breeze is saturated with smoke and spice. Saffron, pepper,
others I can't place. The buildings around us are inlaid with mosaics, intricate spirals painted above doorways, laundry laid out
to dry on wooden steps. Metal fans spit air through open windows, curtains fluttering.

Beneath the market's fabric canopies, men and women laugh
and chatter, their fingers stitching, smoking, strumming instruments, but their eyes watch us as we walk the square.

Cautiously curious.

I struggle to catch the fragments of wavering conversation, the
offers made by vendors as they barter with customers, some of
them even offering to me. I hardly recognize any of the words
from my lessons, which annoys me. I'm supposed to be good at
this language thing.

"Keep moving," Wick instructs. "They know we don't buy
from them."

That's an easy order to follow when the sellers are old men.
But soon enough, a little boy's tugging at my arm, green eyes
wide and expectant. He opens a case holding golden strands, a
small stone on each end. Necklaces. Not very grand ones, but
still pretty.

"For good luck," he says in Landori, tiny smile bursting with excitement.

I have no choice. I hold out a few coins and let him decide what a strand's worth.

Wick looks back and sighs. "Lieutenant. Don't encourage this."

I ignore him. The boy studies the coins, then carefully extracts two from my palm. I choose a necklace with an amber-coloured stone, and thank him in Thurnian.

He offers me a plucky salute, then he's disappeared into the crowd again.

"Well done!" Greycap announces, his arm around my shoulder. "You got robbed blind. And it doesn't even seem like your colour."

"It was for a good cause," I reply. "And it's not for me."

"Tell me who she is."

"Who says it's a girl?"

"Well, it wouldn't look good on Fox either."

I laugh, slipping the gift into my pocket, and suddenly wonder when, if ever, I'll have a chance to give this to Ali. Frustrated by that realization, I change the subject. "I have no clue what anyone's saying here, Nazem. Are you sure I'm studying the right books?"

"Different dialect out here. They have their roots further south."

"How many dialects are there?"

"In Thurn? Five or six."

God, this place is getting more and more complicated. What's the point in trying? I'll never be on the ground long enough to learn this. I'll be thousands of feet up in the air, where I'm useful. Negotiating down here is an entirely different realm.

Sudden shouts erupt ahead, and my hand quickly falls to the pistol at my side. By an ancient fountain, two young women are arguing with a Landorian soldier of local background. One girl leads the charge, dressed in a flower-print dress and heels, brown hair in a braided knot, as impassioned as the soldier and hurling rapid Thurnian words into his bitter face.

"She says one of our soldiers stole from her display," Greycap explains. "She says her mother is Landorian and we'll be hearing about it."

"You think she's telling the truth?"

Greycap opens his mouth, then shuts it. He shrugs.

No one moves to intervene. Everything's silent in the square.

The soldier switches to Landori and says, "You bleed for Seath!" loud enough everyone can hear, and understand, and the woman hesitates only a second before spitting on his boots. The other girl, much younger, searches the rest of us rapidly, looking for an ally, and her gaze falls on Cyar. I've only made it two steps for him when she flings herself against his chest. Her hands grasp his uniform, appealing in her local dialect, and only a few words register—"Listen, Savient" and "Help me, Captain."

Cyar appears stunned by the girl suddenly in his arms.

I reach his side and she glances at me. Her eyes, amber like the necklace, take in my uniform, my face, my fist around the pistol. She says something else to Cyar. I don't understand any of it. Cyar shakes his head at her, visibly torn. He glances at me with a question, but I can't answer it. Neither of us can. This whole place is strange and confusing, filled with rules we don't know.

Landorians. Locals. Nahir.

The vast majority could be one or two or three of those things at once.

Cyar shakes his head again. "Not a captain," he says in Thurnian. "Not a captain."

But it sounds more like an apology.

"They think you Safire are here to save them," Wick says caustically on his way by, striding for the Landorian soldier with spittle on his boots. "We're so wicked and cruel."

He rolls his eyes and a hiss escapes the younger girl. Pushing back, she releases Cyar and runs into the crowd, heels clicking on cobblestone, swallowed by the saffron and smoke. The older girl moves like a cat. With cunning quickness, she snatches the soldier's rifle right from his unsuspecting hands, then her flower-print dress disappears back into the crowd and she's gone.

Local men swiftly close the gap. Staring down Wick.

The Landorian soldier glares at his empty hands.

Everyone else watches silently—above, below, to the side—but now with an edge of anger, their curiosity towards us disappeared.

Anger and betrayal have a palpable feeling.

Somewhere, a female voice begins to serenade the market—soft and clear, echoing off stone walls, luring everyone back to the sunny afternoon—and Greycap gives us a faltering smile. "*Faria*. Only women sing it. Come on, let's listen."

He tugs at our arms.

But I know the truth, and surely Nazem La'hile can see it also. It's too much like Savient. Like Rahmet and Brisal. No one will live forever in subservience, their loyalty forced with a gun. They want something better, as we did. Stuck between worlds, the sides shifting every day, divisions disappearing, colours bleeding together and creating something infinitely more honest and alive and dangerous.

Cyar looks at me.

It feels like true revolution.

VI

EDUCATION

29

Hathene, Etania

Sun warms the deep places of the woods, casting scattered shadows across the dirt trail, filtering through leaves. I fiddle with the reins and press with my legs, and Liberty collects nicely on the bit even as his ears twitch rapidly at the symphony of forest sounds. He's eager as a colt to be outside again. The *jurica* has worked, and I want to kiss Cyar. The groom's impressed enough with Liberty's progress to encourage these slow rides, strengthening his injured leg, and since Reni is currently in Classit, or perhaps Lalia, I'm the one to do it.

Violet trails behind on quiet Ivory. She's a rather helpless rider, perched awkwardly in the saddle, and she keeps jerking at Ivory's mouth every time my mare tries for a passing leaf. They both appear equally exasperated with each other, and I want to apologize to poor Ivory.

"Don't pull so hard," I say, halting Liberty by the river.

"She doesn't listen," Violet protests.

"Because you're confusing her with your cues. You do nothing and then you suddenly yank."

Violet sighs. She doesn't like being hot and sweaty, or wearing pants. Today she has to contend with all three. "Is it true?" she asks instead. "You're touring the University tomorrow with the Ambassador?"

I frown, walking Liberty on. "Who told you?"

"Her Majesty was discussing it with my father. She sounded very pleased."

She was indeed pleased, and also surprised, since I invited Havis along of my own free will. I feigned a desire to get to know my betrothed, but really, I want to find out if he knows the truth about Lark, and if he thinks a negotiation with the Nahir could work. I'll play along with the engagement if it means finding out those answers. I need to know.

Violet seems to believe me, too. "You've finally taken a liking to him, then?"

"He's not so bad. He likes horses." My list of positives ends there. I'll have to work on that.

"But what about the Lieutenant?"

"The Lieutenant?" I ask, like I'd forgotten him altogether.

"Yes, your darling friend, the one you might have got to kiss you if you'd played your angle a little better."

I draw Liberty into a tighter frame. "I'll never see him again, Violet."

"You can't be sure."

"He's only a farm boy."

"Those things don't always matter."

Liberty throws his head, sensing my rising tension through the reins. "Yes, they do matter, Violet," I say, turning in the saddle. We halt. "I don't see any point in giving up someone who has everything for someone who has nothing. It's foolish."

She sucks in an annoyed breath. "Perhaps to some."

I know we're both waiting for the question, so I finally ask, "Have you heard from the Captain?"

It's a mystery I've wondered about since the Safire left, and since I caught her and Reni in the midst of an emotional tangle before he left for the tour, I think I have the right to ask.

It's my brother she's wounding.

"I received a letter this week," she replies, unaffected by my tone.

"And?" It comes out more demanding than I intend.

"He has an uncle in Norvenne with connections to the royal theatre. They're going to see what strings they can pull, to get me an audition, and I should have an answer by the end of summer." Leafy branches flicker light across her resolute face. "I'm planning to go."

Of course he'd fan the flames of her greatest dream. He's clever and Safire.

"What if he's lying?" I ask.

"I trust him." Her look dares me to contest Cock's loyalty, and my hope of talking her back from the edge, for my brother's sake, disappears. "You know nothing about him, Ali. Nothing at all. Garrick hasn't had an easy life. He's very lonely much of the time, and hates to go home."

I resist the urge to roll my eyes.

"His father's quite hard on him," she continues, "always pushing for more. His younger brother is an officer in the Navy, well-accomplished, yet their father's furious that he hasn't been promoted in a year. Family honour rests on their shoulders, and right now Garrick's the one rising. I don't think we can understand what that's like. They must work for everything they earn."

"That doesn't mean he's worth the trouble."

"Trouble? Garrick's brave and honourable, Ali! He willingly puts his life in danger for others. The stories he told me from Karkev were dreadful. He said he once had an oil leak and his engine caught fire. The entire thing went up in smoke, blinding him, and he thought for sure he'd be cooked to death, slowly, like a chicken." She shudders a bit. "There were blisters on his skin."

My stomach clenches. Death in an aeroplane is supposed to be quick. A sudden explosion, then darkness. Being roasted alive, gradually, sounds far more sinister, and the thought of Athan . . .

I can't think of it.

"It's a terrible, noble thing to be a soldier, isn't it?" Violet continues softly, sensing my horror. "I'm sure no one understands. But I tried for him. That's the only thing I thought as I held his body. I imagined how it could soon turn to nothing. How the energy in him, wanting me, needing me, could so quickly disappear."

I frown. "When you held his body?"

She straightens in the saddle. "I mean what I said."

"Violet!"

"Don't look at me like that, Ali. Don't you dare. I'm eighteen years old, and everything was my decision."

Shock gives way to revulsion, the idea of her—my best friend—allowing herself to be used this way. It's beyond improper. It's foolish and impulsive and she's ruined herself without thought! "He has nothing to offer you, Violet. He's an officer and that's all he'll ever be. He won't have wealth, or high status. He'll be gone for months on end, stars know where, and you'll be left behind, wondering every day if he's already dead and the letter simply hasn't reached you yet. Is that what you want?"

I don't care that I could be giving myself the same lecture.

"What if it is?" she replies, eyes fierce. "I'd rather endure a hundred days of uncertainty and love than a lifetime of miserable, wasted days."

"But you might have had a king!"

"Yes, and believe me, he tried before he left! But Reni is *mad*. He thinks he can win me with a crown, but I don't care whether he gets it now or in a year, that's not love. It isn't!"

She cups a hand to her mouth. She knows she's said the wrong thing.

"What do you mean now or in a year?" I demand.

"I don't know what he meant," she says rapidly. "I don't. He was only trying to win me back. Empty promises. I'm sure that's it."

But even she sounds like that's far from the truth. And I know then, at last, what Reni and Uncle have been doing in their secret meetings all these weeks, why they're suddenly off on a tour, presenting the Prince and reminding everyone how very noble and Northern he is.

Reni wants to take his throne early.

Stars in heaven!

I swing down from Liberty and tie him to a nearby oak, then do the same with Ivory. Violet watches from the saddle, bewildered, but I'm already pulling off my shirt, down to my underslip. The boots are next.

"What are you doing?" Violet asks.

"Swimming."

She gapes at the river. "Now?"

I shrug. My pants are already off, bare feet touching cool mud and wet leaves. The banks of the river lined with grass and weeds and *jurica*. Then I throw off the last bit of cotton and jump in. It's magical. Cold and fresh, everything bare and smooth in the water, like a fish. Beneath the surface are muffled sounds. Shivering light above and murky haze below. My hair billows round me, and when I peer at my naked skin through the foggy water I wonder at how strange it really is, holding all these pieces of me together. Pieces that wouldn't exist without my mother or father, my very heartbeat an act of grace from them. And somewhere, unseen in my blood, a fragment of Prince Efan, and beyond that, somewhere distant, the faded colours of Lark and Mother and Resya. This strange, fragile skin holds too much.

We're all mosaics no one sees.

I break the surface again, gulping in air, and find Violet immersed to her neck. Her clothes are in a heap by the bank.

She paddles closer, soaking wet, and I can't tell if it's the river or tears on her cheeks. "You don't understand," she says, pain in her voice. "Everyone thinks I want a crown, but I don't. I want more than that. I don't want to be my mother."

"But your mother is . . ." I don't say the word. *Dead*. It's never a word to be said out loud. I know that well.

Violet nods. "She is. But before that, she fell in love with another man and went to Lalia. She was bored with my father. With me. And so she left." Her lips tremble beneath drops of water. "I'd be happy enough with Reni, and I'd have everything any girl could want. Truly everything this world could offer. He'd be there each day, always loyal, always the same."

I wait.

"But what if that isn't enough, Ali? I won't be like my mother, who left for no reason. I couldn't do that to anyone, certainly not to Reni. Loving the Captain means every day might be my last with him. That's the sort of uncertainty I need. That's the sort of love I want, where it seizes you from head to toe, and you're frightened and breathless and on fire all at once. If I have any of my mother in me, then I know I wouldn't make a proper wife. I feel too much. Perhaps I want too much. But I can't stay here, wondering, when there's even a chance of another life in Norvenne."

Her green eyes beg me to understand, her auburn hair soaked and dark round her pale face. She's holding a mirror up to me and I'm afraid to look. Perhaps her vain dreams aren't worth the trouble, not when there are wars and the Nahir and my own brother quietly betraying our queen, and yet I want as much as she does.

I ache for that chance, too.

"But what if he never comes back for you, Violet?"

It's not an effort to be cruel. It's the truth, and she shrugs, helpless. A frightened, breathless, helpless love. "I'll wait long enough. Then I'll find another way." She swims closer and kisses me on the cheek. "And even if I don't love your brother, I'll always love you. I promise. We were never about him."

She smiles, elegant even naked in a muddy river, and I hope with everything in me that her captain sees how lucky he is, that he deserves her bold and beautiful heart that loves life so warmly.

The next morning, Havis and I take a motorcar to the University grounds. He's dressed in an embroidered maroon jacket and his black hair is brushed smooth. It's as if this is a special outing for the two of us, and the idea is entirely presumptuous. But I play along, as if I'm delighted to be with him, for the sake of the driver and the two armed guards accompanying us.

We drive down the sloping, forested road into Hathene, passing the stately grey homes that belong to those at Mother's court—Lord Marcin, Lord Jerig, and the rest—and over the river bridge. Downtown, people laugh on street corners, riding bicycles, the girls wearing pretty summer dresses cut to the knees. I can't help but gape out the window. I rarely get to see this. They're all fascinating and curious to me, and even though I know the storm has passed, the Safire visit over and gone, it's still a relief to find the city square bright and calm, not a single protester in sight.

"I'm grateful you agreed to have me come along, Princess," Havis remarks with his easy charm. "I can imagine you might have preferred your brother."

"Oh no, Ambassador. I'm spending my afternoon the way I love best—with strange men from foreign countries."

The fake charm lessens. "I knew that feathered creature couldn't hold a secret. I knew it, but it was worth a try anyway."

"Did she give you anything good?"

"Not a word. I asked her if she'd seen you with anyone, and she said no, and when I pressed her further, she said she was 'too busy' and when I asked how busy, she said, 'Oh *very* busy' and smiled in such a way that I admired her for a moment." He looks at me. "Please tell me you weren't also busy."

"Only on some days," I reply, looking out the window again.

I think I hear him chuckle.

A few minutes later, we turn onto a narrow drive and brake beside blossoming lilac bushes. A wide lawn spreads before us, shaded by feathery willow trees, the fieldstone university walls along the farthest edge.

An unexpected sliver of fear jabs inside, and I hesitate when the door swings open to my left. Out there, beyond this motorcar, seems suddenly very open. Exposed. No walls to hide behind, no guards on each corner to ensure loyalty. It's a place I'm not sure I belong.

I'm never outside royal walls.

Havis waits at the door, extending a hand, feigning gallantry. "Shall we, my star?"

I'd like to hit him for that, but it works. I get out, his strong arm quickly round my waist. His irritating confidence manages to make everything else seem small. As we walk the path to the grey walls ahead, I ask him about classes and schedules and exams. It's all for the benefit of the guards following behind, so that they have nothing unusual to report about us, or to gossip with others. And Havis is too good at playing along—smiling in the right places, patting my arm, promising that I'll love his stable of swift desert-bred horses in Resya.

Then he announces, "The University," leading me beneath a stone archway. "The King's greatest dream."

Like entering the grand ballroom of our palace, we step into an elaborate and embellished world, honey-coloured buildings curving up before us, hemming us in on either side, decorated with leafy vines and sacred orchids. Rampant horses and crouching wolves are carved in elaborate facades. Stained-glass windows glow in the light, casting colours on stonework, and there isn't a single alcove that remains untouched by exquisite detail, a reflection of my father's heart, the pleasure he found in artistry, in learning.

This place sings of him, but it's a hollow beauty.

He isn't here—and something hurts.

"To the library," Havis says, sweeping me along, the guards trailing us. "I think it will please your heart, Princess."

I let him lead me. There's no point in fighting his flowery show, and it allows me to say nothing. He carries the weight of our charade.

The tiled walkways are mostly empty, not many students about during the summer season. The few that remain openly stare. They know who I am. When I offer them a hesitant smile, they respond with a half bow, dropping their eyes and hurrying on. If only I could speak with them, find out what they think about my mother, about the Safire, about the protests in the square. I want to see inside their heads, too.

"Here we are," Havis says grandly, halting us before a large building with a domed roof. He turns to the guards. "Clear it for us."

The men nod and swing open the polished doors. Within a moment, they've announced that everyone must leave and the library's closed. The stern words—and the guns at their side—leave no room for debate. Students gather their books quickly, faces registering shock at the sight of me. The girls skirt round us, eyes down, but the young men, about Reni's age, walk by slower. Their surprise ebbs away, an appreciative glint to their gaze that makes me uncomfortable. I step closer to Havis as they pass.

"Boys are always trouble," he tells me, "with or without a uniform."

"So are most men," I say.

"*Se'til er keren!*" he sings with exaggerated offense, gesturing at himself.

"Not this handsome face." It's a well-known line from Mother's favourite Resyan opera, and his voice has an unexpected baritone beauty. I give him a strange look, like he's just made some kind of odd noise, and he appears mildly disappointed, like I should have indulged him further. But he doesn't yet know I speak Resyan. And for now, that seems wise, since I like having a card hidden from him.

The guards position themselves at the doors, and the library becomes mine to explore. It's a welcome place, the scent of books heavy in the air, like Father's library. My heels click on floors of burgundy and cream, wide windows overlooking the gardens, and high on the domed ceiling above spreads a painted mural.

My breath catches.

"And what delight is this?" Havis asks, behind me.

I stare up in disbelief at the unicorn and dragon. "It's Elois and Elinga. Father made me a painting of that story."

"Then I'd imagine this was also picked for you, Princess. A beloved daughter's favourite story, immortalized in the place the King prized most. How charming."

It's beautiful, the most beautiful thing I've ever seen, and embarrassing tears sting my eyes. I want Father here so badly. I want him to come and hold me and speak to me again, just one word.

Please, Father, only a word.

I strain my ears, but there's nothing. Silence. Breeze skittering on the windows.

Havis motions me to a long oaken table, covered in gold lamps, books scattered. We sit next to each other, wordless, and I blink away the wet behind my lashes. Havis is the last person I'll let see me cry.

"I think we should talk about your education," he says, suddenly all business, glancing at the guards far across the room. "I've heard a rumour you don't wish to be married until after you've had a chance to study, and I want you to know, I'm fine with it. I'd prefer to marry an educated woman. Otherwise I might get bored, and then there might be an affair, and then you'd cry, and then what would I tell your mother?"

"I'm not doing this for you," I say.

"Believe me, I'm well aware. Buying time is more how I interpreted it." He chuckles to himself, leaning back against the table. "All things considered, you do entertain me."

I think this must be my moment. He's called my bluff and is still in his insufferably pleasant mood. It's time for the true questions. "Ambassador, do you believe the General is a good man?"

The sudden question fades his amusement. "Well, I believe he's predictable, if not good. He has ways of looking at the world, and they don't change. Once they're understood, you can know what to expect. But his eldest son? He's no good. I prefer the younger one." He sees my confusion and gestures. "The younger son is a naval officer. He's practical and has good sense."

I tuck that observation away, for later. "You sound like you know them quite well."

"Talk travels fast in my circles. It's my business to know."

"And do you trust Lark?"

"To a point. But that's how I feel about everyone, and especially you."

There's slight teasing in his voice, and I know he's trying to deflect this. I won't let him. Not this time. "He explained his father's proposal. Tell me—what would you gain from it?" I'm purposefully vague, to see what Havis might confess.

He raises his brows. "Me?"

"Don't pretend, Ambassador. You would gain something from war just like everyone else."

"I'm not pretending, Princess. I'm no man of war. I'm a man of opportunity, and sometimes peace is the better gain."

I find I believe him. It's the most candid he's ever been, and while he's implicating himself as a selfish creature, at least it's honest. "Is it true that Seath was once a reasonable man? Studying to be a doctor, even?"

Havis's mouth drops open. "Where the hell did you hear that?"

"Lark," I reply, not wanting to implicate Mother.

Truthfully, the knowledge of Lark's involvement with the Nahir has me reassessing every word I've ever heard about them. Lark is hardly vicious or unreasonable. He's rather plain and ordinary, if anything. And if a man like Seath was once sewing up wounds, not hanging necks, then what other reality might I be missing? Something doesn't make sense. There's a current between these two worlds, and I want to find it.

Havis shakes his head. "I know nothing about Seath. And you'd be wise to stop involving yourself in things you don't understand—namely, Lark." He gives me a pointed look.

"Then you don't trust him?"

"I already told you. I trust exactly one person, and that's my-self." He crosses his arms, clearly perturbed, then nods across the room. "Tell me, what do you think is in that locked chest?"

I frown. "Is this a trick?"

"Not at all."

The wooden cabinet before us glows a warm amber beneath the window, ornate detailing and a metal lock on each drawer. "I suppose something important. Perhaps old documents and political treatises."

"Or?"

"Items of importance to our history. Rare books."

"Why do you think that?"

"Because it's locked. There must be something in there that needs protection."

He nods. "Then go look closer."

I follow his strange advice. Walking near, I trace my fingers along the round edges, the etched flowers. On impulse, I attempt to open the top drawer. It slides towards me with ease. "It's un-locked," I say, surprised.

"And what's there?"

"Index cards."

"Interesting."

I face him again. "I don't understand your point."

He grins lazily. "You don't see the power of the idea? I told you the chest was locked, and you believed me without even checking. That one word made you imagine a dozen things that weren't there. The idea led you astray."

I stand in his slightly gloating gaze, aware he's entirely right. A sour thing to admit. Annoyed, I slump back into my seat at the wood table, the surface old and scraped, shined to a luster. "You think I'm a fool, Havis, but I'm only trying to protect the ones who have no choice in this to begin with. It's not right. Not when there's power to change it. Otherwise how can I even keep breathing? What right do I have?"

Havis studies me, glee dissipated. "That's the first time you've ever called me by my name, Princess." The realization is as much a surprise to me as it is to him. "Listen, Aurelia . . . Can I call you that? Since we're on more personal terms now?"

"No."

"All right, *Princess*, let me try to make this clear. You're from Etania. Your ideas are of this earth. If you tried to explain your most sacred memory to me—about your father, let's say—I'd only ever catch a shade of it. It would never be real to me. That's what Lark's world is to you. You can't understand it, so don't treat him like one of your textbooks. Don't underestimate him."

Familiar anger breaks inside. I have no proof yet that Havis knows the truth about Lark's Nahir connections, but I should have known he'd take the easy way out either way. He's right—he's a man of opportunity. He'll play along and say noble-sounding things until he gets what he wants—which, apparently, is me—and never mind how many lives are scattered as ash behind him. The rest of the world can burn and he'll be safe. Stoking his pleasure in the hills of southern Resya, drinking and kissing and racing desert-bred horses. Pretending he's too honourable to get involved.

But I want more than that.

"Enjoy your power while it lasts," I say hotly. "Soon my brother

will take his crown and then you'll never be allowed in this kingdom again. Perhaps sooner than you think."

Havis's face turns in a strange way. "What do you mean?"

I realize the words after I've said them. "I'm saying *if* he did
take his crown, you'd have no chance with me."

Havis seizes my arm, tight. "Aurelia, tell me—is your brother
trying for the throne? Did he admit that to you?"

"No, he didn't—"

"That crown is the only thing keeping your mother alive. Tell
me this isn't true!"

I feel my cheeks pale. He can't be serious, but this isn't the
Havis with the lazy grin and cavalier arrogance. It's Havis from
the hall, the first time I mentioned Seath's name to him, all those
months ago. His eyes scour me, searching for the truth. A desperate man.

"Listen to me," he says, voice low, urgent, "no one will touch
her as long as she is Queen. It's too much of a risk. But the moment your brother takes power? She loses that precious value,
that protection. She becomes a target, do you understand? If you
know anything about your brother's plots for the throne, or your
uncle's, you must tell me. You don't let this happen."

I stare at him. I have no idea what to think. Perhaps he's being honest, or perhaps he's ensuring Mother stays in power and
he remains in her good favour. What good does a crown do?
Murder is always possible, crown or not. Look at my father. Look
at what those rumours did in the dark.

"I know no more than that," I say honestly, because this is all
from Violet's lips, a passing comment, and perhaps she made the
whole thing more grand in her head.

"Don't let this happen," he repeats.

But I promise nothing.

I'm fairly certain Gref Havis is as good at playing desperate
as he is at playing noble.

30

Havenspur, Thurn

High noon.

Engines growl to a start and the long runway wavers before us. Another afternoon in the sky. We fly over the harbour and practice war games with the naval ships, film cameras following our aerobatics, recording our show to take home to the North. The two allies, Savient and Landore, united in flight. Then we land, pass off the planes to ground crew, strip out of our hot flight suits, and drive down to the water for a swim.

In the evenings, the mail arrives, and I pretend not to get too excited when it's a letter from Ali. More often, they're from Leannya. Lengthy reports about school and life in Savient, subtle critiques buried within, as is the Dakar way.

"Thank you for the perfume, Athan, but now I smell like a complete rose garden, so could you send something less fussy next time? I like notes of orange and citrus."

To which I said:

"Leannya, what are these 'notes' you speak of? Musical? Written? If a smell can be a note, then I might be able to send you notes of kerosene and petrol."

To which I only got a one-line reply:

"You're not as smart as they say.-Leannya."

But this lazy schedule isn't enough for the seasoned pilots growing restless. The absence of skirmishes against the enemy brings boredom to a head the night of my birthday. They think I'm turning twenty-two, and every pilot wants to make sure I celebrate right. Which means getting drunk. Garrick, Merlant, and Wick are conveniently off base, so Greycap produces a bottle of local *mezra* and promptly offers it to everyone, excited to finally share it around. It tastes like boot polish in flames, but I choke some down.

Too many shots later, a drunk Ollie challenges a drunk Baron to a bet. Baron can't resist. Even though it's nearing on midnight and planes are grounded, two of the more sober pilots, Greycap for the Landorians and Sailor for the Safire, fly into the darkness. One charging east, the other west. Up to 5,000 feet and then down in a steep corkscrew dive.

The rest of us wait along the runway flare path, watching navigation lights spiral through the black. It's a tense few minutes, breaths held, but it's agile Greycap who lands back on the tarmac first. He emerges from his cockpit and gives an over-the-top bow.

"Landorian supremacy!" Baron announces, taking yet another shot of *mezra*.

A vexed Sailor lands not long after. It's difficult to get our fighters to dive that tight. It takes sheer focus. I'm sure I could have done better, but I've been working hard to prove myself, to everyone, and especially to Merlant. Not going to throw it away on a stunt like this. Not now that I'm eighteen.

Morning comes and a good number of the pilots on base are hungover in bed. Wick's furious. "This isn't a game," he spits at us. "You can't be having your reckless fun with rebels lurking in every corner. Are you trying to get shot down and waste aircraft? Waste your own damned lives? And now look at the lot of you—couldn't fly if you wanted."

He grounds everyone who's sick on their feet—Spider, Baron, even Ollie—then marches Cyar and me to the briefing room and waves at Garrick, passing us off like an inconvenience. "Fill them in, would you? At least they've got more sense than your first officer."

Garrick nods, jaw clenched. I'd take a guess he's less than pleased Ollie got himself into this. "You're both walking straight?"

"Yes, sir," I reply.

"Good." He casts his eyes to the map on the table before us. "You've got your first sortie over Hady this afternoon."

Cyar and I look at each other.

Maybe we should have taken those extra shots.

"Lightstorm's carrying out a strike on the Nahir-occupied airbase," Garrick says, "and they'll be bearing the brunt of the rebel planes. Our job's to lure some over the sea, to help ease pressure on them. It won't be as heavy as what they're facing, but it won't be easy either."

He runs over strategy and formations with us, then Merlant arrives at the table.

"Weather's clearing nicely off the coast. We're set for two o'clock. I've picked my four pilots still able to fly. And I've requested Charm as my wingman."

Garrick straightens from the map, frowning. "These are my rookies, Captain. I'm responsible for them."

"I understand that, but Officer Helsun is now grounded, which means you'll be tasked with both. Two rookies is too many their first time up."

Garrick can't argue with that logic. "Fine. I'll take Hajari. He'll be less trouble, anyway."

The next few hours pass painfully slow. Why the hell do they drag it out like this? I'd rather have gone straight from the briefing into the skies. I force myself to eat lunch, feign excitement. Cyar can't see me afraid. I may not have much practice with being a leader, but this seems important, and I know what Arrin would do. Fear's contagious.

By quarter to two, Filton and Kif are running around my

fighter, Filton hollering orders at Kif as they fuel, test the engine. Cyar and I sit on a wood bench, lacing our flight boots. When we stand, the hot tarmac feels warm even through the thick soles.

"It's going to be easy, Fox. At least we're not with Lightstorm, right?"

He gives a nervous smile. "Yeah, sure."

"See you up there."

"See you."

Then he's walking for his plane, and I wish I'd added, "Be careful."

Merlant marches to each of his pilots, offering final instructions, his gaze alert and determined. Something else I can't place. He strides over to me, helmet on, goggles resting on top. "Once we're airborne, Charm, you stay on my wing. Never lose sight of me."

"Not planning to be anywhere else."

"Good." He doesn't smile.

"Any other advice?"

"If you find yourself under fire, never—and I do mean never—fly straight for long. Understood?"

I nod.

"All ready, sir?" Filton calls.

I turn and he's waiting by the nose of my fighter. He's glossed up the wings until they shine, a fresh paint job on the Safire swords. Prettiest plane in the sky, just like he promised.

"Ready, Filton."

I shoulder my parachute and rest a hand on the wing. Then I jump up and climb into the cockpit. Filton assists with hooking the parachute, the oxygen tubes. My damn hands tremble a bit on the buckles, but only Filton sees. He attempts a smile, his brow furrowed, shoulders tense. He looks at me like he's memorizing details under pressure. "Be careful, sir."

This time when the cockpit shuts around me, it's with a sense of finality. I adjust the gages, checking glycol and flaps. Everything looks good. I prime the engine, faithful propeller kicking to a spin.

Takeoff is smooth and familiar. The same steady voices give us clearance. I follow Merlant's right wing, and the other four Lion's Paw planes, including Greycap, lead the formation. We level out at 11,000 feet, my breath coming a little funny through the oxygen mask. My hands sweat in the gloves.

I glance left. Cyar's not far off, following Garrick. Good to know he's right there.

The sea below churns with whitecaps as we follow the coastline, and miserable thoughts make the thirty-minute flight feel an eternity. Does Kalt know what I'm doing? Should I have said some kind of goodbye? Maybe I won't get another chance. Not to mention, I've hardly sent Leannya any of my promised letters. And Ali? Can't I at least see her one more time? That's not too much to ask, is it?

God, I don't want Mother to see me afraid.

She never wanted this.

I shouldn't be here.

I shut my eyes for a breath, so there's darkness, nothing. Only roaring engine and shaky metal. The memory of Mother in all her gentle glory.

I'm not actually here.

I'm far away and no one can touch me.

Then light again, the world in a sunny flash, and Hady finally appears, a shadow on the horizon.

"We're scaring first," Greycap says over the radio cheerfully. "See you on the other side, fellows!"

He and the two Landorian planes waste no time, diving down, away from us. They're barely above the city buildings. Their olive-green wings zigzag through the sky, growling their challenge, reminding the people below they made the wrong choice and soon vengeance will come.

Merlant's voice crackles over the radio. "Our turn, Charm. Follow close. Stay on my wing."

"Understood, Leader."

Stick forward and down we go. Hady grows in size, coming near, though we don't go as low as the first group. Surprise isn't on our side anymore. But we're still there, moving so fast it's hard to focus on anything except the little bit of reason nipping at my brain. *Why are you here again? Why are you willingly flying over people who'd like to shoot you down?*

Garrick and Cyar circle behind us from the west, then our throttles are opened and we're back in the wide sky, no one in flames.

Merlant orders us to 6,000 feet. From this new altitude, black puffs of smoke appear to the south, beyond Hady. Anti-aircraft fire. The remnants of large shells hurtled into the air. I know exactly the acrid scent of burnt metal and smoke, memories that feel woven into my existence as tightly as charcoal pencils and brilliant skies. Lightstorm's facing that vicious assault, trying to weaken the Nahir defenses. For what? Is there an army on the way?

"Here they come. Stay awake." Merlant's voice is calm.

No time to worry about the big picture. Six dark dots are hurtling close. Colourless wings. My hand clutches the stick tighter.

"Greycap, give them a chance to reconsider," Merlant says.

"Will do!"

The three Landorian planes break away and meet the pursuers from above. We're on the offensive at this height. Greycap holds fire until they're close, then his guns light up the air with red tracers and bullets. A quick burst and away. It looks easy, effortless. One rebel plane chokes out black smoke. Someone was asleep there. Down he goes, spiraling, bits of plane glinting.

A parachute?

Yes. Lucky him.

"On my turn, Charm. We're going next."

We fling our planes to the side, world shifting hard, familiar weight against my limbs. Blood racing to my feet. One of the rebels is alone and Merlant locks sight on him. A burst from his plane forces the rebel to break upwards, a beginner move, and I'm waiting for it. I pull the trigger. A stream of fire from my plane, like a dragon. The rebel pilot dodges, spinning down, and Merlant maneuvers into position. He wounds it in seconds. We're so close behind, going so fast, that we're over the smoking wreckage before I can look for a parachute to appear.

"Thanks for the help, Charm. Couldn't have done it without you."

"I don't need your charity, Knight."

He laughs.

My hand itches on the trigger. I glance around, wondering where else I can point my plane. Voices blur over the radio, calling out victories, strategies. The sky's become a little battlefield. Of the six enemy planes who answered our challenge, three are already down, one still tries to engage, and another flees with two Landorian fighters in hot pursuit. This feels too easy. I almost wish for more of a challenge.

A shadow momentarily blocks the sun and I glance up. Garrick's Moonstrike plane shoots past a hundred feet above me, flying hard. No wingman behind.

Wait, where's Cyar?

I glance side to side, trying to spot him in the fray. Nothing looks familiar. Can't spot one from another at this distance. "Fox, do you copy?"

Breathe, he's fine.

Stupid, reasonable voice. I don't trust it right now.

"At five o'clock," Merlant says.

I twist around. Cyar's plane loops wildly below us with a rebel on his tail. My breath catches, amplified by the oxygen mask.

"Bring him this way, Fox," Merlant says. "We'll get him off you."

"I can't make it!" Cyar sounds scratchy, panicked. "He almost got my left wing. I'm taking him lower!"

He dives, disappearing into cloud cover, the rebel plane behind.

"Do not pursue, Charm," Merlant warns. "We need to do this together."

The warning doesn't register. I don't think. I don't hesitate. It's not even a question.

I'm gone.

"Don't leave my wing, Charm!"

"Follow your leader," Garrick barks.

The only one who seems to agree with my decision is the plane between my hands. She responds immediately, engines spurring to a furious roar as we plunge deep and to the right. We're going far too fast for the dive, and I hang on to the stick with all I've got, plunging through thousands of feet of air. The overwhelming force hits like an anvil against my chest, against my head. Grey smoke appears at the edge of my vision.

But it works.

Through sheer will I level out, and the chase is on.

Cyar's maneuvering his fighter with a light hand—left, right, up, down—trying to shake the enemy. My head spins working to keep up. I give a solid burst of machine-gun fire and graze the attacker's tail, some work for his ground crew. Hady looms ahead. Galloping towards it seems like a bad idea, perhaps why Merlant was against this pursuit. But to hell with reason. It's not going to serve me well up here.

We reach land just west of the city and our three planes are damn close together. Spent shell casings from the rebel's guns rain against my cockpit, rattling glass and nerves. Have to be careful with my shots. Don't want to hit Cyar by accident. I haven't said a word to him over the radio, but conversation seems pointless right now. At least he knows I'm here, that I didn't leave him on his own.

I push up to get some altitude when another dark dot appears ahead, racing straight for us at an alarming speed, smoking from one wing. My pulse scatters.

"Watch yourself, Fox! Eleven o'clock."

"I see it."

Cyar dips his wings deeply to the left, preparing for a turn, and his attacker does the same. But at the moment of spin, Cyar swings his fighter back the other way, breaking up and out. A brilliant move, and the plane in pursuit finishes his now point-less roll to the left. The game's over. Time for me to break and follow. But something still burns inside. I hate this pilot in front of me. This person who thought they could hurt Cyar. I hit the throttle, ready to pounce, then freeze.

Damn it, the second plane!

I jam my feet against the rudder, throwing my stick right, flinging myself into a wild downward roll. Anything to get out of his crosshairs. For half a second—half an infinite moment—I brace for the inevitable red fire, the pounding bullets into my fuselage. But then the enemy wings flash silver above me. Bright silver with glorious black swords painted beneath.

Safire!

My breaths are ragged. The injured Lightstorm fighter passes close overhead, and I'd like to shoot him out of the goddamn sky. What the hell's he doing over here by himself, charging me! My reckless relief and fury are twin flames. But I hate myself most. If he hadn't been friendly, I'd have been shot down my first time up. Top Flight, my ass.

But no time for this. I search the sky for the rebel plane and spot him diving, almost falling, in a frenzy to get away. I've come this far. Not stopping now. I throw my plane into another steep dive, straining to hold it all together. She shudders around me.

The poisonous grey clouds my vision, the anvil pressed to my chest like a death sentence. I ease back a touch. Blacking out over Hady will only turn me into the Nahir's first prisoner of war. But once we're level . . .

He flies straight at five hundred feet. No choice, low as he is, and he uses the speed of his dive to propel him forward. I fling open the throttle and push my plane hard. "Come on," I say, like anyone's listening. "Prove to me you're the best damn plane in the world!" She doesn't disappoint, and we close in. He must be panicking now. He tries a sudden roll to the left.

Not bad. That was good thinking, and I have to check myself.

He scrambles higher again, racing for clouds above. A terrible mistake. He doesn't realize this is our moment of glory, these climbs into the heights. The altimeter ticks our easy ascent and I'm right on his tail. Now I have him. Now I have this person who tried to touch my brother. Finger on the trigger, line up the gunsight.

It's much quicker than I expect.

Easy.

The shot's right to the undercarriage with my deadly twenty-millimeter cannons, and his engine smokes. The nose drops, then it's falling down and away. I finger my trigger again, amazed.

A little parachute appears below.

The plane explodes.

That's right, I tell the pilot. *Go see the wreckage of your plane. Go take a good look at what I've done.*

Heart racing, I head back for the formation.

The pilot in the wounded Lightstorm plane returns to Havenspur with us. Smoking and chased from the rest of his squadron, he'd figured his best bet was to make for our friendly group. As we fly along, he fields the many questions about how the attack on the airbase went. There's lots of laughter, boasting, now that tension has passed.

I ignore the excited chatter. Dizziness and nausea overwhelm me, the weariness sudden and thorough. I just did more high-force maneuvers in ten minutes than I normally do in an entire week. When we land, I sit in the cockpit, sucking in air like I've been underwater, every muscle trembling with exhaustion. I have nothing left to give.

Filton waits below, relief etched on his face as I slide open the cockpit glass. "Not a scratch, Chief," I say, jumping down. My knees give way slightly.

He offers me an arm. "Very good, sir. Very good."

Cyar lopes over, face streaked with sweat, dark hair matted. He looks a bit undone. "God, that was terrible! I was on Garrick's tail and that pilot came right out of the sun. Cut between us and chased me off before I could even say a thing over the radio." He stops and looks me up and down. "Did you get him?"

I nod.

He glances to my plane, then shifts on his feet. "Sorry. I would have come along, but I thought you were right behind me. By the time I looked back, you'd disappeared."

I manage a smile. "Just testing out the plane. She's quite fast."

There's a breath of silence before he says, "Athan, I owe you one."

"You do." I shove his shoulder, grateful I can still do it. Anything for him.

"Lieutenant Erelis," a third voice interrupts. Merlant marches over, mouth set, silk scarf untied. "You were supposed to stay on my wing! You were not supposed to let me out of your sight."

Cyar steps away, but I straighten. "Sorry, Captain. I had no choice."

"You damn well did! Flying alone your first time up is the most foolish thing you could have done. You're lucky we aren't fishing you out of the Black right now."

"If not me, then it would have been Cyar. No one else was running to help him."

He opens his arms. "Because the rest of us were using our heads! Trying something called strategy rather than blind flying. And even after the round was won, you still carried on. Right over Hady! All on your own." He gives me a look of disbelief. "You're a lucky fool that plane you met was one of your own."

Garrick appears around the nose of my fighter. "What's this, Captain?"

Merlant gestures at me. "I'm trying to explain to your rookie what strategy is."

"Not much luck, I'm guessing?"

"You're welcome to take a shot at it."

Garrick looks at me. "You flew off like a devil, Charm. Incredible dive. I've seen pilots nearly kill themselves with moves like that. How'd you keep her out of a stall?"

I shrug. "No other choice."

"Did you get him down, then?"

"Yes, sir."

"You're sure of it?"

"The whole thing was in flames. There's no plane left."

A slow grin lights Garrick's face. "My God, really? Not bad, Charm! Your first time up, too!"

I stare at him. A compliment from Garrick? What do I do with that?

Merlant looks the same. "Captain Carr, you can't encourage this in a squadron."

"Can't encourage what? Bringing down the enemy?"

"No, every other damn thing he did." Merlant ticks off his fingers. "Leaving formation without permission, abandoning his leader, never bothering to radio his intentions, attacking the enemy without support . . . I'm not sure there's a rule he *didn't* break. Sorties aren't a one-man show."

Garrick steps between us. "Captain, my rookie just shot a

plane out of the sky on his first time up. I'd say that's pretty damn impressive. Strategies only get you so far, then instinct and luck kick in." He glances at me. "Though next time it would be helpful if you tried to be a bit more of a team player."

I nod.

Merlant throws Garrick a dark look. "I will be reporting this to Major Wick. The Lieutenant broke direct orders."

That threat stops everyone, even Filton and Kif, who've been checking my plane over. Garrick straightens his shoulders. His voice is low. "Listen, Captain, there are two squadrons here. We may be training with you, and the Lieutenant will show you the proper respect, but he doesn't answer to you, nor will he ever. He answers to me, and I say he did a good job today." He steps away from Merlant and claps me on the shoulder. "Stay on your leader's wing next time, Charm. I'm not going to be the one who has to explain your death to . . ." He trails off, no need to finish.

"Yes, Captain."

He nods, giving me what might actually be a genuine smile, then heads for the barracks. Cyar follows. Filton and Kif disappear into the nearby hangar.

I stand before Merlant, slightly embarrassed, still nauseated. Nothing left to give.

Merlant looks drained, too. I suppose there's no such thing as an easy dogfight. "This is the problem with you Safire," he says quietly. "You think you know everything already, need no one's help. You think that because you got it right ten years ago, and created something from nothing, you can do it again with ease."

I rub my aching head.

"You can't do this alone, Athan. You need to be a part of a team."

"Cyar's my team," I say tightly.

"Not when you're a captain. When you're captain you'll have ten pilots looking to you for guidance. You can't abandon them for one." He walks closer. "I lost a good friend up there last year. I know this isn't a game. You can treat it like one, but up there people die. And you die. It's about victory, assess, victory, assess. Strategy, Athan. You should know that better than anyone."

Exhaustion and reason win out. "I understand, sir."

"Good." He pauses, shaking his head again. "You really made the bastard run, though, didn't you? We usually let them off once they've waved the white flag and headed for home."

"He picked the wrong plane to go after."

Merlant smiles faintly. "I'll be writing the operations report for Major Wick, and I'll be sure to mention your score. Perhaps we'll overlook the rest this one time. But only once."

I glance up, relieved. "Thank you, Captain."

He nods and heads for base headquarters, as sweaty and tired as the rest of us. His black cat runs along at his heels. I didn't even notice it trot over.

Night falls, and I'm still pulsing with adrenaline. Sleep doesn't come, only the feeling of loops and dives in the sky, up and down through the atmosphere, the moment of blinding fear when I was caught between crosshairs. I turn onto my stomach and write Ali, holding the paper in the compound light. As always, I end up staring at the blank sheet for far too long.

How do I share what I've done today? Where do I begin?

It wasn't so bad, really. Some heart-stopping moments, then parachutes. As Merlant said, they often just let the other pilot go after a certain point.

See? There are principles and rules—rules I might have broken a bit today—but we're not out for blood. We're out for the challenge, for the grin of victory. Doesn't that make sense, Ali?

I don't even know why I'm worried about explaining this to her. She'd probably agree with me.

I sigh and lean heavily on my arms, sinking into the mattress.

"This bed is as old as Thurn," Cyar says below. "It creaks every time you breathe."

"Sorry."

"Can't sleep?"

"No."

He slides out of bed and stands beside the bunk. Even in the scant light, he still looks a bit undone. "You know this is only the beginning."

"I know."

"We're going to have to keep going up there, facing better pilots than that. And when this summer ends, who can say what's next? This could be on for years. Years, Athan. And this is our life now. There won't ever be a day when we do our best, and then it's over. It's not like the Academy. The better we do, the more they'll send us up." He pauses. "And they'll keep sending us up, over and over until we . . ."

"Until we win," I finish for him. I won't let him think the other option.

He catches himself. "Yes, until we win."

Neither of us mentions that "win" is a vague term in the South. In Savient, there was an end. We unified. Is that even possible here? I don't know. I don't think anyone knows. If it was up to me, I'd just give the rebels their Free Thurn and then everyone's happy.

But no one's going to ask me.

"We'll be the best and see it to the end," I say.

"We will."

"I won't go up there without you, Cyar—I won't." That's the truest thing I know.

We share a thin smile, vague in the darkness. Then he returns to his bed and I fold my paper. I've survived my first day of eighteen.

Tomorrow, I'll write.

VII

TRUTH

Dear Ali,

Here we go—this week's exciting installment is about a bet.

Two planes, one Landorian and one Safire, raced each other in the absolute middle of the night, then dove a good thousand feet through the air. Before you ask, no, it wasn't very safe, but that's why I didn't participate. It was a bunch of other bored (and very drunk) pilots, and tragically, the Safire pilot lost. He couldn't quite make the winning dive. Though I'm sure if it had been me flying, the Safire honour would remain intact. I'm not bragging here. It's just the truth.

(All right, maybe bragging a little.)

Beyond that, we play kickball, we swim, we drill in the sky. The evening is my favourite, when it's finally cool and I can sit out here in the hangar and find some quiet. I really should be writing my sister, you know. She sent me a strongly worded letter this week about how those who break promises are bound for the worst parts of hell. Well, it wasn't quite so direct, but to that effect. And it's true. I did promise her a letter a week. But somehow they each end up addressed to you. You've captured all my thoughts, Ali, and I don't have any left for her. And before you tell me I'm cruel—don't worry, I'm not even her favourite brother, so I think I'm safe from hell for now. She just likes telling people what to do. It's a habit that runs in my family.

So what should I share with you next, Princess? I feel like I owe you something heroic in here. Something impressive I've done, that you'll read over and over and over again. But to be honest, I don't find this mission very inspiring. I mostly feel a bit overwhelmed. We walked the streets (it's so damn hot, sweat everywhere, sorry for the smudges) and a local girl actually threw herself at Cyar, begging for help. She believes we Safire are here to rescue them. Can you believe it? They think we'll fight against the Landorians, at their side, which just shows how complicated this whole mess is.

I wish there was an easy answer. I know there usually isn't.

Instead, I'm just going to lie here and enjoy this evening, see the sky filled with a hundred thousand stars. I've never seen this many stars, Ali. It reminds me of your eyes. I think I'll always remember your dark eyes when I see the perfect night sky here. So perhaps there is something beautiful here and it's tied, forever, to you.

I'm saying too much now. And I haven't even had a glass of wine. This never ends well. Cyar's the poet, not me. I love your pictures of the woods and mountains. I have them pinned near my bunk here. I've included more of my own—the freckly-faced fellow is my rigger, Kif. (I have my own ground crew. Did I mention that in my last letter? Am I still bragging?)

Thank you for writing me so faithfully. I look forward to each one of your letters.

Yours,
Athan

To my most talented Lieutenant (Star of the Safire pilots):

Of course you'd have won the bet! I have no doubts about that. You once put our own Etanian pilots to shame, and though no one quite realized it, you were in fact the talk of the palace, remember? I should have mentioned this to your General when we spoke. I mentioned your good manners and he said that wasn't enough for a promotion, so I'll be sure to mention your exceptional talent and daring moves in high wind next time. I'm determined to see you awarded the highest rank in your entire air force. What would that be? Commanding Captain or Colonel or some such title of a famous squadron? With golden diamond wings?

I'll allow you the bragging, Lieutenant. It's well-earned, I think. But you really should do something about that younger sister of yours. May I speak from experience? There truly is nothing worse than a brother who says one thing and does another. I know you might hold a differing opinion of Renisala (and I don't blame you) but he is everything wonderful to me. He's a piece of my soul. When he pays me no attention, it's like I'm on the earth and he's in the sky, discovering an entire realm of places I can't follow. My greatest fear is that someday he'll stay up there for good. That he'll lose sight of me below. And you really are in the sky, Athan, so now can you imagine how your sister might feel?

Anyway, thank you for sharing your feelings on Thurn. I like to hear your thoughts, since you're so close to it all, and I agree there are no easy answers. But I believe they must be out there. And I believe we can find them, together, perhaps even before this gets any further along.

Imagine if there didn't need to be any war!

Perhaps there's time to make things right.

Now, for your next letter, you must tell me what it's like to fly. Do you get nervous? Have you had any close calls? You must also write it after a few glasses of wine. I'd very much like to see what you have to say then.

Consider this a royal command, Star of the Safire.

(But write your sister first.)

Yours with affection,
Ali

31

Hathene, Etania

Transpiration, condensation, precipitation.

I spend my days balancing between two worlds—one where I study for my exams and pretend everything is fine, learning the mechanics of the earth, drafting essays for Heathwyn and taking practice tests, and another where I hide in Father's library with Lark while he quizzes me on health and biology, dispelling any illusion I once had about the terrifying Nahir. He knows far too much about the common head cold.

But when we open my history books for our weekly discussions, I discover he lives in another third world altogether. We can't read a single page about the South without him pointing out something that shouldn't be there, or should be there, or is vaguely inaccurate though not quite wrong. Battles. Treaties. Accords. He goes on and on about forced borders and displaced peoples and I listen, wondering what I can trust from his mouth and what might simply be his version of a "locked" chest.

"This," he says, pointing at a page which describes the wasted potential of long-ago Thurn, "is classic Northern arrogance. They pretend there was nothing grand before they came. As if our cities aren't as old and beautiful as Norvenne itself!"

"They don't look that way in the photographs," I observe. "They're usually half falling down."

"The photographs? From the *newspapers*?" Lark draws a deep, balancing breath, and I'm fairly certain I inadvertently try his patience more than I should. "This is exactly what I mean. You'll justify anything to prove you're better than the rest of us. Do you even remember the old monarchies of the South?"

"There really were royals in the South?" I ask, intrigued.

"Stars." He thumps one hand on my book. "Education is wasted here."

I'm wildly fascinated by the prospect of far-away royalty, wondering what they might be like and if they're still there and how their palaces are, but Lark's only interested in war and politics and theories of resistance. When I press him further on the subject, he waves it off, saying monarchies are the way of the past and the South has moved beyond it, to a place where all might be equal and have their say—with or without a gun.

"You remind me of someone else I know," I remark with a sly smile.

He gives me a quizzical look, doubtful, but I keep my Safire friend a secret. I've learned well of Lark's deep hatred towards the General, which might be even greater than his hatred of Landore. Any mention of Athan certainly won't go over well. But this only reminds me that I'm still not sure why Lark cares so much about Thurn. He's from Resya. All of this is closer to him, yes, but it's still not . . . *his*. How on earth did he wind up embroiled in the Nahir cause?

I want to ask, but I feel it's a later lesson. A more personal one. In the meanwhile, I'm beginning to realize Athan might indeed be right about the South, that there is something darker going on than we in the North know, truths you can't understand until you're there to see them with your own eyes. Enough to make a girl beg the Safire for help. It gives further credence to Lark's impossible hope—that my mother, who has lived in both worlds, might arrange a negotiation and invite reason to reign and peace to be restored. If she became the woman who saved the world from war, Lark says, how could anyone in the North ever speak against her?

It's a gamble, and we both know it. But Lark is practical enough about the whole thing it suddenly seems entirely reachable. And I like that.

So, I sketch visions from his Southern life—born of his rambling monologues—and then add them to the little secret box which is the heartbeat of my joy. I've tucked Athan's letters away there, the one place that seems safe and inviting in a world of sheer uncertainty. His folded pages hold the scent of kerosene, and heat. His touch. He tells me stories of Cyar hunting for snakes, of the funny new pilots he flies with and their training flights above the sea. My stories in return must seem painfully dull. But I always kiss the letters before I seal them, though he'll never know.

"*I have a plan,*" I wrote him in the last one, "*and you'd be pleased with my dedication to it. I'm not simply waiting behind these walls any longer. I'm going to do more than anyone imagined. Perhaps I'll make a Safire soldier yet.*"

I don't only mean the negotiation scheme. I have another idea sheltered inside, one that's just for me. It takes me to the University and then to another city, like Norvenne, and Athan's there, older, walking with me down the wide street arm in arm, no wars anywhere at all. The steps in between are hazy, the specifics not entirely sorted out, but the ending's clear. He looks very good with a few years on him, broad-shouldered and handsome. Playful, still, and teasing me.

And every evening, when I'm drowning in his sketches like a lovesick fool, imagining where he's touched them, I also imagine his hands on me. I kiss the side of his jaw, then his lips, and I feel electric all over, wondering at the idea of his bare chest against my skin. . . .

I blame Violet for these ideas.

And then, as the summer begins to turn, General Dakar's eldest son stands before the Royal League, striking in his uniform, bold before a balconied room full of old men at desks, and destroys my impossible hope with his own impossible speech.

Reni's still on tour, and Mother's sequestered away in meeting with Havis. Lark manages to secure a reel for us to watch, since he knows I want to witness our tragedy unfold—and I know he wants to share his opinion of it.

I'm hoping he'll have some practical solution.

Seated together in the quiet of his guest quarters, we watch the General's son on screen as he adjusts his Safire cap and strides for the podium, a reflection of his father—straight-shouldered, focused, handsome. He appears not the least bit intimidated by the sea of impassive faces before him, leading with a brilliant smile. "Gentlemen, I stand before you today as one who was born in war. I knew it long before I ever knew peace. The struggle in Thurn is one familiar to me, the same struggle from which Savient was birthed, and this revolution is not an accident. It's a reaction born of bitterness and frustration. For too long you've watched without mercy, choosing to intervene only when it has promised you reward."

I glance at Lark, since on these points I think he'd be inclined to agree, but Lark doesn't notice, fixated grimly.

The speaker from Landore objects. "You spent a week touring the territory, Commander, and now you've the nerve to pass judgment on us?"

"I do. Because I've seen Thurn with my own eyes, unlike most seated here, who read it all from a report." There's a momentary stir at the desks, but the Commander doesn't stop. "Every day that you wait, the shadow of the Nahir spreads further, inciting them to violence. They won't stop with Hady. Decisive intervention is the only answer."

"We've tried, Commander." That's a speaker from Elsandra. "It's never as easy as that, not in the South."

"Easy?" He laughs. "If that's what you're waiting for, then I can see why things have reached this point."

"You know his meaning," the Landorian man retaliates. "And I'm certain you know as well as us what kind of suffering the South can bring."

"As if any one of them knows what it's like to suffer," Lark mutters.

For a breath, there's a waver of resentment on the Commander's face, acknowledgment of this knifed statement. But he straightens, voice sharpening. "You're right. I do understand suffering. My mother was innocent, had no quarrel with anyone. Whoever murdered her brought the fight to us, and they will be held to account."

"You would go to war because of a personal vendetta?"

"I would go to war for a chance at saving the South."

"And you think your army can do this?"

"Yes, because we will cut the roots that feed the Nahir and bring Seath to his knees once and for all." The Commander swings his hand towards the representatives from Resya, facing them. "There's a certain kingdom on Thurn's borders that has pretended to be a friend of the North even as it works against us. They sit here now, claiming neutrality, yet their king supplies money and weaponry to the rebels who fight you at every turn."

I knew it was coming, heard the rumours preceding the reel, that the General's son had actually condemned Resya before the entire North.

But here it is before us, igniting my anger.

Ugly in its boldness.

Lark taps his foot rapidly, arms crossed. The Resyan representative on screen protests eloquently, but since everyone is in a flutter, no one entirely hears, and it's the Landorian man who silences all with the incredulous question in everyone's mind. "Commander, you're accusing His Majesty *King Rahian* of funding the Nahir?"

"I am," the General's son says evenly, and I want to spit at him through the screen. "Our Safire forces conducted a raid near Hady," he continues, unaffected by the rising controversy before him. "It was carried out with the approval of General Windom, and there we discovered proof of transactions between Rahian and Seath. Money, weapons, all of it. We've also secured evidence of arms exchanges on the Black Sea, done under cover of the Resyan flag."

All eyes turn to the Resyan speakers again. The two men appear shocked, wordless.

"You're sure this isn't a ruse?" the Landorian man asks. He appears more concerned now than vexed.

The Commander nods. "We extracted confessions, have signed documents. The League will be provided with these. There's no doubt in our minds, nor should there be any in yours, that Rahian is guilty. And when you agree to our campaign, we will overthrow this corruption that encourages unrest. We'll see how strong the Nahir truly are without their allies."

"We haven't given consent to war," the speaker from Landore reminds him, eyes narrowed again. "There are questions which must be answered first."

Dakar's son narrows his eyes right back. "I'm not asking for your consent to war. I'm asking for your consent to victory," he announces, opening his arms to the entire League. "If you don't choose to act now, your children will carry the burden and live their days in fear. I swear to you, I will defend Savient and the North. I will avenge my mother's death, and to hell with any of you here who choose the coward's way out!"

That elicits further shock from the room. Even the General raises his brow.

Then the Commander gives a perfectly winning smile and says, "Thank you," as if he hasn't just offended every leader in the North.

The film ends, jumping to scratchy darkness.

I want to leap into the screen and undo everything I've heard. I feel frantic, tormented between hating the Commander for daring to bring Resya into this and realizing he's made a very compelling case, and what if it's true? What if Rahian isn't neutral? Here I am, presented, at last, with evidence which could condemn Havis for good, banish him from my life forever, but now his downfall is my downfall. And also, I have a cousin and ally in the Nahir.

I'm desperately confused by the world.

"Lark," I say urgently, "do you believe King Rahian has aided . . . your cause? I'm asking you as your cousin, not as a princess." He says nothing, and I grip his arm. "Please, Lark. Whatever you know, you must tell me."

My desperation works and he shrugs. "Truthfully, who am I to say what one man would do when pushed? Seath doesn't always request help kindly."

"Then you believe Rahian's been threatened into helping?"

Lark shrugs again, as if it's beyond him, but I wonder if it's actually a polite way to avoid revealing a thing he can't, not as Nahir or as my cousin.

"Nothing will happen," he assures me instead. "The League won't approve a war against a sovereign kingdom. They leave their guns for the likes of us."

His distaste is clear, but I'm not as convinced.

Seeing my expression, he says, "This damned General has at last stepped too far, Aurelia. He can't wage war against a king without the League's approval. They'd turn against him—and he's worked too hard to earn their blessing."

"But it was a persuasive speech," I fret.

Lark snorts, gesturing at the blank screen, where the Commander was. "That one I trust less than the General. He changes with the hour, and that's dangerous."

"I'm sure it would make him a good warrior, though."

"A good warrior?" Lark's laughter is more a hiss. "I doubt you'd say that if you knew the truth."

As always, my cousin knows how to hook me. "Really?" I lean back, uncertain. "What do you know about him?"

"Things that wouldn't make him look this pretty before the League."

A residual of hope returns. "Enough to undo what's just been said?"

"Possibly."

"Lark!" I'm so delighted, I'm nearly grinning with relief, but his expression is entirely grave, and I calm myself, trying to match his practical frown. "Well, what is it?"

He glances at the door, calculating a long moment, then comes to a decision and disappears into his adjacent bedroom. I wait, a bit uncertain now. When he returns, there's a leather briefcase in his hands, his expression familiar—rapidly earnest when wrestling with something big, trying to find its centre. He sifts through papers while I wait.

"My sister served as translator with the Landorian forces in Beraya," he explains. "The city isn't far from the Resyan border, and she speaks the local dialect there. When the revolt happened a month ago, she was called upon to help negotiate a ceasefire." Lark pulls two photographs from a crisp envelope and pushes them before me. "She took these in secret. Now she's distraught, unsure what to do with them, convinced she's cursed herself for not saying a thing."

I look down. The photographs are black and white, slightly blurry, indicating either an older camera or that they were taken in a hurry. In the first, there's a line of men standing against a wall. They're blindfolded, their shoulders hunched. Some are young, some are old, but the ones at the farthest end, nearest the camera, are thin and tiny, no more than thirteen. One child holds the hand of a man. My own hand begins to tremble. I slide the first photograph to the left and reveal the second. The bodies are sprawled on the earth.

Even the boys.

I hear a strange sound in my throat.

"This was only one of many executions in Beraya," Lark continues quietly. "They slaughtered any boy who seemed old enough to carry a gun, then they starved the city. And it wasn't the Landorian general who ordered it. It was Dakar's son."

Fresh revulsion threatens to make me sick. "He couldn't . . ."

"They say he did the same in Karkev, Aurelia. And we know who raised him. I doubt the apple falls far from the tree, as you Northerners like to say."

I stare at the crumpled bodies—an inky black snaking around them, spattered on the wall, on their pale, empty faces staring at the sky—and all of this feels suddenly much darker and more evil than any common war. This doesn't look like a battle should. It looks like murder.

"*This* is the scourge of the Safire," Lark says plainly. "The Landorians? They do what they must to keep the world functioning as they like it, permitting us to live in peace beneath them but never allowing us to rise too high. They like things easy and manageable. But the Safire? They'll destroy our world and rebuild it again as they see fit. They'll do to us what they did in Savient, removing anyone who's against their code, until only the faithful are left. Forging their own version of a perfect nation. Well, it's not. It's simply not, and I won't stand by and watch it happen."

"This can't be real," I say.

"It *is* real," Lark replies, sharp.

"You have no proof it was the Safire commander."

"These photographs speak for themselves. He was there. He knows it."

"But how can any of this be? It's quiet down there. No fighting at all yet!"

Lark gives me a skeptical glance. "How do you know that?"

I open my mouth, then realize it's an answer I can't give. I stare at the photographs, a fierce new anger flowering in my chest, rotten and thorned, strangling me—anger at this injustice, at the world, at all the people who let this happen without objection. Whether it was the Commander or the Landorians, it doesn't matter. Someone did this. They did this while a whole war was fermenting in the Southern heat, with real bullets, real attacks, and I had no clue.

Not a hint.

Furious, I stand and flee for my room.

"Good heavens."

Heathwyn steps through my doorway, a hand to her mouth, staring at me on the bed. I've opened every letter from Athan, every single damn letter sent to me since the beginning of summer, and now they're tossed across the coverlet in a righteous storm. Drawings of cities and sea birds and aeroplanes. Stories of drunken pilots and swimming in the sea and insects larger than my hand.

But nothing of war.

Nothing, anywhere, that speaks of it.

"He's been lying to me." I can barely speak, I'm so frightened and angry. "He said it was quiet and boring, only some drills and practice fighting. But it's a lie. I saw the speech given to the League. I saw more than I ever wish to see, and it's all—"

I choke on the words I can't say, a place she can't follow.

"Aurelia . . ."

I blink back tears. "I deserved the truth!"

"Yes, but what if it isn't his to give? For heaven's sake, he's a soldier! They can't write these things down. It's a surprise to all of us, not only you."

Her pragmatic observation stills my rage, slightly, but I'm not

yet ready to surrender. She sits on the edge of the bed, stacking
a few scattered papers. "I'm sure he didn't wish to frighten you.
He's kindhearted, isn't he? He must be or else I know you
wouldn't have adored him so quickly." She picks up one of his
drawings, studying. "These are quite exquisite, aren't they?"

My head drops into my hands, aching with the weight of
everything. With the knowledge that my Safire lieutenant wears
a uniform that might conceal darkness and he doesn't even know
it. How can he? With the bright optimism he holds?

"You told me the war was young and didn't yet know what
it wanted," I accuse Heathwyn quietly. "What if it's already
decided?"

"Nothing is ever decided."

"Don't lie to me. Please don't."

She sets down the page and looks at me for a long moment.
She's never looked at me like this, like she's already regretting
her words. "I do worry about what will come," she admits. "I
don't know what goes on behind secret doors, the discussions in
high places, and I never will. But I see those mighty ships with
nowhere certain to sail, all those guns waiting to be fired, and
I think that's a lot of power to leave restless beneath men's
fingers."

"But what if someone could make them see a better way?"

"Then pray it comes swiftly."

It's the first time she's ever given me such stark words. She
kisses me on the head, without apology, then walks for the door,
leaving me alone.

I sit and stare at the letters. I finger one, then another, then
the next. Wrinkled paper and familiar cursive words. I sit there
and realize he's very far away, and now that will never change.
He'll go to war with the rest—a dark war, where children
are taken along with the guilty—and perhaps he'll die in a place
not like here, buried in a deep grave, forgotten, and we'll never
know what might have been. I'll be asked to smile every day like

there's nothing the matter. I'll be asked to go on and marry some other person, but I'll still remember this darkness and these photographs. I'll remember the days of early summer, when he was near me, full of life, laughter on his lips and living in a hopeful world.

No one will care that he's dead, that his warm skin has been turned to dust and his laughter's no more. No one else will give a damn about how very lonely it is to be trapped under the earth in a place far from home, to be buried forever beneath the banner of a cause you never even wanted.

No one will care about any of this, because he's small and forgettable.

But I will.

32

ᴈ ATHAN ᴇ

Havenspur, Thurn

The number of sorties we fly increases each week. Sometimes near Hady, sometimes over the distant villages of Thurn. We linger above the supply routes the rebel planes like to prey on, and while we wait, the Landorian pilots take potshots at sheds and empty vehicles, laughter echoing over the radio.

"Here's what you get for Hady," Spider says, and Baron follows close behind. Bullet holes appear from eight blazing machine guns. Twisted metal and clouds of dust rising.

I hang back.

This doesn't feel right.

Gallop's the first pilot shot down by the rebels. His green-winged plane spirals towards the Black in flames, then dissolves into a shower of metal and sea, disappearing beneath the waves. He's lucky. He escaped in time to deploy his parachute, later retrieved by a friendly cruiser.

"Damn them," he curses back at base, covered in dried salt water, life vest limp around his shoulders. "That was my favourite plane."

Baron grins. "Poor girl couldn't have saved you from that last move you made. Lazy ass."

If there's any fear, nobody shows it.

That's one down for us, at least ten for the other side. Garrick leads the tally with three credited victories, then two each for Ollie, Greycap, and Spider. I've managed third place, thanks to my chase the first time up, but Cyar remains cautious. Nothing knocked down for him.

Though Garrick's taken me back as his wingman, I still watch Merlant from the corner of my eye. Always the same—gaining altitude, then down out of the blinding sun like a devil. They never see him coming. But he's also a gentleman. He wounds instead of securing victories, and when we come across a rebel plane with its engine already on fire, he orders us to pass it by. "Not a fair fight," he says, and that's that.

I'm sure he could overtake Garrick's record if he wanted. If he felt like making a point.

He never does.

The morning after the reel of Arrin's speech arrives, it's the talk of the base. Everyone has an opinion on the prospect of this new war, and whether or not General Dakar's son has made legitimate accusations. The debate continues around our breakfast table.

"I always knew there was something funny with Resya," Greycap says, nodding as if he's in on the secret. "They've never caused trouble, but they've certainly never helped us much either. And you have to admit the pilots we've been facing have some skill. They're getting help from somewhere."

Spider points his fork. "Or that goddamn Safire commander's trying to start a war, and we don't need it. God knows one mess is enough."

"But you have to admit he has some guts," Greycap persists, "calling all those politicians cowards. I liked that bit. No one appreciates what we do down here."

"Guts or not, the General's son is a fool." Spider glances to the nearby Safire table. "No offense."

Garrick, Ollie, and Sailor frown, looking ever so discreetly at me.

They'd better quit that.

I swallow what's left of my coffee in a single gulp and stand from the table. I'm done with it.

A breeze greets me outside, flags rippling a lazy rhythm. The black runway heats in silence, and I take a deep breath of the fresh air. Then another. I'm not angry with Arrin because he's trying to start a war and insulting every Northern politician in the process. No, I'm furious because he went so far as to use Mother, to wield her death as a chess piece in his gamble. He should have ignored the baited suggestion. Moved on. But of course he couldn't resist the opportunity to go from cavalier young lion to noble avenger of injustice. And then that only reminds me he's still plotting away about Etania, whispering ideas in Father's ear. . . .

He's too good at turning a spark into a forest fire. All I want is Ali safe, and I feel helplessly far away.

The door creaks open behind me and Ollie slides around it. "Never mind those Landorians," he says. "They're nervous about change. You know we all think it was a brilliant speech."

"Was it?" I ask, and his smile disappears.

He tries again, voice lower. "Your brother spoke the truth, and they don't want to hear it. In time, they'll see it's the right move. We can't let allies of the Nahir go unpunished and—"

A loud, clanging bell interrupts. It echoes from the ops hut urgently. For half a second, we both look at each other, confused.

Then recognition snaps at our heels and we take off at a wild run for the flight line.

The bell. They've spotted rebel planes. They're here, attacking us.

Us!

It's never happened this way before, but I know I need to get to my plane. That's my only thought as I tear across the tarmac.

Filton and Kif are already scurrying around the wings, fueling and arming the guns with incredible speed. I pull on my kit in record time—parachute, gloves, life vest. The vest gets tangled and I throw it off me. Never mind that. I scramble into the cockpit, Filton hollering words at me: "Seven planes, coming northeast," and that's all I need to hear. It's not until I'm buckled in, flaps tested and pump primed, sunglasses on to cut the morning sun, that I realize I have no leader.

I scour the tarmac, a commotion of pilots and crew as they try to get us in the air. Ollie's plane is still being fueled. I don't know where Garrick is. Merlant's the only one already inside his cockpit with propeller spinning. I call to him over the radio, and he looks over, brows briefly raised as if shocked to find me ready to go.

"Follow me up," he orders.

"Copy that."

We're the first two planes off the ground. Arcing north, we follow Control's coordinates to face the oncoming rebel planes, out over the sea.

"All right, Charm," he says. "Don't fall asleep on me today."

"Wouldn't do that to you, Knight."

"And stay on my wing."

It could be a joke, if we weren't the only two pilots facing seven enemy aircraft.

I spot the dark swarm quickly. "Two o'clock low."

"Good eye. Let's get some altitude."

We swing up to 7,000 feet, towards the sun. My fighter hums beneath my hands, electric, on edge in a new way. This time, they've brought the challenge to us.

"On my turn," Merlant says.

It's his familiar strategy. We dive down, side by side, sun at our backs, and fire on the enemy formation. They must be surprised, certainly still eyeing the planes hurtling up from the coast. They scatter in all directions. I push down on the stick and lay into one hard. His wing smokes, the plane falling away, wounded.

"Nice," Merlant says, and the quick affirmation feels better than an entire report of praise.

The enemy formation's now broken, and others are arriving—Garrick, Greycap, Ollie. We charge onward, after the nearest target. Knight locks his sights on a rebel fighter tailing one of the Safire planes. Our machine guns light up the air. The rebel abandons his prey, diving lower, away from us. We stick to him. He's trapped between our two planes. Nowhere to go but forward.

"One's on our tail," I say, instinctively aware of the shadow barreling in behind.

"I'll take care of him."

No time to affirm that one. Knight breaks away with fantastic speed, a tight spin that quickly puts him behind the rebel who's after us. He fires and chases the rebel into a dive.

Now it's only me and the colourless plane ahead. He tries a sudden roll, wings trembling with a rookie's grace. I roll as well, still on his tail, and mimic every move he makes. Left, right. Back and forth. His strategy's nonexistent. He tries to wiggle his wings, like it's some kind of message, and I hesitate. Time to end this pointless game. I dive a bit lower than him, a feigned surrender, giving him a moment to look around in confusion, then open my throttle and surge upwards again, attacking from below. The rebel plane can't outrun this. There's not a chance. I fire at the undercarriage with my cannon. Bright flames shoot from the plating as I pass beneath and away, pieces of metal pelting me, and the little fighter goes into a spin much too steep. There's a violent shudder through its body. Stalling. The right wing tears off, giving in to the pressure. Black smoke erupts from the burning engine, thick and ugly.

Get out of there, I tell him over my shoulder. *Hurry the hell up.*

A flash of orange, bright as noon, explodes five hundred feet below me. Flames streak through the air. I stare, hand still on the trigger, watching with some kind of terrible fascination as it plummets for the sea in a mesmerizing storm of colour and scattering metal.

No parachute.

"Two for you now, Headache," Knight calls, somewhere nearby. "I'm at your nine o'clock."

I fly straight.

"Charm, nine o'clock, understood?"

Silence. My breaths are heavy. Hands frozen.

3,500 feet, the altimeter says.

"Charm?"

"Yes."

"Get back on my wing."

"Yes."

"Quit saying that and do it, would you?"

Without thinking, I steer my plane for the coordinates and follow Knight into the fray.

The battle lasts no more than ten minutes. Ten minutes of life and death before the remaining enemy fighters decide to hightail it home. We land on a runway lined with relieved faces, ground crew and operations officials rubbing sweat from wet brows. The other pilots jump out to greet their grateful crowd.

I sit in my cockpit and ignore Filton's curious glances, pretending to write my flight report, taking my time, anything to avoid facing the questions and congratulations. I hide behind my sunglasses.

3,500 feet.

My grip tightens on the pen and nothing legible appears.

A knock on the cockpit startles me. Cyar peers through the glass, concerned, resting on the wing. I take a breath and open it, swiping off the glasses. Give him a grin. "Better catch up quick, Fox. I've got two on you now."

"Just letting you get a head start. Damn, I never even made it
into the air! Bell sounded right when I was in the shower, and by
the time I got out here, the rest of you had . . ." He pauses, studying me again. "You all right?"

"Fine."

"You're pale."

"Because I'm starving."

I push out of the cockpit abruptly and Cyar jumps onto the
tarmac, making room. There's something dark constricting
me from the inside out. It's going to make me sick. I walk for the
barracks and force myself to move at a regular pace, to appear
normal, but there's a flash of orange, bright as noon, in my vision.

"Impressive speed into that plane, Charm," Merlant calls.
"You've got a talented ground crew, readying it at the rate they
did."

"I do." I muster a hollow smile.

He gestures at my disheveled flight suit. "But remember the
life vest next time. Drowning isn't the way any pilot should go."

"No, sir," I say.

There are other ways to go.

The day passes and I sit on my bunk, thinking, letting my brain
go in circles. It's a terrible habit. I should be outside, distracting
myself, maybe playing cards or writing to Ali. If she were here
right now, I'd kiss her and not think twice. I'd kiss her and maybe
do even worse, because suddenly this moment feels very selfish
to me. It's mine. I've won it. There was me and there was him,
and now there's only me.

The loneliness of that startles me.

Evening comes and I sign out of base with one of the motor-
bikes, the ones we use to ride to the harbour on days off. Down
the familiar curving road, through Havenspur. The long promenade appears ahead. No one's out strolling tonight. The recent

weeks, the awareness of our fights in the sky, Arrin's speech . . . it's enough to unnerve even this quiet corner of Thurn.

The wharf looms along the western edge of town. When I arrive, the Landorian soldiers at the checkpoint flip through my papers. They nod and motion me to leave the motorbike at the gates. Ahead, shadowy ships sleep along the docks. Will the *Pursuit* even be here? Perhaps she's out on the Black, miles across the sea hunting for rebel vessels, for weapons being passed from hand to hand.

But no. There she is, anchored at the farthest dock. Relief floods me.

I haven't visited Kalt in the six weeks we've been here, and the Safire soldiers on guard look surprised at the sight of me. They quickly escort me to his officer's cabin. It's lit from within in the warm dark, inviting.

He sits at a table scattered with reports. Folco Carr's next to him. Folco quickly stands when I enter, his freckled face etched with surprise.

"Sorry," I say. "Am I interrupting?"

Folco shakes his head.

Kalt spares me a cursory glance. "Glad I was finally worth a trip."

"I've been busy."

"Join the club."

He looks tired. His normally pressed uniform jacket is tossed across the bed, and the collar of his shirt has at least three buttons undone. That's a lot for the brother who prides himself on looking the part.

"I'll leave you two alone," Folco says, no hint of hesitation.

He disappears out the door, and I slump into the seat opposite Kalt, ship creaking from side to side.

"What spurred you to make the effort, little brother?"

No words come. A sense of shame rises unexpectedly. We're not the type of family that stops by for sentimental reasons, but

that's why I'm here, and I don't know how to say it. "I'm not . . .
I was . . ."

He sets down his pen, waiting.

Oh hell, I'm desperate to tell someone. Anyone. I'll do it.

I tell him how Merlant and I came out of the sun, how we
trapped the rebel plane, how I chased him and got him in my
sights, then came from below and shot him to the sea in flames.
I killed him, I say. I burned him to death at 3,500 feet and now
there's nothing left, nothing at all, not even a body for his mother
to bury. And I did it.

Kalt listens, his fingers laced together, resting on his elbows.
"You did what you had to, Athan. There's nothing to blame
yourself for."

"I took someone out of existence."

"No, you eliminated a threat. A threat to you and your friends.
You're thinking about this wrong."

"It's not easy to think any other way." I struggle for the words.
"I've . . . I've never done it with my own hand. It's never been me."

"Neither have I."

Kalt says it almost in passing, and I nearly tell him not to
lie to make me feel better. But I realize he's telling the truth. He
hasn't. He serves on a ship with hundreds of men, prowling the
sea, playing games of cat and mouse, and even the times he's
been in battle, in Karkev, he's always been at the bridge, watching, strategizing, while sailors on the gunnery turrets pull the
triggers. It will always be that way for him—death coming as
shells fall miles away across the water, never right before his
eyes. Never a dogfight, two people locked in a blistering moment
with only one allowed to come out alive on the other side.

I look at him and realize, for the first time, I've been somewhere he hasn't.

His eyes are on the papers before him. "Do you remember
the last battle before Valon was won, when I made you hide
under Father's desk?"

The question catches me off guard. Of course I remember. I was seven and it was the most terrifying night of my short life. I knew that whenever Father and Malek began to bark orders, it meant gunfire and explosions would quickly follow. I was used to hiding and covering my ears to it. But that night was different. It happened too fast, too close to our base, and I wound up curled beneath Father's desk, eyes shut, certain the sky would fall on top of me if I opened them for even a breath.

"I said I'd watch the door," Kalt continues. "I told you that Arrin was guarding down the hall."

"Yes."

"I lied." His green eyes flick to mine. "Arrin wasn't down the hall. He was fighting. We were surrounded, and Father had no choice but to arm everyone he could."

I stare at him. "Arrin was thirteen."

"It was the first time he killed."

Nausea spikes again, rolling against my stomach. I lean forward in the chair to lessen it.

"I couldn't have done what he did, Athan. Not at that age. I asked him later how it was, and he said it wasn't so bad. He simply remembered that the other man had chosen to hold a gun, and it wasn't by accident, so how could he feel bad? Both of them knew why they were there. It made a lot of sense, and that's how I look at all of this. We're each here by choice, so why feel guilty? They want to fight, and we meet their challenge."

His explanation seems simple, rational, but something doesn't connect in me. "And Arrin has turned out just wonderful for it."

Kalt doesn't contest that. He only sighs. "I won't make excuses for him. He lives by his own rules, but it's always been that way. You know Father once tried to marry him into some wealthy Rahmeti family? To finalize the unification in a way they'd appreciate down there, or so he said. But Arrin just refused. Ran off and got some other girl pregnant and then slept with one of Father's officer's wives, a woman twice his age. Be glad you missed that one. It wasn't pretty. So believe me, I see what an idiot he can be. It has nothing to do with war. It has to do with *him*, and he suffers the consequences."

I'm not sure I believe that Arrin has ever suffered any consequences, but Kalt leans forward. "The point is, you make the choice for yourself. No matter how high you fly in the sky, Athan, no matter how you pretend otherwise, you were born with our name and you can't outrun it. Away doesn't exist, and you need to accept that. Then you'll be able to do what you should. As I do."

"At least it sounds like I'm getting another war to learn from." Can't hide the bitter humour in my voice.

"Yes. But surely you expected that."

I don't know if I did. Maybe there's always been a piece of me holding out hope that one day Father would decide he's had enough and that would be the end. I've done a very good job of not thinking about reality. I've spent years inventing a fiction in my head that sounds much better. But now I've killed someone, and there's nothing pretend about that.

Kalt's still watching me. "He'll never ask you to do more than you can. He asked Arrin to fight because he knew Arrin could do it. And he was right." He pauses. "You'll figure a way through it."

We sit in silence a few moments, the *Pursuit* creaking in her side-to-side sway. Kalt starts writing again. "I need to take care of these reports."

I don't move.

"You can stay here tonight if you want."

The offer's generous, coming from him, but I shake my head. "I should head back." I move for the door, then stop. "Thank you, Kalt."

He nods without looking up.

To Her Royal Highness (Princess of Royal Commands):

I'm your obedient servant. But as it turns out, there are no glasses of wine here. Wine is too fancy for an airbase full of men and so I've wound up instead with one bottle of watery ale. I drank the entire thing in a single go, now I'm sitting before a piece of paper. I might regret this in the morning (I will), but I'm going to seal the letter up tight when I finish. I've told Cyar to hide it, then mail it. I won't give myself a chance to think. He says all men become poets in love and war (though I really can't say here if one of those is true yet).

So what is it like to fly? It's like this.

You march out into the dawning day and nerves rattle around inside. Of course there are nerves. This isn't the safe sky you trained in. This is anyone's sky. It's always dark at first, thick with clouds from the sea, before the sun burns them away. Your friends laugh as they lace up their boots, your ground crew gives you the rundown, you feel happy to be alive. No one's going to die. Not today.

There's your plane, waiting faithfully. She's beautiful as ever. Up you go, settle in, the cockpit shut tight. It feels awfully tiny at that moment. Please, God, don't let this be my coffin. The rigger gives you a thumbs-up, saluting. Always smiling.

"Go on," he says. "We've done our work and now it's up to
you. You're on your own."

There's a bit of fear at this part. You have to commit.

But you go, of course, and then the runway's stretched out
before you like a shadow. Follow the flare path as you throttle back. They flash by and up you go into the unknown, into
anyone's sky. Steady now, watch the pitch.

3,000 feet.

You break through the clouds and meet a shining world.
Sunlight all around. The wind fights you side to side, but still
you push higher. This beautiful plane won't let you down. She's
on your side. Your ally.

15,000 feet. The birds have disappeared because even they
don't come this high. It's just vibrating metal, endless blue. Up
here in this perfect and untouched world, I see your face in
the sky, Ali. Your warm eyes in the golden dawn. You're the
sky I love so much, the place I want to be, and I feel like there's
nothing that can take that away. You and I, we could run as
far as we'd like and not look back. We could escape earth
and beat her at her own game. Maybe I'll fly away from here
and never come back. Go west and never stop, leave all this
behind.

How far to you, girl of the dawn sky?

But someone calls over the radio and the slipping western
horizon betrays me. It's getting farther and farther, and they
need me here. If anyone challenges our sky, I have to be ready
to fight. Today. At least for today. But I promise you, when
those dark planes come for the chase, I won't let them touch
me. I won't let them touch us, Ali. I was born in war and I
will not let them even come close. We'll go right into the smoking storm, beautiful plane and all. We'll ignore the chaos,
ignore the flaming wings and spiraling metal stars that streak
through the blue. We'll ignore the panic that scrapes like fire

to get free. We'll just keep running. Just be quick enough to stay ahead. It's what I'll always do. Because I have you. And I fly for you.

And that's what it's like, Ali, every day.

Yours always,
Athan

VIII

CHOICE

33

Hathene, Etania

The exam sits before me, taunting with its final questions.

They've allowed me to write in a secluded room of the palace, an instructor sent to oversee, his skeptical gaze and bushy brows bearing down while he circles my desk. I've already taken the first half—three hours of math and science, then a break, and now literature and history. It's asking me about the Wars of Discontent, about the final terrible rout where ten thousand Etanian soldiers were lost at once, but stars, I'm tired. Everything's blurring together.

And as always, Lark's photographs bleed into my thoughts.

Ten thousand men lost a hundred years ago, but what about the mothers today, whose boys were murdered before that wall? Did they watch and beg? Or did they simply cover their eyes and weep? The scene plays out in my head, over and over, in different ways. Sunny. Rainy. Dusk. The soldiers line their rifles, and I'm ordering them to stop, because I'm a princess and they have to do what I say, they must, and then I'm the one being blindfolded, stuck before the wall in the hot sun, waiting for death, and then it shifts again and suddenly I'm the one holding a gun.

I'm staring at the Landorian soldier, with a gun in my hands, and I wonder if I'd shoot.

I wonder if it's the right thing to do. If it would save the boys.

There's a cough, and the instructor gives me another pointed look. I haven't written a thing for at least five minutes.

What would you think about those photographs, sir? Would you care if you saw those children? Surely you would. You're stern, yes, but perhaps you have sons yourself. Wouldn't you protect them in any way you could? Wouldn't you imagine them in front of the wall?

He appears offended by my stare.

I see, suddenly, in this proud and educated man, the vanity of the North, and I'm glad Lark can't witness it. We get to read about tragedies far away and long ago. Study them in papers and presentations, debate solutions and strategies.

We don't have to live them.

He raps his pen on the desk and I hurry down some answers, then surrender the exam.

Three days later, I find Lark alone by the target range. The air is cold and wet, feeling more like early spring than late summer. He fires a pistol at the wood boards. Over and over, like he might right the world with a single, flawless shot. The thick pine trees round him absorb light and sound.

He lowers the weapon when he spots me, and I catch the glint of hope. Of gladness to see me. When I arrive, he kisses me on the cheek and I return it. It makes me feel better about the world, because if we can be friends, then surely this negotiation is possible, and soon.

"You're very good," I greet in Resyan, offering him my secret at last.

His smile warms further. "Thank you," he replies, evidently pleased to hear me speak his tongue. "You look like you have a question. What shall we discuss today?"

I stop beside him, arms wrapped about myself. "Only a small one."

"Then ask."

"What does your father do?"

"Ah, small question indeed." Lark gives me a half grin, then fires a sudden shot like a show-off, making my ears burn with the sharp sound. "He's a translator, in Rahian's court," he explains after. "We're not so impressive as your mother, I'm afraid. She's the one who claimed a Northern king's heart—and his crown."

I shift beneath Lark's teasing gaze. I know how fantastical it must seem to them, that she has risen so high and they've remained behind, forgotten characters in a story I don't know. I've always imagined that moment my parents first saw each other like a childish myth—she visiting from a foreign kingdom, beautiful, wearing Resya's colours, and he watching from across a ball or a reception, young and handsome and with no family left. Only his books. I'm certain my father was lonely. There was no one left to stop him from marrying a woman he shouldn't.

Why, then, did no one stop Lark from following the Nahir?

Desperately curious to hear, at last, how he ended up this way, I ask, "Did you always want to be . . . ?"

For some reason, I can't bring myself to say the word aloud. It's too strange to talk of the Nahir like it is a title, a thing one can be, no different from a doctor. But it is. In Lark's world, it is.

He pauses, sensing my meaning. "No. Not at first."

Unsettled pain wrinkles his face.

I wait.

"My mother was a nurse," he admits eventually, which explains certain aspects of his knowledge. "She believed in healing others. Civilians. Nahir. Even the wounded Landorian soldiers left behind by their own officers. Back then, the revolt was young, and she believed if she could save people, she could save the world."

"*Was* a nurse?"

"Was." He nods. "You can save other people, but you can't save yourself from a misspent bullet."

We stand in silence, in the memory of this woman—my aunt—whom I will never know.

"I've seen the lives that are wasted through inaction, Aurelia," he continues after a moment, his mouth gentle around my name, like he's holding out a flower of goodwill. "It makes little sense to you, here, I know, but I don't want to die for no reason. I want to die with purpose. That's why I am what I am."

"I don't think she died without purpose," I say.

"You haven't lived half your life without a mother," he replies.

I turn away, acknowledging the wet woods so he can't see my face. I don't want to witness his grief, nor do I want him to see my pity.

There's a tap on my arm after a moment.

I find him offering me the pistol. "Your turn," he says.

I shake my head. "I don't shoot."

"Come on. You must. My father says your mother was the best shot he ever saw. She could shoot the tail off a cat."

"My mother?" I make a face. "She'd hate that I'm even here."

"And yet you are."

His excited gaze wears me down. "One time, then," I say, taking the pistol for the sake of our friendship.

I stretch my arms out straight, the way I've seen others do, and aim the pistol at the board with its large red circle. Lifeless, distant. Paint chipping from seasons of harsh weather.

"Keep steady," Lark says. "Watch your breath. If you flinch, you miss."

I try to still myself. Still everything.

"And you need to balance forward more. The force will knock you off your heels."

I grimace, adjusting, standing on the balls of my feet instead, then I focus again, clutching the pistol.

One shot.

"Ali, what the devil are you doing!"

I lower the weapon, spinning.

Reni strides from the wash of pine trees, his face horrified. "You'd better thank your stars I saw this instead of Mother."

"And why shouldn't she shoot?" Lark inquires, irritated.

"Please," Reni says. "This is dangerous for a woman."

"*Why?*"

At this moment, I quite appreciate Lark's dogged Nahir persistence.

But Reni is freshly returned from his tour and armed with the news from the Royal League. General Dakar's son has given my brother a great gift—justification for his enmity. He scowls at our Resyan cousin. "Why? This is a live weapon. In the hands of a girl who has never fired a thing before in her life!"

"It was only going to be one shot," I say.

"Don't make me the villain today, Ali. I was trying to bring you good news, but now you're sour."

I frown at his interpretation, but hand the pistol back anyway, not wanting Lark to bear the brunt of Reni's strained civility. "Then tell me the good news."

"You passed your exams. You're now a student of the University."

The words, announced in the damp gloom of the target range, don't feel very inspiring. Not the way I expected. "Oh," I say.

"And you have a surprise for your birthday." Reni appears even less enthused about this part of the good news. "The General is coming. He's giving you an air demonstration."

"A demonstration?" I ask in disbelief.

This I wasn't expecting, not by any stretch.

"Yes. He says you requested it, and he doesn't wish to disappoint."

Thin laughter slips out. My request from a month ago seems foolish now, like a silly question from a silly girl who asked simply because she could, and of course there are far more important things at hand. Why should he remember it?

"He's not coming for that reason alone," Reni continues, sensing my thoughts. "He has much to discuss with Mother, about Resya. He's also bringing his son, since the Commander's the one who will inevitably be on the ground there."

Thick revulsion coats my mouth, and Lark stares at me from behind Reni, a question in his eyes. I know he's waiting to see what I'll do next. I have a power in my hands, the power he longs for and will never have, and the terrible wall sits between us, an unforgivable crime that no one knows.

But we do.

"No, I don't want the air demonstration, Reni. Not if his son is coming."

Now my brother looks stunned. "I'm sorry?"

"I don't want it. That rotten Commander won't come to Etania. You'll have to tell the General an excuse."

Lark looks a bit in awe.

"But he said he's planning to bring your friends," Reni says. "The Lieutenant and the other one."

At that, my noble certainty crumbles to dust. The offer in those wonderful and unexpected words is as radiant as a hundred suns—Athan, here, far from danger and close enough to touch, to see where it might lead, and the temptation makes me light-headed. But then I imagine the Commander's brilliant smile gloating over his victories, impressing our kingdom. That isn't the sort of show I asked for at the beginning of the summer. There won't be any joy in it, not knowing what I know, not even with Athan in front of me. Perhaps there's another way to see him again. Surely there is, but not like this.

"I don't want the demonstration," I say, surprising myself with how calmly the words come. "Tell the General."

Reni shakes his head, expression drawn, tense. "We can't refuse the General. Not now with the situation in Resya. I don't think it matters what you want."

And I shrug, because really, I never expected it did.

When Reni has left—with a strict order that I not touch the

pistol—I turn to Lark, the two of us alone again in the drizzly silence. "What will you do?" he asks, distressed. "That General isn't interested in talking round a table. He'll have another angle. He could ruin our whole damn negotiation!"

"But what if he *would* talk?" I ask aloud, remembering how he and I did that very thing earlier in the summer. How civil it was, with tea. Surely he and my mother could settle this matter of Resya and do so without force. The Safire and Nahir have too much in common. Surely he'd listen to Seath? We could bring him to the table and—

"You can't trust him," Lark says sharply.

"I have no choice." I look at my cousin helplessly. "The Commander may be bold and reckless—unpredictable, as you said—but I have to trust the General is not. And if I can keep him talking to us, and away from Resya, won't the world be better for it? I can't let these suspicions grow, Lark. My mother needs him as ally."

Lark watches me with hollow copper eyes. "Do what you'd like. But your first and last mistake will always be trusting an ambitious Northerner."

34

Havenspur, Thurn

Father arrives at base one morning with no warning.

His motorcar rumbles through the gates just past noon, flanked by armoured carriers. The vehicle halts and everyone on the tarmac stares. Father steps out, greeting Wick with a handshake, and armed Safire soldiers surround him. Casually, as if this isn't a show, he and Wick peruse the compound, walking across the runway, pointing, smiling. Wick has to look up, since he's at least a head shorter.

Inside the hangar, I clean my plane with Kif. He sits on the wing, rag in hand, and I pretend to work, watching Father. Waiting for him to wave for me.

Kif chatters about his theories of gun alignment, cleaning as he goes, but eventually, his voice lowers a touch. "I have to say, sir, that whole speech at the Royal League has got me thinking."

"Yeah?" I'm still looking out the doors.

"I've been wondering since we got here, you see, about the camouflage on these planes."

Father and Wick have stopped, isolated together on the far edge of the runway.

"I mean, these wings are still grey," Kif continues, patting the metal he's seated on. "I got here and the first thing I said to Filton was 'When can I paint them?' and he says, 'We're not painting them,' and I thought 'Not painting them?' Everywhere inland from here's mostly desert, right? These wings need to match. I told him just that and he said to wait, because the orders hadn't come."

Father and Wick turn, heading back this way.

This is it. He's going to wave me over.

I set down my rag.

"But see, here's the funny part, sir. Why would we wait? If we're here to help Thurn, setting up a base and all, then we need to change the colours now. Might as well. But Resya . . . see, Resya's mostly mountainous jungle. The jewel of the South. Desert camouflage wouldn't work there. And that's when I started wondering."

I turn back to Kif, his words finally registering. "What are you saying?"

He's earnest atop the wing. "Between you and me, sir, it's almost like they knew we'd need to paint the planes again soon. So they didn't bother to do it yet."

"Kif, no one could have predicted this."

He swallows, hesitating. "It just seems a bit convenient."

I shake off the uneasy feeling and give Kif a pointed look. "You shouldn't talk like this."

He drops his eyes. "Sorry, sir." Freckled cheeks red, he begins to clean the metal again, and I glance out the hangar doors.

No sign of Father anywhere.

The day shifts forward, hours passing, and still no invitation comes. It's nearly dinner now and I'm getting impatient. He wouldn't leave without seeing me, would he?

I sit in the lounge, hands idly constructing a little ship out of newspaper. Folding, folding.

Distraction.

Right when I've talked myself into marching over on my own, Wick stomps through the door and points. "Lieutenant."

God, that took long enough.

Inside HQ, he motions me down a hall to the back offices, the place Merlant and Garrick usually go for their private briefings. It's hushed there, away from the busy main room filled with maps and typewriters and phone calls. The sound of pilots and personnel fades. Wick points to a closed door, wordless, before returning the way we came.

I take a breath and step inside.

Father's seated at the desk. Early evening light filters through narrow windows. He glances up and gives a small smile. "Look at you. Hardly recognizable with all that sun on your face." He gestures to the seat across from him.

I sit.

He continues to scan whatever it is he's reading. "A moment."

"Yes, sir."

It's been seven weeks and five long hours. What's one more moment? I wait quietly, analyzing my boots, while Father reads, signs, repeats.

Clock ticking.

"You've done well here," he comments. "Captain Merlant's impressed."

"I downed two planes, sir."

He nods, still reading. "Very good."

Silence again. Ticking. Flies buzz behind the window blinds.

Eventually, he finishes and sits back in his seat. "Did you see your brother's speech?"

I nod. "It was something else."

"Indeed. Windom helped him with it, so he can't claim full credit."

"I'm guessing it wasn't Windom's idea to grin and call them all cowards?"

"No, but he did hope to provoke a reaction. Arrin may have taken it to the edge, as he often does, but the insult woke them up. They know they're guilty of what he said."

"And whose idea was it to bring up Mother?" I can't hide my distaste.

Father pauses. "It earned us sympathy from the skeptics. Windom got Arrin in the right frame of mind this summer—never an easy task. I'm sure Arrin learned some humility." And that's the end of the discussion about Mother, conversation diverted easily around it.

No choice but to follow. "Arrin wasn't excited about working with Windom. Said it was his own personal hell."

"No doubt."

"Why?"

"The problem, as always with Arrin, is a girl." I give a questioning look, but he ignores it. "And Kalt? Did you see him with that Carr boy?"

I forgot about Father's sudden switches. They're like mental flick-rolls. I never know what's next. And the intense question in his gaze, bordering on aversion, suddenly illuminates the whole "reporting" thing.

"No, sir," I say quickly. "I only visited him once." Which is true. I just don't mention that they were together, in his cabin, Kalt half-dressed.

I steel myself for Father's inspection. I feel like I can hear the blood in my ears as he looks. Then he tilts his head and sits back in the chair, no evidence of whether or not my half truth worked. "I'm returning to Etania next week. I need to ensure Sinora knows the position she's now in—and Resya. I've decided an air demonstration would be a nice reminder of our power. And I did promise one for the Princess. It's very generous of me to indulge the request of a sweet girl, for her birthday."

Something like excitement spikes inside me cautiously.

"And I can't do that without you," he adds, like it needs to be explained. "I want to know how the winds are blowing."

Yes, it's excitement now. Undeniable. There's a protest inside me somewhere, that noble part of me that feels whatever I've

done so far is enough of a betrayal, and anything more only
amounts to the kind of sin that can't ever be forgiven. But the
protest doesn't come. I want to see her again, more than I want
to think about whatever comes after.

"Yes, sir." She'll be thrilled to see me, that's certain at least.

"See what you can find out about Resya, what Sinora's been
up to this summer."

She'll smile at me with that secret smile that says everything
and nothing, then disappears, making me try harder, making me
desperate to win it back again. Instead of the dreamlike vision
she's become, she'll be real and welcoming and brighter than the
nightmare of 3,500 feet.

"Arrin's coming too."

I snap back. "Arrin?"

He gives me a wry look. "I think you just went pale, even with
the new colour on your face."

I stare at him. This was inevitable, but it still sucks the heat
from my skin. Too soon, too soon. A shadow on my wings, waiting for me to maneuver. "Why is he coming?"

"That isn't your concern. You have one job, and only one job,
and you're doing well at it. Still writing letters?"

I nod, scrambling for an opening. Something to put myself in
the middle of this. With her. Not just in my damn airplane, which
will be useless against whatever Arrin's planning.

"There's a birthday masquerade, Father. She invited me."

He looks unimpressed. "A masquerade?"

"Yes. You know, with masks."

"I know what a damn masquerade is. How is this helpful?"

A very good question, but I hold his stare. "I'm sure you and
Arrin will be busy with other . . . priorities, and I think I make a
good decoy. A distraction. Because I doubt Sinora's very fond of
me at the moment. If you needed a distraction, I mean."

I'm stabbing in the dark, hoping to hit on something that

makes sense for his secret mission, and interest flickers on his face. "A distraction?" He nods slowly. "That could be helpful."

"I should go?"

He glares at me. "No, you should stop talking. Your mouth irritates me more than Arrin's sometimes. At least he's honest."

"I was trying to help, sir." It sounds convincing enough, a touch hurt even.

He says nothing to that, leaning back in his chair again, cracking his knuckles, and doesn't speak for a long stretch. The flies continue to buzz behind the slatted blinds. Crawling, falling, flying in little bursts.

"Two planes down?" he finally asks.

I nod.

"All on your own?"

I nod again.

Silence.

"All right," he says, "you'll go."

I glance up. "I will?"

"For God's sake, is this a question now?"

I shake my head quickly. "No, sir."

"Bring me something useful. Make this worth it."

"Yes, sir." I pause, then give a guilty smile. "But I might need a mask."

He looks at me with what's nearly a shred of humour. "Son, you need a lot more than that at this point."

IX

A THOUSAND
DAYS

35

Hathene, Etania

The morning of my birthday, I wake to a palace on edge.

The halls around me quiver with nervous voices and twitching hands, faces vainly trying to give me a bright smile, though they never break the hushed mask of uncertainty.

Down in Hathene, the protesters have gathered again, far beyond their usual numbers. They've swelled out of the square, trickling into side streets and luring more to their cause. We can hear them from Mother's drawing room above the palace entrance. With the windows open, there's a faint noise on the balmy breeze. Distant, yet palpable. Shouts and chants that won't be silenced, along with the purr of our aeroplanes patrolling the sky.

Alone, Mother and I stand at the windows. I keep waiting for the faint sound to die down. Hoping.

"My star, this has nothing to do with your birthday," Mother assures me, arm round my shoulders, "and everything to do with the General."

This makes sense, of course. We can't hear the protesters' words from this distance, but the Safire will soon arrive, returning with the fresh controversy of new ambition in Resya, and certainly these crowds are as angry as when they threatened my Royal Chase this spring. They still despise the Safire and their bloody boots in our kingdom. But this time, I can see both sides, both worlds, and it's not as simple as they imagine. I want to run before them and say, "I'm on your side, I swear it. I'm trying to bring peace in the best way I can!"

Instead, I have to stand here and simply listen, wrapped in a pastel-blue dress with ribbons and suffocating lace. I feel as tiny as the pearl pins in my hair.

Finally seventeen.

"Mother, I know this may sound presumptuous, but I'm wondering if I might host a meeting with both you and the General this evening. In honour of my birthday," I add, so it might sound more qualified.

Her dark gaze turns from the window, holding me now with a question. "A meeting?"

"It would be very important to me. Could you arrange it?"

She lifts a hand to my cheek, the scent of saffron lingering. "And what do you wish to say?"

I pause, uncertain exactly how much to share with her in advance—these weeks since the Commander's speech have upturned her usual gravity, leaving her weary and drawn, a fragile shadow beneath her eyes, but it compels me even further to do what I must. After everything else she's endured, she doesn't deserve a kingdom divided and a homeland bound for flames. We have too much at stake. There's no choice but to be bold and play a step ahead, keeping the General on our side.

I lower my voice. "I have an idea for peace," I say in Resyan, "and I simply need you and the General to hear me out for but fifteen minutes. I promise it would be worth everyone's time."

A thin smile brushes her face. "My darling, you can no longer speak that tongue in this place," she replies in Etanian, glancing cautiously at the door. "Please, speak as you should."

The command feels suddenly wrong. I never thought of Resyan as mine. It's always been the language I speak for her— to comfort her, to warm her in her loneliness. But now that it's being taken from me, for no other reason than an unproven and distant allegation, I feel a sense of loss. Injustice.

It's half mine, at least.

"I will speak what I wish," I say in Resyan, annoyed by the larger world, not her.

She covers my lips with her hand, firm. "You have to be your father now, child. Do you understand?"

I step back. "I think I'll be myself," I reply shortly.

She shakes her head with another weak smile, then kisses my cheek, and a loud drone envelops the valley, announcing the arrival of the Safire flight in all its vainglory.

When it's time to make for the western balcony, I find myself trailing behind Mother and Reni and their retinue, stalling the inevitable. A tremble of nerves has me filled with anticipation. I feel both brave and scattered at once, and a sudden hand on my unsuspecting wrist makes me jump nearly out of my skin in surprise.

"Lark!" I hiss, realizing it's him.

"Sorry," he says, a sheepish expression on his face. Apparently he's been lurking in the alcove. "I wanted to tell you I've left a gift in your room. For your birthday?"

His hesitant offer, and the fact that he's tucked away in the shadows, drains my annoyance. I know why he's hiding, and I glance towards the balcony. "Will you be all right?" I ask, suddenly not wanting to leave him—a Nahir fighter—alone anywhere with the many Safire uniforms soon about.

"I don't particularly trust them," he agrees bleakly.

"Then stay away," I order. "Just stay put in your room."

"Yes, but—"

"Stay out of the way," I repeat, more firmly, putting my hand on his chest. "You don't owe them anything. Leave it to me."

He says nothing, but he knows I'm right. I have the luxury of trust.

He certainly doesn't.

I give him a halfhearted smile. "I have to try this, Lark. For my mother. For all of us."

He looks at me, his gaze distant. Some inner sorrow warring with his luminous fire. "You needn't worry this much about your mother, Cousin. You should worry more about your uncle."

I shake my head. I don't have time to concern myself with Uncle Tanek, not now. His little plots with Reni feel so far from the larger danger of war.

Lark saunters back down the hall, alone, and I head for the sunny centre stage. Warmth greets me on the balcony. Etanian and Safire flags fluttering together. Facing the hangar and the forest, everything seems normal and bright, a crowd of loyal courtiers gathered for the display, the only change the plentiful liveried guards patrolling the grounds, many on horseback. The Queen's Royal Mounted Guard. Their horses are lovely, large creatures, like Liberty, trained in the barracks outside the city, and today they're groomed to a gleam in honour of my birthday.

My eyes skim past them, searching the seven planes shining silver on the tarmac, and something warm and wonderful nips inside my stomach, easing the uncertainty.

Athan.

Where is he? Which plane is he waiting in?

I'm ready to run to the railing and find him, but Mother diverts my plan with a polite wave, and I step back reluctantly. The General is with her, wearing a sanguine smile, formidable today in his slate-grey uniform, adorned in medals, a force that won't be intimidated. "I'm sorry these protests must happen on your birthday," he says to me, as if he should be the one apologize. "But rest assured, we can still celebrate without fear. We'll send our squadron over their heads afterwards, how about that? Get them to reconsider?"

"Thank you," I say, unsure if his confidence makes me feel any better.

Lark's photographs have already blurred my perception of him.

"There's no reason to be alarmed," he assures firmly. "It won't last the afternoon."

"Regardless, General, I'm grateful you even thought to bring me this demonstration."

"It's your doing," he replies. "You made an impression, and I haven't forgotten our first meeting."

We share a smile then, thanks to our private memory, and I try to convince myself that such a calm and reasonable man would surely be willing to hear me out. That he might even listen to a man like Seath, who also wants to defy the order of things.

Mother leads him off, and I spot Lord Marcin waiting with Violet in a shady patch of the balcony. Her lips are painted red, but the look on her face approaches despair. I assume this means her captain hasn't made an appearance. Then I look beyond her and nearly choke on my own breath.

There's Reni, with the General's son.

The *Commander*!

They're at the farthest end of the balcony, laughing together in some sort of friendly conversation that defies all reason. The Commander has his arms crossed, leaning against the railing. No indication of the blood on his hands—children's blood. Instead, he looks comfortable as a lazing dog, trussed up in his fancy uniform and cap, and my hatred burns, thick and sour. I want to go right up and ask him about the photographs. I want to demand he admit the truth. But I need to be subtler than that, I know, and I force myself to take a breath.

I march for the railing and my eyes sweep the seven planes assembled below.

Searching, searching, wanting only one thing, the one thing that makes sense, that needs to be true, and then I find it.

My heart skips.

Athan.

He's there and I'm up here, and even that feels much too far at the moment. He pushes the tousled blond hair from his forehead, sharing words with a mechanic, and then, as if written in the stars, glances up to where I am. He gives a beautiful smile. It's all for me, and I return it to the point my cheeks hurt. I'm ready to abandon this balcony and close the now crossable distance between us, no sea to swim, no letters to speak words for us. There's nothing else I want in this moment but to fling my arms round him!

"I've never seen a girl this delighted by a bunch of silly airplanes," a silvery voice observes.

I spin, startled, and look up into the face of the Commander. He grins, holding an iced gin in one hand.

"They're impressive," I manage, and immediately regret such a mindless answer.

"Perhaps in show, Princess."

"They're *your* aeroplanes, Commander."

"Oh, did I say silly planes? I meant the pilots."

His rude comment nips even though it has nothing to do with me. I'm about to tell him to show more respect for his men, but he laughs, a nice-sounding laugh, the sort that makes whatever came before it seem entirely like a misunderstanding. "Beautiful mountains," he remarks instead. He's even more handsome than in the film reel, all perfect angles and glamorous confidence. The one who'd shoot boys holding the hands of old men. The one who dared condemn Resya before the entire world.

I'd like to spit in his vain face.

"Yes," I agree, straightening. "What were you talking about with my brother?"

"Politics. But I won't bore you with that." He leans his arms on the rail. "You have a friend down there?"

"Lieutenant Erelis."

"Never heard of him."

I raise my chin. "He's new to the squadrons, and I'm sure you'll hear of him soon enough." I indicate Athan on the tarmac, still readying his plane. "We happened to meet earlier this summer. I was impressed by his manner."

"You happened to meet? How?"

"Why do you care?"

"Because if some low-rank commoner has managed to tempt a princess, I'd like to know his strategy." He grins again.

"The Lieutenant isn't common," I say pointedly. "He's an officer, and I don't appreciate your insinuation."

The Commander raises a suggestive brow. "I'm only saying I was that age once too. No one ever put a princess in front of me, but if they had, I sure as hell know what I would've done."

"Not everyone lacks a moral compass as you do," I say, thinking of the blood-spattered wall more than anything else.

"Princess, he's a boy and you're a girl, and"—he leans closer, lowering his voice—"please don't take this the wrong way, but you'd certainly leave the compass pointing north."

I gasp.

He frowns, as if offended that I'm offended. "I'm not talking about me. I'm talking about *him*." He waves at the tarmac.

"Do you have no manners at all?"

"When I feel like it." He flags a passing servant, and holds out his empty drink. "Another one, please. Less ice this time, extra gin—in fact, bring a larger glass. Thank you." He turns back to me. "How was that?"

I refuse to look at him. "I'd like to watch the silly pilots now, if you don't mind."

"You're still on that?"

"It was insulting to your men."

"It's not my fault they're useless," he says, glancing at the sky. "They spend their time in a pristine cockpit, playing tag two miles above the real battles, and—no, don't look at me like that, Princess. I know what you're thinking. You're thinking 'What do you know? You sit behind a desk and get medals while they do the real fighting.' That's what you're thinking, isn't it?"

I hate that he's right. "They're shooting down your enemy," I say hotly.

"In theory, yes. And I have no problem with the ones who do. To them, I say thank you and please do it again. But too many of them are show-offs. They get a thrill from the game of it, and while my men are being torn to bits on the ground, strafed by enemy planes, I look up and find these idiots spinning around the sky like a flock of goddamn sparrows." He shakes his head. "War isn't a show."

"It's not like that."

"You're speaking from your vast military experience?"

"You should watch your tongue, Commander."

"Why? Because I'm honest? People never like the truth, Princess. They don't like discovering that the Jewel of the South is actually a den of the Nahir. They hate the ugliness of that reality, but there it is, whether anyone likes it or not."

"Truth?" I spit furiously, stepping too close, into his minty scent. My whisper is fierce. "Resya isn't what you believe it is, Commander. The real truth to be discovered is what *you* did in Beraya."

This wasn't how I planned it happening, but here we go.

He stares at me. "What did you say?"

"You heard it."

"How do you . . . ?"

"Photographs," I say under my breath. "I've seen them."

Anger flares behind his clear blue eyes, and he leans down closer, voice equally low. "The *Landorians* did something in Beraya. Not me."

I'm certain he's lying. The denial's too quick, too practiced, and his sudden hostility borders on guilt. "You should be careful, Commander. You'll tarnish your father's reputation, and I don't think you can afford that. Not with the League still considering your petition for war."

His gaze darkens. "Good God, I certainly don't need a lecture from *you* on strategy. You have no idea what it's like down there."

Someone clears a throat. "Excuse me, sir."

He turns from me abruptly, facing a nervous servant holding a drink. The Commander grabs the glass, waving the man off, and then takes a very long drink—most of it—eyes on the tarmac again. "You tell me to preserve my father's reputation?" Unfriendly laughter growls from his chest. "I did nothing, Princess, and even if I had, where do you think I learned it?"

That unrepentant observation saps my burst of confidence. The aeroplanes below suddenly glint in a sinister way, creatures of prey, blood on their claws, and I hate that I must smile on it.

"I don't want your show!" I snarl. "I didn't want it before, but they made me accept it and I wish I'd refused. I want nothing to do with you or your father!"

He blinks down at my fury, stunned by the rude words. I realize I might have just ruined my own plot for negotiation. In this moment, I don't even care. But then he smiles. "Nothing to do with us?" he repeats. He looks at the runway, at Athan's plane, then bursts into laughter. He laughs so hard, with such sudden delight, that I'm certain he's finally drunk.

I spin to leave, but I'm not quick enough.

"We're set to begin, Your Highness," the General calls, his steady voice like firm ground. "Are you ready?"

I force myself to face him. "Yes, of course."

"Got my second drink," the Commander adds, raising it. "Now I expect this show will be spectacular."

The General shoots a look at his son. It holds a sliver of pure derision, reminding me, at this very important moment, that they aren't one and the same. He walks over and places himself between us. "Would you like me to tell you about the planes, Your Highness?"

"Please," I say.

He does just that, pointing out pilots and aircraft, explaining how he pulled them from three different squadrons since he couldn't very well pull an entire operational unit home from Thurn. My gaze drifts to Athan again. He's inside his plane now, Cyar in the one beside it. I'm hardly listening, but I nod every now and again while the General explains this and that about firepower and special cannons, and then the planes have come to life. Flames licking from exhaust pipes and propellers spinning.

They roar into the sky, and from where we stand, it's like they're mere feet apart, nearly touching. Three of them separate, spiraling. Three more do the same, and soon they're moving in pairs, diving far too steeply, a whistle screaming as they devour hundreds of feet of air. The crowd cheers, but I can scarcely breathe. Didn't Cyar say pilots can become disoriented and lose sight of the horizon?

Two planes pass above the crowd, rolling their wings and flying inverted. They make it look effortless, like a skip in the sun. Even Reni appears impressed.

Other pairs take their turns, the General explaining each maneuver to me, and finally the two planes with no squadron symbols on their flanks approach from the west. Athan and Cyar. The leading plane does two wild spins as if caught on an invisible string, snapping over twice before swooping high again.

"A double flick-roll," the General observes.

"Is that difficult?"

"This low to the ground, yes. It can easily become a stall and you need room to recover from that. A bit of a risk."

I've no idea what a stall is, but secretly I'm pleased to see Athan showing off for me. Of course it was him.

A Safire man approaches the General. "There was a request for a low pass, sir."

"Was there?"

"For the Princess."

"Very well," the General says, glancing sideways at me. "You'll like this one."

I find his kindness wearing my anger down, yet again. It's like we're the only two on this balcony and he's forgotten anyone else who might be wanting his attention. He's interested only in my happiness.

I steal a glance at the Commander nearby. He's idly sipping another full drink—his third? fourth? He covers a yawn, then catches my eye and gives a bored smile. "Father, how about we get some Etanian pilots up there? Make this an actual match?"

The General ignores him.

As I turn my gaze back to the sky, a growl of thunder skims the palace behind us, erupting across the balcony. A lone fighter passes right over our heads, impossibly low, propeller raging. There and gone again in the space of a petrified breath. Everyone ducks, glasses dropped, shattering.

Everyone not in Safire uniform, at least.

The General sips his drink. "That's a low pass," he says to me, as if we're sharing a private joke.

I clutch the railing with white knuckles. "I thought for sure it was a low crash!"

He laughs. "Rattles your bones, doesn't it?"

"Stars in heaven, General!" Mother exclaims nearby, hand over her heart. "I hope that's a punishable stunt."

"I believe it was in honour of the Princess," he says. "If she objects, then yes, it might be punishable." He looks down at me. "What do you think?"

I glance at the retreating plane, its flank empty, and recognition dawns. "That was Lieutenant Erelis, wasn't it?"

"I hope so," the General replies. "The older pilots wouldn't bother with such a stunt."

"No, I loved it. I'll never forget it! Can he do it again?"

"Stars, once was enough," Reni says nearby. He looks pale, as do Jerig, Marcin, and Violet.

The Commander raises his drink in my direction. "I'll remember your pilot's name now. The one who terrorized an entire balcony of royalty. That might deserve a medal!" He laughs again, that good-natured laughter, elbowing Reni in the arm.

My brother smiles reluctantly.

The aeroplanes perform a few more figures in the sky, then land, lining up proudly to rousing applause.

"Would you like to see one up close?" the General asks me. "That's Captain Nevern in the third plane. Leader of our first squadron, Greydawn. He'd be happy to show you."

I spot the older pilot, stepping out of his cockpit. "Yes, of course. I've so many questions for him," I lie. Before the General can suspect my deception, I hurry down the steps, past the courtiers, and onto the tarmac. Smoke lingers in the air. Pilots hop from their planes, speaking with ground crew, and I offer a brief stop at Captain Nevern. "Very nice show," I say, "and thank you."

He bows from the neck. "Of course, Your Highness." He looks about to add more, but I march on, winding through the planes, ignoring the surprised stares of the pilots I don't know. My heart begins to pound quicker. I wish more than anything there weren't a hundred eyes watching, no rules to follow or manners to remember. Then I round the nose of a plane and they're in front of me.

Athan Erelis and Cyar Hajari.

No longer a memory but real, both leaning against Athan's plane. They're a splendid match. The same height. Funny I should notice this now, but it seems very perfect.

"So you weren't lying," I announce, and they straighten quickly. "You really are pilots."

"We tried to be modest about it," Cyar replies cheerfully, "since not everyone has this sort of talent."

Athan holds up a rag. "I was even blindfolded." His face, golden from the sun, splits with a grin that's more infectious than I remember.

Oh stars, I want only to throw my arms round him! Why must I feel this nervous now that he's three feet away? An army of butterflies has me light-headed and flushed, entirely undone. I turn and study the plane, covering my nerves with curiosity. "It was an incredible show. I swear my heart stopped more than once."

"And what was your favourite part?" Athan asks.

I run a hand along the hot wing. "I don't know. I'll have to think about that." Of course he's hoping I'll mention his stunt. Surely that's what he wants. But I'll keep him guessing awhile yet. "You know, the Commander believes you pilots aren't very helpful in battle. That's what he told me. You'll have to practice some more if you hope to impress him."

Athan glances to the balcony. He gives a slight roll of the eyes, a bold move for a rookie, but I don't blame him. "Do you know how difficult it is to impress him? Almost as difficult as impressing you."

"Oh, I am impressed, Lieutenant. I thought Officer Hajari did a very fine spin on that last lap."

Cyar bows, and Athan nudges him. "Are you trying to make me look bad, Hajari?"

"Not trying at all, though the Princess is entitled to an opinion."

"But how could she even tell whose plane it was?"

"That's a good point."

"So we'll say it was mine."

Cyar salutes. "You're the higher rank."

Athan smiles at me. "Thank you for the compliments on my spin, Princess."

I laugh and continue to circle the plane. "And where do your orders take you next?"

"Hopefully, home," Athan says. "At least for a bit."

"I'm sure your family misses you with autumn harvest coming."

"Harvest?"

"Yes, for the crops. I've done a lot of reading this summer for my exam. Water cycles and irrigation and all the things farmers must think about. It's very fascinating to me. There's quite a lot of work that goes into it."

Athan nods. "You're right. A lot of work."

"Good thing your family only has cows," Cyar says. "No crops."

"Yes, exactly," Athan agrees. "No harvest for us."

Two little marks on his plane catch my eye, and I touch them. "What are those?"

"My count," Athan explains. "How many planes I've knocked down so far."

"You mean shot down?"

He nods, and this blunt admission shadows the mood. Somewhere in this world are graves for two pilots, put there by this boy I desire so terribly. I try to shake myself out of the inevitable thought, for his sake, but it still steals some joy.

He steps near, the closest he's yet come. "Don't worry, they both had parachutes. We always hope to see those."

Relief returns. "I'm glad."

"Come on, enough about me," he says. "You've been hinting at rumours of an escape for weeks now. Don't I get to hear about it finally?"

"Perhaps for a price," I say, taking my own step closer, now that we're hidden behind the plane. He's close enough to touch. Smelling of petrol and smoke.

He wrinkles his nose. "Did I mention I'm a poor pilot with a rather meagre monthly wage?"

I reach out to adjust the crooked lapel on his chest. I let my hand linger just a moment, feeling the firmness of his chest, wondering if I might feel the beat of his heart, even. "There are other things I'd accept, Lieutenant," I say softly, and this time he's the one who looks undone.

⊰ ATHAN ⊱

Being with Ali again is as exhilarating as flight.

I'm wearing a uniform smudged with oil and engine grease, sleeves rolled to my elbows, but she notices none of it. She doesn't care, breeze tugging the curves of her perfectly pressed dress. She's different and the same and new all at once.

Cautious and inviting.

I don't understand it. I love that I don't understand it.

Out on the tarmac, it feels safe together, our own little world. We're far from the dark horizon—Sinora, the Prince, Father, Arrin. But every time I start to get distracted by them, by the storm I know is brewing, she turns on me with those beautiful eyes, asking another question about Thurn or my plane, and I keep saying things that seem satisfying enough she won't push further. Eventually, though, I slip up. I make a joke about saving Cyar's life and realize the misstep immediately.

She stares at me with the kind of furious precision that rivals Father's.

I'm dragged down a narrow stone path deep into the gardens, away from the crowd, dodging green-coated men on horseback who hold our Safire vintage. A reminder of our fake unity that sets me on edge all over again.

We make it far enough into the flourishing grove that we're nearly to the stables, and then she faces me. "You never mentioned the knock-downs in your letters," she accuses. "You can't go off and do these things without even a warning."

"I'm sorry," I say honestly. "I didn't want you to worry."

"I know, but if anything ever happened to you . . ." She sighs, a new kind of heaviness in her gaze. More like grief. "Everything down there, it's not as simple as you think."

Bitter laughter escapes my lips. I can't help it, since nothing is simple, not here nor there, and I know it well.

But she narrows her eyes further. "I mean that. You've only seen your little corner of it, and there are terrible—" Her annoyance changes to distress. "There are terrible things that have happened and you don't understand," she whispers.

"Understand what?"

"You won't believe me."

"I will."

"Do you promise?"

I nod, and she looks at me, as if trying to determine if I'm lying, but she's not very good at that anyway. I wait.

"Your General's son did horrid things in Thurn, and no one knows. I saw the photographs. I swear I did. There were children. Little *children*, and they were shot."

She clutches my arms, bare skin against mine, and no words come. I'd like to have a hundred of them right now, a hundred reasons why she's wrong, reasons why it can't be true, but I don't. We just stare at each other, her hands clinging to me. Her words demanding an answer.

"Children?" I say finally, wanting to hit something. Wanting to hit Arrin.

I hate that I don't doubt it right away.

I hate that it feels like it could be truth.

She can only nod. "It's not right. It isn't, and someone must do something before this next war begins."

I push an escaped dark strand of hair from her face. I've waited too long to do that, liking the way she stills beneath my brief touch. "There won't be another war, Ali. The League will never allow it."

"But they could, Athan! It's all so very complicated. You were right when you said that the Nahir might be justified in their revolt. I see what you mean now."

I stare at her. "I never said the Nahir were justified."

"No, but you implied it strongly, and now I've heard the truth, from someone there. It's more than—"

"I believe you," I interrupt, wanting her to stop talking. I don't want to hear things I shouldn't, not this time. "Whatever the Commander has done, I promise the rest of us are trying to do the right thing. I swear it."

She leans up on her toes and kisses my cheek. "I know you are."

But the feel of her lips doesn't send my pulse into a flick-roll. It's too much like a blessing, like an offering of trust, and I don't deserve it. Not with what's happening today.

I force a laugh. "God, it's your birthday. Why are we talking about war? We should be talking about your masquerade and what the hell I'm going to wear to it!"

Her eyes widen. "You're coming tonight?"

"We don't leave until first light tomorrow."

"Oh, Athan, you can wear whatever you'd like. It doesn't matter!"

"I might have to," I admit. "I haven't been planning on this for months like you."

"Come as you are. That's the best gift you could give."

"I have something else, but it's quite small."

"You do?"

"Close your eyes."

She obliges, and I pull out the amber necklace, placing it in her outstretched hand. She opens her eyes, her face lighting up all over again. "From Thurn?" she asks, fingers moving over the sharp-edged gem. "It's very crude, isn't it?"

"Exactly the reaction I was hoping for."

This is why pilots don't give gifts to princesses.

"But it's perfect all the same," she says quickly. "Put it on for me, please. I'll wear it now." She turns around, sweeping the dark hair off her neck, waiting.

I glance left and right down the path. Not that there's anything wrong with this, but guilt still prickles as I bring my hands up and fiddle with the clasp, fingers brushing her skin. I imagine kissing her neck.

I imagine kissing a lot more than that.

She turns and faces me again. "Thank you."

There's too much trust in her gaze, and the thought of lying to her for another minute seems beyond shameful. But then what would I say?

Ali, nothing in my life makes much sense, but I know I'd fight for you if you gave me the chance. But my father, he wants to destroy your mother, and truthfully, I think I want that too, because my mother was the innocent one and yours stole her from me. But maybe when this is all over, if it ever can be over, we'll meet in the middle and try to—

Her eyes study my face so intently that I take a step back, embarrassed. "What's wrong?"

"Nothing," she says, and her hand moves, as if to reach for me again. "The sun made more freckles across your nose. They look very sweet." Her lips part softly, curved with invitation. There's no question about it. It's an offer for me to take more, honest and true, and I would if it wasn't the worst thing I could do to us both.

I resist the fierce temptation and hold out my arm. "We should go back. They'll be wondering where we are."

"I don't care what they think."

"Please don't force me to answer to the Queen." I try a smile.

She relents and slips closer, her hand taking mine unexpectedly. "I wouldn't do that to you." She smiles in return. "And at least we have tonight."

36

≥ ATHAN ≤

"Nice mask," Cyar says to me from across the room, the same one we shared during our first visit, "but I don't know what you are."

"Hm?" I'm staring out the open window, at the rainy evening. Glorious mountains and all.

"It's a masquerade. I think you have to be . . . something."

"I am." I turn, holding the mask to my face. "A Safire pilot. The General's son. Take your pick." I laugh at my own joke, though it's really not that funny.

Of course I know why I picked this mask and not the dozen others in Norvenne. I just can't quite admit it to him. She's going as Elinga, the unicorn, and that makes me Elois, the dragon. Cyar's a romantic, yes, but maybe not enough to waltz around as creatures from a damn painting.

He smiles wryly at me. "Don't waste your ace, then. I think you'll need it."

I'm not sure what he means. Presumably he's pleased, as always, to hold his experience with women over me—though technically he's only ever kissed one, and he hardly sees her as it is, so really, his expertise is entirely hypothetical and in his head.

"I have a very clever ace, in fact," I say, "and it's—"

I stop.

"Go on," Cyar says. "Does it have anything to do with your remarkable ability to waltz?"

My hands grip the mask, the satin-trimmed purple and black, the little gems like fire along the edges, and I can't move or breathe. My brain is turning cylinders.

Cyar frowns. "Athan, are you all right?"

A very clever ace.

One very clever ace.

The throttle releases and I'm charging through the truth, all of it there and ready to be captured. Every clue. Everything I should have seen long ago if I hadn't been so blinded by my own self-misery. Every perfect piece that fell into place right on time to the ticking clock—the loss of Hady to the Nahir as we arrived in Landore, the subsequent attacks as we bartered for our right to be in the South, our fighters sitting there with no desert camouflage, the Nahir suddenly armed with weapons and airplanes, and now, like divine fate, their trail leading right to Resya, the homeland of Sinora Lehzar.

And the plea of the man Father shot in the back alley.

The name Seath on his lips.

"I have to see my father," I hurl at Cyar, wheeling for the door wildly.

"What the hell?" Cyar says, blinking at me.

"Wait." I swing back and toss a folded paper at him. "Stay on my wing, all right?"

He doesn't question it. He's stunned by my madness, gaping, but he nods and takes the paper, staring at it likes it's a scorpion.

Thank God for Cyar.

I arrive at Father's quarters and bang on the door. I'm past worrying, past fear.

Just desperate.

Father opens it with an annoyed expression, and the scowl deepens when he finds me on the other side. Around him I see

Arrin and a young man who is Southern-looking, not in uniform, and my suspicion turns to raging certainty.

"Would you excuse us, Ambassador Gazhirem?" Father says to the man. "I need to deal with my son in private."

It's partly polite, partly a threat directed at me, but I no longer care.

The Ambassador doesn't hesitate. "Have a pleasant evening, General," he says with a slight bow, then stalks by me for the door, smiling warily, brown eyes curious.

Then he's gone.

Father looks at me, something like expectation in his gaze—like he's been waiting for me all night. Waiting for me to show up at his door in a fury.

I don't like that.

"Your ace in the South," I say, watching his face. "Tell me it isn't Seath."

There's only a flicker in his expression, a slightly raised brow and then a subtle twist at the end of his mouth. He fills a glass with brandy and glances at Arrin. "There, you see? He is the brilliant one. It took you months to figure it out—and you had every report at your disposal."

"In my defense," Arrin replies, arms behind his head, "you were the one who specifically said the Nahir cutting out my tongue would be a favour to you. It didn't cross my mind you'd be encouraging your friends to do that. But then, when have I ever been given special treatment?" He looks at me. "Not like Lieutenant *Erelis*."

Neither one is denying my absurd claim.

This can't be true.

"Father, what are you doing?" I demand, and I know I sound stunned, a step behind.

He eyes his brandy in the lamplight. "It's as you said, Athan. Seath is helping me take the South. I supply him with the weapons, he wages the war. He's uniting that place, far faster than anyone has before, and with him on my side, I'll succeed where every other Northern king has failed." He tastes the brandy. "And in return, I'll one day stand with Seath as ally. He'll have the Free Thurn he's fought so long for—once we've cowed the royals into submission. Fear of him is a helpful motivator for now."

I stare, horrified. "You're arming the *Nahir*?"

"Seath isn't the monster they believe," Father admonishes quickly, "and he's certainly more reasonable than many down there. He's a revolutionary, Athan. A man who wants a change of power, a new order to things. And who better to help with that?" Father indicates himself, as if that needs to be clarified.

And suddenly it does make perfect and terrible sense. Two revolutionaries challenging the established, royal order in a secret alliance. Two leaders who fought their way from nothing, who are demanding attention whether anyone wants to give it to them or not.

Of course Father would admire a man like Seath.

Of course Seath would admire a man like Father.

"If Gawain catches wind of this—" I stop. There's an edge of desperation in my voice. "If *anyone* in the North finds out, we're ruined. The united kingdoms would outnumber us easily."

"I don't leave a trail," he says simply. "Nothing on paper or otherwise. I have a man to go in-between."

The pieces shift together with my dread. . . .

"Havis," I say.

It's too much, too fast. Seath and Father have together conspired to put an innocent kingdom in the crosshairs. They've convinced the North that Resya is to blame for all this trouble. They've made sure the evidence leads there, not to Father. When the kings of the North wonder who is arming the Nahir, they'll see Resya in their reports, in their suspicions.

And Resya is Sinora's homeland.

She'll be the only Northern queen with ties to the kingdom that armed the Nahir.

"Seath is helping you bring down Sinora," I say, feeling helpless before the scope of all this. "You're going to make her as guilty as Resya when you go to war there."

"Don't look so glum about it," Arrin remarks.

Father nods. "That was the idea, though Seath has his own quarrel with her. It goes back further than mine. Fortunately, I now have an even better sin to condemn her with which won't take quite so long."

In this moment, I'm not sure whether to be in awe of him or terrified. He's feigned friendship with the Landorians to get his army into their Southern territory. He's feigned an alliance with Sinora to lure her into the right trap. Now, he's mobilizing the Nahir and supporting their revolution and blaming it on another kingdom entirely. It's all a charade. The weeks Kalt spent out on the sea looking for Nahir, the aftermath of the arms exchange we passed on the *Pursuit* . . . Those exchanges were with us. We gave them guns and mortars and better aircraft, pinning it on Resya. And that reality brings a bitter truth, hollowing me out and leaving a fierce hurt.

"You mean I've been fighting *you*?"

Father shifts and won't meet my eye. "I wouldn't put it quite like that."

Not quite, but close enough. Those Nahir pilots who tried to kill me are on our team. It's all a show—a deadly show—to make it look real.

Do their pilots know the truth? Or are we all in the dark, committing ourselves to this lethal game, believing it counts for something?

I look between my father and brother. Twin masters of madness. I'm scared to be in the same room as them, to know they don't give a damn about anything, not even me. "I don't know what it is you're planning here tonight, for Sinora, but please swear to me the Princess won't be involved. She has nothing to do with this."

Father frowns, vexed. "She'll be fine."

I don't believe him.

Arrin rolls his eyes at me. "Despite what you think, that girl knows far more than she should and is liable to start slandering our mission. Good job winning her to our side."

"She says you murdered children, Arrin."

"You too?"

"You're not denying it?"

Arrin looks to Father, disbelieving, then throws his hands in the air. "You created this mess, Father. How'd you not guess he'd end up too far in to see straight?"

"Tell me what you're doing tonight," I growl at my brother.

"Me?" Arrin's usual stupid grin returns. "I have a date in Hathene."

Of course. The entire city is in a state of unrest and he's there like a moth to easy flames. "Don't stir something that's already boiling, Arrin. This kingdom, and every kingdom around, will pin it on us and then—"

"They won't pin it on us," Arrin says.

"Why not?"

"Because those protesters were bought by us."

The shock of this revelation is significantly lessened, thanks to the Nahir one. I realize my hand has worked itself into a brutal fist.

"Well, they were ours at first," Arrin continues, "back in the spring. And we might have given them some rifles for tonight. But actually, it was much easier than expected to get Etanian tempers riled. They really feel strongly about getting this Resyan woman off their throne. I wanted ours to storm the palace tonight, to deliver the coup, but to be honest, the group's grown since my speech to the League and I'm not sure what they'll do when they reach here. Might have to have an actual battle with them. Take a few out before we can win and look like heroes."

I stare at him. "Who the hell is going to fight with *us* against Etanians?"

"I don't know. Maybe supporters of the Prince. Civil wars are messy, Athan. Anything can happen!" He sounds disturbingly intrigued about the possibilities.

"*Civil war?* You're going to burn all of Etania for one woman?"

Arrin holds out a hand. "Yes, but for once I won't take credit. I'd like to, but really, this is your moment. Because let me tell you—the protesters weren't very happy when they learned a Resyan woman *murdered* their beloved king. That was the moment they truly wanted her head. They'll help us get her under house arrest, and after that we'll do some investigating. I bet if we looked hard enough we'd find proof she personally helped her homeland arm the Nahir. Can you imagine where that would lead, Athan? To a noose, I'd imagine. Sinora Lehzar and her Southern sympathies. The woman who murdered her husband in a spectacular plot for a Northern throne." He pauses. "A murder confessed from the lips of the Etanian princess, in fact."

Blood disappears from my face, flooding me. Strangling me. *The murder.*

The fatal weakness Arrin needed to make this all possible. Now we don't have to let this build with time, slowly gathering evidence against Sinora. We get to seize everything, right now, because we found a crime that is all hers, the crowning sin of a traitorous woman linked to the kingdom now arming the Nahir.

And it's because of me.

Me betraying Ali's trust for a chance to save her.

I pretend I'm not shattered by guilt, struggling to be stronger than the fear in me, because now I have no choice. I have to finish this betrayal and actually save her.

"I'm going to the masquerade," I say, like I'm giving my own order.

Father downs his brandy, then gestures at me. "You're certainly not."

"Why?"

"Don't you dare question me, boy." It's the sharpest command he's given me in months. I forgot how it takes the heat from my skin. How it takes everything from me, leaving me empty. He's at me in a stride, gripping my shoulder, hard enough to throb. "I'm taking this palace, Athan, and you stay out of it. I've worked too hard to let your weakness get in the way. Don't be your goddamn mother."

His words are worse than any fist to my face. They bruise my soul.

Anger suffuses my throat viciously. Anger that he'd take this incredible risk and not think twice. Anger that even though I'm trying my best, even though I don't want to hurt Ali, there's no way for this to end without her despising me.

I've condemned her entire world.

Father's still got me by the shoulder. "You need to use your head, Athan. You think only a step ahead when you should be thinking ten. You need to think on the ground the way you do in the air."

I almost laugh in his face. He doesn't know a thing about the air. In the air, you react within the space of a second, you make up everything in the breath of a brutal, terrified moment, and if you're lucky, someone else ends up burning instead of you. There's no such thing as ten steps ahead.

He holds my gaze, determined, this man who's my father, gambling with the fate of the entire world in his steady hand.

"I understand, sir," I say.

"Good."

I pull from his grip. "And I'm going to the masquerade."

I'm gone before he can do anything. I bolt across the room, and Arrin tries to stop me on the way.

"Don't be an idiot," he says. "Don't try to—"

I'm out the door.

⊰ Aurelia ⊱

It's humid by the time I reach the grand ballroom, the after-effects of an evening rain. The air feels slightly sticky, my hair curling, my satin gown heavy and clinging—freshwater pearls embroidered into the bodice, fastened with petals of lace, silver skirts twirling round me. With the feathered mask, I'm every bit a magical creature. Elinga of the mountains.

At my throat rests Athan's necklace, the precious amber stone, and though Heathwyn says it doesn't match my gown, not even slightly, I don't care.

There's a glimmer of certainty building inside.

Being with Athan again has shifted everything right, illuminating the secret things in my heart, chasing the shadows everyone else tries to bring close. I know the words I'll say to him tonight. I'll mean them with everything in me.

No one will touch what's ours.

"Shall we, then, pretty unicorn?"

Reni smiles, offering me his arm at the top of the promenade steps. He's dressed in a green tunic with gold trim, high leather boots, a sword at his side, and topped with a plain brown mask. He claims to be a pirate, but I think I know which treasure he wants for himself tonight.

Together, we descend the stairs, stepping into a land of fantasy. Flowers gather in archways and windows, colours in roses and peaches, lights like stars across the vaulted ceiling. Green vines wind from chandelier to chandelier, and on each table a burst of

flowers and flickering candles. Hundreds of jeweled masks sparkle, courtiers watching me arrive with half-hidden smiles.

Mother waits for us beside Lord Marcin. Her sweeping red
gown is vibrant and startling, a bright flower in the soft light.
She kisses me on the cheek. "Happy birthday, my heart." Then
she steps back, noticing my necklace. "What is this?"

"A gift from the Lieutenant."

She tilts her head. "It doesn't quite match your gown."

"It's perfect," I say, touching it again. "And I'm going to wear
it every day."

"I think it's hideous," Reni offers with a smile.

I'm about to protest, but his attention is already ensnared
elsewhere. Violet's wearing a strapless dress, slender shoulders
revealed, face obscured by a gold mask of butterfly wings. She
looks fragile and miserable and very alone, standing beside a
table with fresh-cut freesias. He adjusts his sword and strides in
her direction.

I worry for his heart—and hers.

But I do what I must, putting on a polite smile and wading
through the large herd of masks, listening to compliments from
lords and ladies, from aging counts and countesses, accepting
their frivolous praise. It's fine and well for the first little while,
familiar and fluttering voices, but soon an anxious tremor twists
my hands together. The minutes escape.

Where is Athan? Why hasn't he appeared?

I wait in my shimmering gown, alone, the moments ticking,
taunting. Maybe I shouldn't have hoped for anything more.
Maybe this was never his to give, not when he wears a uniform
and answers to all those brutal men above him.

Maybe I've tricked myself yet again.

"Is Elinga missing her dragon?"

I spin round.

Athan stands there, cautious, dressed in his uniform and

wearing a dark-purple mask with black trim. A stark figure in the midst of the florid ballroom sea.

"You came." It's the only thing that finds its way out of my stunned delight.

"I said I would."

"Your mask is perfect!" And it is. Slightly angular at the sides, so very dragon-like.

He glances round the room, nervous, and I don't blame him for feeling out of place. His plain uniform stands out in a tapestry of rich fabrics. The courtly faces watch us, curious, but I take his arm slyly and lead him for the marble floor gleaming in chandelier light. "Dance with me, Lieutenant."

"I was hoping you'd forget to ask."

"Certainly not, and it's my birthday."

He smiles hesitantly. "I suppose I can't say no to a unicorn. But, please, let's be terrible in a corner where we won't hurt anyone else." He's leading me now, by the arm.

"Say *unicorn*."

He looks over his shoulder. "Unicorn?"

"It sounds lovely with your accent."

"Unicorn."

"Again."

He turns and brings me closer, stopping us in a lonely corner. "Unicorn, unicorn, unicorn," he whispers softly, turning the silly request into something that trips up my breath.

Heart pounding in my palms, I place my arms round him. I catch the scent of soap, but also lingering smoke from the runway. Perhaps it's saturated into his very skin. Together, we dance in our little corner, and though the slow waltz is easy to keep pace with, I have to remind him again what to do. He's distracted and still nervous. To think he can perform those fabulous breathtaking stunts in the air but be so perfectly helpless with his feet on the ground.

"I think I'm starting to get the hang of this," he says, bumping into me again.

"I hope you haven't been practicing."

"With who?" His grin appears for a moment. "Cyar?"

"I don't know," I say. "Those pretty girls in Thurn."

He pulls me even closer. "Are they?"

The sudden nearness of his lips distracts me momentarily. He makes me want so much more, and I'm desperate to learn what kind of kiss he'd give me. But not here. Not in front of all these people. I step back to give us space. "What's the first thing you'll do when you're home?" I ask instead, as if he hasn't just set me breathless.

He thinks. "Be alone for a while. Everywhere I go, I'm always with someone else. Morning, afternoon, night. It's tiring."

"And then?"

He glances over my shoulder. "And then I'd like to fly for an afternoon. No one after me. No targets. Just for the joy of it, not any other reason."

"And once you're back on the ground?"

"Then I'll probably sit there, realizing how much I'd rather be with you." His gaze is serious.

He recaptures the polite distance I've put between us, and I'm sure my cheeks are glowing pink. I feel the many eyes on us—hundreds of them, bejeweled, tipsy with wine, laughing through the night. We must look very strange and romantic, the princess and her handsome, common pilot. But once upon a time, many of them saw my father do the same. They watched him love a woman who didn't belong, watched him give his crown to her, and a sense of rightness moves through me, all the way to my fingertips draped across the back of Athan's neck. His skin is warm, his uniform rough, and his lips are close enough to my face I can feel his breath there. I rouse courage for the words I want to say.

But first.

"Tell me again there will be no war."

"No war," he says, glancing over my shoulder for the hundredth time. He really doesn't need to worry so much. We dance a moment in silence, before he pushes me back gently from him. "No, I'm not going to lie about this." There's a new heaviness in his voice, but his hand briefly brushes the skin along my neck, delicious fire. "In truth, I don't know how the League will rule. I'd rather plan for the worst."

I stop waltzing. "You're the one who said you didn't like reality, that you preferred to dream. Do we need to flip a coin for this now?"

"Ali, that was—"

"And yet here you are. You made it to my masquerade, didn't you? The League won't rule against a sovereign kingdom. You know this. They won't. So tell me what it is you're truly afraid of."

He doesn't speak for a long moment. Then he says, very quietly, "Sometimes I'm afraid that no one—not a single person—will notice that I don't belong here."

In this place, alone together in the corner of the dance floor, surrounded by too much unknown, too much unspoken, I know what he means.

"Here" is this uniform, this ugly thing that sends him to battle.

"Here" is a world where the League might surprise us all and announce war.

"Here" is anything that goes against his desperately gentle nature.

I bring myself closer yet, looking into his face, fervent, at the light freckles and sun-dusted skin pulsing with life, into his grey eyes that seem as weary and layered as the sea. I can't imagine him harmed. "You can be expected to do and be many things, Athan, but know this—you don't always have to be brave."

He looks like he wants to kiss me.

I know he does, then his gaze is torn away again.

"Look at me," I insist, and he does. "This is important. I've known you hardly more than a summer and yet it feels like it might as well be a thousand days. I feel like I know all of you, and I want us to have a chance. I don't care how long it takes. I'll escape and meet you somewhere. Anywhere. I'd wait a thousand days for you if you promised you felt the same. A thousand days, don't you believe me? You simply have to stay alive. Promise me that."

He looks down at me, not smiling. Oh, I wish he'd smile at a moment like this! I'm trembling to have admitted all of it. I know I sound childish and desperate and willing, but it's true as the sun, starting here and ending there, certain to follow the same path.

He slips the mask off his face, resting it above his forehead. "I have to tell you something."

"Tell me."

"It isn't easy to say."

"It's all right."

His eyes dart beyond me, arms tensing round my waist, distracted again.

"Tell me what?" I ask, confused.

I'm about to turn and see what he's staring at, the thing that's apparently more enthralling than me, when he grips me by the shoulders and holds my gaze fiercely with his own. "That I've missed you more than anything," he says in a breath. And then his lips are on mine, sudden and warm and overwhelming, like a dream, like everything I've imagined. But it's all so wrong and unexpected that I push him off me.

My face is aflame behind my mask.

"What are you doing?" I whisper, mortified.

He appears briefly hurt, and then a blistering crack shatters the moment. I wince with the sharpness of it, my hands gripping him, still pushing him away. Then another crack, and another.

The room splinters to chaos.

Screams and shattering. Limbs falling, scrambling. A table overturned.

I'm still frozen, but Athan grabs me, yanking me from our lonely corner of the floor, dodging panicked faces. The mask covers my peripheral vision, and I tear it off in time to see a guard fall with red seeping from his chest. He stumbles right into me on his way down, eyes strange and distended. I turn and see others crumpling. Scarlet stains on satin and silk. But Athan drags me between the narrow side doors, and the harsh thrum of bullets fades to bursts behind us. Awful screams.

We hurtle down the stairs, recognition clawing through my terror. It's the same way I took him weeks ago on our tour. I want to grab at something, beg him to go back, but he's sprinting us through the maze of halls, then pushing the library door open.

My father's library.

He has me by the wrist and it hurts. "Stop, stop," I say more as a gasp. "Reni!"

He ignores me and shuts us inside, pulling me before the wide windows. Outside, propellers are already growling into the night sky, the glass trembling as they pass above the palace. It's far too many aeroplanes at once.

What the stars is happening!

Athan points his sidearm at the window. "Can I?"

I look at him, wide-eyed. "Yes?"

He fires, glass imploding, and the sudden sound forces a cry into my throat. But it doesn't get out. There's a desert inside me, sucking away my voice.

Before us, a few feet down, is the dark lawn and the gardens beyond. He gestures for me to jump, and there's no other choice but to do it. My gown tangles round my legs. Muddy earth soaks my knees, and the scalloped lacing turns brown. I stand quickly and trip, but Athan's hand grabs me again, helping me up.

We run for the dark edge of the forest, keeping to the shadowy gardens. The hangar to our left is lit by floodlights and shouts, and a plane flashes close overhead, black swords glinting from the bottom.

Safire.

Once in the woods and hidden by leafy darkness, breathing hard, Athan says, "We're safe here for now." He kneels beside me on the cold, wet ground.

I nod numbly, smelling the sweet pine, the smoky trail of aeroplanes, and stare at my ruined gown. A gaping tear mars the delicate fabric where I tripped. Blood is speckled on the bodice from the wounded guard.

Stars, I'm going to be sick.

I feel gentle hands on the sides of my face. "I'm taking you away from here, Ali. You'll be safe, I promise." When I don't respond, he says, "Cyar's coming. He's going to help."

I peer up at him, confused. "How does Cyar know where to find us?"

Athan doesn't answer. His face is pale and tense in the flickering illumination of the distant spotlights.

"What's happening?" I demand, trembling, finding something sharp to grasp. Something like anger. "What do you know?"

He leans back against the tree opposite me. The mask still rests on his forehead at an awkward angle. "The protesters aren't happy to have us here, you know that."

"And you thought they'd attack my damn masquerade because of it?"

"I didn't know anything! God, what do you think?" He sounds as panicked and frustrated as me. "I just had a fear inside me, and I've learned to listen to that fear. It's often right."

I lean forward and snatch the mask off his forehead. It looks all wrong.

Tense moments go by, the sky filled with engines, staccato sounds erupting from the distant palace. But then a shadowed figure approaches the woods cautiously, and Athan readies his pistol.

"First into the fray, Charm?" the familiar voice calls.

It's Cyar, looking shaken when he nears, but relief softens his face at the sight of us. Athan also looks relieved. He jumps up and they begin to speak in Savien, but I stand and clear my throat behind them.

"Please," I say, arms wrapped round myself. "Whatever it is, I want to hear."

Cyar glances at me warily, and I raise my chin higher. He relents. "It's the protesters," he says. "They came disguised as guards. We've captured them, and our General has secured the palace, but there are rioters still marching up from the city. They're armed, demanding the Queen be arrested."

Coldness seizes me, indignant. "This isn't her fault!" I say. "She has nothing to do with this. They're angry at *you*. They've been in the square all day!"

Cyar hesitates. "This . . . this is larger than Hathene, Princess. There are three other cities in revolt."

"Then what are they saying?" My panic builds with the growing discomfort on Cyar's face. "If it's not about you, then what is it about?"

"They're saying . . . she murdered your father."

My body turns to ice. My heart, my blood, my bones. Everything. They know—the kingdom knows the truth. They know my father was murdered. But how? And how could they ever blame her?

"Where's my brother?" I ask frantically.

"He disappeared. And they're searching for you now." Cyar looks at me, helpless. "The General wants to put you with your mother, for the time being."

"He wants to arrest me, too?" My voice nearly breaks on that, stunned.

Athan remains silent, fist tightening on his gun.

"Our General doesn't wish to arrest anyone," Cyar says quickly. "It's only for your own protection until the protesters are dealt with. It's much too—"

"No, we have to get to the hangar," Athan interrupts.

"The hangar?" both Cyar and I repeat.

Athan looks at me. "I told you. I'm taking you away from here."

"You can't steal a damn aeroplane!" I say.

But he's already striding for the tree line, off to plot this mad strategy. Cyar turns to me once he's disappeared. We stand together awkwardly, my dress torn and bloodied, my arms still clutched to my chest.

He removes his Safire jacket and hands it to me. "You look cold, Princess." That's what he says, which is truer than he can know, but I also see what he means, gentle beneath the surface. He's aware of my trembling horror. I put it on gratefully, savouring the sudden warmth, covering up the splotches of brutal red. The blood of my people.

Then he holds his pistol out. "And put this in the pocket."

I stare at the weapon. "No, I can't—"

"You need it more than me tonight. But don't let him see. He won't let me leave here without it."

I know he means Athan, and I'm about to protest, but my mad dragon-boy is already back, and I hide the gun quickly.

Athan looks me up and down, now wrapped in Safire uniform.

"Tonight's not the night to be running around in a dress," Cyar says to him simply.

Athan nods, and I see a bit of embarrassment in his gaze. Perhaps he knows that he should have thought of this. That he should have been the noble one to give me his coat. But there's no time to worry about being a gentleman.

"Cyar's going to make our diversion," Athan says to me, "and I'll borrow one of the Safire planes."

"Borrow?" I ask.

"Commandeer." He shrugs.

Stars, they're going to get themselves both court-martialed—or worse!

But he takes my hand, earnest. "We have to run, all right?"

There's urgency in his touch, and I see the loyalty in his gaze, feel the strange sense of having everything I want right in front of me . . . and yet nothing at all. And then I see the orange glow south of us, rising higher. A devilish horizon of blood red. The hazy air.

It isn't the fuel of aeroplanes I smell.

The Safire boys see my fresh horror, and they turn.

Flames dance in the distance, beyond the front gates of the palace. Thick, dusty smoke blots out the stars, billowing south, and shapes of aeroplanes pass between the dark plumes.

The forest is on fire.

The rioters have done this, or perhaps one of the metal machines in the sky. I don't know anymore, but my world is burning.

"Good God," Cyar says.

"Get to the hangar," Athan orders, grabbing my hand.

I'm not sure if it's the Safire uniform I'm wearing or the pistol hidden in my pocket, but suddenly, with absolutely certainty, I know what I have to do.

"No," I say, pulling from Athan. "I'm not leaving my mother behind."

He stares at me. "Ali, there's no way we can get to her. Not without you being found and locked up as well. Look around you! There's an entire militia demanding your neck!"

"I have a way." I sound more confident than I feel. "Because I know it's a lie."

"What's a lie?"

"The damn murder, Athan!" I could hit him for looking so perplexed right now. "My mother didn't do it! She must speak to them. They'll listen. I know they will. They adore my mother, I swear it! If they heard the truth, they could never blame her."

Athan tilts his head. His face is fire and shadows. "The truth?"

I don't have time to explain. Not now. But we have an answer, the secret rumour about our royal line, the reason he was truly murdered. My mother didn't want to share it with the world, but now she'll have to find a way to redeem herself. A half version of it, perhaps. There's no other choice.

I grab Athan's arm. "Take me to your General."

His eyes widen. "What?"

"Please! I need him, and I believe he'll listen to me. I know that sounds mad, but we have an understanding. He won't arrest me."

"You *are* mad," Athan says. "You don't know what fear makes people do. They don't listen."

"Oh, he'll listen, Lieutenant. He has to, because I have leverage." I raise my chin, finally feeling some power in this. "Photographs of his son's war crime."

Another Safire fighter snarls above us, and Cyar raises his hands, stepping back. "Maybe commandeering the plane was the better idea."

But Athan says nothing. He simply stares at me for a long moment, the feeling of an eternity passing between us, the brilliant little wheels turning in his head. Like he's trying to run through every possible outcome of this gamble. I don't blame him. But I'm going back for my mother, with or without him, and I think he knows this, too.

He waves to Cyar. "All right, you're scaring first. But I guess we're doing it inside the palace now."

Cyar sighs. "Copy that, Lieutenant."

"Is this pilot talk for 'yes'?" I ask.

Athan's hand is already clutching my own again, the only answer I need. The fever dream of this strange night retreats in the wake of renewed conviction. Whatever he's concerned about, it's not large enough to kill his determination to help me, and he's quickly leading me at a run towards the monstrous, glittering shape of home now wrapped in a fog of smoke.

We drop down behind the garden hedges. Faint dark figures loom in the haze, patrolling the grounds, guns raised. Safire uniforms. Cyar makes his move, approaching them with a Savien greeting. They lower their weapons in acknowledgment. One pats his shoulder, asking a question. Cyar points in the opposite direction, towards the stables, urging them to follow, and then they're gone.

"That was easy," I say.

"Who wouldn't believe Cyar?" Athan replies.

Quickly, we dash for the back doors, the ones I always take through the kitchens. It seems the safest bet. We stumble into the scullery, greeted by wide-eyed faces. Hall boys, footmen, maids. They're all crouched behind tables, gaping at me and my muddy gown and Safire jacket. But I see the one thing I need to see in their gaze—relief. They may be following the General's orders, panicked, but they're glad to see me alive. Safe.

It means more than they can know.

"Your Highness," a hall boy says tentatively. It's the one who always delivers my breakfast. "Are you all right?"

"I'm fine," I say, trying to sound confident but wildly grateful for a familiar face. "I need to get to Her Majesty."

"Those rioters in the city are saying terrible things," one of the maids blurts out. Another elbows her, but she keeps on. "We know it isn't true, Your Highness. How could anyone believe it?"

The others nod, and I want to cry now. Their loyalty bolsters my courage and touches my heart. My mother has to address the kingdom. These liars don't speak for everyone and they must be silenced.

"I need to get to Ambassador Gazhirem's room," I tell the nearest footman. "We'll need to use your service stairs, to avoid the main halls. Can you work out a diversion?"

The man fidgets nervously. "We've been ordered to stay here, Your Highness."

"By who?" Athan interjects. I'd almost forgotten him standing behind me.

"Safire orders," the man stutters in reply.

"Then I give you a new order," Athan says. "You're making a diversion. Where are my comrades posted?"

Athan's words do the trick. It's almost comical, all these grown men suddenly bumping round, discussing the best way to go, and all because of an eighteen-year-old farm boy who wears the right uniform tonight. But I'm sure it's reassuring to have a Safire soldier working in unity with me.

Like they're gambling on both sides at once.

The older footmen go out the doors to the hall, and after a moment there's a sudden argument in Landori—the Etanian footmen saying they need to check on the injured in the ballroom with the physician, and the Safire saying the injured are well taken care of and about to be transported by the General's plane to proper facilities, and then the Etanians saying it's still their duty to check, and back and forth they go while the younger footman slips Athan and me across the hall and into a narrow service door.

We dash up the spiraling stairs for the wing of the state apartments. I pray to Father that my mad idea works.

If Lark is hiding there, let him give me those photographs. Let him see the dire situation we're in. And if he isn't, then at least let me find them. Somehow.

Stars, it all sounds worse now that I'm in the palace. My cousin will never let me waste his evidence to save myself. I wonder, briefly, where Havis is but it doesn't matter. He's off saving his own neck, for certain.

We're nearly there and I feel I've been running a lifetime. There's a smoky veil to the air. Someone has opened the windows, letting in the stench of burning trees and flowers and earth. The gunfire and shouts are very close now, just outside the palace.

Silently, the servant boy leaves us at Lark's room, darting down the hall to scout for Safire. I try to open the door but it's locked. Athan pushes me back and swings out his pistol. No choice. I say another silent prayer that Athan's shot will blend into the stammering cacophony of the night, but the report is still loud. Echoing.

I push the wounded door open and—

"Your Highness!"

We both spin.

Three Safire soldiers approach with guns raised, but Athan swings his pistol at them, and they halt abruptly.

"Where is the General?" Athan demands. Again, he sounds far more bold than I expect, as if it's only natural they should be following his orders, answering his questions.

But it works. They swallow, step back, eyes still on me.

"He's in the throne room," one says. "We're under orders to—"

"To leave her to me," Athan finishes for him.

The man blinks, then nods.

They retreat down the hall, casting suspicious glances, and we disappear into Lark's room, shutting the door firm. He isn't there. Perhaps he's run off with Havis—which is a relief to me. At least he's safe. I pull out every drawer, scattering papers and books and maps. I don't think. I just grab at things, searching, throwing, scouring. But then at last, it's there, the simple paper folder smudged from sweaty fingers.

I grip it in relieved victory.

"That's it?" Athan asks, staring like I hold a serpent in my hand. His face is pricked by shameful curiosity, and I know he'd like to look, to see the horrible truth that could condemn his fox and crossed swords forever.

I nod and flip it open. He needs to see.

For a long moment he studies it silently, the wall, the murdered boys, then says, "What, exactly, do you plan to do?"

The realization that he's just followed me into all this madness without asking that question humbles me. He trusts me. I don't think anyone has ever trusted me quite like this before.

I shut the folder. "I'm going to demand your General speak on my mother's behalf. He has control of the palace, so he must announce that these horrid accusations are lies, then let her address our people with a broadcast. If he doesn't, these photographs go public. To the League. To everyone. It would ruin him before the North."

"And if he does what you demand?"

I stare at the photographs, reality suddenly shifting with his question.

"If you do this," Athan continues, "if you use these photographs against my General, you must honour your word and hide them forever. No one can see them. Not your mother, your uncle. Not even your brother. You have to forget the children."

My chest aches, the images before me begging for justice. Little bodies covered in mud and blood. My hope at bringing two worlds to the table of negotiation. A reason to make people stop and listen.

And the only way to save my mother is to destroy it forever.

"This is important, Ali. Please listen. My General won't take betrayal lightly. He'll find his revenge if you lie to him tonight, if you reveal these later and shame him before the North. He doesn't give second chances." Athan swallows. "You have only one chance. Do you understand what I'm saying?"

I do understand. It's fear I hear in Athan's voice now. I'm playing with a man—a warrior—who knows how to protect himself, who built his own nation from nothing. He won't let me play him, not with so much at stake. If I go ahead with this move, I'll be bound to it forever, and the children killed in the mud will be forgotten.

"Tell me, Lieutenant, how much trouble will you get in for this?"

He takes my hand. "We're long past that point, Princess."

His sacrifice sharpens my resolve, dissolving doubt. He's given up too much already. "Then I have to help my mother first," I say, not wavering from his solemn gaze. "The children must wait. How can I stand by and watch my own family burn? I can't."

He nods. A lonely smile plays on his lips. "You can't."

It's only a moment that passes between us, alone in the emptiness of Lark's room, holding this darkness together, but it makes me love him. I don't know exactly what love is, but I believe it must feel very much like this. He won't turn back now. He's with me to the end of this night.

He stalks towards the window, peering outside carefully. He listens. "There's still gunfire at the gates. I'm not taking you into a battle."

"But if the General is in the throne room, we need to get to him. We need to—"

Athan returns to my side. "Not yet. I want to be sure the palace is settled, under our control. Those men in the streets . . ."

He doesn't have to finish that. He said it earlier. They want my neck. A fragment of my own people, convinced we're liars and murderers. Would they shoot open my chest as they did the guard's? Or would these rough men simply put a rope round my neck?

It feels suddenly very alone here, all kinds of horrors beyond these walls, and in this room, I have only him.

Only us.

And in some mad way, that seems written in the stars.

I grip his neck, his familiar, safe warmth. "Kiss me. Properly, this time."

He looks startled.

"Hurry!" I whisper desperately, willingly, and he does.

At last.

Those perfect lips on mine. Gentle and hungry. We both smell like smoke and woods, his hands touching me like he'll never get the chance again—in my hair, along my neck, following the curve of my ribs beneath the Safire wool. I want more. I want everything, and I don't even stop to think if I'm doing it right. None of it matters. Only his mouth moving with mine, gaining confidence.

"I'm sorry," he whispers beneath my ear, his lips kissing me there, kissing my neck.

You have nothing to apologize for, I want to say, and I could cry at the regret aching behind his touch, like he knows it should be better than this, yet we're here.

This is all we have.

Then his hand moves down my hip and I pull away. I'm afraid he'll feel Cyar's pistol in the pocket.

He accepts the retreat, bringing his warm hands back to my face. "Don't ever forget this. Don't ever forget what's ours."

I shake my head. I trace his lips with a finger. "I never could."

We wait, and he whispers his mouth against mine once more, tasting, learning, and eventually the gunfire lessens, fading.

I don't want to leave this moment. I don't want to ever move again if it means a step away from him.

But we look at each other and know this is where we make our gamble. I turn to the desk to retrieve our evidence. I grasp for whatever of my mother is in me. I call upon the girl inside of me who refuses to wait for fate.

"Drop the photographs," a voice growls softly, and I freeze.

Lark.

37

⸭ ATHAN ⸭

Father's Southern man steps through the door, a dangerous look on his face, and I don't think.

Not that I've done much of that tonight.

I swing my pistol at him and consider just pulling the trigger, no questions asked. I don't care if he's bought by Father. I don't care if he's on our side. My only thought now is for her. That's it.

And I will shoot him.

"Get out of our way," I order. "We're going to the General."

If he has any kind of sense, he'll take the hint.

But he doesn't, and his gaze shifts from me to Ali. "What are you doing?" he asks her, and the danger on his face transforms to something like betrayal.

She holds the photographs close. "Saving Etania."

"With something that belongs to me, Cousin?"

"They don't belong to you," she says firmly. "They belong to the ones who were murdered."

"And are you helping the children or yourself?" He strides to her side, and my brain is too busy processing the word *cousin* for me to realize what he's doing. He snatches her to his chest, gun at her head. "Please, Lieutenant. Drop the weapon."

"Lark, stop it," she says, struggling against his grip. "You're mad! This isn't the Lieutenant's fault!"

Lark looks faintly amused. "Isn't it?"

"He's helping me here, Lark. We're going to make sure the

world knows what happened in Beraya. We're going to expose the General's son for the criminal he is."

I have to admit, she lies really well.

But Lark holds her tight. "I think, Cousin, you overestimate Safire promises. Now put the gun down, Lieutenant. I will shoot her. Blood or not, I'll do it."

"He's bluffing," Ali tells me fiercely.

But I know he isn't. He's with Father, and I have no choice. I set my pistol on the floor, hands raised. Then I kick it out of reach.

Lark nods, pushing Ali from him. He motions for the photographs. She's about to protest, then sees Lark's gun now on my head. An easy shot. Trapped as well, she surrenders them, and with it our one chance of ending this nightmare.

"You can go now," I tell Lark. "You have what you want."

"I'm not sure that I do," he replies, gun still trained on me.

My hands are raised. "You're not going to shoot me."

He won't. He can't. If Father's truly allied with the Nahir, shooting me would only put the whole thing in flames, and right now both sides have something the other wants. They give us victory—against Sinora, against the South. We give them freedom. Both get something greater than they'd secure on their own.

Lark fidgets on the gun, his eyes narrowed. "Wouldn't I shoot you? There are some who believe the General will save us in the South, but I think that's a fool's wish. I think we've been fed yet another lie from one who wants only to gain for himself. Just like every other Northerner who has come before."

My hands falter slightly and raw fear crawls along my spine. This isn't a dogfight. I can't spin from one moment to the next. I can only stand here, staring into that hateful gaze and see all my father's plans burning to nothing with one traitorous Southern gun pointed at my head. And I'm the one who'll take the shot.

There's nowhere to run, not anymore.

"You don't want that," I say. "You will regret it."

"I won't." His finger fidgets to the trigger.

"Do not—"

He takes a step for me. "I don't give a damn about you! Your kind always—"

A *crack* shatters the air.

It hits my ears, too close, obliterating all sound, and I expect pain. The scorching pain of a bullet in my stomach. Blistering darkness. But nothing happens. I open my eyes and find Lark twisting on the floor before me. Red spurts from his neck in little gasps.

I turn.

Ali's beside me, a pistol clutched in her hands and still pointed at the air where Lark was standing.

What the hell?

She's pale as her muddy gown, shaking, and I'm about to reach for her when she falls to her knees and scrambles on all fours for the one she just shot. She crouches over him, her hands hovering above his neck like she might try to staunch the blood herself. Her mouth makes tiny sounds. I realize she's apologizing under her breath. Over and over and over, like a prayer.

Boots near in the adjacent room, a silhouette appearing in the doorway.

Havis stares at us.

He absorbs the scene, stunned—Ali on her knees with a pistol, Lark writhing and gurgling on the floor, me useless in the middle. Then his horrified face darkens and he shakes his head. "You're going to start a goddamn war, girl!"

"I didn't mean . . . ," she whispers, her hands trying to comfort Lark now, a futile effort.

The endless gurgling continues.

Havis pulls out his own sidearm. "I know, but you can't take it back. If he speaks of this, we're all dead, do you understand?"

She nods, more a knee-jerk reaction.

"Step away, Aurelia."

She doesn't move, and he glances at me. I reach for her hesitantly, drawing her up to her feet, and she reluctantly allows it.

Havis holds the pistol to Lark's temple and fires. There's a spray of blood and brain. Lark stills, a river of red around him, dark as oil in the night. I've been here before and I hate it. I hate how easy it is to extinguish life. How meaningless and cold.

But the strangled noise at my side reminds me she *hasn't* been here before. I hold her closer, but she hardly notices. I know the feeling. I lived it this summer, in the shadows of the airbase, but I had silence to process. She has only this fiery night, and I whisper into her hair, "You did what you had to."

Because I know she needs to hear it the way I did.

For some reason, it sounds hollow saying it to another person.

Havis watches us silently. Then he shakes his head again and waves us to follow. "You don't ever speak of what's happened here. We'll say it was suicide."

"He was shot in the neck," I point out.

Havis is in front of me with two long strides. "I said you don't *ever* speak of what's happened here, Lieutenant. To anyone. And I mean that. I don't think my king would appreciate hearing the Princess of Etania murdered one of our own."

Ali holds my arm, still shaking—or maybe it's me.

"You wouldn't do that to her," I say, but I'm beginning to doubt all these things I thought were certainties. This night has changed everything.

"Wouldn't I?" Havis smiles coldly, then glances at Ali. "And you, Princess?"

She looks up at him, pale and furious. "You are a snake."

"Good," Havis says. "Now let's get out of here. Things are not going well for the Queen. I assume you have an aeroplane somewhere, Lieutenant?"

This man makes no sense to me. The entire place is under siege and he wants the three of us to run for the hills together? If Father finds out . . . Wait, unless Father arranged this? I don't know what to think anymore. I'm not even sure how that would work, but Ali decides for me.

"We're going to the General," she says, chin rising. "I'm not leaving my mother behind."

"It's too late for her, Aurelia. The General is preparing to make his broadcast to the kingdom, assuming emergency powers until this is solved. Come now and at least you'll have your lieutenant to keep you safe. Let the dust settle."

"No!" Her voice snaps hotly. "I'm saving my mother. Tell her that, Havis. Tell her I'm safe and I'm coming."

"You'll never make it to the General!"

"She will," I say.

"Lieutenant," Havis begins. "You can't—"

Ali grabs the photographs and we sprint for the hall, always running, leaving Havis behind with Lark's mangled corpse. Father's in the throne room. We have to get there—and fast. The halls are silent tombs, an orange colour still faint beyond the windows. No gunfire. I hope to God Arrin has settled the rioters. For once, I want him to be right so this war doesn't have to spread.

We turn a corner and run right into an entire flood of Etanian uniforms.

Two dozen of them.

I freeze, as does Ali, and her hand tightens on mine, ready to run. Then the Prince pushes through them.

"Reni!" she cries, abandoning my side and throwing her arms around her brother's neck.

The armed royal guards stare me down like a viper that might slither off with the slightest movement. I'm not sure if I should raise my hands.

Did we just lose somehow?

Then I spot Lord Jerig staring at me, white-faced, and I see his weak betrayal. The Prince has won him over. Our bought traitor has been bought right back.

"Stars, Reni, what's happening to us?" Ali asks.

"It's a mess," he replies. "A rotten mess. They've revolted in three cities, and a thousand men came marching from Hathene alone. Armed to the teeth. I don't know how they could have rallied such a force."

He doesn't know, but it suddenly makes perfect sense to me. Father's vintage weapons bound for the Queen's Mounted Regiment. A traditional gift, as Kalt said. Generous. Expected. But I saw them being loaded in Norvenne. There were enough crates there for a sufficient amount to go "missing," numbers erased, rewritten, the rest disappearing to be repainted, refurbished, and stripped of Safire design. Ready for these men to march on the palace, not with fancy machine guns, but with exactly what everyone would expect from a home-grown militia.

It's clever.

Arrin clever.

"But I have the Air Force," the Prince continues. "Colonel Lyle has mediated with 3rd Squadron outside the city. We're going to order the Safire planes down and get our sky back."

"Can anyone help us?" Ali asks.

"Lyle tried to radio Classit straightaway. They're closest to assist, but they refused the requests. Said we should let the experienced General deal with this." He sounds thoroughly hateful.

So Father's visit to that neighbouring kingdom paid off. I wonder what he gave them for the loyalty. Or maybe they really believe the myths about him? No bribery required. Whatever the case, it's left Etania and its outdated planes alone in a sky against Safire. One word from Arrin and this will be over.

"The truth is getting out, Ali," the Prince continues. "Uncle and Lyle have also gone to the army. They're loyal, I know it. He'll have them deal with the ones in the city. And I'm bringing my guard to the General. We'll stop him before he addresses our kingdom."

"You won't convince my General with that," I say. "They'll hold you to trial, just like your mother."

The Prince scowls. "Do not dissuade me from this. I see through your lies."

"I'm not lying, Your Highness. You're the son of a woman now accused of murder."

The Prince looks at me fiercely. "I am a king, Lieutenant, and I will bring an entire kingdom. I will bring the rest of the Heights!"

A king.

If I'm stunned, Ali is even more so. "What are you doing?" she whispers fearfully.

His face is elegant iron, his hands wrapped gently around hers. "I'm doing what I must, Ali. It's time, at last, for me to rule."

God, this little faction of Etanian men is declaring him their new leader. Just like that. In the middle of a coup against his own mother. I don't know how royal politics work, but this seems more like something we Safire would do, not a proper Northern prince. Maybe I really have underestimated him. But still, he's wildly outnumbered. If Father's about to make his own address, then he'll be quick to muddy the waters with half truths and bold lies, putting the Prince and Sinora in the worst light, and all he needs is a wireless radio and some airtime. He'd have everyone in the Heights convinced the whole family is in on the murder cover-up.

Trying to stay a step ahead, I leap through the possibilities as fast as I can. If Arrin is still suppressing the rioters, then we have a chance. Father cares about appearances. He'll listen to what Ali says, as dangerous as that is. But Arrin? Never. He'll take one look at her photographs—and his guilt—and order the Safire planes to attack. I'm certain of it. He'd rather take everything out at once than play politics. He'll come up with his reasons later.

And if the Prince already has his factions on the move, then we're running out of time.

Once again, though, Ali beats me to it. "You can't take the risk, Reni. If you're our leader now, then the people need to see you." She steps away. "I'm going to reason with the General. I can get him to speak on our behalf."

Now it's the Prince's turn to look stunned. "You're going to what?"

"I have a way and you have to let me go."

He looks about to protest, but she throws her arms around his neck again, whispering something in his ear.

He pales, visibly, eyes flickering to me.

"No, Ali, you can't be—"

But she's already away from him, grabbing my hand and dragging me down the hall in the other direction. I don't need to be convinced. We sprint side by side, the final stretch. The nearer we get to the throne room, the more Safire uniforms appear. They're all gaping at me but I plough right through them. No time. Two of Father's officers try to step in front of me before the large doors. They look angry.

"Lieutenant, you need to stop—"

"Get the hell off," I say in Savien.

This might mean a firing squad later, but I'm still hoping I can redeem myself.

I drag Ali past them, flinging open the doors and throwing us through them in front of the startled expressions of Father's men. But there's no sign of him.

Only Arrin.

All hope and colour drains from my face. I've run her right into the lion's den and there's nothing I can do.

I let go of her hand helplessly, retreating as she strides forward.

Uncomfortable silence reigns in the darkened room. The velvet curtains are drawn tight, routine protection from snipers, and everyone stares at Ali, trying to register where she's come from.

Then Arrin grins. His casual grin that's all danger on the inside.

"Princess," he says, eyeing her up and down. The ruined dress. Cyar's crumpled jacket. "Have you been running around outside?" Then his eyes jump to me. "Wait a minute. Don't tell me. Is this Lieutenant Erelis? The one who frightened the balcony of royalty?"

"It doesn't matter what's happened to me," she says, chin raised in her usual show of force. "There isn't time. Right now, you must let my mother speak to the kingdom. She had nothing to do with my father's death."

I'm impressed she's still going to try her scheme on Arrin. It will never work, but she's not afraid to try. Guilt works at my stomach. I could speak up and defend her. A no-name lieutenant can't mouth off to the Commander, but his little brother can. And I want to. How I want to give him a piece of my mind for all of this! But then she'd know the truth, and this is the worst time and place to hear it.

I'd lose her forever.

So I stay behind and pray Father shows up fast.

Arrin meanders over to her, a hint of concern on his face. "You think so? You think it's coincidence that a king was murdered and a Southern woman now conveniently sits on a Northern throne? I'm not sure, Princess. I don't think it looks very good."

"And don't you think these protesters know that also?" she replies. "We've been set up. They want to tear Etania apart for their own gain. It's obvious."

"Well, it might have been obvious if Resya wasn't now also accused of aiding the Nahir."

Ali tenses at that. I can see her hands tighten on the envelope. "Those are *lies*. There is no proof, and most of our kingdom is still loyal to my mother. You'll see."

"I will see, yes, but first what is that?"

His hand whips for the envelope, no doubt having zeroed in

on it right from the first moment, but she's even quicker. I don't know how she saw it coming, but it's already behind her back. "Photographs," she says calmly, looking up at him.

The false humour on Arrin's lips fades. "I hope it's a portrait of you," he says. "I'm sure the Lieutenant would love to carry it into battle."

"Of your crime," she declares. "And if your General doesn't release my mother and speak on her behalf, everyone will see them. I've already sent the other photographs with a trusted ally. Take these if you like, but the evidence will get to the Royal League. I'll make sure of it."

It's another bold lie, but she sells it too well.

"I told you before," Arrin says to her, voice dangerously low. "I didn't do this."

She reveals one photograph. "Were you not in Beraya, quelling the revolt there?"

"Yes. But I didn't do that."

"Well, it doesn't matter. Whether it was you or whether you were complicit with the ones who did, I'm sure the murder of prisoners—and children, at that—is something the League would like to be informed of. There are already enough rumours about your campaign in Karkev as it is."

Arrin sucks in a breath and turns from her. From him, that's restraint. But I don't trust it.

Speak, you coward, my bit of conscience says, but I can't.

Not like this.

"Princess, you have nothing to go on but hearsay. It's *my* honour at stake. I'm the one you will blackmark for all of history, whatever the truth may be. Do you think that's fair?"

She doesn't look away. "You needn't worry. God favours the innocent, doesn't he?"

He reaches for his pistol and turns on her. "You damned little—"

"Arrin, step back!"

Father's cold voice whips like a leash as he strides into the room.

Arrin's hand is still on the sidearm, but he steps back from Ali.

This is progress. Now I just need to stay alive long enough to explain it all to Father. He wouldn't put a bullet in me, not in front of everyone. But Arrin might, and he's glaring at me now like the thought's definitely in his head.

Father walks to Ali without hurry. "You're sweet to care so much for the Southern children, Your Highness." It's the tone he saves for the public. Calm. Gracious. "Now how do you want this to go? You know I'm only trying to protect your kingdom from revolt. Such unrest must be dealt with decisively."

This fatherly angle—like none of this was his idea and he's only assuming the role forced onto his shoulders—works. Ali relaxes, lowering the photographs. "I know," she says, equally gracious. "And we're so grateful you've secured the palace. You've saved us tonight from these vile men. But I swear to you that my mother is innocent. She lives only for Etania, for the kingdom of my father."

Father cocks his head. "May I talk plainly, Princess?"

She nods.

"I wonder," he says, "if you might be blinded by your affection? That's understandable, of course. We would all believe the same in your position." He gestures at the men around. "But honesty is the only thing that can quell the storm tonight. All cards on the table so that an understanding may be reached."

"An understanding?" she repeats.

"Yes. No one wants your mother slandered, Princess, I assure you. Dangerous men can persuade even the most noble into terrible things. And that isn't the fault of the noble ones, but of the dangerous men." He pauses. "I think we all know the Resyan king has put quite a lot of pressure on her lately. With his ambassador . . . Ambassador Havis, I believe?"

It's a cruel trap, an invitation to innocently implicate her mother by placing the blame on someone else, but she shakes her head. "He has tried, but she refuses. She wants nothing to do with Resya."

"You know all your mother's private dealings, then?"

"I know enough. And she is innocent." Ali's dark hair has escaped its elaborate style, strands sticking this way and that. She's a mess. Torn lace and wearing a jacket too big for her shoulders, dried blood splattered all over. A miserable, muddied star fallen in disgrace. "Now let *me* say plainly, General, if you do not release my mother and speak on her behalf, the entire world will know what your son did to the unarmed boys of Beraya."

She's glorious.

The whole room waits for Father's reaction, his men shifting in their boots, sharp glances filled with nerves.

This is the precipice, and I'm ready to throw myself in front of her. Beg him, as his son, not to hurt her. Destroy Sinora, but never Ali. Shoot me, even. I'm the worst traitor in this room. I let her kiss me when I knew her world was ending. When I knew my brother wouldn't hesitate to pull a gun on her.

I'm the worst, but I will fight.

But then a small smile appears on Father's face. "Persuasive, even without the blackmail." He waves to one of his men. "Bring Her Majesty. Perhaps together we can make our address and right this night."

His attaché nods, disappearing into the hall.

"You have protected our home and done us a great service," Ali says to Father, playing beautifully, putting him in the best light, "and you will see the truth."

"I do hope so," he replies.

Then he looks right at me. Wordless. Razor-sharp.

I want to disappear.

"It's not his fault," Ali says quickly. Father turns back to her. "The Lieutenant," she explains, gesturing at me. "He didn't know

I had these. I said I needed to speak with you, that's all. I ordered him to it."

Father smiles again. "Of course. My soldiers are bred to follow the orders of the higher rank, even those from a girl."

Arrin smirks darkly at me and kisses his pistol before holstering it.

Father's attaché creeps back through the door almost as quickly as he left.

"Yes?" Father demands.

"The cities have been dealt with, sir. Our planes are returning."

"Returning?"

"The Etanians have taken the sky. And the Lalian Air Force is patrolling the eastern region, settling the city there."

There's a stir, everyone trying to figure out the change in events, and Father narrows his eyes. "On whose order?"

The man swallows. "The Prince's order."

Everyone stares.

"He issued a wireless address to Etania and the surrounding Heights," the man explains nervously. "Every kingdom except Classit has responded. He's already made arrests."

Father's frown turns to vague darkness. I'm sure he thought the Prince was locked tight with Sinora. We both underestimated him.

Then it dawns on me.

I look at Ali and find her wearing an almost invisible smile. Her whisper in her brother's ear. She stalled for enough time with the photographs, luring Father here, away from his emergency address of lies, and her brother went and took the kingdom back from us.

I stand, exhausted by shame, and think the Isendare siblings might be better at this than we Dakars.

38

When the Prince arrives, he's greeted like a damn hero. The plain brown and green costume he wears looks like something anointed, like he's made of this mountain earth, the son of his father, wooing his kingdom with a single speech and saving his own mother from a wrongful coup. He strides the room, giving orders, patting shoulders, and the Etanian men no longer offer him simple obedience. They offer him admiration. True and pure.

Respect has a tangible quality, but so does anger, and I can feel that as well, radiating from Father and cinching my neck.

It's Sinora Lehzar who gives him the perfect punishment.

She arrives in a show of trembling gratitude, embracing Ali tightly, thanking Father, praising her son. She plays the fragile flower, only a woman and mother.

How could she ever breathe a dark word?

"The Lieutenant saved me," Ali explains, grateful weariness in her voice, as if to reassure Sinora, though it certainly has the opposite effect. Ali also leaves out anything to do with the photographs, the blackmail, the death of Lark.

She plays the fragile flower, too.

"Ah, Lieutenant," Sinora says to me, sighing over my title. "You bring honour to your mother." I bite the inside of my cheek to keep from glaring, from playing any less than her. "Now, Captain," she continues, motioning at a uniformed Etanian man, "escort my daughter to her room. I want three of your men outside her door the rest of the night."

Sorrow graces Ali's face. The realization that this is our good-bye, here and now.

She comes near, offering me Cyar's jacket, the edge of the pistol glinting from the pocket. "Thank you," she says, and her voice is so perfect in its aching love, such a mirror of the thing I hold inside, that I want to kiss her again. I would, if it wouldn't sign me a death warrant—from both Father and Sinora.

But Ali is braver than me. Her arms are suddenly around me, boldly, all of her nestled against my chest, and I feel her lips against my neck. It's brief and secret, burning like wildfire.

A promise for me alone.

Then she's away from me and following her captain out the wide doors.

Sinora watches me with a neutral gaze, less warm than a moment earlier. But she smiles. A flowering smile of polite interest. "General, might I have a private word with your lieutenant? I wish to properly thank him for saving my daughter."

I don't think he'll say yes. He's furious with me, true, but if someone is going to kill me, I think he'd rather it was him.

For practical reasons. Diplomatic ones.

But he says, "As you wish, Your Majesty," and Arrin gives me a look that is partway between disbelief and delighted approval. He's not going to defend me from her anymore—he's going to urge it on its way.

"You've done an impressive job this evening, Lieutenant," Arrin says to me on the way by. "Perhaps you've earned a promotion."

And with that, everyone in uniform departs, Safire and Etanian alike, and I'm left behind, entirely alone in the throne room with Sinora Lehzar.

An empty feeling of betrayal echoes.

I wonder what I'm supposed to do.

"How quickly he abandons you," Sinora says after a moment, the trembling gratitude gone, replaced by something raw. "That's the one you wish to obey?"

I say nothing.

She walks nearer, moving in such a way it feels more like stalking, like narrowing in on prey, softly, and I think of the *si'yah* cats and their haunting cry. I think of silent, shadowy creatures that are rarely seen, yet painted in beauty to decorate halls.

I think of the frustration of doing one thing and being another.

"What will I do with you, little fox?" she asks, halting before me. Her accent is pronounced when not speaking formally, effortlessly lilting. She has to look up into my face. "That's the trouble with foxes, you see. They're pretty and clever. They frolic in the garden and make you forget they're headed for the roost . . ."

"I never—"

"Who does your father say I am, Lieutenant? What did he tell you?"

The sudden shift throws my conviction off balance. I was on the defense, bracing for her claws, but now her questions—and gaze—are quiet daggers of honesty. She's alert and tranquil before me. Breath from her lips, the heady scent of saffron from her hair. The lines of an aging beauty heavy around her eyes.

"You're a false queen," I say. "You're from the dirt."

"The dirt?" she repeats.

I realize I don't know where exactly that is. In the South, somewhere, I assume. A name comes back to me, a sudden memory from Father's council room. "Rummayan," I say. "You bury hearts."

She doesn't speak for a long moment, dark eyes a veil. "I see," is all she says.

It dawns on me this all sounds too vague when she's standing before me, an enemy with thoughts and imperfections, with beauty and softness and an infinite world of memory behind her searching gaze. I feel, as always, a step behind.

"Do you want to know the truth, Athan Dakar?"

I'm not sure that I do. I've heard enough truths tonight, all of them stealing from me, darkening my past, destroying my present, condemning whatever's to come. I've seen the game and it's too large for me. She'll only spin a false truth. I know that. And yet she's waiting, patient as a cat, and I'm not sure I'm in the position to decline.

I nod.

The dark eyes hold mine, unafraid. "I was your age when my father was imprisoned. I was the only one left to care for my family. My elder brother was gone to make his fortune. My mother was dead. The younger ones could do nothing for themselves, so I did it all. I made something of us. I made certain we'd survive. My only dream was to ransom my father from prison—the man who should never have been there, who stole only to protect his children. When we'd managed the money to do it, I went myself, on horseback, and felt wonderfully victorious. I was seventeen. I thought the world might yet bow to my dream. But do you know what those Landorian soldiers did when I offered the exchange?"

I say nothing. I try not to think about the way this story is told, the way it's pulled up through some ancient grief, forced in front of me like a card to play.

It's all in her eyes. Her voice doesn't change.

"They laughed," she says, "and they took the money, took the horse. I adored that horse. The one thing I called mine. When I tried to protest, they threw rocks at me. They treated me like a stray dog that had pestered them long enough." Her flint breaks on those last words. A flicker of a tremor. "Now let me tell you, Athan Dakar, I will not live my life like a dog. I will not be chased away by stones or threats or anything else. No man can frighten me."

Silence fills the throne room. Somewhere, the forest is burning, my father is raging, and the kingdom staggers. But in here,
she is only this story. This dream that was ruined long ago. I
don't want to understand where she comes from. I don't want
to know her like this.

"Will you be a dog?" she asks me. "Will you follow the whistle like your brother?"

Startled and offended, I almost shake my head. Then I think
of tonight. I think of the summer, the spring. I think of my whole
life up until this breath, and I stay silent.

A hint of a smile appears on her lips. "Your father has a way,
doesn't he? I was his comrade once, too. My gun was hot for his
cause, and I remember his rising star, the way it pulled us all into
its fire. He made it a joy to burn. He gave my anger what it needed.
That's what he does, you see. He offers a glorious rage that feels
very honest, very grand." She steps closer. "But it isn't. It's his star,
not yours, and with him you'll always be the dog."

I feel sweat along my neck, an ache in my shoulder blades
from looking down at her so fiercely. "Why are you telling me
this?"

"Because I know his path, his ways, and you deserve better,
little fox." She tilts her head at the failing expression on my
face. "I had a father worth fighting for. When he died in that
prison, he died for me. He ruined himself to save us. That's the
man I bled for, the dream I chased. But yours never deserved to
be a father. He never had one himself, never knew the meaning
of the word, so how could he do any better than this?"

Something aches, and it's no longer my shoulders. It's deeper.
Heavier. Perhaps I'm what I always imagined—a useful thing, a
weapon, an ember to be nurtured and fed to flames. It's the fear
that's always haunted. The thing that Mother always—

"Your mother saw the truth," Sinora says, seeming to read my
thoughts, "and it's why I considered her loyalty a—"

"Never mention my mother!" I say suddenly, violently, too far into my own misery. In my confusion, I want to grab Sinora by her slender throat. "You killed her. *You* took her from me."

Her certainty is unflinching. "No, only your father takes from you, clever boy. Understand this and you'll never see your world the same again. You'll see how perfect her death was. How it gave him the war he longed for, the respect he needed to become strong. Wasn't it all very perfect?"

Her meaning strikes, and I struggle against the words, terrified by the suggestion in them. Everything lined up, ticking to the clock, but not this. Not this one thing. It can't be true. It isn't.

"I've said enough now," Sinora continues, "but there is one last thing I want to share, and I hope you'll hear my heartbeat in this. Are you listening? Think you are honouring your mother's memory and bury me in hatred, yes. Think of me what you will. But I believe there is still a gentleness in you, a thing he hasn't ruined. The thing she gave you. I won't bury you in hatred yet, Athan Dakar. You may follow your father of steel if you wish, but I have a daughter of warmth, and you don't have to live as a ghost. Not if you lived here."

Before I can acknowledge her impossible offer, she's taken five steps back. Her gaze doesn't falter. "Now return to your father, little fox. Run to his side again and prove your loyalty. But you might also tell him this—you tell him I will not be chased like a dog, not even with all the armies of the earth behind him. You remind him this old comrade still holds his secrets in her clever palm."

And then she smiles again, the silent promise of war.

◗ AURELIA ◖

It's been hardly an hour since the terror began, yet I'm sure an entire century has breathed and died in it. There's nothing in me anymore. No fear. No sorrow. No relief. I'm a murderer now, a pale shadow, and truthfully, all I want is to sleep.

I've had enough of being seventeen.

As I lie in bed, heavy and weightless at once, fighting tears, Heathwyn tells me about the battle at our gates, about how Lord Marcin himself was wounded at my masquerade and it doesn't look good.

I listen, far away, as Safire planes rise once again into the night. They're leaving for Norvenne, Heathwyn says. The General will speak for us there. He's going to explain what's happened, defend the Queen's innocence before the allegations of murder, and though I'm grateful, I know what it cost me, a gamble and betrayal that will haunt me the rest of my life. A gamble no one, not even Heathwyn, can ever know.

I try to soothe myself by remembering what we've gained. Reni, who trusted me when I whispered the only thing I could in his ear—that if he took the crown, Mother would die. Perhaps he should have become king like this, as a hero. Perhaps this was the right path. His fate. But in that moment, when I realized what he wanted to do, it was Havis's face in my mind. Havis's dark desperation, in the University, clutching at my neck.

I couldn't explain anything else to Reni, hoping the horror of this night made anything seem possible. I could only pray to Father that Reni would trust the bond of blood between us, the place where we meet, where we speak only truth to each other. I'm his sister. And he heard the fear in my voice.

Now he remains a prince, his address issued on behalf of our Queen.

This is a victory, I tell myself numbly.

Heathwyn leaves me to my thoughts, since I have no words, and I lie watching the smoky haze lessen beyond the window. It's gradual. A slow clearing of sky and stars, the fire doused in water and smoldering, skeleton trees left in its wake.

I feel Lark's gun resting against my temple.

I wonder if he would have shot me. Did I never imagine that he, a Nahir fighter, might be capable of it? Did I underestimate him, as Havis predicted? But no matter how I try to rationalize it, I keep seeing his panicked eyes. His lungs filling with blood, struggling for breath, and all because of me. The girl he considered his friend. The girl he taught to shoot the gun. I hear Athan's voice saying, "You did what you had to," but something deathlike heaves inside me.

What if Lark hadn't meant to fire at all?

What if it was only a threat?

The truth is—I shot first.

In my fear and panic, I left him tortured on the floor, terrified of the thought of losing Athan, of losing the evidence that could save Mother. It was me, choosing between the worth of lives, and I pray Father didn't watch from his world of lights and stars. He'd be ashamed, his own daughter abandoning children and firing her gun in a selfish fury.

Oh, Lark . . .

I rise from the bed in a daze, remembering suddenly, from another lifetime, from a time when I was not a murderer, that Lark said he'd left a gift for me. It doesn't take long to find it. A simple, tiny package on my desk, an envelope beside. With trembling hands, I pull apart the brown paper. I find a pair of turquoise earrings, elegant and lovely as anything I own.

I open the letter.

There's an address listed first, from Resya.

Dearest Cousin,

Whatever happens tonight, you cannot forget our mission. If I have to leave, please meet me at the place I've written here. Find your way there. The only hope we have is for your mother and Seath to talk, or else we'll all be in hell.

*I'm sorry to say this on your birthday. I've included a gift
from my sister. She wanted me to give these to you. Meet us
both in Resya and we'll find a way through this.*

There's always a way, Cousin.

—L.G.

I stare.

I read the words again. Then again.

One after another after another.

And that's when I cry. At long last. I curl up on the bed, shivering even though it's warm outside, and cry and cry until there's nothing I have possibly left to give.

39

ৰ ATHAN ৰ

3,000 feet.

I know I'm in trouble by 3,000 feet.

I've spent the better part of tonight jumping without thinking, right from the first shots. When a guard approached us on
the dance floor, reaching for his gun, targeting Ali, I did the only
thing I could. I took evasive action, a maneuver of quick thinking. A way to let these men, bought by Father, know she's precious to the Safire and can't be harmed.

I kissed her.

Admittedly, it was far more enjoyable than an inverted dive
out of crosshairs. Everything after that was a dogfight in itself,
waiting to see what opportunity would appear, looking for weak-
nesses, openings, and now it's led me here.

3,000 feet

That's how long it takes for Father to forbid me to fly my own
plane, passing it off to some other bootlicker pilot like it isn't
even mine, then speak in muttered tones with Arrin, with his
men. How long it takes him to work his way towards me, hiding
alone in the back of the wobbling plane. The wings break above
the lingering smoke, through the turbulent evening clouds,
and a midnight sky stretches endless outside the windows.

I want my fighter. I want to leap into that dark sea of stars.

Instead, I'm cornered by Father behind a metal partition, in the cargo area. He seizes the neck of my uniform, his cold voice snarling, "You goddamn traitor. You idiot boy."

And then in his fury, his fist goes up with my name on it, and I say, "I saved you, Father!"

I'm shaking, but it might just be the plane.

The fist halts, and he stares at me, black as the night outside.

"Aurelia would have given those photographs to her brother. I swear it, he was ready to take the crown tonight. He hates us. He wouldn't hesitate to bring that crime and whatever else he could find before the League. Karkev. Beraya. He wouldn't stop until the entire North despised us the way he does. He wouldn't stop until he discovered the truth about your alliance with Seath. We'd have to fight Landore. All their allies." My voice breaks. "We can't win against them, Father. You know that. We can't."

He's still staring at me, at my desperate mouth, but I know I'm right. He's spent too long trying to earn the respect of the North. Every step has been a strategic move in the direction of true power. Not the kind that threatens those kings. The kind that's welcomed. Power that Landore and the other royals envy.

But if they turn against us right now, it's over.

If we go back to being the rustic commoners with too much blood on our hands, they'll grow suspicious, renege on everything gained.

And those small photographs would launch the case against us.

But Father doesn't acknowledge any of it, only yanks the sidearm from his hip. It's glaring and angry in the low lights. A dark flare of terror. Everything disappears from my chest. I'm only fear and bones.

"You can't fire that in here," I say, my voice sounding panicked, unfamiliar.

The plane wobbles sharply.

"No?" he asks, steadying the weapon. "You think I can't fire my pistol in this airplane? You think it's a risk?" He cocks it at my chest. "It's only a risk, boy, if the bullet doesn't find a body first. It needs the right target. The flesh to absorb the blow and silence the shot."

I hover like a ghost before the barrel.

He pushes it an inch closer. "I have my target, Lieutenant. I have Resya. It will take the fall and light my triumph. And if you ever disobey me again, you can forget being a captain. You can forget the squadron. You'll be at my side every minute of every day and Hajari will be at the front of our first wave into Resya. Without you."

He lets the gun loom on me a moment longer, the awareness of it burning my chest. A phantom pressure of heat. He won't forgive me a second time. I've wasted my promise, the promise that once made him believe I'd be the best. Then he abandons me in the tiny, vibrating metal space at the back of his plane, and I slide down to my knees, lungs wrestling for breath. I'm alone. Burned up in his star. I'm too afraid to move, desperate for him to have shown me otherwise. I don't want Sinora Lehzar to be right. I want him to be who he was on the floor of the study months ago, tamed by drink. Seeing me.

Knowing me.

I shut my exhausted eyes. In the darkness, twin weapons flicker coldly—Father's pistol and the one that was wielded by Ali's cousin. Two guns hot for war. Two barrels that don't flinch. I think of Sinora's warning for Father, about the secrets she holds. Her infinite shadow. Have we only woken the cat, this woman with endless ties to the South? How do I tell him that? How could I convince him? Would he even care anymore?

I can't think of anything.

I'm too damn tired to jump again.

The airbase outside Norvenne greets us with startled questions. The news from Etania consumes everyone, and Father has to explain a dozen times what happened there, the unexpected coup, the accusation of murder, and I've seen at least three Landorian officials quickly look at whatever map is nearest them, searching for Hathene, confused. It's not a place anyone thinks about much. Buried in those mountains.

Two days later, the League denies Father his war.

"A sovereign kingdom must not be dealt with in bloodshed," they declare in writing, "and furthermore, there must be firmer evidence to convict His Majesty King Rahian of dealing with Seath of the Nahir."

I expect to find Father and Arrin furious. Their carefully measured plot isn't enough to convict a king. It's the truth that's always lingered over this, ever since Mother's death and revenge was brewed against Sinora.

In the North, nothing trumps a crown. That royal blood of Prince Efan.

But when I find Arrin with Kalt in one of the airbase lounges, Arrin's half-dressed, a bottle happily in one hand. Father's disappeared to meet with Windom, and here's my brother reveling like the world's suddenly been handed to him on a silver platter.

Kalt just watches him, a cigarette in one weary hand.

I ask Arrin what the hell he's doing.

"Celebrating," he explains, lifting the bottle. "Time for another war!"

"You failed, Arrin. Try again."

"Failed?" He laughs, glancing at Kalt. "God, our little brother is the best. At times brilliant, at times so far behind I'm not sure he'll ever catch up."

Kalt sucks on his cigarette, like it's giving him strength. "Athan, we're still going to war with Resya. Please tell me you knew this."

I realize I didn't.

I stand there, mad at myself for actually thinking the League's verdict mattered. Of course we're still going to war. The Nahir are on our side, and when we invade—and win—Rahian will look guilty as sin and all the proof of his dark dealings will be at our fingertips, courtesy of Seath.

We'll be the heroes of the North.

The ones who exposed Resya as traitorous—and brought the kingdom to account.

I hate that I ever believed there was a chance for peace, for home. That I believed Sinora did this and what other truth could there be?

This silent, shrewd war.

My father's war.

"Get yourself ready, Lieutenant." Arrin smirks. "Resya won't be Havenspur."

I snatch the bottle from his hand. "This isn't a game."

He looks up, sour. "Now, Lieutenant. I'd have had Mother's murderer if not for you. *You're* the one playing games."

"You were ready to shoot an innocent girl to make your point!"

"At least I have loyalty," Arrin snaps.

I'm numb with fury. Exhausted still. But my anger is alive.

He scowls through his drunken fog. He tries to get the bottle back, but I move it out of reach, and he looks up at me with dog eyes. "What the hell do you think of me?"

Kalt sucks on his cigarette again. Smoke stinking the room.

"For all your apparent virtue," Arrin observes, "I happen to know Leannya has hardly heard a word from you this summer. It's a good thing I made sure to send her the letters I promised, since you were too busy betraying us all."

One of the great mysteries in life will always be how he manages to stay this sharp even when drunk. Practice, maybe. "I didn't betray you," I get out through my teeth. "I *saved* you."

Ali's the one I've betrayed with every word, every breath.

I *am* a traitor, just not how Arrin thinks.

But he shrugs, nonchalant, and I know he's about to outmaneuver me. "Did you hear Leannya took her testing two weeks ago? She's always kept such a low score, so I told her to try her best this time, to make Mother proud, because I know she's better than that. And you know what? She did. Turns out, she's as smart as you. Perfect scores."

My grip loosens on the bottle.

"Yes, that's right, Athan. Another brilliant child. Better make some room."

My anger reaches a new level, one I didn't know was possible without an entire forest burning around me. "Now she's useful, Arrin! Is that what you want for her? Right as we're heading into another war? She didn't want others to know! She doesn't want to get involved in any of this."

He succeeds in snatching the bottle back. "No, that's you. *You* didn't want to get involved in any of this. Leannya's just never had anyone tell her she could, which is a shame, because she's got enough spirit for it."

Now I've reached furious. If I could, I'd hit him dead in the face and anywhere else I could manage before he pinned me to the ground. He can't want her thrust into the middle of this hell. He'd better just be drunk and forget everything tomorrow. I'd like to forget everything tomorrow. That's not going to happen.

"You're taking us to war," I say. "For God's sake, don't do it through a bottle."

Then I'm headed for the door.

"You know what your problem is?" Arrin says at my back. "You don't know what the hell it is you're fighting for. You've never known."

I whirl around, ready to hate him, finger on the trigger and ready to fire. But then I stop. He looks damn pathetic sitting there, hiding in this office while everyone else plots the war he'll have to win, Kalt leaning on an elbow, lighting another cigarette with shaky hands.

It's too quiet in here. Too empty and forgotten, like a grave.

"No, I do know what it is I'm fighting for. It's the thing I've always wanted. The thing I'll never stop wanting." *Away.* "But I also know what needs to be done, and I'll do it, even if it means destroying a part of myself. Because there's no other choice. I get that now."

I look at my brothers and everything aches, not just the past, not just this moment, but the future. I walked into a Southern gun and almost took the fall for Father. But if this goes bad with the entire Nahir, it won't be a single gun Arrin faces. It will be an entire army that falls betrayed. It will betray him, betray Kalt. Even Leannya.

But I can't tell Father what happened in Etania. If I tell him, he'll confront Havis, his ghost, and God knows what would happen then. Havis would slander Ali if it meant some sort of gain for him. He'd never think of Ali first, only himself.

I'm trapped between loyalties.

Losing either way.

I hit the doorframe with a fist. "You're my brother. You know I'd fight for you. Where you tell me to go, I'll go. What you ask of me, I'll do. And I hope you get everything you want. The entire South and whatever else you need to please him. But this isn't who I'll be forever. I'm not you and I don't give a damn what anyone else thinks about that."

Then I turn and leave.

Outside, the sun's sinking lower in the west, casting shadows along the runway. My fighter's fifth in the lineup of Safire planes, and I crawl inside the cockpit and hide, sketching the squadron logo I want to use when I'm captain. The bright sun of Rahmet for Cyar. A chamomile for Mother. And a dark horse rampant against the whole thing, for Ali. I have nothing of my own to put on here. But I have her. And in the days to come—years to come—I'll make sure she's with me every moment, through every foot of breathless sky, glorious on the flank of my plane.

She promised me a thousand days. Of course I can promise the same.

That's three years, and then I'm only twenty-one. Maybe I can stay alive that long. Maybe I can at least give us that, because I won't give it up without a burning fight. I'll fight for my days with everything I have, every scrap of nerve I've inherited from this rotten family.

I scrawl the squadron motto against the bright sun.

There's a knock on the glass.

Cyar's sitting on the wing, leaning against the cockpit, and I hand him the sketch. He studies it thoughtfully.

"Eyes on the horizon," he says, reading the motto.

"Always. Looking to the end, to the hope."

"I like that."

"Me too."

He smiles, then together we watch the sun disappear, exhausted and frightened and damned determined.

40

❧ AURELIA ❧

Hathene, Etania

The days after the coup are exactly my worst fears come to life. I'm confined to our palace, ten guards in every hall, while soldiers prowl the gardens, the woods, and beyond. I'm trapped. The sad faces and confused whispers only add to the sense of imprisonment. Eight of our courtiers are dead, including sweet Lord Marcin. I know I'll have to stand beside Violet at his funeral, holding her, and the thought unnerves me. I'd rather it were me crying.

It was my masquerade that killed him.

Lark's body is also in a casket, ready to be sent back to Resya with Havis, and no one says anything about the hole in his neck. They're too relieved that Havis, Lark's compatriot, is declaring it suicide and no one's about to contest that and call it something else.

Only Havis knows my terrible secret, and he gives me a sharp smile before he leaves.

It's there, in the shadow of his power over my fate, that I know what I must do.

I find Reni in Father's library, surrounded by the ever-present silence that permeates our home. My brother, like the palace, has been wordless and made of stone since the coup. He's seen the dark side of our tiny kingdom, and now his twentieth birthday taunts from ahead.

There's a metamorphosis taking place, all of him changing beneath the quiet.

I don't yet know what will emerge.

"I'm accepting Havis's proposal," I say, as I sit beside him. "I have to go to Resya, and he'll take me. Someone needs to find out what's happening there, and since you must stay here, it will be me."

He draws my hands into his. "Ali, you can't go there. I won't let him take you from us."

"He's not taking me. I'm going."

"Why?"

I tremble at his question. I can't tell him the truth. I can't tell anyone. "It's safe, Reni. The League has ruled against the Safire petition for war. The General's an honourable man and I know he will accept it. But we have our own trouble there, with Uncle, and now that Lark's dead, Havis is the only one who can help. And . . . I did something, Reni. Something that I must deal with myself."

Lark's last letter to me is an order I must follow. I have to apologize to his sister, to his father, and whoever else might be there. I have to see if I can continue our mission. There's always a way, as he said. But I see the fear in Reni's eyes, and I resist the urge to admit it all. The murder, the debt, the threats to our throne. The fact that I killed our cousin, blackmailed the General of Savient, and kissed a boy I can never have in the shadows of a forgotten room.

I'm not sure how I will emerge from this either.

"You have to trust me, Reni."

"But what about the University?" he asks sadly.

"Perhaps later," I say after a moment, but we both know there might not be a later. To accept Havis's offer is a risk, more dangerous than Reni can know.

I have to go.

I have to make amends with our family, in so far as I can.

"I'll get you a tutor," Reni vows, "in any subject you wish. The best in that field. I'll order him to teach you, even in Resya."

I smile. "A tutor?"

"The best in their field, I swear it. You want to learn a language? Isn't that it?" He pauses. "Savien?" he ventures, sounding afraid of my answer.

"I'd be thrilled," I whisper, overwhelmed by my love for him.

"Then that's the least I can do."

We embrace, and I know that no matter what comes, I will always have a brother I would give my life for. Always, always, until the end of my days.

When the palace grounds are finally declared safe, I'm out the door before Heathwyn can finish delivering the good news. I ride Ivory high up into the beautiful mountains. She's eager, excited to be in the late-summer forest where colours have already begun to turn. Flecks of yellow in the green. She doesn't care that the way is steep and rocky and far from home. She steps carefully along the narrow trail as we get higher, emerging finally to the endless world of the mountaintop. Towering and magnificent. A secret place of stones covered in moss and goldenrod, sun brushing the western horizon before us.

I place my hands on the earth, promising Etania, promising my father, that I won't leave forever.

I won't.

I'll return.

Then I sit down, alone, on the wind-swept rocks and write.

Athan,

Do you know I meant what I said? About the waiting a thousand days? It was such a hurried confession, I'm sorry, but it was all true. Before the worst happened, and even after. I know now what it feels like to live with something rotten on my hands. I look at them and they don't feel like my own. And I know you might have to do worse than me in whatever comes.

But . . . this isn't me.

This isn't you.

We're here on our mountain, always, a special place that is just ours. And there's nothing you could do to make me care for you less. Nothing at all. I suppose that's all I want to say this time—you're precious to me. You'll always be precious to me, no matter what anyone else says, or does, or thinks. Please never forget that. Promise me you won't. When all this terrible madness is over, we can come back here.

Fly west and you will find me.

With affection (forever, for always),

A.